VIOLET THISTLEWAITE *Is Not a* VILLAIN *Anymore*

VIOLET THISTLEWAITE *Is Not a* VILLAIN *Anymore*

Emily Krempholtz

ACE
NEW YORK

ACE
Published by Berkley
An imprint of Penguin Random House LLC
1745 Broadway, New York, NY 10019
penguinrandomhouse.com

Book design by George Towne
Sandwich board art copyright © Emily Krempholtz via Canva.com
Other interior illustrations excerpted from the cover art by Chaaya Prabhat

Library of Congress Cataloging-in-Publication Data

Names: Krempholtz, Emily, author.
Title: Violet Thistlewaite is not a villain anymore / Emily Krempholtz.
Description: First edition. | New York: Ace, 2025. |
Identifiers: LCCN 2025002243 (print) | LCCN 2025002244 (ebook) |
ISBN 9780593954300 (trade paperback) | ISBN 9780593954317 (ebook)
Subjects: LCGFT: Fantasy fiction | Fiction | Novels
Classification: LCC PS3611.R466 V56 2025 (print) |
LCC PS3611.R466 (ebook) | DDC 813/.6—dc23/eng/20250602
LC record available at https://lccn.loc.gov/2025002243
LC ebook record available at https://lccn.loc.gov/2025002244

First Edition: November 2025

Printed in the United States of America
3rd Printing

The authorized representative in the EU for product safety and compliance is Penguin Random House Ireland, Morrison Chambers, 32 Nassau Street, Dublin D02 YH68, Ireland, https://eu-contact.penguin.ie.

For anyone who has ever dreamed,
even for a second,
about leaving it all behind and starting fresh.

And for Angela, who gave me the nudge I needed.

BE GOOD

Until very recently (eight minutes ago, in fact), the blood spattering the outside of Karina's brand-new tunic had pulsed inside the heart of the dark sorcerer known as Shadowfade. Brock, the knight she traveled with who did most of the laundry, would be appalled when he saw it. But Karina the Tempest, Protector of the Queen's Realm of Mereth, chose to think of the stain as a rather dashing and intimidating addition to her look as she strode through the castle grounds, blade in hand.

Karina searched for movement atop the black stone battlements that stood watch like hulking sentinels over the expansive gardens. The carefully groomed paths flanked by topiaries and flower beds were full of poisonous blooms, no doubt, but greener and more cheerful than she would have expected from a villain like Shadowfade.

None of this was as she expected. With as fearsome a reputation as Guy Shadowfade had amassed, vanquishing him should have been much more of a trial. Her lingering concern whispered that this had been some elaborate trick.

But Karina would have time for those thoughts later. One way or another, the sorcerer was finally defeated and his minions scattered, meaning it was up to Karina and her companions to make sure they could cause no further harm to the Merethi people.

"She went into the hedge maze!" Maggie cried, her long legs a blur as she sprinted in the opposite direction, her staff in hand as she chased another foe—hopefully that dreadful alchemist who had burned through Karina's favorite pair of boots with his poisons. "Brock and I will take care of the others!"

Karina nodded curtly, her eyes dragging on her partner's form for only a second longer than necessary before she took off into the hedge maze, sword gripped tightly in her fist. As she navigated the twists and turns of the maze, she kept an eye out for danger. She wouldn't have put it past Shadowfade to fill his grounds with tricks and traps, but the maze was strangely pleasant, its greenery on full display despite the late-winter season, and its corners staged with cheerful pots of colorful flowers. Like everything else about today, it didn't meet her expectations, and it only put Karina further on edge.

At the center of the maze, in a wide, round clearing, she found the one they called the Thornwitch.

To look upon the Thornwitch, it was said, was to look your death in the eye as it reached for you with vines that strangled and flowers that poisoned. The Thornwitch had destroyed the crops of an entire county with a single wave of her hand, dooming them to famine. She had torn buildings from their foundations by roiling the roots beneath them and disrupted trade routes by tearing apart roadways and growing impenetrable forests of the poisonous thorny vines for which she'd been named. She could command anything that grew and twist it to her dark purposes.

She was a monster, or so Karina had always heard. Hideous and deformed, some said, though others swore she was a temptress more beautiful than Evry, fearsome goddess of the second moon. When she'd fought her back at the castle, Karina had gotten only an impression of thorns, spiny like the quills of a porcupine, and eyes glowing like fox fire.

But the woman in front of her was sitting serenely on a garden bench like a young lady enjoying afternoon tea, not like an infamous trafficker of cruel poisons and punishments for the sorcerer's enemies. Gone were the thorns that sprung from her skin like spines and harshened her facial structure. Gone was the unearthly glow from her eyes and the vines that sprouted from her back like wings, slinging clouds of toxic pollen. If not for the iconic purple cloak puddled at her feet, Karina wouldn't have recognized her at all.

She was young, late twenties if Karina had to guess, and without the thorns that she had been named for, her face was soft and round. Pretty, in a homespun sort of way, with pale, freckled skin, thick brown hair that tumbled over her shoulders like vines reaching for a hold, and honey-tinted eyes beneath soft-angled brows. A white scar, perhaps the length of Karina's thumb, tracked down her face just to the right of her nose, slightly puckered where it bisected the edge of her lips and tugged one side of her mouth upward in a permanent smirk.

She would have been popular in a tavern, Karina judged, though of course she had nothing on Maggie's elegant beauty. Still, there was little to liken her to the monster of the stories or the villain she'd seen just minutes ago.

"Hello," the witch said softly, her voice high and clear.

Karina raised Flamebright, putting the sword between her and the witch, though she was realizing now, too late, that she was surrounded by plants. Here, the Thornwitch could incapacitate her with a twitch of her fingers, which were covered in dirt and curled tight around a long, sharp branch, still filthy with blood from the fight. The Thornwitch followed her gaze and allowed the branch to crumble to dust, leaving dark stains on her fingertips that matched the black silk of her tight clothing.

"Why haven't you killed me yet?" Karina asked, her voice like brittle steel.

The witch only blinked her long lashes. "Should I have?"

"We're surrounded by plants."

"Well, yes. This is my garden, after all." The witch paused. "Are you here to kill *me* now?"

Karina hesitated. If anyone had asked her even twenty minutes ago, her answer would have been a resounding yes. "I don't know. Do you *want* to die?"

She lowered her gaze. "I don't deserve to live."

"That's not what I asked."

The Thornwitch's chin trembled, though she quickly got herself under control. Karina hid her surprise. The witch in the stories felt no fear, only anger and hatred. But stories—she knew well, being one herself—were just stories in the end. Made of equal parts truth and lies, and it was often impossible to be certain which was which.

There was more to the Thornwitch than Karina could fathom, and more still she didn't understand. She had fled to the hedge maze, but why did she stop here? Why wasn't she fighting back? Her mind snagged on something the witch had said. Karina looked around at the center of the maze—the ivy-covered bench where the Thornwitch sat beneath a large flowering shrub heavy with pink flowers, the koi pond edged with round, smooth stones, the lush flower beds filled with buttery daffodils and the tall jut of foxgloves. "This is *your* garden?"

The Thornwitch looked around, fondness shining in her eyes. "Yes."

Karina remembered the tidy room she'd found in the castle,

with a small bed and potted flowers and leafy vines crowded in the doorway to the balcony.

And a lock—on the outside of the door.

"You made all of this."

The witch did twitch her fingers then, but instead of carnivorous plants or thorny vines, a flower burst from the ground next to Karina. From amidst its splayed, fingerlike leaves sprung several clusters of vibrant purple flowers.

"It's gorgeous," Karina murmured, her fingers stretching toward a flower, half afraid it would sprout teeth and sever her fingers.

The witch tossed her head back and laughed. "It's monkshood. Incredibly toxic."

Karina snatched her hand back.

"All of this is poison." The witch gestured at her garden. Bitterness stained her words. "Nightshade. Foxglove. Oleander. Even the ivy—it might look pretty but all it does is destroy."

"But what else could you do?" A thought bloomed in Karina's mind, tickling her with the gentle press of a hunch. "With Shadowfade gone, you could create something good."

"*Good* is not in the Thornwitch's nature." The witch's words were scornful, but there was curiosity in her brown eyes.

"And the woman behind the Thornwitch?"

She jerked back as though Karina had drawn her sword, her jaw tight. The hero studied the villain whose name was spoken at a whisper throughout the countryside. There was something in her expression, behind that angry, suspicious mask, that looked a lot like wistfulness. Uncertainty. *Hope.* Karina thought back to the castle, to Shadowfade's final moments. The words on his lips with his final breaths.

Truth and lies, she thought. *Both stand before me, but which is which?*

Karina decided. "The Thornwitch dies here today. But you—whoever you are without her—don't have to. You could do so much better. You could be good."

The Thornwitch looked confused as Karina sheathed her weapon. The ivy on the bench detached itself to curl gently around the witch's ankle in what looked like a gesture of comfort.

"Just be good," Karina told her. "And don't make me regret this."

WELCOME TO DRAGON'S REST

Grimy puddles filled the missing cobblestones in the streets of Dragon's Rest, pockmarks of muck that spoke louder than words of what had become of the town. In the decades since Shadowfade had built his fortress on the craggy peak that towered over the edge of its borders, Dragon's Rest had gone from a prosperous community to a mountainside ghost town full of closed shutters and chipped paint.

The letter Violet had retrieved from the post office said she could meet her new landlord at Wingspan Green, and the postmaster said she'd know the town's largest park when she saw it, but despite the directions she'd scrawled on the back of the parchment, Violet was hopelessly lost.

"How does anyone navigate this place?" she wondered aloud, looking up at the darkening sky. Rava and Evry, two of the three moons, had already come to life for the evening, illuminating the hand-painted street signs on the corner. Evry was nearly full, and Violet was glad—she could use some of the goddess's bold nature now. Dragon's Rest wasn't a large town, but its winding, sloping streets curved and twisted like an errant vine creeping up a stone wall, looking for purchase.

"Are you lost, dear?" A tall elf woman with pale skin and a saffron-colored hair wrap approached Violet, her smile kind.

Violet ducked her head behind the potted plant in her arms. There was no reason for anyone in Dragon's Rest to recognize her, not unless she lost control of her magic, but still, she felt a spike of concern at having to interact with strangers.

No one will recognize you, she convinced herself. Still, Bartleby the pothos, with his broad, heart-shaped leaves, was a good disguise. Sensing her hesitation, the potted plant patted her on the shoulder, his flat leaves either smoothing the wrinkles in her cloak or trying to strangle her. It was often hard to tell with Bartleby. "I'm looking for Wingspan Green?"

The woman pointed back in the direction Violet had just come from. "You just missed the turnoff. Head that way and take a left at the first corner, then keep going straight. You can't miss it."

"Thank you," said Violet, peeking out from behind Bartleby to offer the woman a smile she hoped didn't look threatening. She was leaving that life behind. She was going to be good now, like Karina the Tempest had told her to.

Sure enough, now that she was headed in the right direction, Wingspan Green was easy to spot from several blocks away. The large, circular park was surrounded by battered storefronts with faded awnings. It was carpeted with green grass and lined with trees, which were just beginning to bud in defiance of these last stubborn days of winter, and the very presence of the greenery made Violet breathe a little easier. Paths meandered through the space, dotted with benches and a few small tables as well as what seemed to be a platform near the center, though it was blocked by a huge rock formation that looked as though it had tumbled down from the mountains sometime in the last thousand years and had since been tucked into bed beneath a blanket of moss.

Bartleby shuddered.

"Oh, shush you," Violet scolded him.

Before he had been turned into a plant, Bartleby wouldn't have just argued with her, he'd have towered over her and threatened bodily injury for shushing him like a child. He still managed to find ways to menace Violet on a near-daily basis, but she'd been careful to remove all sharp implements from within reach of his vines before they set off for Dragon's Rest.

"I think it's lovely," she said now, both to herself and to him. "The place has loads of potential." She stepped onto the grass, wishing she were barefoot so she could feel the soil beneath her toes. No flowers anywhere, but then, without magic like hers, it was too early in the season yet. Cesenne, the goddess of the third moon, whose phases heralded the changing of the seasons, would soon wax anew as spring began, and Violet suspected the park would liven up then. Perhaps once she'd settled and opened her shop, she could add a few flower beds to give it some splashes of color. A pang of longing for her gardens struck her, quickly suppressed by complicated relief for her own freedom.

She would plant a new garden here in Dragon's Rest and open a shop where she could sell her flowers. Just the thought of surrounding herself with blooms all day made her feel lighter. No one would have to know who she once was or how she'd once used her magic. She bent to stroke the grass and couldn't resist releasing just a bit of power from the well deep in her core. As easy as exhaling, especially under the moons, her magic spilled into the grass, making it grow tall enough to tickle Violet's wrist and wrap lovingly around her fingers in the one embrace she'd cherished her whole life. It was hard sometimes, when she did little things like this, to remember that her plant magic was evil at heart, but she'd done enough terrible things as the Thornwitch that she couldn't deny it.

Your own mother knew the truth about you, whispered a voice in her head nearly as recognizable as her own. *She saw the darkness in your magic and she abandoned you for it. You are so lucky I found you, petal. You will always have a home with me.*

But now Shadowfade was dead and that home was gone.

If she could keep that dark part of herself locked away, perhaps Violet could call this place home. Yes, it was dingy and a little weather-beaten, but then, so was she. Here, she could finally start over. Maybe she would learn who she could be without Guy Shadowfade. Without the Thornwitch.

The Violet who opened a flower shop in Dragon's Rest would have no idea what it was like to watch the life leave someone's eyes. She'd never have heard the wails of an entire village as she sank their homes into a bog that hadn't existed before she swept into town. Bartleby was simply a fondly named houseplant, not one of her former adversaries who'd spent the last half decade transformed into a potted pothos.

Violet Thistlewaite, she decided, was kind and generous. She came from a loving family with parents who had wanted her, and maybe some siblings who teased her about moving so far away. Nieces and nephews whose faces lit up in delight when Auntie Vi conjured flower crowns for their hair and grew playhouses for them of hardy-yet-thornless bramble. Violet Thistlewaite had no dark side looming behind her like a shadow. She could sleep through the night without waking in a cold sweat from nightmares of her past. She could—

A scream cut the air like one of Guy's enchanted daggers through her rosebushes.

Violet stood fast enough to make her head whirl, which reminded her she hadn't eaten yet today. There, just behind the rock formation, was a flash of movement that Violet soon recognized as a woman running.

"Get away from me, you bloody nuisances!" she cried, turning to throw what appeared to be her shoe behind her.

A moment later, a creature rumbled into view. Violet gasped as she took in the blocky granite legs and massive height of the beast. It was two-legged and ungainly, with no visible head and a long tail that appeared to be missing great chunks. The whole thing seemed to be cobbled together from stone. Its rocky body scraped as it moved, and although it wasn't very quick, it definitely wasn't the type of creature anyone would want chasing after them.

Be good, the Tempest had challenged her. Violet placed Bartleby carefully on the ground, raised her hands to chest level, and shouted, "*Oy!*" The woman noticed her then, her eyes widening, and Violet cried, "Duck!"

Unleashing her power was like opening a tap. Magic flooded Violet's chest and spread eagerly through her veins like roots through soft earth, until even her toes were warm with energy. With a sweep of her hands, Violet pulled tree branches into clawed fingers that reached menacingly for the beast and sprouted vines from the ground, which wrapped tight around its limbs.

Her eyes were glowing, as they always did when she used dark magic, but she reserved a sliver of her attention to making sure her skin didn't burst with thorns as it did when she was the Thornwitch. She intended to make a home here without anyone knowing who she was, and that meant not letting them see the fearsome face on the wanted posters. Violet focused as the bespelled plants snatched at the creature, breaking it into dozens of pieces that flew across the park and, to her surprise, scrabbled away on legs of their own, making small, croaking noises as they ran.

Rock goblins, Violet realized. She knew groups of them, called slides, could combine to become a much larger creature, but she'd never seen one before. Her magic begged her to follow them, to give chase, to become the predator she had always been. It was a siren call she was well used to heeding, and for a moment, she almost did. But no. Violet coaxed the trees back to their original shapes, closing her eyes and willing their appearance to return to normal as well. She'd almost lost control for a second there, and it couldn't happen again. *No more dark magic*, she'd promised herself when she left Shadowfade Castle. She was starting over. She was *good* now.

It was too bad dark magic was all she knew.

"Quick thinking," said the woman, panting, as she trotted over to Violet. "That slide is obsessed with me."

Violet couldn't tell whether she was joking or not. She settled for a simple "Ah."

The woman winked at her. "I'm a musician. They like music, I reckon. It's always been more amusing than anything, but they're getting out of control lately. Ever since—" The woman looked behind Violet, and a chill strummed her spine as she realized she was referring to the silhouette of Shadowfade Castle, just visible on the crags of the mountain above Dragon's Rest like a sinister sentinel peering down at them.

Violet felt suddenly embarrassed.

The woman continued. "I've never seen anyone get rid of them with quite so much . . . *oomph*. That was a hefty bit of magic you just did there."

"I panicked a little," Violet admitted with a nervous giggle. She had gotten used to being around power when she was surrounded by Guy and his associates. Shadowfade had collected powerful mages like toys, and Violet had stood out even among them. In a place like Dragon's Rest, among ordinary folk, she'd have to be careful not to show too much of herself. She didn't want to draw any questions.

The woman nodded. She was about Violet's age, maybe a few years older, and tall, with warm brown skin and dark brown eyes. Her long hair wound down her back in an elaborate braid that swung to the rhythm of her steps, and she wore a bright patterned dress with colorful, intricate embroidery on the bodice, and a number of scarves around her waist and neck. Violet's own clothes were expensive and well-made, but much simpler: wide-legged gray trousers and an oversized men's shirt, accented with a fur-trimmed cloak of midnight blue.

It had been weeks, but it still thrilled her to wear them—Guy had always insisted she wear tight leathers spelled against damage so she could move easily without being caught or snagged, as well as her recognizable purple cloak, all the better to strike fear into the hearts of her enemies from a distance, long before they were within her range. He had been a showman, but now that he was gone, Violet would be pleased if she never saw the color purple ever again. The looser men's clothes she'd stolen from the castle before she left for good were overlarge and made her feel like she could disappear in them if she wished. Become truly invisible. Truly free.

"You wouldn't happen to be Violet Thistlewaite, would you?" the woman asked, and Violet felt that surge of panic rise in her once more, like the woman would be able to smell the dark magic on her.

No one knows your name, she reminded herself. *No one here knows the identity of the Thornwitch.* She cleared her throat. "Yes. That's me."

"I thought as much. It's not often we get newcomers here." The woman's grin lit her whole face as she thrust out a hand for Violet to shake. "I'm Prudence Marsh, your new landlord. Welcome to Dragon's Rest."

THE LANDLORD

"You did what?" Nathaniel Marsh pinched the bridge of his nose and mentally recited alchemical laws to stop himself from strangling his twin sister.

"She saved my life," Pru argued.

"From a slide of rock goblins?" Nathaniel snorted. "Hardly."

"Excuse you." Pru huffed like he'd delivered some great offense. "I could have been crushed! To death!"

"The worst they would have done was build a wall around you for a few hours until they got bored."

"They could have turned me to stone!"

"That's a myth, Prudence."

"No, it's not. A few of them got into Corrin's glass studio just last week and turned half a dozen vases to stone before she found them! And there's that table at the Claw & Hoard with the stone leg, that was them too!"

"There has never been proven evidence of a rock goblin having enough power to turn a *sentient, living being* to stone," he corrected impatiently.

"But the stories—"

"—are just stories, and you know it."

She stuck out her tongue at him. "Well, it was getting cold! I didn't want to be out there for hours."

This was so like Pru, being magnanimous for the sheer sake of it, despite the fact that she knew quite well the state of their finances. "Be that as it may, it was no excuse to offer her a discount on her rent. We can't afford to be charitable if we want to keep the shop open."

"Any rent is more than what we're making right now," said Pru, flapping a hand in his face. Nathaniel resisted the urge to swat at her, knowing it would only fan the flame of his sister's drive to irritate him. "And besides, you should have seen them scatter, Nat. The poor woman's going to be recovering for days after a display like that. Now she'll be doing it from the warmth of a bed."

He rolled his eyes. "She could recover from magic burn just as well from the bed she is renting *at the asking price to which she already agreed.*"

"Pah!" Pru flapped a hand. "We're too young for you to be such a curmudgeon already."

"On the contrary, thirty-one feels an entirely appropriate time to begin the journey to curmudgeonhood."

"By thirty-five you'll be a bona fide grump," she teased, rolling her eyes. "And by forty you'll be the terror of every child in Dragon's Rest. Oh, and speaking of terrors, I need you to clear your mess out of half the greenhouse."

"What?" His attention sharpened. "Why?"

"Well, I mentioned the greenhouse in the lease posting, and that's why she was interested. She's opening a flower shop, isn't that sweet?"

"Prudence," Nathaniel said slowly. "We are an apothecary."

She looked around in mock astonishment, her eyes widening

at the bundles of herbs hanging from the rafters and carefully measured vials of ingredients lining the shelves. "Is *that* why we're surrounded by so many medicinal teas?"

He glared at her. "I use that greenhouse, Pru. We need somewhere to dry herbs and plants."

"Well, yes, that's why I only offered her half of it."

Nathaniel gritted his teeth. He should never have left this to his sister. He knew she couldn't handle it, that she'd get distracted or miss the point, and clearly he was right. But of course Pru had insisted. She wanted to help. She could contribute, she'd argued, if only he'd let her. And this was what had come of it!

He found himself suddenly very glad he'd decided not to show her the letter he'd received last week from the bank, which even now weighed like a bar of iron in his pocket. He couldn't imagine what sort of preposterous mess Pru would get them into—under the guise of "helping," of course—if he told her about the debt they'd inherited from their parents.

"She's kind, and very sweet," continued Pru, pulling a little leather purse from her bag. "A bit shy. You'll love her, I just know it. Won't even notice she's there. Besides, she paid up front for her first three months. In soli!"

Any tenant who could afford to pay in gold soli, thought Nathaniel as he took the purse from his sister and recorded the currency in the ledger, didn't need a discount on their rent.

"I finished clearing out the upstairs rooms on the western half of the house," Pru called out as she locked the front door, lowering the shades so they could no longer see the words MARSH APOTHECARY painted on the windows in their father's sure hand. "And locked the hallway door separating her half from ours. All that's left is the greenhouse, and I'm not touching your potion-making toys."

"Alchemical instruments," snapped Nathaniel automatically, the next lyric in an oft-sung duet between the twins.

"Mmm," hummed Pru musically, then swung a graceful leg over the dusty velvet rope that blocked customers from the stairs and disappeared up them.

Nathaniel checked the front door to make sure it was locked, then glared at the new wall that cut the shop in half, as though this was its fault and not his own for ordering it constructed in the first place. He shrugged on his coat and stepped out the back door into the neglected garden behind the shop.

His parents had built the greenhouse back when the apothecary was successful enough to warrant occupying the entire ground floor of the building. His mother had commissioned the wrought iron metal vines that curled over the panes, and the green-and-yellow stained glass panels that checkered the space above the doors. Outside, his father had grown a beautiful garden, full of vegetables they ate throughout the summer and colorful flowers he cut early in the morning so he could surprise Nathaniel's mother with bouquets when she awoke. Inside the greenhouse, pots of medicinal herbs had grown year-round with the help of an annual weatherproofing spell from a traveling warlock. The enchantment was enough to keep out even the worst of the harsh mountain winds that thrashed Dragon's Rest each winter.

Nathaniel remembered sitting on the floor of the greenhouse with Pru when they were children, watching their mother bundle herbs and hang them from the beams above their heads even as snow swirled outside the warped glass.

"Dried, these herbs are more potent," she taught them as they played in the dirt, her voice low and sure. "But it's more than plucking the stems and leaving them to dry. We harvest our herbs in the morning, after the dew has dried but before the sun has a chance to diffuse the oils from the leaves back into the stem. Then we bundle them at the stalk like this, see?"

Nathaniel remembered running his fingers over the twine while Mum held his hands and guided him through the process, laughing softly when he experimented with different knots and made a mess of his bundle of feverfew.

"Be gentle, my love," she said when he dropped the bunch in frustration. "Or you'll bruise the leaves. Here, like this, see? Try it again."

Now, his breath puffing in a cloud before him in the cool night, his father's garden was little more than some scrubby grass and stubborn mint that still poked its head from the ground each spring. He pulled the letter from his pocket and smoothed the paper as he unfolded it, his eyes skimming the neat, orderly words he'd practically memorized by now. Phrases jumped out at him, phrases like *condolences* and *grace period is ending* and *three months* and *apothecary* and *collateral.*

He shoved the letter into his pocket and looked up at the moons in the sky. Rava would wane and wax three more times before he had to start making the new payments. A bit less, now, because he'd felt absolutely frozen in the week and a half since he received the letter.

Nathaniel was trying his best to follow his mother's example, but he didn't have her patience or knowledge, and besides, the warlock who bespelled their greenhouse had disappeared a few years back, probably a victim of Shadowfade's paranoia. He still had a few potted plants, but most of their supplies came from merchants these days, though Nathaniel still insisted on blending the teas and tinctures himself. It was what they'd always done, which meant it was what his mother would have wanted. Besides, it was the closest he'd come to alchemy in the apothecary.

He feared, with the kind of dread that weakened everything it touched, that he wasn't cut out for this. Nathaniel didn't have his mother's skill with herbal medicines or her ability to charm customers. His original plan for saving the apothecary had failed with the kind of epic tragedy that had his neighbors trailing off their sentences and grimacing rather than speaking of it, and now he was barely holding his head above water. Pru was insistent that downsizing the shop and taking on a tenant was the answer.

He hoped for both their sakes that she was right.

Light spilled through the warped glass of the greenhouse already, and Nathaniel eyed the dark silhouette inside, preparing himself for the unpleasant task of interacting with the new tenant. His mouth tensed with the smile of a man held hostage by propriety, but the door caught on something as he opened it—a stack of boxes that shouldn't have been in its path.

As if in slow motion, Nathaniel watched, horrified, as the tower of crates wobbled and then toppled over, spilling glass vials and flasks that crashed and shattered on the ground. One crate struck a pile of boxes, knocking those over too and creating a clamoring eruption of sound and shattering that seemed endless.

A small "Oh!" of surprise cut through the crash, but Nathaniel could only stand frozen, his hand still on the doorknob. Amidst the chaos, he dimly registered a pale face, a tangle of brown curls, a pair of lips slack with dismay. Eventually the cacophony came to an end, and his eyes swept the mess before landing on the woman who stood, hands clutching another crate, amidst the destruction.

THE TENANT

"What," said the man calmly, though his words hissed with underlying steam, like a kettle about to boil over, "do you think you are doing?"

"I . . ." Violet cleared her throat. "Pru said I was free to explore. I only wanted to see if the floor was dirt or stone. I was going to move the boxes back. I didn't expect . . ." She trailed off, thinking that calling out this man, whoever he was, on his own part in the mess—the door would never have knocked over the crates if he hadn't opened it, after all—would only deepen that crease between his brows.

She took in the stranger's lean height and long limbs beneath the worn sleeves of a forest-green coat, and the thick black hair that swept tidily back from his forehead, as though he'd run a hand through it that morning and told it sternly to stay put in that low voice that brooked no argument. He surveyed the mess before them and said, "Those flasks won't be easy to replace."

"I'll pay for them," she said quickly, feeling small as his gaze landed, unblinking, upon her once more. His scrutiny unsettled her, like he was taking note of every feature and every flaw, and Violet felt thoroughly stripped bare by the analysis, as if he could sense all the thorns of her past and prick *her* with their sharp points. She drew a shaky breath and set the crate in her arms on top of another stack, which collapsed under the added strain. Of course it did. Violet clenched her eyes shut in an extended, horrified wince as another chorus of shattering glass detonated among them.

"You will," he agreed, his glare sharper than any of the shards that lay smashed around them. "How could you be so careless, and with someone else's belongings no less?"

Violet bristled at his cold tone. *How dare he speak to you like this*, said a voice in her head that sounded an awful lot like Shadowfade's. *You are the Thornwitch. You could tear him to shreds where he stands.* The thought triggered a reflex, one that filled her to the brim with power. The energy inside her clambered to escape, to make, to create, to grow. Thorns, vines, it didn't matter—Violet's body was a conduit for roots and leaves, a seedbed for natural destruction, just as Guy had taught her.

Her limbs buzzed with unspent magic, begging her to grow vines that would tear his arms from his torso, tempting her with sweet promises about opening the ground and swallowing him whole, pulling him into the dirt with strong, grasping roots so she could be left in peace. She could make him regret looking at her with such patronizing scorn.

No. Violet forced those thoughts down and screwed a lid tight over them. Hadn't she *just* vowed to be done with dark magic when she was back in the park with Pru?

Holding this much energy made her feel like the very seams of her were ready to burst. Her vision sharpened, and she knew her eyes were glowing green.

Oh no.

Violet sometimes imagined herself like a sieve—she could slap her hand over the mesh all she wanted, but magic would still find places to seep from her pores. She could feel it coming now whether she liked it or not, plants and poisons budding from the power within her, the only thing she was ever any good at. *But what else could you do?* Karina the Tempest's voice was still fresh in her ears. Violet squeezed her eyes shut against the onslaught of magic pushing its way out, until—*there!*—in her mind's eye she sensed a glimmer, like sunlight winking from the shimmering surface of another spring. Power that was pure, uncorrupted. Power that was *good.*

Violet reached for the new spring, barely a puddle compared to the deep well of the other one, but what plant could grow after a lifetime of being starved for air and light? She yanked her thoughts away from thorns and poisons and breathed relief as the Thornwitch's power dissipated, spreading back into her body. Violet focused on that other spring, pulling it through her fingers like a rope, and thought, *Be good.*

Now hollyhocks in shades of red and pink exploded from the ground, tall and towering where they burst between the other stacks of crates, and blue clematis began to climb the walls of the greenhouse, wrapping its vines tight around the legs of a table. Bright yellow dahlias with their thick masses of raylike petals burst to life, shards of glass trapped between some of the blooms from the force of their growth, and delicate pink-and-white phlox sprung to soften the ground beneath her feet, the shattered instruments glittering among their leaves. Tall sunflowers and fragrant lilacs completed the scene, splashes of color at strange odds with the detritus of broken glass and dusty boxes.

It stung, this new magic, like nettles against her skin, but perhaps this was Violet's price after so many years of doing evil. She kept her hands in the air for a second longer than necessary, marveling at the difference, the way the new magic receded without complaint. Then she turned to face the man who was gaping at her with something between anger and shock.

She looked around sheepishly; she hadn't expected the garden she created to be quite so . . . much. It was beautiful, at least—and didn't seem likely to try to murder anyone, so that was promising. "I'll pay for the damage," she told him. "And I can clean this up."

It would hurt a bit to cut it down, this wild and beautiful thing she'd made, but she could use the flowers for bouquets and arrangements. That was why she was here, after all. One could not open a flower shop without cutting a few stems.

His jaw was hanging open like a door with a broken hinge, eyes scanning the garden she'd created. "You're the new tenant, then."

"Violet Thistlewaite," she said, brushing her hands over her shirt. "And you must be Prudence's . . ." She trailed off, and when he didn't fill in the blank, she tried, "Husband?"

He barked out a sound that might have been a laugh. "Brother."

"Ah." Another landlord, then, and this one not quite so impressed with her as his sister.

Now that she thought about it, he did look an awful lot like Prudence, if someone had dressed her in drab colors, dusted a layer of stubble over her brown cheeks, and removed any trace of humor from her expression. He and his sister were both tall, with the same eyes like an ink spill, framed by the same thick lashes and bold brows, though his were pinched in distaste. But unlike Pru's open warmth, there was a sharp, elegant clarity to her brother's features, as if he'd been drawn in sure strokes and angles rather than the smudged, shadowy pencil sketch of her own silhouette. If not for the scowl that twisted his mouth, Violet might even have called him beautiful.

He cleared his throat, his dark eyes still caught on the garden that had bloomed to life around them. "Nathaniel Marsh."

"It's a pleasure to—"

But he interrupted her as though she hadn't even begun to speak. "Miss Thistlewaite, I must ask that you refrain from treating the equipment in this room as your own. I conduct delicate work in here, and Pru should never have offered the space to you." He strode to the other side of the greenhouse, where a large, metal worktable held a collection of meticulously organized vials as well as a small cauldron that had been upended by the creeping clematis, which was still, she noticed, growing throughout the space, tangling with a small potted mint that had been carefully pruned into submission on the corner of his table.

With a small yelp of dismay, he leapt back and turned his glare on her.

"This is exactly what I mean!" Violet shrunk from his anger, her thoughts turning to Guy and his punishments when she'd displeased him. *Shadowfade is gone*, she thought. *And who is this? You are the Thornwitch. Why should you cower from him?*

She huffed and straightened her shoulders, drawing herself to her full height. Thorns prickled beneath her skin, threatening to burst from her like the claws and horns that had for so long made her a monster. Her mind flashed with ways to scare him, to stop his disdain and questions in their tracks, but they were Guy's solutions, folded into the steel of her being after decades at his side, and with him gone, she felt like an impure metal, a forge long grown cold.

Violet wasn't sure what her own solutions might look like, but she knew they didn't involve using the clematis—which was creeping ever closer to her new landlord—to string him up from the rafters until he apologized. She was *good* now, and what her instincts begged of her was decidedly not.

"I'm sorry," she said carefully, tasting the foreign word on her tongue. Guy had never allowed her to apologize for her failures. He preferred for her to atone for disappointing him by proving her worth in other ways. Once, she had blinded one of his enemies using the thorns of a rosebush and felt relief when her master smiled. Now the memory made her sick. "As I said, I'll replace whatever was broken."

"Can you replace the weeks I've spent working on it?" he snapped, and tension filled Violet at his tone. This man had no intention of keeping the peace, and Violet strained to hold on to the frayed rope of her own fractured manners.

"I cannot."

"Then perhaps next time you won't be so careless. You had no idea what was in that cauldron! What if it had been volatile? What if someone had been hurt?" He scolded her like a child, and she clenched her fists.

"Mr. Marsh," she said carefully, "I have apologized, explained the accident, and offered to help as much as I can. But I won't be spoken to like that." Not anymore. Violet could feel her temper rising. She searched for that new spring once more, and with a stinging twitch of her fingers, the clematis lunged down to reach for the broken glass, sweeping it into the empty crates and setting them upright.

He swallowed whatever he had been about to say. "I apologize for my frustration. I could have paid closer attention when opening the door."

Violet nodded. "I'll put everything back exactly as it was." She glanced at the garden now around her and amended, "*Almost* exactly as it was. But I was promised half of this space, and I need it if I'm to do the work I have planned. Work that will allow me to pay you rent." She eyed him with disdain, allowing just a touch of the Thornwitch to show in her expression.

His jaw flexed, but he said nothing.

"We must come to some sort of understanding here," she said, her scorn collapsing into a plea. This was not how she wanted to begin her relationship with her neighbor—her *landlord.* He could make her life very difficult, which was the exact opposite of what Violet wanted.

"Clean the rest of this up," he said finally. "And try not to break anything else. I'll have your half of the space cleared out tomorrow." He scrubbed a hand through his hair, and she toyed with whether to tell him that a single lock had escaped the rough comb of his fingers, curling outward like a ram's horn. She pressed her lips together, deciding against it as, nose in the air, Nathaniel Marsh stalked back out the door.

Well, this was just great. Violet waved aside the phlox that wound around her ankles.

"Stay," she told the plants. "We've caused enough trouble."

At least "trouble" was a good deal less serious an accusation than "Thornwitch, right hand to Guy Shadowfade and Scourge of Silbourne," though neither worked in her favor. She set Bartleby and the clematis to cleaning up the broken glass and began restacking the fallen crates, careful not to jostle the contents any further. She could sense plants inside some of them, dried herbs and medicines for the apothecary, but others moved with the sound of clinking glass. Violet winced, knowing this meant she'd likely broken more than what littered the ground. An apothecary needed plenty of vials, she supposed, though looking over at the ruined solution on the worktable, perhaps it was more than that.

She'd never heard of an apothecary who brewed potions any more complicated than a cup of medicinal tea or a tincture enchanted to cure a cold. They sold potion ingredients, not potions themselves. That was alchemy, not medicine.

Violet had known a few alchemists in her time with Shadowfade. Nasty pieces of work, the lot of them, concerned only with their explosives. One had thought it would be funny to mix one of his powders with her plant fertilizers, and when she had fed her garden, he'd blown the whole thing up as a lark. He and the others had laughed, though not for long.

The Thornwitch didn't have a reputation for nothing.

Over near the glass wall, Bartleby reached out a vine and poked one of the crates she'd just set right.

"Stop that," Violet snapped. "You won't find anything explosive in there—and if you do, you'll just hurt yourself." His nosiness successfully plucked out her own curiosity by the roots like a weed. She'd made enough of a mess, and as she shouldered her bag and headed back to the empty building that would soon become her shop, she vowed to keep her head down from now on.

The sting in her hands had faded, and Violet itched to try that new magic again with an excitement she hadn't felt since Guy had given her free rein over the castle grounds landscaping. There was *another* well inside of her, she thought happily, searching for it again, though the glimmer she'd sensed before was nowhere to be found. It wasn't as strong as her dark magic, she suspected, but if she could learn to harness it, she didn't need it to be.

Tomorrow, she promised herself. Tomorrow she would try again.

USEFUL

Nathaniel straightened his shoulders before knocking on the door to the new tenant's half of the shared storefront. He felt uneasy, just as he had every day since he'd paid the carpenter to build a wall splitting the apothecary in half. Was he really to be a guest in part of the building he'd called home since he first learned the meaning of the word? What would his parents think if they knew he and Pru had been forced to rent out half the shop and the rooms above, where his own childhood bedroom had once been?

Nathaniel could practically hear his father's booming laugh. "We do what we must for family," he always said. "And we do it with pride, because family is everything."

He was certainly doing what he must for his family, Nathaniel thought, but he couldn't drum up much to be proud about.

The tenant—Miss Thistlewaite, he corrected himself—saw him through the shop window before she opened the door, and he winced when he saw her tense smile.

He'd gone back to the greenhouse this morning to clear out some of his storage, as promised, and marveled some more at the garden she'd grown from thin air. He'd never seen magic quite like it before, and had spent some time studying the blooms, touching their petals as though they might be an elaborate illusion. A potted plant in the corner had even touched him right back, wrapping its long, leafy vines around his wrist and gripping so tightly that he'd grown nervous it was about to eat him and so detached himself. It wasn't that the encounter *scared* him, exactly, only that he felt it most practical to meet Miss Thistlewaite in the shop and determine whether the plant posed any real danger before he attempted to venture back into the greenhouse.

He was still miffed about the ruined decoction, but when he'd seen the careful way she had restacked his crates, guilt rose in him, choking him like smoke. Pru had scolded him too last night, and explained that she'd given the new tenant permission to settle in.

"Hello, Miss Thistlewaite," he said when she opened the door. He was trying to sound pleasant, though he suspected it came out a bit brusque.

Her hair was swept out of her face with a spotted kerchief, and her cheeks were pink with exertion, a broom held tightly in her grip. He felt that unsettled feeling again, the one that had struck him last night and had him staring at her like a fool. There was something about her that drew his eye and held him captive—and Nathaniel Marsh did not like feeling trapped.

"Mr. Marsh," she said by way of greeting, her tone suspicious.

"Nathaniel," he corrected. "Please."

She nodded, studying him with those eyes like sunshine through a cup of tea. "Nathaniel, then. And you must call me Violet."

She leaned against the door frame, and his gaze dropped to her attire, a pair of breeches several sizes too large for her and a men's shirt and waistcoat, with a few stray flowers woven into her buttonholes like their stems had snapped and she couldn't bear to discard them. The clothes obviously hadn't been made for her by any tailor, and Nathaniel let his eyes wander for a moment, wondering whose they were. Was their owner the reason she'd come to Dragon's Rest? Not that he cared, of course. Her history was none of his business.

"Is there something I can help you with?" she asked, and her voice was like the unexpected scent of smoke during one of his experiments, warning him, *Danger. Be on your guard.*

"I've emptied the half of the greenhouse nearest your side of the building." Nathaniel hovered on the doorstep. He hadn't set foot in this part of the apothecary since the wall went up, and before then, not since—well, no use dwelling on that.

"Thank you."

"I ask only that you keep any of your plants away from my worktable in the far corner." Nathaniel cleared his throat, awkward under the scrutiny of her amber eyes. "Please."

"Of course. It won't be a problem." She cocked her head, sheepish, and a smile teased her lips enough that he very nearly forgot his irritation. "Well, it won't be a problem *again*."

He dug in his pockets for a ring of keys and dropped them into her hand, careful not to touch those long fingers that had brought blossoms to life. "My sister asked me to give these to you. Spare keys for the upstairs apartment and the back door."

"I appreciate it," she said again. "I should get to work. I'm, er, clearing out the shop today. Trying to get set up. Is there—I mean, is there anything in here I shouldn't touch? Pru said I was free to make it my own."

He swept his gaze over the empty shelves and countertops behind her, where his parents and grandparents had once blended teas, mixed poultices, and carefully measured medicines on the brass scales he'd loved to play with. He tried not to focus on the hastily constructed wall.

"No." His brow creased into a frown. "Do with it what you will."

"I did find a crate of supplies upstairs. I thought they might be yours. Looks like more flasks and vials." Her smile turned crooked. "I didn't break these ones."

He nodded stiffly. "Yes, they're mine."

"For the apothecary?"

"No. They're my—that is . . ." Nathaniel cleared his throat. "I used to be an alchemist."

Those honey-gold eyes widened. "I wondered, when I saw all the—well." She winced, clearly trying to avoid mentioning all his smashed implements. Nathaniel probably deserved that. He'd been rude.

He cleared his throat again, wondering if perhaps he was coming down with something. "I left the Crucible last year, when I moved back to Dragon's Rest."

"Homesick?"

His mouth tightened, and his eyes flickered toward the worktable in the corner of the room. The phantom smell of burning chemicals filled his nostrils. "Something like that."

Violet was already flitting over to the table in question. "Well I imagine you'll want your supplies back, then. What are you doing running an apothecary if you're an alchemist? I suppose it's helpful to source your own ingredients for potions, but do you sell any of your creations in your shop?"

Memory fled him like a rabbit from a hound, and Nathaniel's eyes narrowed. "Absolutely not," he said sternly. "Herbal medicine and alchemy have no place at the same table. The alchemical arts are for weaponry or entertainment, and an apothecary provides a real service to the community." He was halfway through the sentence before he realized he was quoting his mother.

Violet's head snapped up sharply. "Oh. I'm sorry, I didn't . . ."

"It's fine." Nathaniel tried to brush off his reaction. He strode toward her. "Now where are those boxes?"

"Just over here," she said, waving him closer.

Nathaniel stepped next to her, trying to ignore the sharp floral scent of her hair as she hefted the large wooden crate onto the worktable and pried off the lid. Ah, there was his barrier set. Used to prevent contamination, particularly when working with volatile solutions that had a high chance of exploding, it wasn't something Nathaniel expected to have much use for in Dragon's Rest, but the sealed glass box was a pain—not to mention expensive—to replace, and he'd thought it lost.

"I'll just take this back to my shop," he started to say.

Violet interrupted him with a vehement "*No!*" and he shook in surprise, jerking back until he felt something cold and sharp against the back of his neck.

"Put it down," said Violet, her eyes flashing with a strange light. "Bartleby, put it down."

The sensation left his skin, and Nathaniel turned around to find the same viny houseplant in the blue-glazed pot that had grabbed him this morning. He would have been relieved to find she'd moved it out of the greenhouse if not for the fact that it was now brandishing a knife. He lurched back, bumping his hip into Violet, who stared furiously at the plant.

"We've talked about this," she said in the exasperated tone of a parent disciplining a child. "No more knives, or I'm going to build you a terrarium and lock you inside."

The vine around the knife's hilt unraveled, and the blade clattered to the floor.

"Three moons!" Nathaniel cursed. "What is that thing?"

Miss Thistlewaite flapped a hand at him, her attention still on the plant. "That's just Bartleby. I promise, this won't be a problem, he's just not used to the new place and he's a little skittish around strangers. Even though he promised me *no more stabbing*." She hissed this last part quietly enough that Nathaniel wasn't sure he'd heard her correctly. The plant had done this before? She tapped her foot and held out a hand, approaching the plant—er, Bartleby. "Come on now, give me the other one."

Bartleby heaved its—his? Violet had used *his*, hadn't she?—leaves as if in a sigh and extended another vine, this one wrapped around the handle of a pair of sharp pruning shears. Violet waited until the plant dropped the scissors carefully into her hand and then set them down on the worktable out of Bartleby's reach.

"And the one in your pot too," she chided.

Sure enough, Bartleby reached a vine into his pot and dug through the soil until he produced a folding pocketknife. Violet stared him down for another hard moment, as if trying to determine whether he had any other sharp weapons hidden away. Finally she gave a curt nod and dropped the third knife on the table next to the others.

"Sorry about that," said Violet, turning back to Nathaniel. "He and I are going to have a serious conversation about how to be neighborly."

"What . . . is he?"

"These days he's a golden pothos." She shrugged. "Sometimes called devil's ivy. I'm sure you can imagine why after that display." Her tentative smile, trying to assess his level of anger, brought his attention to the scar on her face, which was much more noticeable in daylight than it had been last night.

Where would she have gotten a scar like that? he wondered. Had she been unlucky enough to cross paths with Shadowfade or one of his ilk? Certainly not, or she wouldn't have settled so close to his castle. But she was definitely not from Dragon's Rest, Nathaniel could tell, and unless news of the sorcerer's demise had spread quicker than he thought, he struggled to understand how a magic user would come to be here.

"What brought you here?" he wondered, then started when he realized he'd spoken the question.

Panic flared in her eyes for a moment, and he clocked the way her gaze darted around him, as though looking for an escape route. "I needed a change," she said at last. "A fresh start." She ducked her head so her scar was out of sight.

"Hmm." He covered his own embarrassment at being caught staring. *None of your business*, he chided himself, but couldn't help adding, "And you ran a flower shop where you came from as well?"

She shook her head. "No, but I . . . gardened."

He remembered the way those plants had sprung from the ground, blossoming like it was midsummer, not the last stubborn dregs of winter. "I imagine you did. And you truly expect to find success here?"

She blinked at him. "I beg your pardon?"

"It's just that Dragon's Rest seems a strange place to settle, of all the places in the world. We're not much for flowers here." The mountain climate was harsh, for one thing, and the summers short, though he supposed she didn't need a good climate to make things grow. Not with a power like hers.

"*Yet*," she added, a smile tugging at her mouth. "You're not much for flowers *yet*."

"I'm sure you know that until quite recently the sorcerer Shadowfade lived in the castle just at the edge of town."

"Oh?" When he frowned, she amended, "I mean, yes, I know. Everyone knows that. Of course it's common knowledge. There's no reason for me not to know that. But he's gone now, isn't he?"

"And good riddance," said Nathaniel. So she *had* heard. "He and his band of ne'er-do-wells have held this place beneath his thumb for far too long."

"Oh," she said again.

"What I mean to say is that folks around here haven't had much use for flowers, not when we've lived in fear of the sorcerer blasting us off the map when he was in a bad mood, or of one of his associates finding their way into town and taking what they pleased."

Her voice was quiet. "Perhaps it's time for something new."

"Perhaps." He shrugged. "But in this town, I reckon you'd find more success selling something that's actually useful."

"Useful?" Her eyes narrowed. "Flowers bring people happiness. Isn't that useful? Especially now?"

"Hardly. Herbs, maybe, or vegetables. Many of us barely made it through last winter, after Shadowfade's pet witch destroyed Silbourne and the surrounding trade routes." Nathaniel watched her wince, and he wondered if she'd been affected by the Thornwitch too. Maybe that was how she'd gotten that scar. "Believe me. A bouquet that sits on a windowsill for a few days before wilting and dying is only going to remind people in this town that they should have spent their money on something that will help them survive."

"Well," she said stiffly. "I suppose we'll see."

And then she ushered him to the door and shut it in his face. Anxiety pulsed through Nathaniel as he stared at the shop windows. He had an uncanny ability for saying the exact wrong thing in a situation. He knew that the memory of it would haunt him for days, the moment repeating with perfect clarity in an endless cycle that would, in turn, probably affect every other interaction he had until a worse one took its place. He had a potion for times like this, but he was nearly out, and the unfinished next batch he was working on had faced an untimely death at the hands—or leaves—of a troublesome clematis last night. Two weeks' work down the drain. Nathaniel felt frustrated all over again.

He marched back over to the apothecary, where Pru was measuring dried vervain for a customer. The jar was almost empty—he made a mental note to add it to the order list for the next time their supplier came through town. Perhaps with Shadowfade gone, and word spreading that Dragon's Rest was no longer an undesirable place to be, he'd have more options. And more customers.

Hopefully it would happen sooner rather than later—preferably sometime in the next two and a half months. He still hadn't told Pru about the letter yet. *Maybe*, said the little voice in his head that dared to be hopeful, *it will all go away and she'll never have to know.*

He stood behind the counter scowling until the customer left and Pru rounded on him.

"Smile," she hissed. "You're going to scare everyone away."

Nathaniel did not smile, but he did make an effort to relax his face.

"Marginally less disturbing," said Pru, pinching his arm. "Has anyone ever told you that customer service is not your calling?"

"Neither is running an apothecary," he snapped, immediately regretting that he let his sister needle him so. "And yet here we are."

"Oh, whose fault is that?" Pru's tone was teasing, but the moment the words were out of her mouth, she snapped her lips shut. "I didn't mean . . ."

"It's fine."

It wasn't, but Pru knew that already. Belaboring the point would do nothing but make them both feel worse. Nathaniel much preferred his emotions like his workspace: tidy, uncomplicated, all the messy edges swept neatly out of sight.

Pru looked like she wanted to say more, but Nathaniel was grateful when all she asked was, "You gave Violet the keys?"

"Yes."

"How was she?" In perfect Pru fashion, she seemed content to change the subject. Fine by Nathaniel. "Poor thing must be exhausted after all that magic she used at the park yesterday. I should have had you bring over some pixie dust to ease the magic burn. I know we still have some left around here somewhere . . ."

But Nathaniel had stopped listening after "magic she used at the park yesterday."

Any average mage who had managed to dispel a slide of rock goblins with the ease Pru had described would have exhausted herself. And yet Nathaniel had seen before his very eyes the garden Violet created from thin air barely an hour after she saved Pru in the park. He could practically still smell the scent of her magic—tart blackberry and nutty almond—as the garden burst to life.

He'd seen the effects of magic burn before, the way it brought a person to their knees, sometimes causing fever, chills, or even a magically induced sleep that could last for days. People who overextended their magic looked exhausted if they managed to stay conscious, with dark circles under their eyes and a pallid tone to their skin. He'd even heard of extreme cases where their magic became permanently diminished. It was one of the risks of using innate magic rather than drawing upon an external source as in alchemy, because there was no known way to prevent magic burn and no way to speed the recovery. Magic was above all else a balance, a give-and-take—and this was part of the cost.

But Violet had been bright-eyed and alert when he'd seen her just moments ago, as if yesterday had never happened. Could she have some sort of amulet? A device that allowed her to draw on some other source of power?

Or could it be that his new tenant was much more powerful than any small-town florist had the right to be?

FIRST SALE

Violet was an early riser, but not so early as her new landlord. Each morning, she found him already in the greenhouse when she came downstairs from the little suite of rooms above what would become her shop, frowning over a cauldron or measuring pots of dried herbs on the brass scales that winked in the glare of the sunrise.

After the third or fourth time his eyes skittered away from hers when she looked up, she realized he was watching her. Did he think she was going to steal something? Knock over more of his belongings, which he'd now stacked carefully in the farthest corner of his half of the greenhouse? Did he think to scare her off?

She supposed in a way she understood. She didn't know the particulars of the Marsh twins' situation, but it was clear that Violet renting the shop had been more Pru's decision than Nathaniel's. Having choices thrust upon her was something Violet could relate to, and she knew it wasn't always comfortable. It made sense that he would chafe at the restriction.

But she wasn't used to being looked at this way—not with fear or envy but with such blank indifference that she could not read it. He looked at her like she was nobody, and she hated the way it nettled her.

Don't you know who I am? she wanted to ask in a seething hiss. *Don't you know who you're dealing with?*

But no. As Violet left the greenhouse that morning, shaking off the weight of his stare, she reminded herself that she *was* a nobody now. And being a nobody in this town—being a nobody to Nathaniel Marsh—was a good thing.

Violet pushed open the back door to her shop and forcibly pruned away further thoughts of her inscrutable landlord and his inkwell eyes—they couldn't watch her here. She took a deep breath and looked around the open space, marveling again that she was really giving this dream a go.

Potential bloomed in every corner of Violet's new shop. The rounded oriel window with its mullioned panes was lined with shelves that would let in the perfect amount of light for plants, and the beams above her head looked plenty strong enough to hold more of them as soon as she had time to make some woven hangers. The space was airy and bright, with plenty of room for her to work—and now if Violet could only master the skill of conjuring plants without drawing on dark magic, she'd be up and running in a matter of weeks.

It turned out that while using the Thornwitch's near-inexhaustible spring of power was like dunking her head beneath a waterfall to drink her fill, Violet the Recovering Villain had to haul this new magic up by the heavy bucketful from a deep well. It was growing easier the more she practiced, but there was no eager jolt of magic through her veins, no flood of vicious joy like she usually felt. She hadn't realized until she left Shadowfade Castle just how much she'd come to revel in the evil within her. Being good felt hollow by comparison.

She held out a hand to try it once more, picturing a lily, imagining silky, freckled petals and a long stamen dusty with pollen. The Thornwitch's magic leapt to her fingertips, eager and thrilling, but with it came the familiar sensation of thorns that prickled beneath her skin. Violet stanched it and forced her eyes to remain their golden brown, but it was like a tap had been turned off.

"Come on," she muttered. Finding the other spring took concentration. It helped to imagine she was running her hands along a rope in a dark room, her fingers blindly but methodically searching for a place where it knotted.

There.

Violet grabbed hold of the knot and hauled on the rope, bringing the magic into her and bracing against the sudden sting in her fingers. After a moment, a lily appeared dutifully in her hand, though its petals were a touch wilted. Violet stared at it, wondering if she could *supplement* with dark magic, at least until she got better at going without. But no—that was the point. She was done with all that. No exceptions.

Using this morally virtuous brand of magic felt like she was exercising a muscle she hadn't realized she even had.

"I just need to practice," she reasoned aloud to Bartleby, who was idly attempting to juggle a letter opener. She flexed her hands, trying to rid them of the nettle-like sensation, and squinted at the lily, breathing a bit of life into it until the wilted petals perked up. *There.* She conjured a full bouquet of colorful blooms, each a little easier than the last, though the stinging in her hands increased to a dull burn.

"See?" she said through gritted teeth, showing the flowers to Bartleby, who had begun using the letter opener to fence with an invisible opponent. "Practice! A bit of that every day and I'll be ready."

She arranged the bouquet in a little glass vase and placed it in the window, smiling at her handiwork. She'd have to find a supplier for pots and vases, she realized. And for ribbons and paper and twine and all the other supplies she couldn't just grow from the ground with her magic. How much would that cost? And how much would she have to charge for her floral arrangements to turn a profit anyway? That seemed the sort of thing a proper non-evil shopkeeper needed to think about.

Violet wasn't too worried about funds—the jewels she'd taken from Guy's treasury would tide her over for years, once she was able to trade them for coin at the bank. Oh dear, she'd have to set up an account in town, wouldn't she? Violet had never had a bank account before. Would she need a letter from one of her landlords to vouch that she lived here?

And speaking of living, the sparsely furnished little rooms above the shop that she now called her own could use a touch of something. The tiny sitting room had an armchair and a writing desk where she could do her bookkeeping, and the kitchen, clearly converted from some other purpose, had a woodstove and a little round breakfast table, with a hutch she planned to fill with colorful, mismatched dishware and as many varieties of tea as she could get her hands on. The bedroom with its big double window and faded quilt on the bed, and the cramped copper tub in the washroom, were nothing compared to Violet's apartments at Shadowfade Castle, but they were *hers* in a way nothing had ever been before. Perhaps she should brighten them up a bit and put her own stamp on them.

Violet stopped, broom in hand, pile of dust unswept on the floor. She had dreamed of finding a place to call home, of course—a cottage deep in the woods, perhaps, with a cheerful fire in the hearth and a gated garden out back. An apartment in a bustling city and shopkeepers who knew her name and greeted her with a smile. A ship with purple sails and a captain who— But no. Home had never been anywhere but her master's castle. Nerves grew over her like weeds then, and their taproot dug deep. What was she doing?

Guy had told her dozens of times: She was good for one thing and one thing only, and this? Opening a flower shop? This was not it.

She looked at the broom, which was beginning to sprout thorns that pricked at her palms. She startled and they disappeared, the handle budding with leaves instead.

"Just be a *broom*," she grumbled, huffing until the broomstick was just a broomstick once more.

This was what happened when she stopped paying attention. Her magic was always itching to leak from her, as if all her broken bits could never mend and the darkness at her core was constantly oozing from the cracks. She was trying to stop, but *how*, when it was so easy to let it out?

Violet was evil, and Guy had known it from the moment he found her. *Four years old and abandoned by your mother on an island in the Stained Glass Sea*, he'd told her. *You were too powerful, and you couldn't control it. She must have thought you too much of a risk to keep.* As she grew up under his care, Guy reminded her often that if she didn't master her dark magic, it would master her instead.

Your mother didn't understand you, Guy had cooed. *The rest of the world will never understand you.*

But he had. He'd kept her isolated throughout much of her childhood until they were certain Violet could control her powers, and then her training had really begun. Violet had lived among other murderers, ones who were proud of their deeds, who would laugh at her if she showed shame for her own. By all rights, Violet should have grown to be just like them, and for a while it seemed like she might have.

She was an angry young woman with an incredible amount of magic, and Guy had encouraged her to use it to his advantage.

We are building our future, petal. Securing our power. With you by my side, we'll be unstoppable.

It was all he wanted—to be unstoppable, to defeat even the threat of death. In exchange for helping him hunt down legendary artifacts like the Tideheart and the Eye of the Serpent, he'd offered Violet exactly what she wanted most in the world: A place where she wouldn't be alone anymore. A place to belong.

So she'd worked for him, using her magic as he taught her to. No siege could stand against an enemy who could putrefy the food supply, after all, and the dreaded Thornwitch, who could destroy a way of life with a twitch of her fingers, quickly became Shadowfade's most trusted pet. There was a time when Violet even liked it, found that she could channel out all the busy thoughts in her head while she was using dark magic. Violet had been horrible enough to drive away her own family, but she didn't have to be Violet when she was the Thornwitch.

Then came the sack of Silbourne and the collapse of everything Violet had thought she knew. And now Guy Shadowfade was gone. All his talk of immortality, his quests for greatness, his experiments with alchemy and his endless hunt for the Eye of the Serpent—gone.

Violet could feel her dark magic calling to her as always, seductive as a ripe berry on the vine, singing sweet sounds of despair and the euphoria that would come from letting loose a volley of the power she knew lived within her. She wanted to be good, like the Tempest had told her to be. To try for something more. To create happiness rather than misery and to grow roots rather than rot, and if this new magic hurt *her* instead of other people, then she would accept that. She didn't *want* to be the Thornwitch anymore, and so she wouldn't be. Maybe it was as simple as that.

Maybe Violet Thistlewaite could simply live out her days here. At peace.

A crash from outside the shop broke her from her thoughts. For a moment, her body tensed, the broom falling at her feet as she freed her hands, her mind halfway to conjuring thorns beneath her skin or calling the roots of the trees in the Green to lift from the ground and crush the life from her attackers.

No.

No one here is trying to kill you, she reminded herself, forcing a breath into her lungs and some pliability back into her stiff limbs. *No one knows who you are.* The broom had sprouted thorns again, which she quickly banished as she turned her gaze to the front window and drew the curtain. She was surprised to find stalls and carts had appeared as if by magic, dotting Wingspan Green in orderly rows.

"A market!" she marveled aloud, eyes darting to the woman in front of her shop whose overturned cart had been the source of the noise. She had a large, twisted bun of snowy white hair, dark brown skin, and wide eyes beneath pinched, concerned brows. Her mouth was as overturned as her cart, though her frown shifted to an "Oh!" of surprise when she noticed Violet through the window. Someone who was *good* would go out to help, so Violet opened the door.

"Are you alright?" she asked, crouching down to help the woman retrieve the ceramic jars that were rolling around the cobblestones.

"Quite alright," confirmed the woman, gesturing to the broken wheel. "Just frustrated. Not exactly sure how I'll manage this one."

"Let me help."

She and the woman righted the cart, and Violet placed her hand on the wheel. She closed her eyes and urged the dead wood back to life, to grow and mend until the broken pieces were whole once more.

The woman was staring at her, mouth hanging open, and Violet blushed under her scrutiny.

"Sorry about the leaves," said Violet, swatting one of the twigs that had grown out the side of the wheel. "I'll fetch some shears so you can trim them off."

"Well now." The woman blinked at her thoughtfully a few more times, like she was trying to puzzle out whether what she'd seen was real.

Violet's cheeks heated even more. "It's nothing."

"No, I'd say that was *something*. Thank you." The woman's gaze turned studious in a way that began to make Violet uncomfortable, and she repeated to herself once more, like a mantra, that no one here could recognize her without her face full of thorns and that vile purple cloak.

"Oh, you've a—" Violet gestured to the honeybee that buzzed near the woman's head, but then noticed several more. "Bees."

"Almost thirty years together and my wife still claims she's not used to them, but it comes with the territory."

Violet's eyes dropped to the jars that had fallen. One of them had shattered, and a sticky, golden substance was oozing into the cracks between the stones. Honey.

"You're a beekeeper!"

"Yes!" Whatever spell the woman had been under seemed to break. She beamed at Violet. "I'm Quinn, of Quinn Bee Honeybees. You're new here." Her eyes were friendly, but Violet immediately felt defensive.

"Yes, I'm—I'm Violet. I'm opening a flower shop." Her hands were suddenly clammy. Quinn's eyes followed Violet's to the storefront behind them.

"Ah, so you're the Marsh twins' new tenant," she exclaimed. "I'd heard they'd fixed up the place enough to let. And a flower shop! What will it be called?"

Oh, right. A name. "I . . ."

"No matter! It will come to you when you're ready. But you simply must let me talk pollinators with you sometime. Will you import flowers or grow them in your back garden? If you're interested in a hive, I can get you set up. They're great for flowers, which of course you must know already, being a florist."

As Quinn chattered on, Violet felt a thrill at being called a florist by anyone besides herself.

"Oh, but is this one of yours?" Quinn rushed to the big oriel window and marveled at the bouquet Violet had placed there, evidence of her hard-earned practice. She inspected one of the spiky, colorful flowers that nestled among the lilies with awe. "But these—what are these?"

"It's called a protea," Violet explained. "They grow in the Shards."

Quinn marveled at the yellow-and-orange blooms. "Gorgeous! I've never seen their like. And you imported them?"

"Not exactly." Violet wiggled her fingers like she was performing a spell.

"Of course!" Quinn let out a laugh. "Oh, this is wonderful. You're going to do so well here. No one will have seen anything like it! I can't wait to tell everyone. How much for this? I'll draw more customers at market if they have something to look at besides jars of honey."

Violet's eyes flitted to the simple arrangement. "I don't have prices for them yet."

"Two silver stelle," said Quinn, her eyes flashing. "And I'll tell any of my customers who ask where to find you."

Excitement, tinged with more than a little panic, crawled its way up Violet's spine. "I—yes, okay."

Her first sale.

Violet was a florist. She was really creating her own life, and on *her* terms, not Guy's. She fetched the bouquet from inside, smiling at the flowers as she relinquished them to a real customer from her new home. This felt different. This felt good. Dragon's Rest would be a place to start over, to build something of her own, away from the taint of her past.

"It's early for flowers," said Quinn, her nose buried in the blooms, "and I just know my bees are going to love having you around. They usually have to fly all the way to Shadowfade Castle for nectar this early in the season. The Thornwitch was a lot of things, but she kept flowers growing year-round, she did."

"What?" Violet nearly jumped out of her skin at the mention of her past life. She felt like she'd just finished one of Guy's training "games," which generally involved running for her life after he set something unpleasant and deadly loose in her bedroom after she fell asleep.

Best to be prepared for anything, petal, he'd always said.

Violet did not feel prepared for this.

"The Thornwitch," Quinn continued, peering at her. "Oh, but don't tell me you've never heard of her. One of the Dark Lord's most trusted servants. Devastated crops, trapped entire armies in fields of poisonous thorns. Once used her vines to pull a man's entire estate into the sea because he owed Shadowfade money."

That last one was a lie, Violet was tempted to tell her. An earthquake had taken down the entire cliffside before she'd even arrived; she just hadn't denied the rumors. *We are thieves, petal,* Guy had told her. *And if our reputations are in part stolen, well, they still line our pockets.*

Quinn was still talking. "No one's seen hide nor hair of her since he was defeated. Most likely she's gone just like the rest of them. But I've heard her gardens were beautiful."

Violet looked at the crates of honey on Quinn's cart, and another wash of homesickness overtook even the shame of hearing

Quinn recount her past deeds, real and exaggerated. A little piece of her gardens, here in a jar. All she had left of it.

Build a new one, she repeated to herself. *Build a better one.*

"I'd love to talk about installing a hive once I've got everything set up," Violet said with a smile. "And I'd love your thoughts on what I can do to plant flowers the bees will love best."

"Anything's better than nothing at all," said Quinn cheerfully. "But we'll talk. I'll find you!" She managed to make it sound vaguely ominous. *But in a good way?* Violet thought. She got the sense that Quinn was a walking, talking information machine. Violet would be more concerned if she wasn't already being careful of her words around *everyone* she met.

Quinn continued. "I should get going. I need to claim my spot by the trees before Fallon and their ceramic bowls take it again. Corrin—that's the glazier, you'll love her—says they bet her three stelle they could usurp my place! But here." Quinn shoved a jar of honey into her hands. "As a thank-you."

"Oh, I—" Violet held the jar awkwardly. No one had given her a gift in years; even Guy's "presents" were thinly veiled rewards and bribes to keep her in line.

"Come visit my stall once I'm set up," said Quinn, oblivious to the tangled weeds of Violet's thoughts. "I'll introduce you to some of the others."

Violet dragged a shaky smile to her lips. "That would be lovely."

"We watch out for our own here."

She tried not to hear the words as a threat.

LIES

Market Day meant more foot traffic, and Nathaniel wasn't about to turn it down. He was contentedly explaining to one of his customers the differences between ginger and peppermint to ease nausea when the bell above the door tinkled again.

"Be with you in one moment," Nathaniel said to the newcomer, and finished measuring herbal tea, tossing in a sample-sized packet of candied ginger for free after his customer paid. As she left the shop, he turned to the new arrival and the display of skin creams he'd been examining.

"Did you change the scent on these?" the man demanded. "The old one was better."

Nathaniel suppressed the urge to admit that the pearlflower petals he'd used for the scent had grown too expensive, so he'd substituted the ingredient in his grandmother's recipe for another, cheaper fragrance.

"We're trying a seasonal change," he finally said, forcing a stiff smile to his lips.

"Seems like lots of changes being made around here." The

customer looked pointedly at the wall that separated them from the workroom turned rental.

"We don't need all the space," said Nathaniel as casually as he could. The unfinished follow-up to his sentence—*we don't do enough business to merit it*—hung in the air like an apple on a branch that both refused to pluck.

It was no secret in Dragon's Rest that Marsh Apothecary was struggling, and Nathaniel knew what he looked like to the people who had shopped here for decades. He'd been gone too long. He was too different now. He didn't belong here in this town the way he once had.

When Nathaniel Marsh was nine years old, he'd decided he didn't want to be an apothecary. He was on a trip with his mother to select new stock for the shop directly from the merchant ships that docked in Lokoa. The great port city had enthralled Nathaniel as much as it had scared him with its staggering sheer cliffs and floating docks that rose and fell hundreds of feet with the dramatic tides of the three moons. Dragon's Rest seemed outdated and tiny by comparison.

He'd stuck close to his mother's side as she bartered for rare herbs and ingredients that he'd never heard of and watched in awe as a gray-haired woman in dark robes swept past him to a stall that sold stranger items—faceted crystals, feathers that shone gold, and delicate leaves that looked made of glass.

"Mum," Nathaniel had asked. "What is that?"

His mother had glanced at the stall with derision.

"Alchemists," she said scornfully. "Pretty showmen turning one thing into another. They could be of such use—put their skills to making medicines more powerful than any tincture of mine!—yet all they do is craft baubles for the rich and tools of war for the Queen."

Nathaniel had watched as the man behind the stall poured a

concoction onto an onyx hair comb and ran it through the woman's hair. As the comb passed through her locks, it turned the silvery gray to a lustrous chestnut brown. She beamed, looking at least ten years younger.

"I think it's beautiful," said Nathaniel.

"Pah!" his mother spat, and he felt burned by the sudden acid in her voice. "Parlor tricks and criminals."

She led him away, but Nathaniel couldn't get the alchemist out of his mind.

"Why is it so bad to make things that are pretty?" he asked her that night over a hearty bowl of beef stew at the inn where they were staying.

His mother put down her spoon. "Well, darling, it's not. But they rarely stop there. I had a sister who was an alchemist, did you know that?"

"Aunt Althea." Nathaniel nodded sagely, as though he knew more than just the hushed whispers he'd gleaned from adults around him.

His mother's nod was curt. "She made pretty things once. But pretty things have sharp edges, and other people can wield you like a blade if you're not careful." Her voice caught. "Althea died, Nathaniel. Do you understand me? Her alchemy was dangerous and she paid the price. Better to be of use, to be able to help people with something *real*. That's us, my love. We do good. We do something of substance. Not like her. Not like them."

He wasn't clear on who *them* was, but the conversation stuck with him, a constant flame burning just this side of too hot even as his aspirations grew. At nineteen, he told his parents he wanted to join the Crucible, the royal university where the Queen's alchemists trained.

"I want to make it useful," he pleaded to his mother. "I want to apply alchemical practices to make our medicines more effective.

Create cures and methods to make our family's business unlike any other. I don't need power. I don't need baubles. I just want to help."

Da smiled and congratulated him, but his mother hesitated.

"It will change you," she said mournfully. "Five years you'll be gone from us at that school, and then you won't want to come home."

"That's not true, Mum," he said, feeling confident. "I'll experiment and send back ideas for ways to help the shop, and when I've finished my education, I will come home and we'll bring Marsh Apothecary into a new age."

But his mother had only smiled sadly. "We'll see, my love. We'll see."

On the day he left for Lokoa, she told him, "Remember there's more to it than pretty tricks and flashy explosions. You, and only you, oversee your destiny, Nathaniel. Never forget it."

"Five years, Mum," he promised.

It was the first big lie he told his mother.

Once Nathaniel was happily settled in Lokoa, his fingertips blackened with ink and soot, his leather apron smelling of magic and science and all the things he loved most, he was never quite sure how to tell his family that he'd fallen in love with school, and with the city.

He finished university at the top of his class, and with a twinge of guilt, he accepted a research role in the Crucible developing new alchemical solutions for the Queen. He immersed himself in a world of innovation and scholarship, drinking deep from the chalice of knowledge in a quest to quench his ever-worsening thirst.

Before he knew it, ten years had passed in the blink of an eye, and his youthful naivete had evaporated like a decoction left too long on the flame.

If he'd known from the start that his parents would take out a second mortgage on the shop to pay for his schooling, would he have chosen differently? If he'd realized the harm he was causing with his experiments, would he have left the Crucible sooner? If he'd known the violent, disastrous results of his work, would he still have gone? If, if, if . . .

Now, as Nathaniel wore a mask of pleasant goodwill in front of surly customers who knew he didn't belong, knew what he'd done, he wondered at what a waste his education had been. Here he was anyway peddling the same tea and herbs his parents had—only his parents had been able to keep the business afloat.

"If you'd like the pearlflower scent back," Nathaniel said now to his customer, "I can put your name on a list and let you know when we have it in stock once again."

"And when might that be?"

"Ah, well." Nathaniel cleared his throat. "Shipments have been delayed since Shadowfade's defeat—merchants aren't sure what to think." This wasn't a lie, or at least not quite. Several merchants had indicated that they worried news of the sorcerer's death was some kind of trick. Unfortunately for Nathaniel, it was a sentiment that had been accompanied by a steep increase in their prices; now that they were no longer forced to trade in Dragon's Rest with the sorcerer himself, they were giving his town a wide berth until they could determine where the dice had fallen—and what sort of entity might be picking them up in Shadowfade's absence.

To his relief, the customer's expression softened. "Aye, you and everyone else in town," he said. "I work down at the inn, and the brewer from Shadow Springs, where we get our ale, told us we can come and get it ourselves but he won't be delivering to us for the foreseeable future. Now our options are a day's journey to Shadow Springs every other week or purchasing from the Barrel."

Nathaniel sympathized—the Rusty Barrel was the only brewing operation in Dragon's Rest, and its beer was about as appetizing as its name promised.

"We'll come through the other side of it," Nathaniel said with more conviction than he felt. "Now that Shadowfade's gone, Dragon's Rest will find its balance."

"We should tear down his bloody castle," muttered the customer, heading for the door without making a purchase. "That would prove to everyone he's gone for good."

Shadowfade had made his mark upon the town, and Nathaniel would be lying if he said it wasn't part of the reason he'd fought to get away from Dragon's Rest.

He looked around the shop, his eyes lingering on the too-wide spaces between products on the shelves and the jars that were nearly empty. Like all of them here in Dragon's Rest, those merchants were holding their breath because they knew change was on the horizon.

And just like those merchants, Nathaniel was terrified of what that change would bring.

As he waved goodbye to his customer, his eye caught on a now-familiar head of curls just outside, watching the market stalls in Wingspan Green with a certain wistfulness in her eyes. He couldn't forget his suspicions. Something about Violet Thistlewaite was *off* somehow, and like a kernel stuck between his teeth or a stubborn stain he could not scrub out, Nathaniel had become fixated. She was a distraction he did not want or need, especially at a time like this when he should be focusing on his business—but she presented the exact sort of puzzle he couldn't resist, the kind that urged him to pull out paper and ink to start cataloguing hypotheses, to put on his best gloves so he could carefully measure and examine to determine exactly what it was about her that drew his attention so.

Nathaniel told himself that he watched her so closely because he wanted answers. He wanted to know how she was so powerful and why someone with her abilities would open a flower shop in a town as small and sad as Dragon's Rest. He told himself it had everything to do with his own self-interest and nothing at all to do with those amber eyes or the way she always seemed to miss a few strands when she tied her hair up out of her face. It was about the survival of his business, not the high, clear sound of her laugh, which had shocked him like lightning only that morning when Pru ran into her outside the apothecary. He didn't need to make her laugh. It was perfectly acceptable that Violet liked his sister better than him.

Nathaniel Marsh had grown accomplished, over the years, at telling himself lies. Most of the time, he even believed them to be true.

MARKET DAY

A basket clutched to her side, Violet threaded her way through the throngs of vendors and curious customers that had gathered in Wingspan Green. The paths were lined with carts and booths; Quinn waved from hers with a grin as Violet passed her stall. A heavenly smell, thick with spices and sugar, wafted through the air, and a little girl marveled at the small posies in Violet's basket.

"Oh," said the girl on a breath, wistfulness in her blue eyes. Violet smiled at her and willed a spark of magic into a small, pink-daisy bouquet to give it a little extra life. She held it out to the girl.

"For you," she said, but the girl's mother pulled her back.

"No, thank you," she said curtly.

Violet's smile wilted. "That's—of course."

She took a step back, right into someone else. "I'm so sorry."

"Not a problem," said a familiar voice. "Oh, Violet! It's you!"

Pru was dressed in another of her bright dresses, tied seemingly at random with scarves, her hair coiled on top of her head and pinned with a large and cheerful red feather. There was a violin slung over her back like a quiver of arrows. "Enjoying Market Day?"

"I—"

Pru followed her darting gaze to the daisies in Violet's hand, and the mother who was tugging her daughter away by the arm. Her face twisted for a moment before resuming her usual grin. "Elis! It looks like you've met my friend Violet. She's new in town and opening a flower shop. Isn't that just what Dragon's Rest needs?"

The woman—Elis—froze.

"A flower shop, you say?" An unsteady smile settled on her features, though it did nothing to calm the storm of nerves that had snapped the branches of Violet's budding confidence. "We've not had one of those before."

"I'm hoping to be open in just a few weeks," said Violet, her voice timid. She had brought entire cities to their knees! She had wielded power beyond imagining! And this sharp-eyed woman could make her cower all because Violet was afraid she didn't *like* her?

"What are you called?" Elis asked.

"I'm Violet."

"No, what's your shop called?"

"Oh." Heat flushed her cheeks. "It doesn't have a name just yet."

"Hmm. A business worth remembering merits a name worth the same, don't you think?"

Violet had given some thought to it, of course, but like a water lily in the desert, she was coming up dry.

"It will be something wonderful, I'm sure of it," said Pru smoothly. She swiped the daisies from Violet's hand and pressed them to her nose, inhaling. "Ahh. These are gorgeous. Violet, how much did you say you were charging for them?"

Violet startled again. "Oh, there's no charge."

"None? You're sure?"

Feeling suddenly embarrassed, Violet explained, "I just wanted to explore the market and get to know the town."

Pru's expression was still friendly, but her eyes were on Elis. "Of course, because Dragon's Rest is your new home. That's incredibly kind of you, wouldn't you agree, Elis?"

Elis nodded, and Pru handed the flowers to her young daughter, who by now was bouncing on her toes, completely unaware of any subtext between the adults.

"Tell the nice lady thank you," said Elis uncertainly, nudging her daughter until she looked up shyly from her treasure and thanked Violet.

Pru's grin widened. "And remember, once she's open, come see her sometime for more! She'll be just on the other side of the Green, next to the apothecary. If you stop by both our shops, we might even cut you a special discount!"

"We will," promised Elis, and though her smile was tentative, at least now it looked real. Pru waved as Elis led her daughter away to a stall selling whittled wooden spoons and utensils.

"You didn't have to do that," Violet said, and she wasn't certain whether she meant scolding Elis or referring to Violet as a *friend*. She stared down at her basket of flowers, which she'd spent most of her morning growing, exercising her new magic muscles. Some of the flowers looked a bit wonky, but overall, Violet was pleased to find it was getting easier.

"Of course I did," said Pru. "You'll have to forgive her, and anyone else who acts like that. People around here, we—well, we haven't had much reason to trust outsiders in a long time."

The understanding of what Pru was talking about hit Violet like a punch to the gut. Guy was the reason people in Dragon's Rest were suspicious and scared. *She* was the reason.

They had every right to reject her.

Pru nudged her. "Don't worry, they'll come around. Things are changing for the better around here. You're proof of that!"

If only she knew.

Violet allowed herself to be led around the market, handing out flowers with a smile as Pru introduced her to bakers and innkeepers and farmers and craftsmen. With every new interaction she felt more and more on the outside, more and more like Pru's forceful "And we're *so* happy to welcome her to Dragon's Rest" was a stake driven deeper into dried soil, cracking the surface and making clear it wasn't ready for planting. Still, she had to admit that, as word spread through the market and Pru introduced her to more people, Violet received fewer hard stares and more kind smiles.

"How often does this happen?" Violet asked after they walked away from a friendly candlemaker, who had insisted on giving Violet a floral-scented candle in exchange for a bouquet.

"Market Day? Once a week. It's grown smaller over the years, mind you, but perhaps now that Shadowfade is gone, some of the old merchants will return." Prudence looked around the market wistfully before settling her attention back on Violet. "How are you enjoying your new space?"

Violet beamed, brightening up for real. "It's perfect. The ceilings, the shelving, the windows, the—" She paused, and Pru laughed.

"The greenhouse? I imagine that takes more getting used to than the rest. You weren't anticipating having to share."

"Neither was Nathaniel, it seems." She didn't bother hiding her grimace.

"That's my fault, I'm afraid." Pru gave her the courtesy of looking sheepish, at least. "My brother's never been good with change—he's always been a bit rough around the edges. I hope you won't let him intimidate you."

"I've tangled with worse," Violet said truthfully.

"He's been through a lot. Don't get me wrong, he could do to loosen his collar a bit, but I promise you, he's a dragon who only blows smoke."

A gruff voice from near Violet's waist growled, "Are you gonna play, then, or chatter like a pair of squirrels?"

She looked down to find a squat gnome with a shapeless yellow, knitted cap perched on his head, his hands on his hips and his skin blotchy red like he'd been yelling. He eyed Violet with suspicion and scowled at Prudence like she'd done him some great offense, but Pru only smiled back, wrinkling her nose at him.

"Hello, Jerome, you old bat," she said fondly, then winked at Violet. "Duty calls."

Pru leapt up onto the low stone platform Violet had noticed the other day and, in one fluid motion, pulled her instrument from her back like she'd done it a thousand times.

"Hello, Market Day!" Gone was the friendly landlord, and in her place was a performer, her voice booming, her eyes glittering with energy. "I'm Prudence Marsh and you're all in for a *treat.*"

She tucked the violin beneath her chin and immediately launched into a lively tune, her fingers flying across the neck so fast they blurred. Pru's eyes fluttered shut, her foot stomping on the platform until someone on the other side picked up the beat, clapping along. Violet soon joined in, and once Pru was satisfied, she began to dance, her body bending and legs kicking up her skirt to reveal underskirts in contrasting colors, all the while keeping to the beat set by the crowd. Suddenly the scarves at her neck and her waist made sense; as she twirled and leapt across the stage, they billowed out behind her in mesmerizing streams of color.

The crowd thickened, but though she was jostled by bodies,

Violet couldn't take her eyes off her new friend. The bliss on Pru's face was totally foreign—it was clear that this was Prudence in her element. Violet couldn't imagine letting her guard down so completely; her own instincts constantly urged her to watch for threats and gauge the weaknesses of those around her.

How can you turn a situation to your advantage? Guy had taught her. *Look for things that grow. Look for what you can bend to your will. This is how you keep yourself safe.* Violet's instincts had already homed in on the wooden instrument and bow and how easily she could twist them into something sharp and violent.

She felt suddenly exposed, vulnerable, like her root system had been entirely unearthed. The voice inside her that was the Thornwitch was waking up, telling her she needed to prove she wasn't weak or timid. That she wasn't someone to be bossed around and messed with and called "friend" by any of these small, silly people. Up there on that stage, Prudence was vulnerable, her instincts told her. Now was the time.

The time for what? Violet asked herself, and her treacherous thoughts had no response. *You're not a villain anymore. Be good.*

Still, it felt strange and wrong to watch someone throw down their walls and invite the world in for a peek. Although the music was beautiful and Pru's steps graceful, Violet found herself backing away from the stage, the crowd eagerly filling in the space she'd left. By the time she reached the edge of the throng, her breath had crawled up into her throat, refusing to go any deeper into her lungs, and her vision was swimming with dark magic that ached to burst from her. *Let us protect you*, her thorns coaxed, pushing their way to the surface of her skin. *Let us make everything go away.* Violet crouched by a tree, her basket dropping from her arms, and shut her eyes, trying to remember how to breathe.

She wasn't sure how long she sat like that, but when she came back to herself and opened her eyes, the song had ended. Pru was calling out, "Now who among you would like to hear 'The Tale of the Witch and the Warrior,' and how the great stone dragon came to rest beneath this very mountain?"

Violet squeezed her eyes shut and focused on the grass that, in her panic, had grown tall enough to wrap around her knees and had even sprouted little yellow flowers. It nuzzled against her fingers like a cat seeking attention.

Focus on Pru's words, she instructed herself, trying and failing to pay attention to the fantastical story she wove of two lovers fighting a dragon. When she opened her eyes again, there was a wizened old man sitting next to her, carefully placing her flowers back in her fallen basket.

Violet yelped, leaning back sharply. She felt sweaty and clammy and out of control. Her instincts told her it was a feeling that someone could take advantage of if they wanted to, and dark magic threatened to flare within her again at the thought. Her eyes sharpened in suspicion at the old man, who only looked at her with a kind smile and pushed the basket back toward her.

She cleared her throat, smoothing the thorns and calming the tempest of power that raged within her. She clenched her hand around a bit of rock, squeezing to calm herself. "Thank you."

He raised his eyebrows and pointed at her, clearly asking if she was well.

"Oh, yes, I'm fine. I don't—I mean, that's never happened to me before."

The old man stood and offered Violet a hand. She took it and rose to her feet, brushing her dusty hands on the tails of her jacket. She was still holding the rock, and as she dropped it she realized it was shaped exactly like a spoon. *Rock goblins,* she realized. They must have transformed it.

"Thank you," she said again, turning her attention back to the old man.

He waved away her thanks, but then gestured for her to follow him. Violet glanced around her, that voice in her mind once again convincing her that he meant to lead her into a dark alley and pull a knife on her. But he was old and frail, and she was surrounded by soil and trees and things that grew. Like a child might count sheep before bed, she counted the ways she could take him down if she needed to as he led her toward a row of stalls just on the other side of the path. She chided herself for her unkind thoughts when he reached a cart set with a charcoal stove and several rotating spits above the open coals. It turned out to be the source of that incredible smell she'd noticed earlier, which she registered the moment he handed her a warm package wrapped in brown paper.

"I don't have any coin on me," she protested, but he waved her off and motioned for her to open it. Inside the paper was a long, spiraling pastry, shiny golden brown and rolled in glistening sugar. It was cylindrical and hollow inside, and the scent of cinnamon that rose from the cake made Violet nearly faint again for entirely different reasons. The man smiled at her and gestured like she should pull at the edge of the spiral and eat it, so she did.

Violet practically moaned when the pastry hit her tongue. It was sweet and yeasty, with a slight crunch around the edges where the sugar had caramelized. Flavors of cinnamon and vanilla overwhelmed her—it was like nothing she'd ever tasted before.

"This is amazing," she said to the man. "What are they?"

He pointed to the sign on his cart: DRAGON HORNS.

"Making friends, I see?" They both turned to find Quinn standing there, arms crossed, smiling at them. "You fool, you didn't even give her any of my whipped honey for dipping."

"It's perfect the way it is," said Violet, before she remembered who she was talking to.

Quinn laughed. "I see you're in league with Guy, then."

Frost settled over Violet's nerves. "What?" she spluttered.

"Guy." Quinn nodded to the old man, then seemed to realize what she'd said. "*Oh*, not big bad evil Guy. Just regular Guy. Good Guy. It was a popular name for a while, not that it helped our Guy. Shadowfade took his tongue when he was a young man."

The old man—Guy—waved cheerfully, but Violet only felt nauseous. Of course, they were so close to Shadowfade Castle, and Guy Shadowfade had been in power for over a century. It stood to reason that some of the townsfolk would name their children after him to try to please him, just as it stood to reason that people here would bear scars. "I see."

"Guy's dragon horns are fantastic, aren't they?" Quinn winked. "Though not as good as my honey cakes. You'll have to come by for tea sometime and I'll make them for you."

Guy made direct eye contact with Violet, his face losing all traces of humor, and shook his head vehemently.

"Oh, stop it, you," said Quinn brightly. "They were much better last time!"

Guy didn't look convinced.

"Well," tutted Quinn. "I have a new idea for the recipe, so we'll see, shall we?"

Guy made a movement with his hands, and Quinn nodded. "Great idea." She turned back to Violet. "A few of us get together every Thursday and chat. You could come, tell us a bit about yourself and how you came to be here."

But Violet couldn't agree to that. How could she? She still felt cold, and the clamminess she'd felt watching Pru was returning—these were real people who'd been affected by Shadowfade's reign, who had suffered under him. The kind old man who had helped her and fed her—he'd been mutilated by the closest thing Violet had to a father. She didn't deserve their kindness. No matter what she did now, she'd never be worthy of a normal life. Violet clutched the paper that held the dragon horn, crushing the cake in her hands. It tasted like ash now.

"Perhaps," Violet said finally, holding back her tears. She selected the biggest bouquet left in her basket, thrusting it at (Regular) Guy. "For the cake," she choked out. "Thank you."

And then with a shaky smile at the two merchants, Violet turned tail and fled.

LEGACY

The A-frame signboard caught on the cobblestones as Nathaniel dragged it inside. As he shut the curtains in the front windows, he watched from the corner of his eye as the last of the market stalls packed up their wares.

Pru slipped in through the door just before he closed for the night, her violin tucked beneath one arm.

"Hello, brother mine," she said, singsong, as she removed her hairpins and shook out her mane of black hair, dropping the pins all over his clean counter. "How goes life at the apothecary?"

Nathaniel grunted and turned back to counting money in the strongbox. A busy day like today helped, and with Violet's rent money it would go a long way toward their bank payment, but he'd have to find a way to boost business if they wanted to restock their supply of burnroot, whose wholesale price had tripled since the last time they needed to purchase it.

"I saw Violet at the market today," Pru continued, ignoring his bad mood as usual. *Pretty things*, he thought darkly. *Sharp edges.*

"I introduced her to a few people—can you believe the cold welcome she's had? I thought better of everyone."

He ignored the pointed barb, knowing she included him in that sentiment. "We've got every right to be careful," he said, his eyes still on his work.

"Pah!" Pru tutted, sounding so like their mother for a moment that the invisible band around Nathaniel's chest tightened a notch. "Quinn said she had a bit of an episode, poor thing—apparently she's not used to crowds."

"Quinn's a busybody," he muttered. The beekeeper meant well, but part of him would never forget the way everyone already seemed to know his business before he'd even moved home and how she seemed to be at the heart of it. "Why are you listening to her gossip?"

Pru ignored him as though he'd never spoken. "She had a basket of the most gorgeous flowers she was giving away."

"That's no way to run a business."

"I'd call it advertising, I think."

"And when she uses up everyone's goodwill and interest before even opening her doors?"

"You really think that will be the case? Besides, it sounds like her problem, not ours."

"It's our problem when we're collecting her rent money."

Pru tutted again. "I think it's nice what she's doing. Dragon's Rest could use a little brightness. A little hope."

"Hope doesn't pay the mortgage."

His sister leaned back against the counter, crossing her arms over her chest. "When did you get so boring and *old*, Nat? Listen to yourself!"

He narrowed his eyes. "Don't disparage me for speaking sense when you won't. I have a right to be concerned and so do our neighbors. I know nothing about her! Is she fit to run a business? Where did she even come from?" *And what could she do with that peculiar magic of hers?*

"Should have thought of all that before you let me handle leasing the shop," she quipped.

"Don't think that thought hasn't crossed my mind." Nathaniel threw his hands up. "Why don't you seem at all worried about this?"

"Nathaniel." Pru's tone shifted. She wasn't playing anymore. "You've barely been back a year, and you were gone a long time before that. You've seen the shuttered windows of shops and homes, yes, but you weren't here to watch the people flee. You weren't here when Harriston's closed their doors or when practically the entire elven population up and left Dragon's Rest in the dead of night."

"You're forgetting I served with the Queen's alchemists. I saw—"

"I *know*." Something in Pru's voice snapped his head up to look at her. Her playfulness was gone, her eyes as serious as he'd ever seen them. "I know," she repeated, gently this time. "It hasn't been easy for you, and you haven't escaped this life unscathed, even aside from what happened to Mum and Da."

She put up a hand, stopping him before he could even open his mouth to interrupt.

"But it's different here. Your experience counts; I would never try to tell you it doesn't. But ours does too, here in Dragon's Rest—and it's *allowed* to be different from yours. It's alright if other people deal with it differently."

Nathaniel pressed his lips together, trying to force the emotions away. This conversation did not fall under his usual confines of neat and tidy, and therein was his problem. He couldn't organize his grief or guilt in one of his ledgers. He couldn't make it fit into a formula or balance it with alchemy. Even if he could, he didn't want to.

He just wanted it to *go away*.

"Dragon's Rest was dying under Shadowfade," said Pru quietly. "We were holding on out of sheer stubbornness, but always looking over our shoulders in case today was the day he or one of his minions decided to destroy us for fun or use us in one of his schemes. And now that he's gone and someone wants to settle here and build something new, why would I choose to see anything but hope in that?"

"But she could be *anyone*," he said weakly, ignoring the guilt that itched like a too-tight sweater at his twin's words. "We don't know her."

"That doesn't have to be a bad thing." Her voice took on a note of warning. "And before you go any further, I know *you* of all people aren't going to begrudge someone for wanting to start over in a new place. Isn't that exactly what you did?"

Nathaniel grunted. "Yes, and where did I end up?" He looked around him, gesturing to the apothecary that had been in their family for four generations. The apothecary he never wanted. "Right back where I started."

"All the more reason for you to be supportive of someone else trying *not* to end up there."

Pru's words stung. Properly chastened, he turned his attention to his varnished countertops, swiping specks of the cherry bark he'd measured earlier this morning into the palm of his hand so he could dispose of it neatly.

Pru ducked her head until Nathaniel had no choice but to look at her. "Look, I don't want to argue with you or dredge up unpleasant memories."

"Great, then don't."

She sighed at him, the long-suffering sigh of someone who had been exasperated with him since they were in the womb, and he turned back to his paperwork. The jangle of coin turned his head, and he found Pru smirking expectantly, a fat purse in her hand.

"I played a few ditties before the rock goblins came for me," she said airily, her eyes sparkling. She was going to change the subject, then. Fine by him. Mentally, he swept the conversation back out of sight, where it belonged. There. Nice and tidy once more. "They're really cutting my shows short—I'm trying not to take it personally. Anyway, add these coins to the count, why don't you?"

He scowled. "You might have asked if I needed your help here before you left."

"Nathaniel," she said dramatically, batting her eyelashes. "Did you need my help here before I left?"

He'd had barely a dozen customers all afternoon, and she knew it by the meager sum in the box. "That's not the point. We're a team, Pru. We need to work together."

"Work together like you telling me you'd received a letter about Mum and Da's debts?" Nathaniel froze, and Pru's eyes narrowed in triumph. "I ran into Travers from the bank."

"I was going to tell you," Nathaniel said listlessly.

"Were you?" His sister didn't look convinced. "Or were you going to ignore it and hope it went away on its own?"

"I was not—"

"You can't just run away from things that scare you," she said quietly, and suddenly they weren't just talking about their finances anymore. "I feel it too, you know. I miss them too."

His new anxiety potion wouldn't be ready for at least another week, but Nathaniel craved it like a stiff whiskey. He forced a breath through his lungs and turned back to the ledger, focusing on the numbers. "I know," he said without looking at her. "And I'm not running. I'm here, aren't I?"

"Are you?" she echoed, managing to make it sound like an entirely different question.

"Yes," he responded firmly.

"Well then, as you said, we need to work together." She shook the purse she'd earned playing music and shoved it closer to him, smiling a playful, infectious smile that was just so *Prudence*. This was the magic of his sister, that indescribable *thing* she had that he didn't. She could turn her mood around, could summon optimism like she was turning on a switch. He was as envious as he was annoyed. "And this is me working together with you."

"I'd still rather you help me out behind the counter every so often," he grumbled.

Pru clucked her tongue at him. "Oh, come on, Nat. We both know I'm rubbish at the shopkeeper thing. I've got a three-night gig at an inn in Westkeep next week—that'll help, won't it?"

It was true, Pru's music brought in just as much as the apothecary these days—sometimes more. *But there are too many ghosts in this place when you're not here*, he wanted to tell her.

Instead, he sighed and took the purse, spilling it out onto the counter so he could begin to assess how much was there.

"You know," Pru added as he counted, "we could put in a few little tables over there in the corner. We already sell tea, and there's always a kettle going because you're an addict, so if we get a few people in here to drink it, I could play for them every day. I'm sure Guy would sell us a few pastries we could offer."

"We haven't the space. And besides, you'd knock over the shelves with your dancing." He pictured the mess of the greenhouse the night he'd met Violet. She hadn't considered for one second that she'd placed those crates too close to the door. Her face had been so shocked when they tumbled, her golden-brown eyes so wide as she blinked those long lashes at him.

"What about the back garden?"

"No."

"I'm sure we could convince Violet to plant us a lovely patch of flowers. We could clean it up for the summer and—"

"I said no, Pru."

She actually *growled* at him. "Well, what then, you ridiculous grump? You're going to keep your eyes down until we run ourselves into the ground?"

"I'm just doing things the way Mum and Da always did. The way things have always worked."

"But they're not working anymore," she argued. "We need to change course. Wasn't that your plan all along? I know it's a risk, but why don't you try picking up your alchemy agai—"

"We're not talking about this." Nathaniel snapped the ledger closed. His thoughts were mixing with memories again.

"We *never* talk about this!"

"Because there's no point!" It was no use now. There was no way he could keep it all together; his emotions had spilled, shattering from their delicate glass vials to spout toxic fumes he couldn't help but breathe in. "My plan was a disaster. I failed spectacularly, Pru. That's what changing course got us."

"Nathaniel, what happened wasn't—"

"I'm not an alchemist anymore," he insisted. "We'll keep the shop afloat *without* any dangerous new ideas. We always have and we always will. Collecting rent will help, and you can keep performing at the market."

"Right." She laughed humorlessly. "Running the shop. Performing at the market. The lives both of us always dreamed of."

"It's the hand we've been dealt, Pru. There's no point trying to reshuffle the deck now."

"So you'll just keep on being miserable in a job you never wanted, here in a place you should never have come back to?"

"Yes!" He caught his words. "I mean, I'll keep things running here at the shop. I'm—I'm not—"

"Nathaniel." Her tone was pleading; suddenly he didn't want to look her in the eye. He knew what he'd find there, and he needed her pity like he needed another bill to pay.

She laid her hand over his ink-stained fingers and squeezed tightly. "They'd understand, you know." She sounded like she wanted to cry. He still couldn't look at her. "If we changed things, I mean."

"It's their *legacy*," Nathaniel said desperately, as though this could make her see.

"I hear you," she said finally, squeezing his hand once more. "I don't agree, but I hear you. We'll keep going for a bit. We have three months, right?"

"Two and a half."

"Right." She nodded, as if that decided it. "Maybe business will pick up."

She disappeared up the stairs, and Nathaniel realized he'd lost count of the money before him. He started over, his brow furrowed, until the front doorbell rang and he realized Pru had left it unlocked behind her. With a sigh, he schooled his features into something pleasant and friendly and said, "I'm so sorry, we're closed for the evening."

The man who stood in the entryway looked around with interest before turning to Nathaniel with a too-wide smile, like he'd stretched it a bit too thin over his face.

"Are you the proprietor?" His voice was reedy, as though his words were being carried to Nathaniel on a gust of wind that warned of a storm.

Nathaniel straightened. "I am," he said, studying the tall, pale-skinned man. He looked to be a few years younger than Nathaniel, with long blond hair pulled back with a black silk bow and piercing blue eyes. He wore a thick, fur-lined cloak made of fine wool and tall leather boots with pointy toes edged in gleaming silver. A man of means, then. Perhaps looking to part with some coin. Nathaniel urged a smile to his lips. "Can I help you?"

"In fact, you can." The man swept forward until he stood before Nathaniel and held out a hand for him to shake. His grip was cold from the outside air. "I'm an alchemist, and I'm new to this . . . *charming* little town." He said *charming* like someone else might say *ghastly* or *decrepit*. Nathaniel straightened his shoulders. "I'm looking to replenish some supplies for my work."

The skin at the back of Nathaniel's neck prickled. More newcomers. A young witch looking to sell her silly flowers was one thing, but this smarmy, wealthy-looking fellow on top of it? And an alchemist at that? He smelled trouble.

"We'd be happy to help you get set up," he responded as pleasantly as he could. "Tomorrow. During business hours."

The man's mouth twitched. "But of course. You wouldn't mind if I leave you with a list, would you? I know what I'm looking for." He pulled a folded sheet of paper from the pocket of his cloak and slid it across the counter.

Still watching the man, Nathaniel picked up the paper and opened it. His gaze flicked down the list of ingredients, written in a slanting script.

"Several of these are quite difficult to procure," he said in a low voice. His breath hitched as he reached the bottom of the list. He looked sharply back at the man. "Minotaur horn? Powdered hellstone?"

The two ingredients were not only rare but extremely volatile even on their own. *Combined* they were pivotal ingredients in a number of dangerous weapons.

"Familiar with alchemy, are you?"

"I spent ten years in the Crucible." He scanned the rest of the list. Acacia and rue were easy enough to obtain, but curare was a dangerous paralytic, and mane of marea? That was outright illegal.

The man smiled. "A man after my own heart! What in Rava's name are you doing in this craggy mountain backwoods?"

Nathaniel's mouth tightened. "This craggy mountain backwoods is my home."

The man smirked, and the anxious ball of unease in Nathaniel's chest grew and hardened into dislike.

Nathaniel knew when Guy Shadowfade was defeated that his death created a vacuum. For years, they'd been under the sorcerer's thumb, and that had been no picnic, but in a way, his power had kept them all safe. No one had dared to interfere in Dragon's Rest and risk angering a dangerous mage like Shadowfade, but now that he was gone, there was nothing to stop anyone else from moving in and staking their claim—and the people of Dragon's Rest, left all but destitute from decades of hardship, were in no position to fight it. Nathaniel wasn't inclined to feel positively about anything that troubled the waters of his careful life, and the man before him might as well have been a giant rock tumbling off the mountain toward the surface, ready to make waves.

"I'm afraid I'm unable to sell you some of these ingredients," he finally said, his voice several degrees cooler. "We don't keep them in stock."

"Ah." The man paused, assessing Nathaniel with new eyes. "Might you be able to procure them for me?"

"No," said Nathaniel without hesitation.

The man's eyes flashed. He understood the message. "I see, Mr. . . . ?"

"Marsh."

"Mr. Marsh, then. Thank you for your time, and for allowing

me into your . . ." He looked around the apothecary, one corner of his mouth curling. "Fine establishment."

Nathaniel bristled, hearing a *tone* underneath his words, the thread of an insult snagged and pulled taut.

"If anything changes, do send word my way, would you?"

"Certainly," said Nathaniel politely, but something about the man made him know he wouldn't.

"I'll be staying at the Claw & Hoard. You can ask for Sedgwick." He smiled again, with his whole mouth this time, and it brought to mind nothing so much as a dog baring its teeth in warning. *Come closer*, that smile seemed to say. *I dare you.* "You never know. Perhaps something will sway your mind."

ROUGH AROUND THE HEDGES

Marsh Apothecary, read the A-frame sign in elegant, curling handwriting. *Today Only, 10% Off All Teas.*

Violet sidestepped the sign—she'd need one of her own, she decided, adding it to her mental to-do list—and slipped in through the front door, smiling cheerfully at her landlord behind the counter. "Good morning," she said. "I wonder if I might have that shipment you so graciously received for me?"

She'd awoken before the sun this morning after a sleepless night, sure she must be the first one in all of Dragon's Rest out of bed, only to find a note on her worktable in the greenhouse in the same neat script that was on the sign:

A crate for you was delivered to my shop yesterday evening. In future, please be more precise when indicating your address.

Sincerely yours,
N. Marsh

The N. Marsh in question was visibly repressing a scowl at the sight of her now. He wore a sweater vest today, bottle green over a cream, collared shirt that lay unbuttoned at the neck, just enough for Violet to notice the way his throat flexed as he strained to be civil around her. Was it really so difficult for him to be friendly? She'd worked for Guy Shadowfade most of her life, and even she was having an easier time of it. Violet recalled Pru's words from last weekend—*He's always been a bit rough around the edges*. With an internal grumble, she wondered how long it would take her to get past that gruff exterior. She didn't *want* him to dislike her. Moons, she was supposed to be *good* now! Being good meant being likable, didn't it? Maybe she needed to try harder.

"I've put it in the back room," Nathaniel said now, his tone clipped. He spoke to her the way he always did, with a voice like velvet rubbed against the grain: a bit prickly, and enough to make her body flash with the sense she'd done something wrong. "One moment, if you don't mind."

"I don't mind," she said sweetly, and he disappeared through a doorway. Violet contented herself looking around the apothecary. It smelled pleasantly of herbs in here, a cacophony of scents both familiar and foreign. She browsed through the shelves and display tables, delighting at the names of ingredients she'd never heard of before and opening a jar of skin cream marked SAMPLE so she could inhale the eucalyptus and lavender scent. She dipped a finger into the pot and rubbed some onto the underside of her wrist, savoring the creamy feel of the lotion on her skin.

When Nathaniel reemerged from the back room, a bulky crate in his arms, Violet was just putting the lid back on the jar.

"This is lovely," she said, holding it up so he could see what she meant.

"Thank you." He cleared his throat. "It's my mother's recipe."

She almost cracked a smile at managing to squeeze civility out of him. Maybe compliments about his family were the way out of the pit of derision he'd clearly dropped her into. "Is she an apothecary as well?"

His expression soured. "Was. She and my father owned this store until their passing last year."

"Oh." She swallowed. "I'm so sorry for your loss."

The words tasted foreign on Violet's tongue—she'd been around her share of death but never the aftermath, never the expression on Nathaniel's face now, fleeting pain quickly bricked up behind his usual mask of indifference. It was enough, though, for Violet to see what she must have done to those left standing after she decimated fields of crops or destroyed someone's home.

You're good now, she reminded herself like a mantra. *Be good. Be better than before.*

"I'd like to buy it," she blurted, holding up the pot of cream when Nathaniel's brows furrowed. "Please."

"Oh. Well, yes. Alright."

She met him at the front counter, where she slipped a few coins his way. He left them where they were and rolled up his sleeves, exposing surprisingly muscular forearms as he wrapped her purchase neatly in brown paper and twine. Violet froze, staring. It stood to reason, of course, that he'd always had nice arms, that they'd always been there just beneath his sleeves. But she'd had no cause to look at them before. Now she knew they were there, and something about the way he flexed as he tied the package with a length of twine and slipped a sprig of dried lavender through the bow suggested to Violet that she would always be aware of them now, whether she liked it or not.

She turned her attention nervously to the shelves behind him. *Think about something else, Violet*, she urged herself.

"So many empty jars," she blurted. It seemed much better than exclaiming, *You have surprisingly attractive arms*, but he stiffened as if she'd said it anyway. She hastily added, "You must do good business to be so low on stock."

Judging by his expression, she might have been better off making the arms comment.

"Some of our ingredients are quite costly to replace," he said coldly, all but throwing her purchase at her. "Not all of us can grow our stock from thin air."

Just like that, the brief allure she'd felt turned right back to frustration. Violet fought the thorns that rippled suddenly beneath her skin. *Control, Violet. No dark magic. Be good.* "I only meant to pay you a compliment."

"Then you should choose your words more carefully."

Magic bubbled up inside of her like soap suds. "What is it that you want from me?" Violet snapped. "What can I possibly do to make you happy?"

She focused on one of the jars behind her and concentrated hard, pulling magic like a stubborn weed whose roots clung to the soil. She swung her arm toward the counter where he stood, her fist clenched around a thick handful of fresh mugwort, its root system bare from the air in which she'd conjured it.

Nathaniel stared at it, then at her. "I . . ." he said weakly. She didn't move, still holding it out to him. When he finally reached for it, she clasped her fingers around his, holding the mugwort between them.

"I'll tell you what *I* want," she said forcefully. "I *want* to make a home here in Dragon's Rest. I *want* to stop stepping on your toes with every move I make."

His expression was void of emotion, a handsome statue upon which she wished she could read a smile, some kindness, even pity—*anything.* Her voice was softer, woven with a plea when she asked, "Moons, can't you find it in you to at least *try* to like me, even a little bit? *I'm* certainly trying."

"I . . ." he said again, staring at their conjoined hands. His skin was warm, and his strong fingers tightened around hers in a way that wasn't entirely unpleasant. Violet suddenly remembered his stupid gorgeous forearms and realized just as suddenly that she didn't remember the last time she'd held someone's hand.

Nathaniel withdrew from her grasp with a stiff sort of urgency and examined the mugwort. Violet ignored the way her palm felt cold without the contact. After close inspection, he said, "I don't believe your plants will have the same level of medicinal efficacy, if any, as true herbs."

Oh, not the "useless" argument again.

Any goodwill she had mustered for him withered away. "There is no pleasing you, I see," she snapped, piling her purchase atop the crate she'd come for in the first place. "Good day, Mr. Marsh."

His face flashed with alarm, as if realizing at last that he'd been a royal ass, but he said nothing, only watched her as she turned tail and left the shop.

Back in the safety of her own store, Violet let loose a growl, and a wave of power rippled from her, knocking over a display of seeds she'd set up only that morning. Bartleby shuddered and brandished a knife at her, but Violet was too irritated to do more than roll her eyes at him.

"Do me a favor and throw that at the bad-tempered apothecary next door," she snarled, but when Bartleby's aim turned rather enthusiastically toward the wall that separated her shop from Nathaniel's, she relented.

"I didn't mean it," she said with a sigh, disarming the petulant pothos before she became an accessory to murder. "We're good now, remember? That means no homicide." Bartleby grasped angrily at her wrists, swiping for the knife back as she danced out of his reach. *He* had never promised to renounce his ways, she supposed.

She set her newly retrieved blade to the task of levering open the crate.

"He's an infuriating man, though," Violet grumbled. "Rough around the edges, indeed."

But Bartleby had retreated to his pot, curling his vines into a tight ball as he pouted. Just as well. He was a terrible conversationalist anyway.

Having a landlord, Violet was beginning to discover, was a lot like working for an evil sorcerer. They were always watching for her to make a wrong move. Always showing up right when she was in the middle of something and demanding she do something else, because of course they were smarter than her and had better ideas. Granted, her landlord wasn't demanding that she destroy entire villages or extort resources from local nobility or threaten people in his name, so perhaps the analogy wasn't quite as apt as Violet first thought.

Idly, Violet practiced growing peonies, sprouting half a dozen from her fingers before she realized their petals were sharply pointed, as though her angry thoughts had fed tainted water to their roots.

She much preferred flowers to people anyway, she thought as she tried again. Flowers were simple. They were beautiful and made one smile. They didn't go out of their way to antagonize the poor woman who was just trying to start a business, and they didn't—well, it was quite possible Violet was once more getting a touch too personal with that line of thinking.

She tossed the peonies on her worktable and turned to the crate of supplies she'd ordered. Wires thick and thin for shaping and supporting her arrangements, rolls of paper for wrapping bouquets, and small glass tubes for keeping stems hydrated. Violet ran her fingers over a box of decorative floral pins, her anger softening. This week she hoped to receive the order she'd placed with Fallon, a local potter she'd met at last weekend's market, for clay pots that she could sell live arrangements in, and any day now, she was expecting her shipment of glass vases from Corrin, the quiet, kindhearted dwarf who ran the glassworker's studio.

Violet hadn't lied to Nathaniel; she wished for nothing more than to make a home here in Dragon's Rest. She'd taken more than her fair share of riches from Shadowfade Castle, and after seeing the havoc Guy's rule had wreaked upon the town, she felt there would be no better way to supply her own shop than by supporting the local artisans of the town. Her bouquets would be resplendent in Corrin's vases, just as the garden soil she planned to sell would use composted manure from a local farmer and her flowers would be pollinated by Quinn's bees.

She wanted to be a part of this community; she did. But there was more to Dragon's Rest than Nathaniel Marsh, and Violet was done trying to make him like her. He wanted nothing more than to put down her business and make her feel small? Well, she'd let him have his way then, but she'd not give him the satisfaction of any more reactions. She needed to prune Nathaniel Marsh from the garden of her mind before he took over and strangled the rest of the flowers that were slowly beginning to sprout there.

Dragon's Rest was supposed to be a new start. Violet was still trying to figure out who she could become without Guy there to guide her path, and she didn't want to let Nathaniel provoke her into being someone she no longer wanted to be.

Violet supposed, after all, that she was a bit rough around the hedges too.

SCIENCE

He dreamed of the way her magic smelled, his sleep soaked with the scent of blackberry and almond as if she'd steeped herself in his sheets like tea. With every breath, he became more convinced she was right there next to him, and then suddenly she was.

Nathaniel knew this was not real. He knew he was imagining this.

He did not care.

He greedily took in the sight of her, eyes gluttonous for her hair, her lips, the flash of her gaze beneath her lashes. His hands took their fill too, skating reverently across soft bare skin, cataloguing curves that those loose-fitting shirts—and his own brittle intentions—had tried and failed to hide in the light of day.

Because of course he had noticed them; of *course* he had, and here in the safety of the dark he could admit she was a gorgeous little thing. He could savor the amber of her eyes in a way he couldn't the night they met, glass shattering around them. He could luxuriate in the warmth of her hand against his without his own thoughtless words from his thoughtless brain tumbling from his mouth like hurdles for him to trip over. His lips could skim her neck, drawing sounds from her throat that he bottled like specimens for later study.

"What is it that you want from me?" she asked again, but this was more than the conversation he'd spent the rest of the day wishing he could redo. This time, her voice was hoarse with desire, her head thrown back in wanton surrender. This time, he could nip at the skin there, soothing the bite with his tongue almost languidly, like he had the rest of his life to do it, like there was no urgency to the way he made her his.

This time, his words did not catch in his throat, because this time, here in the dark, there was no reason to suppress what he already knew.

"You." He molded himself to her, his body humming as she moved against him, threading her legs with his. She was graceful. Sensuous. *His.* "I want *you*, Violet."

She murmured his name like a promise, and aching to hold her to her word, he ground his hips against hers. This woman would undo him, he realized with prophetic certainty. She would overturn everything he thought he understood. With the same mad conviction, Nathaniel knew that once she led him to the sharp edge of that cliff, he would gladly plummet so long as he fell with the taste of her on his lips.

"I'll tell you what *I* want," Violet said to him on a sigh then, and this too was an echo, a redo, some alternate (and infinitely better) version of their interaction that day. This Violet *knew* things—things about the way Nathaniel felt and thought and *wanted*, things Nathaniel barely admitted to himself in the light of day. Her fingers traced his collarbone, nails scratching lightly at his chest as her attention—and hands—drifted lower. She smirked, her eyes alight. "I want—*oh!*"

Her exclamation was dismayed, and it struck a sour and

unexpected note in Nathaniel's consciousness. It wasn't the kind of *oh* one wanted to hear from one's bedfellow. The dream began to slip from him.

"Tell me," he begged, his mind clinging to her even as he staggered on the edge of waking. He was achingly hard, he realized dimly, and there was a muffled sound that came from—

He sat up in bed, eyes wide as he blinked away sleep.

Hell and Undersea, *that* had been unexpected.

Nathaniel registered the sound that had woken him, a muffled cry from the other side of his bedroom wall, and realized it was one of the rooms they'd leased to Violet—clearly she'd made it her bedroom. His dream-soaked thoughts remained lewd for only a second before he heard the noise again and realized it for what it was: a nightmare.

He didn't like the thought of her in distress. She was smiles and sparkling eyes to him, not cries of dismay in the dark. What troubled her, he wondered, his mind still deep enough in the dream to be unburdened by the confines of propriety, and how could he put a stop to it? He could admit, at least to himself—and especially after *that* display of his imagination!—that he was attracted to Violet Thistlewaite. There was nothing wrong with that; people were attracted to other people every day. Nathaniel was a scientist, and he knew that, in large part, he could blame the dream on biology. But what field of science could possibly account for the urge that struck him then, to march to the hallway door that separated her half of the house from his and break it down so he could wake her and offer *comfort*?

Nathaniel Marsh had been told—by family, friends, lovers—that he was not the comforting type, and he believed it to be true. The fact that he wanted to be for Violet Thistlewaite—even if just here in the dead of night, even if just a little—surprised him. Concerned him. It was more than science somehow. More than something he could quantify. How much of his persistent preoccupation with her these past weeks was the result of actual dislike, he wondered then—and how much came from the way she challenged the status quo of his own feelings?

Moons, can't you find it in you to at least try *to like me?* Violet had asked. *Even a little bit?*

With a defeated sigh, Nathaniel pressed his hand absently against the wall that separated them, as though this could conceivably console her. If only she knew that *liking* her was not at all the problem.

Here now!
Marsh Apothecary,
where you'll find plants
you can actually use.

DAISY

Wind pulled Violet's hair across her cheeks and eyes until, frustrated, she tucked it all back into her cloak and held her hood tight over her face. The Smokewood, just outside of Dragon's Rest, was named for the fog that curled between the silvery trunks of the spindly trees, as well as the bare gray rocks of the mountain around which their roots twisted and wound. A bee buzzed near her head, blown off course by a gust of wind.

"You're a bit early, my friend," said Violet to the insect. "But another month or two and there will be plenty of flowers for you."

Spring was slow to arrive in the mountains, but it was beginning to show signs, the ground spotted with saffron-centered crocuses, dainty snowdrops, and clumps of purple hellebore. The color combination would look lovely in her designs for opening day, which was drawing ever closer. She spotted a young sapling, impressionable and perfect for her uses, and took her knife—reclaimed from Bartleby *again* that morning—to one of its green boughs.

It felt good to be here in the woods. Since Pru had introduced her at Market Day and Quinn had taken her under her wing,

Violet had faced no more suspicion at the hands of the locals, but she had come to discover that socializing and interacting with them was difficult for her.

The other villains at Shadowfade Castle had never been Violet's friends—they were her competition, and abandoning that suspicious mindset did not come easily. She suspected—or hoped, at least—that the practice of being friendly would grow on her, that it would become more natural with time, but for now, it left her feeling exhausted. A day in the woods, with no one else around her but the early spring wildflowers and the birds that sang from the treetops, was like drawing a bucketful of fresh water from a well she'd thought dry.

Behind her, leaves crunched.

She turned, her magic already rushing to the bare branches in that direction, ready to command them to her bidding. Twigs grew sharp at their ends like knives on the whetstone of her power, and the dead leaves on the forest floor rustled, ready to whirl around her like a cyclone, blinding anyone who might hurt her.

But it was Nathaniel Marsh who appeared through the trees, a wicker basket hanging from his elbow. His attention was on a patch of moss slung from a branch, and she watched with interest as he reached to collect it. He wasn't scowling for once; in fact, he looked tired, those coal-dark eyes heavy-lidded but intent on his task, lips slightly pursed, black hair tossed by the wind. He had allowed his stubble to grow longer than usual, and it roughened the sharp edges of his jaw, cast his cheekbones in a shadow that made him look . . . "gaunt" was the wrong word, but foreboding. Secretive. Intriguing.

Violet released the dark magic, cheeks burning with shame for letting the Thornwitch's instincts take over and for the thought that escaped before she could cage it—that it had felt *wonderful* to use magic the way she always had when she was wicked.

"Hello," she said, stepping out from behind the tree. She winced at the change that settled over his features, something like panic, and then the stern mask that hardened his expression to stone.

"Miss Thistlewaite." He nodded to her, staring down at his basket to rearrange his goods. *Forearms*, she thought dimly, watching his coat sleeves with something like resentment. There was something jumpy about him today; he seemed less willing than ever to make eye contact with her. He hadn't caught her staring during her brief lapse in judgment yesterday, had he? He was one to talk if he had—all those unreadable looks in the greenhouse! All that scowling! The exceptionally indecent way he had rolled up his sleeves and wrapped her purchase! And now he wouldn't even meet her eyes! It was rude, wasn't it, to spend so much time watching her and then turn it off like this with no notice? How was she supposed to figure out the rules of the game if he kept changing them?

"I wish you would call me Violet," she said coaxingly, banishing the odd sense of frustration she felt when he wouldn't meet her eyes. "Really. I want you to."

His face spasmed like he was in pain. "You *want*—" He spluttered, choking on his words. "You *want*," he said again, this time more to himself than to her.

Three moons, he was strange. "Is it such a difficult ask?"

"It's not *that*." The poor man looked like she'd thrust him beneath a spotlight in front of a packed crowd—and she might not know him well, but she knew enough to guess that was his worst nightmare. "Violet. Yes, I can call you Violet."

She caught her lip between her teeth—this was the most

they'd gotten along since, well, ever, and she wouldn't ruin it by laughing. "What brings you to the woods?" she asked instead.

He lifted his basket with those arms of his. "Foraging. Crow moss is quite useful for making poultices. And there are a handful of herbs that start their growth season out here this time of year. I'm looking to harvest them before someone else does."

"So you can sell them in the apothecary?"

"Cheaper and more efficient than ordering from a supplier."

She cracked a smile. "Plus this way they're local."

"Exactly." He finally met her eyes. "What brings you, then? To the woods?"

Violet held up one of the boughs she'd collected. "I'm building shelves for my shop. Green wood is much easier to persuade than anything fully grown or long fallen."

"Persuade?"

"I can create growing things from nothing or convince already growing things to do my bidding. It's easier to ask green wood to grow and shape itself the way I'd like than a fallen log or hewn lumber."

He narrowed his eyes, and she understood that something she'd said had set the wheels of his brain churning. Fascinated, she watched as he clearly set his thoughts aside and said simply, "So you're foraging too."

"I suppose I am." She wanted desperately to ask him what he'd been thinking about, but it felt private and they were barely on civil terms. "It's nice to be out here in the quiet, I suppose. Dragon's Rest is a bit more crowded than I'm used to. Busy. Noisy."

He *hmm*ed. "I'll admit, I took you for someone who enjoyed that."

"Because I haven't rusted my mouth into a permanent scowl, you mean?" She cocked her head and grinned so he'd know she was teasing. "It might surprise you to know I've never lived in a city. Or among many other people at all, really."

"That does surprise me." He leaned against the tree trunk, watching her with inscrutable eyes. "You've adapted to it quite naturally. Everyone in town seems very taken with you."

She narrowed her eyes, waiting for a veiled insult or scorching remark. But it never came.

"Is that a compliment?" she asked finally.

He had the decency to look embarrassed. "Is that so surprising?"

"From you? Yes."

He looked abashed at that. "I deserved that."

Violet softened. "It's nice, sometimes, to escape the noise. To feel none but your own presence."

"Sometimes, I suppose." His expression darkened. "Though it depends which thoughts are there to keep you company."

"That's certainly true." She nodded behind her and beckoned for him to follow. "Come on, I found a patch of crow moss over here earlier. I'll show you."

Crow moss, so named for its iridescent black sheen and feathery texture, grew best in early spring before the cold fully released its hold. Here in the Smokewood it was abundant if you knew where to look. Violet picked her way over roots and logs, checking back over her shoulder for Nathaniel to make sure he was still following her, and showed him to a large, flat boulder where it grew in thick patches. They dropped to their knees in the dirt and, side by side, set about gathering. While the basket steadily filled with downy black moss, a gust of wind carried his scent to her, a whiff of sharp mint and fresh rosemary that clouded her senses like stirring up a riverbed. She wasn't sure what she expected, but the herbal mix suited him. She . . . liked it.

When they exhausted the boulder, she was almost surprised to find he kept to her side as they set off in search of more.

"Is business going well at the apothecary?" she asked politely.

"It's . . . fine." Once again, quiet settled over them like snow, broken only by the crunching of leaves and twigs beneath their boots.

"I'm hoping to open my shop next week," she chattered to fill the silence. "Just a few more finishing touches and I'll be ready to grow!"

She regretted the pun immediately, but after a stilted pause he responded, "I can't be-leaf you managed it all so quickly."

Violet whipped her head around to stare at him, but he avoided her eyes. Had Nathaniel Marsh just made a *joke*? Wordplay, even?! She wasn't certain what to make of this new development.

He changed the subject before she could probe any further. "Why do you forage for branches, green or not, when you could conjure them from nothing? Is there a difference in the strength or longevity?"

She shook her head, bristling as she thought of the mugwort she'd conjured for him, and his reaction to it. "My magic does hold up, you know, regardless of whether you think it has any medicinal use."

Violet took a startling amount of pleasure from his abashed expression.

"I didn't mean to imply otherwise."

She settled and, after a moment, relented. "Growing them from nothing sometimes . . . stings a bit," she said truthfully, flexing her hands and debating how much to tell him. "Starting with a living plant rather than air is easier for me."

"So you *do* get magic burn," he said, sounding strangely victorious. "I was starting to think you were some sort of legend."

"Hardly." Violet cocked her head and laughed nervously. "I have limits, just like anyone else."

It felt like those limits had been staring her in the face lately. Her darkness still called to her, and though the new way of doing magic had grown easier, it wasn't the same. Even before, she had not been infallible—after all, it had been five years and she was no closer to figuring out how to turn Bartleby back to a human than when she'd first transformed him by accident. (It was likely for the best, though she didn't ever say so to him directly. Murderous as Bartleby the plant might be, he had been far worse when he had opposable thumbs and could lift a greatsword.)

"I certainly haven't seen any limits," said Nathaniel, drawing her from her morose thoughts.

And you'd know, wouldn't you? she almost responded. *With the way you've been watching me.*

"Mostly," she said instead, returning to a safer route of conversation, "I just forage because I like being out in the woods."

He nodded slowly, accepting the olive branch. "You said you didn't grow up in a city. Where did you come from?"

Violet prickled, though for once not physically. Still, the spindly boughs of a nearby hawthorn reached for her like it meant to wrap her gently in its branches.

"I was born on a ship in the Stained Glass Sea," she said, reciting what little truth she knew. The hawthorn leaves tickled her shoulder, and she let them. "My mother was captain of a merchant ship. But I've spent most of my life inland."

"Near here?"

"Sort of," she said vaguely. Was he prying? Did he suspect her identity? Violet took a deep breath to calm herself. She was getting carried away. People were allowed to be curious, to take an interest in her life. It didn't mean he—

"What brought you to Dragon's Rest, then?"

For a split second, Violet considered showing him, letting the thorns that lived beneath her skin come to the surface and the green light of her sorcery shine through her eyes like a predator in the darkness. She could destroy him where he stood, pull roots from the ground to trap him in place or bury him beneath the still-thawing ground. Force poisonous plants to grow all around him, leaving him senseless or sick or hallucinating from their toxins. She could—

No.

She quashed the instinct, pruning it from her will like a branch that grew in the wrong direction. Violet Thistlewaite wasn't the Thornwitch. Not anymore. *Shoo*, she thought, banishing the hawthorn back to its natural position. *This* was why she needed to be in constant control of her magic. It was too easy to slip back into old habits otherwise.

Nathaniel was still waiting for her response. With a sigh, she finally said, "Haven't you ever wanted to start over?"

When no answer drifted back to her over the wind, she looked over her shoulder to find him watching her with a frown. For once, she could easily decipher the language of his expression, and she was surprised that it read like understanding.

"Yes," he said at last. "I suppose I have."

There was something in the way he looked at her then—sad and real—that made her think perhaps she was seeing him truly for the first time. They couldn't be more unalike or come from more different backgrounds—and yet some inner sense told Violet that he understood and wanted her to know he understood regardless of whether he liked her personally. It made her feel warm all over, like she was on the cusp of casting off her cloak even in this harsh wind, but at the same time like she should clutch it closer lest he see more of her beneath. Was there a word for that feeling? And if there was, did she want to know it? Violet clenched her fists to brace herself against the rocking wave of that strange emotion and stared at him until she tripped over a root and careened into the soft floor of the forest, effectively ending her line of thought.

He dropped to his knees next to her in the dirt, his hands hovering as she brushed damp, silty soil and wet, decaying leaves from her trousers.

"Are you hurt?" he asked, scanning her carefully.

She shook her head and he leaned away, settling that mask of indifference back over his features as if the moment between them had never happened. Violet found she craved seeing him without it again.

"I'm quite used to having my hands covered in dirt." To prove her point, she waggled her fingers, tugging at her magic until a white daisy crept up from the ground between them. Violet plucked it by the stem, handing it to Nathaniel. He took the flower from her, tucking it into his breast pocket like a boutonniere, and used his other hand to help her up.

For the second time in as many days, she felt that zing of awareness at his touch, only this time he didn't let go or say anything rude. They just stared at each other, neither making any move to let go of the other's hand. Violet wasn't used to touching people—she wasn't accustomed as Pru and some of her other new neighbors were to a hug goodbye or a casual nudge to punctuate a point, so she wasn't sure how commonplace this was to feel so alert, so alive at the touch of another's skin.

As a lock of Nathaniel's thick black hair blew over his face, Violet could see her own reflection in his eyes, pale and unsure of herself, her hair whipping in the wind. Every time she'd found Nathaniel Marsh looking at her, she'd lamented how difficult he made it to read his expression, only today it seemed he had briefly pulled back the heavy curtains and thrown open the windows, inviting her inside to a room that felt surprisingly cozy and welcoming. *Come and warm yourself by my fire*, his eyes said to hers. *Stay awhile with me, if you want.*

A small part of her—perhaps the Thornwitch, perhaps the florist, perhaps some part she had not yet met—thought she rather did want that actually.

A small yelp broke the moment and had them both whirling around, hands still clasped.

"Did you hear that?" Nathaniel asked, sounding strangely breathless.

From beneath a scraggly bush that hadn't yet budded any leaves for the season, a pair of onyx eyes watched them.

"What is it?" Nathaniel whispered. Violet realized her hand was still in his and jumped away, the cold air chilling her palm as soon as she let go. For someone who had so little experience in the act of hand-holding, Violet could already see how it could become an addictive drug.

"*Crrrrreaugh?*" A croaking sound came from the bush, and Violet let out a squeak of recognition as an odd creature the size of a small dog crept timidly closer. A rock goblin! Was it one of the ones she'd seen that first day in Wingspan Green? She couldn't be sure.

"Hello," she murmured as it—she? He? They? He, Violet decided capriciously—crept closer. A greenish yellow crystal made up the front of the rock goblin's chest, translucent and prominent against the dusty granite of the rest of him like a gleaming breastplate. The goblin opened his blunt-nosed snout, displaying a row of smooth polished rocks where teeth would normally be, and let out a little croaking bleat that Violet took to mean *Hello back* or perhaps *You look delicious, I'm going to eat you now.* She didn't speak rock goblin so she couldn't be sure.

But Violet knew what it was to be feared, and she also trusted her magic enough to know she wouldn't go down easily even if the rock goblin tried something, so she remained still.

"Where's the rest of your slide, little friend?"

The creature let out another one of those bleating sounds and skittered a few steps away. He looked back and whipped his blocky little head around in a passable imitation of a nod.

"Are rock goblins intelligent?" Nathaniel asked. "Is he asking us to go with him?"

"I have no idea." But Violet was already following him, and with every step she was more convinced the rock goblin was indeed leading them somewhere.

"We should be careful," Nathaniel said. "Rock goblins travel in groups. He could be leading us into a trap."

As if in response, they heard that yelping again.

Violet frowned at the rock goblin, who remained still, watching her with unblinking, stony eyes. "That wasn't you, was it? It didn't sound anything like the noise you made before."

The rock goblin took three steps toward another scraggly bush and then sat on his haunches, staring up at her again expectantly.

With Nathaniel's warning in mind, Violet knelt to the ground, her magic at the ready.

"Hi there," she said, and leaned down to peer beneath the bush.

A flash of pale fur caught her eye. Not another rock goblin, then. Violet grew bolder, leaning toward it. A rumbly growl rang from the space, followed by another barking little yelp.

"I think it's . . ." She laughed, clapping one of her filthy hands over her mouth. "Nathaniel, it's a dog!"

Sure enough, a small puppy cowered beneath the bush. She had pale yellow fur, speckled with mud and matted against her body, and dark brown eyes that regarded Violet suspiciously.

The rock goblin had disappeared.

"I won't hurt you, little friend," she said in a low, calming voice, reaching out a hand. The dog barked back and growled again, cowering away from Violet.

"Here," said Nathaniel, squatting down next to her. He pulled a small, wrapped item from his pocket and handed it to her. Violet pulled back the paper and was suddenly overwhelmed by the mouthwatering scent of roasted ham, sage, and gooey cheese, all wrapped in flaky golden dough and kept warm by some enchantment on the wrapping paper.

"A family friend of ours makes them," Nathaniel explained, tearing a corner from the pastry. His eyes were on the puppy and softer than she'd ever seen them. "Guy—not the *bad* Guy, he's—"

"We've met."

"Yes, well." Nathaniel's eyes went back to the pup. "Perhaps our new friend might be hungry."

Nathaniel Marsh was evidently a dog person. Her heart thawed as he knelt next to Violet and held the piece of pastry out with an open palm. "Hello there," he said in a low, coaxing voice that was kinder than she'd thought he was capable of. "Would you like a bite to eat?"

The puppy stopped growling when she smelled the food and crept forward. A thin scratch wove across the side of her nose, and there was a small notch missing from her ear.

"She looks young." Nathaniel's low voice, much closer to Violet's ear than she'd anticipated, carried a slight rasp that sent an inexplicable wash of heat through her. Surprise, she reasoned. She hadn't realized they were so close.

"Much too young to be away from her mother," she agreed, smiling when the puppy swiped the food from his hand and dashed back to safety beneath the bush. She tore another piece from the pastry and handed it to her. "Another?"

It took three bites before the puppy would let Nathaniel

scratch behind her ears. After the fifth bite, they were nearly out of food, but the puppy barely protested when Nathaniel scooped her into his arms.

"Hello, sweetheart," he said, scratching her neck. "Where's your mama? Your siblings?"

Violet eyed the scratch on the pup's nose, the mud caked into her fur. "I don't think she has any."

The puppy nuzzled into Nathaniel's coat and sniffed at the daisy in his pocket.

"Ah," he said, pulling her away from the flower. "I don't think that's going to be good for you."

Violet smiled. "They're just about the same color. Maybe she just wants to wear it instead."

"She sprung from nowhere like one as well. Perhaps we should call her Daisy." Nathaniel's eyes were firmly on the dog as he scratched her neck and checked her over for injuries. He murmured sweet words into her ears and allowed her, his face stern as ever, to lick his stubbly cheeks. Any thoughts Violet might have harbored about taking the puppy for herself dried up like a leaf in the desert when she saw that his look of fondness never wavered, even when the puppy left muddy paw prints all over his clean clothes and upset some of the herbs in his basket during a particularly energetic bid for belly rubs. It was clear where she would find her home.

"Daisy it is," Violet agreed quietly, smiling at them.

Rough Around the Hedges
FLORAL & GARDEN SHOP
NO BETTER MEDICINE
FOR A BAD
DAY THAN
A BEAUTIFUL
BOUQUET!

No Better Medicine
Than Actual Medicine
MARSH
APOTHECARY

GRAND OPENINGS

Nathaniel was halfway through his second cup of tea before he even noticed the increase in foot traffic outside his front window. He strode across the floor of his empty store, teacup in hand, to see what the fuss was about.

Behind him, Daisy barked and padded over to stand beside him. Nathaniel used his free hand to scoop the puppy into his arms, as had become their custom over the past week. She left pale fur all over his clothes and had a habit of gnawing on the baseboards when he left her unattended, but Nathaniel already couldn't imagine his life without Daisy. Pru had immediately taken to her as well, as he'd known she would.

"What's going on, sweet girl?" he mused quietly, scratching her behind the ears and gently prying her razor-sharp puppy teeth away from his lapels. He peered out the window and found a tiered display of flowers outside his neighbor's shop, partially blocking his view.

Ah.

So Violet had opened her doors.

Daisy whined, nosing his teacup until some of the hot liquid dribbled onto the saucer. Nathaniel set aside the cup, holding the puppy with both arms as he stepped outside. The front windows of Violet's shop were framed inside and out with flowers. Wisteria hung from the roof, big bright blossoms wafting sweet smells up and down the street, so garishly out of season—particularly in their mountain climate—that it felt like some kind of ruse. Inside the window, shelves were loaded with greenery and flowering plants in pots and vases of all shapes, sizes, and colors, and in front of the door was her A-frame sign, much like his own, with a message written in chalk that he hadn't been able to resist a response to.

Nathaniel scowled at the people who streamed in and out of Violet's shop, completely bypassing his own front door. Daisy wriggled in his arms. Violet would do well for the first week or two, he predicted, but as soon as the people of Dragon's Rest whetted their curiosity, they'd realize she offered nothing of real use to them. His apothecary, on the other hand . . .

Hadn't seen a customer all morning.

Mum and Da would have known what to do.

Nathaniel's grief for his parents was like the tides beneath the three moons—it came and went in dramatic cycles. He felt it threaten to flood him now, the deep melancholy, the *guilt*—and shoved it back down, clutching Daisy to his chest like a lifeline. He could do this, he thought, nuzzling his nose into her soft fur. He could keep their legacy alive.

He narrowed his eyes at his neighbor through the window. He could only catch a glimpse of her through the glass, shaking with laughter at something one of her customers had just said. Unbidden, that blasted dream rose to the forefront of his mind once more, and his face heated with embarrassment. He couldn't get the image of her out of his head. Couldn't *un*remember what she had felt like beneath him, for even if it had been just a dream, it had been the most vivid one he'd ever had. Still, it felt rude to think of her that way. Invasive not just to Violet but to his sensibilities. It wasn't as if he'd done it on purpose, after all!

Of course, he supposed she did cut an appealing figure—objectively, he meant—in the gray trousers he'd come to think of as something of a uniform for her, and her green half apron embroidered with flowers did—again, *entirely* objectively—draw a rather interesting amount of attention to the tapering of her waist beneath her oversized shirt. If he were to ever buy a bouquet of (Pretty! Cheerful! *Useless!*) flowers, she would be the type of person he would want to buy them from.

Not that he would ever become a patron of her silly little store.

And besides, there was still the matter of her display blocking his window.

He marched inside, noting the sky-blue accent wall behind her with something like surprised approval and the rows of shelves that appeared to have been grown directly into shelf-shape from live trees. He hadn't quite understood what she meant when she was cutting those boughs, but looking at the shelves now, it was clear she'd done exactly that, encouraging the wood to grow and twist and create surfaces where she could display her products, with extruding branches for hanging plants. Garden tools hung from hooks, their wooden handles with that same natural style gleaming and softly curved in a way he suspected would fit into his hand like a well-loved walking stick. And everywhere—*everywhere*—were flowers. Live houseplants and potted blooms in soil filled every available gap on the shelves, with little handwritten signs stuck into their edges to show the buyer how much sun and water each one needed. And permeating the entire shop, amidst the smell of fresh flowers and damp, earthy soil, was the blackberry-and-almond scent of her magic.

It had barely been a month since her arrival, but the whole space was transformed into something bright and pretty. Pru's words came to his mind: *Dragon's Rest could use a little brightness. A little hope.* Looking at the space, for just the barest moment, Nathaniel found it a little less hard to believe that his smiling neighbor could bring that hope to a town that was starved for it.

Arrangements of cut flowers were everywhere in vases or wrapped in paper, and buckets filled with individual varieties hung behind the worktable Nathaniel still could not look too closely at. A sign hung above the buckets that proclaimed Custom Bouquets in what he now recognized as her scratchy, rushed excuse for handwriting, and that murderous plant she called Bartleby had wound himself in loops over the edges of the sign like a snake dripping from a branch, one of his vines reaching for the pruning shears Violet must have left on the table.

"Nathaniel!" Violet looked at him with a smile that sparkled with joy. The effect of that smile aimed directly at him for once, combined with his name on her lips, made Nathaniel forget momentarily why he had come. "And Daisy! Welcome!"

Daisy, the adorable little traitor, wagged her tail so hard that Nathaniel got a mouthful of fluff. She'd met Violet a dozen more times since that day in the woods, and she never failed to pull a glowing smile from the florist.

"Are you being a good girl?" Violet asked, rushing over to hold Daisy's face between her hands. Daisy offered her a slobbery lick on the nose, her little furry body practically vibrating with joy. He could not rationalize the satisfaction that tingled through him whenever he saw how much his dog had taken to Violet, so he chose instead to take no notice of it whatsoever.

"It looks so different in here," said Nathaniel, uncomfortably aware of how close Violet was standing. He held Daisy nearer to his chest, watching how the movement pulled Violet's hands, still scratching behind Daisy's ears, closer to him too. His eyes dragged across the soft bow of her lips, the slope of her neck, the skin that he suddenly wanted to— But oh no, *that* would certainly not do. Nathaniel prided himself on his self-control. It didn't matter how much the imagined memory of her in his arms occupied his thoughts; not even her pretty smile and captivating eyes would tempt him into doing something reckless like *acting* on this feeling. So he cleared his throat and ignored the acid drip of disappointment when she straightened, backing away to a more suitable distance.

"Yes, different was the idea." She hesitated. "Do you like it?"

Nathaniel was halfway through a nod when he remembered the reason he came. "Your display," he said, his mouth tightening to a frown. "It's blocking my window."

He could have shivered in the sudden absence of her sunshine smile. It appeared again a moment later, but without any of the warmth that had struck him the first time. "I'm sorry," she said, and her voice was friendly but distant. "I'll move it."

Nathaniel knew he would jot this moment in excruciating detail onto a little card in his brain and file it in the thick stack of others just like it. He could—and would, ad nauseum—pull it out later and berate himself for his inability to talk to Violet without going all anxious and curt. Pru would have had her laughing by now. Quinn would have coaxed her life story out of her. *Anyone* would have done better than him.

"Thank you," he said softly, trying to sound like he was truly grateful. There, that was better. He didn't sound like he hated her at least.

"You're welcome." She narrowed her eyes at his abrupt change in tone. "Is there anything else you need?"

"No. I'll just be—" He cleared his throat and focused his attention on Bartleby, who waved menacingly at him, the shears now proudly wrapped in his vines. He hadn't known a plant could be threatening before Violet came to town. He turned back to her, afraid to attract more attention from the pothos. "I do like it. What you've done with the space. It looks lovely. Very . . . it looks like *you*."

An irritated flush warmed his skin when he realized he'd effectively called her lovely.

Well, it was the truth, wasn't it?

"Thank you." She looked like she would say something more, but a customer stole her attention away. Just like that, her brightness returned, and Nathaniel amended his earlier thought. Her business would survive three weeks, not two, on the power of that smile alone.

He slipped back over to his store, shaking off the flower witch's spell, and realized his cup of tea had long gone cold. He set Daisy down behind the counter and put the kettle on the stove for another.

"It doesn't mean anything," he told the puppy, who was too busy chewing on a piece of knotted rope to pay him much heed. "I was being kind to a neighbor, that's all."

But moons, that smile of hers had jumbled his brain, and that simply would not do. This—this *infatuation* of his was becoming inconvenient.

Nathaniel had just poured himself another cup of tea when he heard a throat clear behind him.

"Excuse me?" A man stood before him, an infant in his arms. "The woman at the flower shop said you sell herbal remedies?"

Nathaniel's jaw dropped. She was sending customers to his shop? "I . . . yes. Yes, we do," he said, snapping into customer service mode.

The man shifted the baby in his arms. "Do you carry mugwort?"

Nathaniel's eyes flashed, remembering the handful of herbs Violet had conjured for him.

Was she *mocking* him?

Any goodwill he'd dredged up for her during his visit to her shop evaporated. Perhaps it was retaliation for asking her to move her display. He felt bad about how he'd responded to her gesture that night, he did, but now she was sending some of her customers over here to prove her superiority, knowing full well that his stores of mugwort were all but empty. He'd been right that the conjured herbs from Violet were not the same as the real thing—the alchemical tests he'd done on the plants had all but turned them to dust, as opposed to the glossy effect it would have had on an authentic sample. They were organic certainly, but they weren't the same as the real thing. He wasn't sure what the effects of the herb would be if taken medicinally, but he wasn't about to use his customers as test subjects.

"I'm sorry," he said to the man. "We're out of mugwort at the moment. Our new shipment should arrive next week."

The man nodded with a weak smile. "No matter. I can get it from the new apothecary down the street."

Everything inside Nathaniel's head ground to a scraping halt. "Excuse me?" Marsh's was the only apothecary in Dragon's Rest, and had been for more than a decade. "What new apothecary?"

The man pointed with his free hand, and the baby cooed at the motion. "Sedgwick's, down on the corner of Bank and Wyvern, where the mapmaker used to be."

"The mapmaker? What happened to Digby?" But Nathaniel's mind was already whirring. Sedgwick was the name of that man who had come into Marsh's a few weeks ago asking about dangerous ingredients. His stomach sank as the man confirmed his fears.

"Retired and drinking rum on a beach somewhere by now, I

'spect. Rumor's that he received a generous offer—far too generous for Dragon's Rest. Some outsider. Got it up and running right quick too."

"I see."

The man shrugged. "So if you haven't got any, I'll . . ."

"Yes, yes, of course." Nathaniel smiled apologetically. "As I said, we'll have a new shipment in next week, so please check back with us then if you have any further needs."

"Perhaps," said the man, and sauntered off.

Another apothecary, Nathaniel mused. And run by a man of means. This did not bode well.

"Prudence!" he hollered up the stairs. "I need you to watch the shop!"

A moment later she appeared at the landing, bleary-eyed and still in her nightdress. He remembered belatedly that she'd performed at the Claw & Hoard last night. "Can it wait?"

"It cannot. Get dressed and get down here. Keep an eye on Daisy."

Several protracted moments later—Pru behind the counter with a strong cup of tea and Daisy curled up at her feet—Nathaniel marched up Bank Street toward the building that had formerly housed the mapmaker's. In the matter of days since he'd last come this way, the facade had been painted with a garish orange trim around the windows and on the door. SEDGWICK'S HOUSE OF ALCHEMY proclaimed the carved sign, painted in tones of purple and orange to match the door. Nathaniel's heart sank into his stomach.

The man on the street had been wrong: It wasn't another apothecary that had opened its doors.

It was an alchemist.

An alchemist had moved into Dragon's Rest and opened up shop.

And that alchemist wasn't Nathaniel.

A peculiar sensation swept through him then, some poisonous concoction of anxiety and bitter disappointment, tinged with jealousy. Nathaniel clenched his jaw in an attempt to stem the panic that swelled in him like the tide. This was better, wasn't it? No competing apothecary to interfere with Marsh's.

Still, all his dreams for his family's business flashed through his mind in an instant, of using alchemy to create medicines and cures. All of Pru's half-baked ideas of teahouses and gardens and expanding their scope. He'd done none of it, and with a dreadful sort of certainty, he thought perhaps now it was too late.

Nathaniel had already lived his worst-case scenario. A competing shop was nothing compared to what he'd already dealt with, he reasoned. Logically, he knew that.

But the cold queasiness rising in his chest like a rogue wave hadn't received the same message.

He swallowed the prickly lump that had appeared in his throat and laid his hand on the gold knob, entering the store. There were half a dozen people inside, Nathaniel noted with resentment, and from behind the counter, the proprietor's mouth opened in a delighted *O*.

"Mr. Marsh!" Sedgwick's sleek blond hair was tied back neatly in what Nathaniel suspected was his regular look. "I wondered if I might be seeing you. Give me a moment to help Madame Bixby here and I'll be right with you."

Nathaniel glanced nervously around the shop. It had clearly been assembled in a hurry, with temporary shelving shoved into the found space, but that didn't matter much when the shelves behind Sedgwick and his counter were loaded with vials of potions and solutions. Everything in the well-stocked shop was neatly labeled with engraved metal placards that looked much nicer than Nathaniel's own yellowing letterpress-printed labels.

The bulk of the supply, he was relieved to see, was standard alchemist fare—solutions that would change nonliving organic matter to glass or metal or stone, some fireworks and minor explosives for entertainment at parties, and more of the same useless alchemical drivel that had so irritated his mother—though in one sizable nook near the back, he found shelves of herbs and tinctures, some of which exceeded his own stock considerably.

"You've settled in quickly," he said when Sedgwick finished with his customer and approached.

"Yes, yes, it all happened in a flash." The man smirked at him. "After finding out you didn't have what I needed, I looked into procuring it on my own, and wouldn't you know? I found just how easy it was to obtain—if you have the means, of course."

Nathaniel bristled. "Indeed."

"It shocked me to learn there was such a lapse in stock here in Dragon's Rest. But, I thought, if a fine establishment like yours wasn't going to fill the gap, why shouldn't I step in?"

It was so clearly a dig that he didn't know how to respond.

"Now, what can I help you with today?" Sedgwick leaned closer. "A potion to put a smile on your face, perhaps? Something to take those silvery strands out of your hair?"

Nathaniel resisted the urge to touch his hair and check if he was lying. "Your supply here overlaps with my own," he said, nodding to the corner of herbs and medicines.

"Ah." Sedgwick had the decency to look abashed. "Well, you understand, of course. Business is business, and when it comes to the needs of my clientele, I'm simply meeting demand."

Nathaniel's face burned. "Demand."

"It's nothing but a bit of friendly competition," he said, grinning a too-wide smile. "Perhaps it will do you some good!"

"Perhaps," he said stiffly.

"We are professionals, Mr Marsh," said Sedgwick. "And this

is business, not personal. My stock is more abundant than yours, true. But being competitors doesn't mean we need to be enemies." There was a promise in his words that bordered the shadowlands of a threat.

Nathaniel's eyes flashed. "Unfortunately for you, I'm not very good at making friends."

This isn't just a whim, this is our family's legacy.

BLIGHT

The first week of business surpassed even Violet's wildest, most far-fetched dreams. Each night, after her doors closed, she retreated to the greenhouse and let her imagination run wild with growth. Ranunculus, peonies, tulips, lilies, and daffodils; lavender, daisies, sweet peas, and orchids. By now she had been practicing for weeks—she was pulling flowers into existence with a flick of her fingers, and she barely noticed the stinging sensation anymore. Perhaps this "being good" thing wouldn't be so difficult after all. Still, she'd never grown so much in so short a time, not even in Guy's gardens, and some nights, she found herself collapsing into bed too tired to even dream.

Last night was not one of those nights. Violet woke before the sun, sweating, feeling the weight of that damn purple cloak, the itch of thorns sharpening her features. Guy's voice was still in her ear.

You are nothing without me.

She quickly made her bed, got dressed, and combed her fingers through her hair, disappointed when Guy's ghost followed her to the kitchen.

What do you think you're doing, petal?

The dream had been nothing out of the ordinary, but as she poured her teakettle with shaking hands and pocketed an apple from the bowl she kept on her table, Violet wondered if the memories of what she'd done in her past life, not to mention the imagined judgment from a dead man, would ever truly leave her.

It had been over a month since he was defeated, she reassured herself as she slipped downstairs and out the back door, her fingers brushing over the jagged trench of her scar, trying not to remember how she'd come by it. Shadowfade's was the only world she knew. Healing would take time.

"Good morning," she said to Nathaniel when she opened the greenhouse door. He was at his worktable, Daisy curled up on top of his feet, fast asleep.

Violet still caught him watching her, but after that day in the woods she'd begun watching him right back. She'd acquainted herself with the way his brow furrowed when he measured ingredients, how he wrote his notes with his left hand but stirred his cauldron with his right. How he chewed on a leaf from his mint plant when he was thinking, and hummed snippets of melodies to Daisy, and smiled most reliably whenever Pru brought him a steaming mug of tea.

Her observations had grown to quite a comprehensive list, she found, though she had no idea what to do with it all.

"Good morning," he said politely back, his eyes on whatever he had set bubbling in the tabletop cauldron at his workspace.

She hadn't seen anything like this concoction when she went into the apothecary, and her interest was even more piqued, though she was hesitant to ask him lest she stain the stilted kindness he'd shown her when he came into her shop on opening day. Alchemy, she supposed. Her thoughts turned to an alchemist she'd known at Shadowfade Castle—one of Guy's best, and one of Violet's most bitter rivals. From the moment he'd arrived, he'd set his sights on making her life miserable, and in a lot of ways, he'd succeeded. He was a cruel manipulator and had given Violet no cause to feel kindly toward alchemists.

Prickly though Nathaniel Marsh may be, it was a good reminder to Violet that he was nothing like the villains of her past. The man swung her patience like a pendulum, making her resolve to ignore him one moment and befriend him the next. Violet prided herself on being able to present a calm face to the world, even when a storm brewed inside her. But something about Nathaniel oiled the inside of the mask she wore, making it difficult to keep it on her face without slipping, even when she used both hands and all her considerable might.

As she arranged bouquets and magically propagated a few clippings into pots of soil until they were lush and leafy, working side by side in silence with him in the greenhouse, Violet tried to puzzle out why that was. She failed.

By the time lunch rolled around, Violet's mood had lightened. She took orders for a birthday bouquet, her mind ablaze with possibilities for the design. She finished taking notes, Bartleby's vines drooping lazily over her shoulders from his perch on the shelf above her, and absently swiped him aside whenever it seemed he was trying to strangle her.

"Who will water you if you kill me?" she muttered with a dark sigh, slipping from his hold for the third time.

Bartleby retreated, and a moment later, the bell above the door jingled.

"Hello!" she said brightly, her eyes shifting when she realized her new customer was a gnome, and therefore about three feet shorter than she'd anticipated. At the sight of his shapeless yellow hat, she smiled in recognition. "We've met, I believe. At the market a few weeks ago. Jerome, right?"

Jerome the Gnome nodded curtly. "Aye. I suppose that'll make you Violet Thistlewaite."

"That's me!"

"Tell me, Violet Thistlewaite, do you carry garden soil?" He sneezed suddenly, procuring an enormous red-and-white polka-dot handkerchief from his pocket and dabbing at his nose.

"Yes!" She ushered him through the door to the back garden, where she had neatly piled sacks of soil and compost. From the other side of their shared yard, Nathaniel nodded curtly and scooped up a wriggling Daisy before she could bound over to say hello.

As they disappeared into the apothecary, Violet turned her attention back to Jerome. "I carry several different varieties and blends. What are you looking to plant in your garden?"

"That's a racist stereotype."

"I beg your pardon?" She stopped short, looking at him.

"Just because I'm a garden gnome, see, doesn't mean I'm gardening. I don't even have a garden, mind."

"I . . ." It was more the fact that he was looking for garden soil in a garden shop that did it for her, but Violet supposed that line of argument would end about as well as she suspected. "My apologies. I should not have made assumptions."

"S'alright," said Jerome the Gardenless Garden Gnome.

"Erm," Violet replied, unsure how to proceed with customer service. "What kind of soil are you looking for?"

"Something soft," he said, "and with the right scent."

"I . . ."

"For me bed," said the gnome, taking pity on her at last, it seemed. His eyes sparkled with mirth at her discomfort. "Garden gnomes get our best rest tucked into a flower bed. Course, as I'm allergic to flowers, a bed o' dirt's the next best thing." He sneezed again, as if to punctuate his statement. "If you've any I can sample, I'll be pleased to tell you exactly what I think of it."

Based entirely on this interaction, Violet had no doubt he would. She obligingly opened one of each of her varieties of soil and provided Jerome with a bucket he could use to sample each one and create a blend that suited his needs. She watched in fascination as he felt the soil in his fingers and lifted it to his nose, eyes closed, inhaling deeply, even placing the tiniest speck of each kind on his tongue, his lips smacking as he deliberated. Finally he settled on two sacks of compost and one sack of manure so he could blend it at home. He stared at the bucket with apparent dismay and sighed gravely.

"It'll have to do."

"Er, certainly," said Violet.

"I'll need to replace it 'bout twice a month."

Violet, perking up, offered a ten percent discount if he placed a recurring order.

"Delivery?"

She grimaced. "Not yet. It's just me in the store, so I haven't—"

"S'pose it was too much to ask, place like this. I'll come pick it up. Now, would a tall lady like yourself be willing to help load all this dirt into me cart?"

"Of course," said Violet, hefting one of the sacks into her arms. It was easily bigger than Jerome himself, and she wondered how he was going to get it off the cart once he was home.

"Once, I'd have been able to do this meself," he said mournfully, watching Violet heave the bags up onto her back. "Used to be a lot stronger in me youth."

"It's no problem," Violet gasped, clutching the soil. She was a strong woman, but she needed to purchase a wheelbarrow. Immediately. Out front, Jerome's small cart waited, hitched to a pair of goats tethered to a post at the edge of the green. Violet dutifully loaded the bags one by one, smiling and waving to Pru as she strolled out of the apothecary, cup of tea in hand.

"Rava's tits, that's ripe!" Pru exclaimed, waving her free hand in front of her face. "Manure?"

Violet brushed bits of dirt off her apron (a process that, as a person who spent her entire day embroiled in dirt, was entirely in vain). She wrinkled her nose at the putrid smell of decay on the air. "No, *that's* something else."

"Aye," agreed Jerome. "That's no soil I'd ever sleep in."

Violet settled the last of the bags on Jerome's cart, waved goodbye, and ran back across the street to flip the sign on her door so it read BACK IN A FEW!

"Looking to investigate?" Prudence remarked from her perch against the Marsh Apothecary windowsill. "I'll come with you."

She hopped down, maneuvering gracefully around Nathaniel's A-frame sign. Violet tried not to roll her eyes as she read his words again—she suspected she was the only one choosing to see their daily chalkboard exchanges as playful. She thought back to what he'd told her during her first week here. *I reckon you'd find more success selling something that's actually useful.* The truth was, his words had struck a match against the flinty surface of her heart and ignited her innermost doubts. What if she couldn't do this? What if all she was good for was carnage? What business did a villain like her have trying to open a business like this?

Pru followed her gaze to the signs. "Nathaniel's been in a bit of a mood lately," she said, clearly noticing Violet's sudden scowl.

"Only lately?" Violet blurted out before she could stop herself, but Pru only laughed.

"He really is the worst, isn't he?" she said fondly. "I forget not everyone's used to him."

Suddenly Violet felt defensive. "He's not so bad."

Pru pressed her lips together, poorly disguising a smile. "No? I suppose he's put himself under a lot of pressure, not that it's any excuse. But that's a story for another day. Shall we suss out the source of the stench?" She smirked. "Say that five times fast."

Violet wanted to know more about that story for another day, but she shook off her curiosity. It was none of her business, and she wasn't interested in being branded a gossip by prying. She took Pru's arm and smiled back at her friend. "Certainly, let us suss."

The two women traipsed into the park, noses in the air, sniffing at the acrid, damp smell of mold and decay. It didn't take them long at all to find the patch of black near the platform where Pru performed on market days.

"Oh, it's awful!" Pru declared, ducking her nose and mouth beneath the neckline of her blouse. "Like a giant's armpit after a journey through the plains in summertime. Like a bowl of stew left under the bed with unwashed laundry and locked in a windowless room for weeks. It's like something died covered in its own vomit and then came back to life, swam in a pool of raw sewage, and then died again."

"That was so . . . specific," said Violet, but she didn't disagree. The smell was much stronger here, and clearly originated from the patch of black rot. The grass hadn't so much died as been liquefied into strings of sticky-looking goo. She plucked a twig from the ground outside of the patch and poked at the rot, dropping the twig in alarm when it began to blacken as well.

Pru clucked her tongue. "It spreads by touch—that's not good."

"No. It's not."

"Can you do your whole"—Pru wiggled her fingers in what Violet supposed was an approximation of her magic—"thing?"

Violet concentrated on the spot, drawing some power from

her well, pulling it toward her, and channeling it toward the rot in an encouraging sort of way, thinking, *Grow. Heal.*

But to her surprise, the rot pulled *back* at her, oily and heavy in a way she'd never experienced before even when using dark magic. The smell grew stronger, and Violet gagged, letting her power dissipate around her before she choked on it. Her hands felt like they were on fire, and she looked in horror as the ring of blight grew to encompass more of the grass surrounding it.

"That's a no," she gasped, holding her hands in front of her face, half expecting them to be red and blistered. She massaged them, trying to banish the pins and needles that stiffened her fingers.

"What could have caused it?" Pru stared in shock, rubbing circles into Violet's back as her breathing evened once more.

"A blight that looks like this, smells like this, and apparently spreads to other plant life by touch?" Violet shook her head vehemently. "This reeks of magic."

"It reeks of something, to be sure."

Before Pru could launch into another volley of colorful analogies, Violet said, "We should find your brother."

"You think this could be alchemy?"

"Perhaps?" Violet threw up her hands, at a loss. "I don't know enough about it to guess, but he might be able to see something we can't."

"I'll go get him."

Violet stood watch over the patch of blight until Pru returned, her twin brother striding alongside her, looking businesslike as ever. He nodded curtly at Violet and then crouched next to the blight, leaning in to sniff it as though the smell didn't incite the same nausea in him as it did Prudence and Violet. He too tried prodding at it with a stick, tossing the blighted wood into the circle once the black goo began to spread, then pulled a thin metal wand from his pocket. He touched it carefully to the rot and frowned when it didn't spread the way it had on the wood.

"Perhaps it reacts only to organic material," Violet suggested, and he looked up in surprise, as though he'd forgotten she was there.

"My thoughts exactly." His eyes met hers, alight with something like interest. Excitement perhaps. Agreement for once. Then he cleared his throat, and his gaze shuttered again, back to his normal mask of stern indifference. "I'll have to study it further."

He was back to the Nathaniel she recognized, but it was too late. Violet knew he was under there now, and she knew something about him she suspected he tried to keep hidden: that this kind of work, this kind of scientific question excited him in a way she'd never seen when he was in his role as apothecary. Again, her interest spiked—what was a man like him doing running his family's business when his passions so clearly lay elsewhere? Their eyes met again, though he quickly averted his as he procured a small glass vial from another pocket and inserted the rot-covered wand.

"I'll run some tests on it in the greenhouse," he said, pocketing the vial.

"Near all my plants?" Violet was horrified. "If one of your experiments gets even a drop of that substance on my—"

"I'll take precautions. You can approve them before I so much as unstopper the vial."

She searched his face and found sincerity. "Thank you."

Nathaniel held her eye, nodding.

"We should make a sign warning people to stay away from this," said Pru, gesturing to the plot of black.

"I think the smell will do most of the work, but yes, you're right," agreed Nathaniel, breaking Violet's gaze. "Can you take care of that?"

"Of course. I'll—"

A rumbling, scraping sound had thorns prickling at Violet's skin before she whirled around to find the rock goblin from the Smokewood, the one with the big greenish stone in his chest, ambling slowly toward them on legs of jointed granite.

"Oy!" Pru wasn't so pleased to see him. "It's one of the little bastards that chases me around the park!"

"I don't think it wants to hurt anyone," said Violet, watching him carefully. "I saw this one in the woods the other day, before we found Daisy."

"Where's the rest of his slide?" Nathaniel asked, looking around.

But Violet only crouched down, ignoring Nathaniel's and Pru's sputtering as she held out a hand, waiting patiently until the rock goblin approached, sniffed, and gently butted her fingers with the top of his head. He was warmer than she expected, like sun-drenched stone in summertime, and as he rubbed against her hand, she scratched a bit with her fingertips, which he seemed to like.

"I wonder if the rock goblins caused this," Pru mused darkly. Violet looked up, surprised at the thought.

"I doubt it." Nathaniel's eyes were fixed on Violet and the rock goblin, expression unreadable. "Their magic is limited to stonecraft."

"Maybe they escaped from Shadowfade's castle. Maybe he experimented on them and they—"

"He didn't," said Violet, more sharply than she intended. "I mean, look at this one. He's like a cat." She looked down at the rock goblin, who was now softly gnawing on the edge of her sleeve. "You didn't do this, did you?"

The rock goblin bleated at her again.

"That's a peridot, isn't it?" Pru asked, pointing to the gemstone in his chest.

The rock goblin looked sharply up at her, his black eyes brightening as he bleated again.

"I think that's a yes," Violet said with a little smile. "Hi there, little peridot goblin."

"I think he likes you," said Pru. "I'm almost jealous."

"Thought you were the only one who could attract pests?" Nathaniel teased.

"I said *almost*, didn't I?"

The peridot goblin—Peri, Violet had already decided she'd call him—peered around Violet to the ring of rot. He released her sleeve and trotted over to it, head moving as though sniffing the air. He opened his mouth again and let out a different sound, lower and louder all at once. The ground rumbled. From the roots of trees and the base of the platform and the edges of garden beds, more rock goblins began to appear.

Violet watched them in amazement. They were all shapes and sizes, made of smooth, round river stones and others of jagged chunks of granite. Some were as small as mice, and the largest was about the size of a sheep. Some had strange markings and textures, and a few hinted at shapes that just escaped her recognition. Peri let out that sound again, which Violet suspected was for the other rock goblins in the same way she suspected his croaking little bleat was especially for human ears, and the rest of the slide gathered around the blighted spot of land, flowing around the humans' legs while Pru hopped and squealed nervously. The peridot goblin rubbed against Violet's ankle, scratching her skin in a not-entirely-unpleasant way until she got the hint and dutifully stepped back.

Almost immediately, the space where she'd been standing

filled with rock goblins, who launched themselves atop one another until they were near indistinguishable. They formed a ring around the blight, climbing and melding together into a spiraling shape like a snake coiled over itself, enough that Violet convinced herself she could even see scales. It was a wall of rock tighter and cleaner than any mason could replicate.

"They're covering the rot," said Nathaniel wonderingly.

Sure enough, in a matter of minutes the rock goblins had built a stony dome over the blight, blocking it from the rest of the park. Peri stood aside from the pile and stared up at Violet with onyx eyes. He croaked again in the sound she now recognized was for her. She bent to pat his head, and he leaned into her hand, letting out a rumbling sort of purr. "You did very well."

"He did," Pru agreed.

But Nathaniel wasn't so optimistic. "It doesn't solve our problem."

"I know." Violet frowned at the rock goblins, and the rot hidden beneath them. "What *was* that stuff?"

Their eyes met. "And what do we do if there's more?"

Rough Around the Hedges
FLORAL & GARDEN SHOP

COULDN'T YOU "USE" A SMILE TODAY?

DAY-OLD BOUQUETS 50% OFF

Herbal remedies. Because our stock doesn't wilt.

MARSH APOTHECARY

NOT MY ANYTHING

The rock goblin was waiting for him outside the greenhouse when Nathaniel awoke the next day.

"Get out of here," Nathaniel told him, shooing with his hands. The gemstone in the little goblin's chest caught the light as he cocked his head at Nathaniel, but he—Violet was calling him Peri—did not move. "Shouldn't you be with the rest of your slide?"

He'd woken twice in the night to check on the blighted spot in the Green, and both times, he'd found the slide of rock goblins still at their post, no sign of the rot outside their tight wall. He'd gone back to bed both times with a frown as he clocked the troubled sounds of his neighbor, clearly in the throes of nightmares, on the other side of the wall. How did the woman manage to look so bright-eyed each morning if she was up half the night tossing and turning?

Nathaniel, on the other hand, had been bereft of any dreams of his own lately. He was less thankful for that fact than he'd wish.

He narrowed his eyes and warned the goblin, "If you turn any of my belongings to stone, I'll . . ."

He didn't know what. No one knew how to harm a rock goblin. They were simply pests to be lived with.

"Stay out here," he told the goblin finally, feeling strangely defeated by the one-sided exchange. He opened the door to the greenhouse and slipped inside like Peri was a cat that would steal past his feet, but the goblin made only a croaking sound and stared at him, motionless.

Inside the greenhouse, he stepped up to the large glass box he'd erected on his desk and plucked a leaf from his mint plant, chewing it thoughtfully as he put on a pair of thick gloves.

He opened the two arm-sized holes in the side of the box and slipped his hands through to where a small cauldron simmered above a vibrant pink alchemical flame. Nathaniel wrinkled his nose as the smell reached him—no doubt he'd be hearing about it from Violet, but such was the nature of his science. He tied a handkerchief around his nose and mouth, then got to work.

Nathaniel had already tested the substance for organic properties and found it entirely changed. Although it had undoubtedly begun life as a patch of grass in the Green, it no longer had any chemical resemblance to plant matter. He knew of several alchemical processes that could do this—turning a flower to glass or gold was a staple of the industry, after all, and people paid good money for it, frivolous as it was—and a few others that worked in the opposite direction, but none of his experiments last night had made the spot of black goo so much as jiggle. He'd hoped the morning would bring some speck of inspiration, but he stood now, scratching his head, and wishing desperately for a pot of tea.

"Knock, knock," said a familiar voice. Pru slipped into the greenhouse, a steaming ceramic mug in her hand.

"That was perfect timing," he told her. "I was just about to go inside and put the kettle on."

"Call it twin intuition," she said with a wink.

Twintuition, he mused but did not say, though the sparkle of her smirk told him she guessed at his thoughts anyway. Pru set down the mug and jerked a thumb over her shoulder at the door. "You know that rock goblin is outside your workroom, yes?"

"I can't get him to leave," said Nathaniel, removing his gloves so he could touch the tea with clean hands. "But seeing as the rest of his slide is currently doing us a favor, I'm inclined to look the other way."

Pru leaned against the edge of his desk, eyeing the glass box with curiosity. "That's probably wise. Maybe they'll get attached to *you* and leave me alone."

Nathaniel scoffed, his eyes still on his experiment. "I wouldn't want to take that away from you."

"How very kind," she responded dryly. Pru followed his gaze. "Any luck reversing it?"

"Not even a little." Nathaniel shook his head.

"Why don't you ask Violet?"

"What on earth could she do? She's not trained in alchemy."

"Right, but she's your—"

Something akin to panic jarred him. "She's not *my* anything."

"We'll *definitely* return to discuss that tone in your voice," said Pru, her eyes bright with laughter. "What I was trying to say is she's *your best resource* when it comes to plant magic. Perhaps the solution is somewhere between your two areas of expertise."

Heat crept up his neck. "Ah."

"But since she's *not your anything*, I suppose—"

"Prudence," he warned.

"Nathaniel," she teased back, her smile only growing. He knew he'd stepped in it now. She'd never let this go.

Ignoring her smirk, he said, "I'm not entirely certain what she's capable of or if her magic will be of any help."

"Why not?"

"I ran some tests on some herbs she conjured for me before any of this business began to see if we could use them in the shop, and while they're certainly plants, at least to an extent they're also . . . not. They're somewhere in between."

Even as he spoke, Nathaniel was already snatching the bundle of mugwort Violet had given him. He laid it on [illegible] glass surface, then dipped a metal stylus into the blighted [illegible] nd carefully transferred it to the mugwort. The rot pulse[illegible] ly, just as it had with his other experiments, and began to [illegible] d to the rest of the plant . . . but then it stopped.

Pru *hmm*ed thoughtfully. "So her plants are resistant to the blight?"

"The *magic* she used to make them resists the blight," Nathaniel corrected.

She nodded seriously. "Ah, yes. A distinction I *definitely* understand without any further explanation."

He threw his sister a look, which she caught and threw right back.

"If her magic resists the blight, wouldn't it be a good starting point for reversing it?"

Nathaniel squirmed at the thought, suddenly uncomfortable. "I don't know."

"Well, we could always ask her," said Pru reasonably, though of course she had to add, "Even though she's not your anything."

"Prudence," he warned, groaning. "Please. I'll ask Violet, but I'm begging you, don't—"

"Ask Violet what?" said the witch herself from the doorway of the greenhouse. Her face brightened when she noticed his sister. "Pru! What brings you here?"

Nathaniel felt a twinge of *something* at the realization that Violet never smiled like that at him.

"Just watching my brother fuss over his chemistry set."

"Alchemy," corrected Nathaniel automatically, which only made Pru cackle. He was determined to make himself the butt of her teasing today, it seemed.

Violet turned her attention to him, and that, for some reason, was worse. Her scrutiny was a flame to the cauldron of his nerves. She scanned his setup and then, worse, his *face* and asked with genuine curiosity, "Can you explain to me what you're doing?"

It was the exact right thing to say. Nathaniel relaxed and launched into teaching mode. "Alchemy is all about balance. It's about knowing your intention for the result and creating magical parity with what you put into it. Turning a substance to gold, for example, is one of the most common understandings of what alchemy *is*, but actually achieving it means using gold—the desired end result—as a focal parity, or centering force. If I wanted to turn this leather glove into gold, for example, I'd have to combine it with a substance that is, to say, *more* gold than gold just as much as the leather is *less* gold than gold."

He could see from both Violet's and Pru's expressions that he'd lost them, and he pulled his brass scales to the front of his worktable. "It's a puzzle. If the blight is on one side"—he pressed his finger to one of the scale's bowls, weighing it down—"and a healthy plant is the result we want, then to cancel out the blight I need to find the exact mix of ingredients that forms its alchemical opposite." He put another finger on the other bowl until they evened out. "That, along with some magical and alchemical techniques, will serve as the basis of the solution."

"It's as simple as that?"

He barked out a laugh. "Insofar as it's the foundation of the science, yes. But alchemy requires delicate precision, and often finding the balance means accounting for components and details you can't see from the start." The sound of Pru pretending to snore drew his attention. His face heated, embarrassed. "Sorry. I have a tendency to lecture, as Pru is quick to remind me."

"I don't mind it." The softness in Violet's tone surprised him. "Where I come from, people wielded knowledge like an advantage. You had to figure it all out on your own or appear weak. I'm, ah, I'm not used to someone being kind enough to explain things to me when I don't know them."

If he could have dived into the pleasure that filled him then and swum in it like a pool, he might never have stepped foot on dry land again. He was so used to being ridiculed, even teasingly, for the way he talked about his passions. But the waters tinged with sadness as the rest of her words caught up to him. *Where did she come from?* he wondered for the thousandth time.

"Yet another reason you should use Violet's plants to help," Pru interjected. "She's not bored to tears by you answering questions with a whole sermon!"

"Ah." Violet's eyes found Nathaniel's again, sparkling with mirth. "So you're saying you might find my plants *useful*."

Her A-frame sign today took on new meaning as he recalled his own words. "That was not intended to—"

She flapped a hand, waving him off. "I'm only teasing. You don't have to fill your shop with my flowers or wake up to them on your bedside table."

This was the part where an apology was required of him, but Nathaniel was distracted by the image she'd painted. Waking up to her flowers on his bedside table, opening his eyes each morning to something she'd crafted from her magic and touched with her clever fingers.

He'd never considered how *intimate* her work could be.

Violet refocused those honeyed eyes on Nathaniel. "Have you made any progress? With the balancing?"

He sighed and leaned back against his worktable, careful not to jostle the glass box. "Not yet. It's as we suspected; the substance infects surrounding organic matter and eventually slows a bit, like it's eating away at other plants until it starts to get full. I haven't worked out a safe way to find out whether that extends past plant matter." If the blight could hurt living, breathing creatures, Nathaniel didn't know what he would do. "It only comes to a full stop when it reaches an inorganic barrier, like stone, metal, or glass. And while the blight does affect your conjured plants to a point, it doesn't seem to destroy them entirely in the same way as natural plants."

Violet looked over his shoulder at the stalk of mugwort, still partially black. He could feel the puff of her breath on his skin as she *hmm*ed in thought. "I wonder if I could conjure a wall of thorns—or any plant at all would do, of course, it doesn't have to be *thorns*—to strengthen the defense by the rock goblins."

He shook his head. "Since your plants are at least partially organic, it wouldn't be a perfect system. If even a speck of rot reached the outside of the circle, it would spread."

"Why don't we just burn it all?" Pru asked. "The blight, I mean."

Nathaniel scraped a hand through his hair. "I tried to incinerate a pair of gloves that became contaminated last night and all it did was create a horrid black smoke. Took ages to get rid of it. I was afraid it would spread."

"What did you do with the gloves?" Pru asked.

"Nothing yet." He jerked a thumb behind his shoulder so they could see the blackened leather in a glass jar where he'd shoved them until he could figure out how to dispose of them.

"It's good you're taking precautions," said Violet, eyeing the setup with approval. "I assume the glass box on your desk is the one we discussed that would protect against contamination?"

"Yes." He felt suddenly nervous under her scrutiny, wanting to assure her he'd been careful to protect her plants in their shared space as he'd promised. "The box remains tightly closed when I'm not actively working inside it. It's spelled against breaking, and even the air vents are designed to filter what comes out."

"Incredible." She leaned closer, examining it.

"It was designed originally for experimenting on alchemical bombs."

She glanced at him. "And is that entirely necessary? Is there a risk of them exploding?"

His mouth tightened, his memory full of the smell of smoke and chemicals. "It's not a risk I'm willing to take."

"Well done then," she said, homing in on the hard expression he wore. He watched her next thought as it occurred to her and dreaded the question even before it left her mouth. "Are you well acquainted with experimenting on bombs?"

He hesitated. "Much of my work in the Crucible was contracted by the royal military."

She took in this information with a slow nod. "And what would the royal military make of our discovery yesterday, do you think? What would they do to destroy the blight?"

"They wouldn't," he said immediately. "They'd find a way to weaponize it."

"Villains, the lot of them," Pru added. "No offense, Nathaniel."

Nathaniel rolled his eyes. After his time in the Crucible, his relationship with his country had grown complicated, to say the very least. He'd led projects that still kept him up at night worrying about how the science had since been applied. So it was safe to say that his sister wasn't exactly wrong.

"Villains," he agreed quietly.

Violet's eyes had shuttered at some point in the conversation in a way he worried meant they'd start arguing soon. Anxiety rose in his chest; he found he did not want to quarrel with her anymore. Perhaps it was the blight, or the memories of the Crucible, but Nathaniel was sick of fighting. She'd offered him olive branch after olive branch, and he wished he'd been wise enough to accept one.

Luckily, Pru was there to step in before things escalated. "Nathaniel will find a way, don't you worry. He's the smartest person I know—when it comes to alchemy, anyway." Her words had the intended effect, and the tension in the greenhouse dissolved.

"We'll fix this," Nathaniel said awkwardly to Violet, clenching a fist at his side so he wouldn't do something foolish like pat her on the shoulder or push back the lock of hair that had sprung in front of her face. "And I'll answer any questions you have."

Her throat flexed as she swallowed whatever emotion had tightened her expression. "Thank you," she said finally in a soft voice. "I have every faith in you, Nathaniel."

The wave of shocked longing that racked his body at the sound of his name on her lips was entirely inappropriate for polite society; his fingernails dug brutally into his palm while the other hand clamped down on the mug of tea Pru had brought him. They held eye contact, and though Nathaniel had long since perfected the (complicated, expensive) alchemical practice of turning a material to gold, he had a ridiculous notion then that he'd been doing it wrong all this time, because he'd never in his life seen a result so lustrous as the shade of her eyes.

Pru, the monster, chose then to clear her throat, and the moment fell away like untempered glass cracking in hot water.

"I should get going." She leaned in to hug her brother and said low in his ear, "Not your anything, eh?"

"Don't," he growled, returning the embrace, but his sister only laughed.

Nothing "rough"

about

our products!

ROSES AND THORNS

"I'll get right to work drawing up these sketches," Violet promised the young couple on the other side of her counter. She looked down at her notes, with all the requests and schematics for their planned nuptials later this spring, her imagination already alive with possibilities.

"Thank you," said the bride-to-be, with a grin matching the one on her groom's face. "I love roses, but I know they're out of season. I can't wait to see them."

"They'll be gorgeous, I'm sure," said Pru with a smile from where she leaned against a wall, Daisy wiggling in her arms. "All of Violet's arrangements are beautiful."

"And I don't even pay her to say that," quipped Violet. "Come see me after the weekend. I'll have the plans ready for you then, and we can talk specifics for the wedding."

The couple left with a smile and a wave, and Violet hummed to herself, feeling content as she daydreamed about building an arch of roses in situ behind the altar, shaping and placing the flowers as they grew under her fingers. As she pictured it, that nettle-like sensation rose once more to her fingertips, where a rose materialized, its stem shiny and smooth. Perhaps a slightly dustier hue for the color, she thought.

"A rose without thorns," Pru mused, watching her as she formed another in the color she wanted. "Something about that feels wrong."

"I'd just have to strip them all down anyway," Violet said with a shrug. "People don't want the thorns, they just want the flower."

"But they're a part of it—without the thorns there *is* no flower. Don't they help protect the plant?"

Violet unclenched her jaw, which had suddenly grown tight. "In the wild. Not here."

"I suppose it does save you a lot of work as you build the arch." Pru clucked her tongue and set Daisy down. "Fine, you little menace. Just don't chew up any of Violet's lovely shelves."

"This arch will build itself. Or I hope it will anyway. I've never tried pruning such a large arrangement as it grows," Violet admitted. "Even the topiaries and hedges I grew in my garden at—" She froze. "Where I used to live. Those ones had been conjured and grown wild. I only shaped them afterward."

"Everything I've seen you do so far tells me you're up for the challenge," said Pru, seemingly unconcerned with Violet's gaffe.

At her feet, Peri appeared with a gravelly rumble, and she watched in amusement as Daisy tackled him, her wet nose snuffling at Peri's neck. Violet had never had a pet before, and she wasn't quite sure a rock goblin who came and went as he pleased constituted one exactly, but she'd grown used to his presence over the past few days. His clear obsession with Violet had only grown, though he forgot all about her as soon as Pru so much as played a single note on her violin. Peri spent the majority of his days exploring her shop, wrestling with Bartleby, digging up rocks along the fence line in the back garden, and wreaking havoc with Daisy in the greenhouse. He spent his nights curled up at the end of Violet's bed, a comforting weight on her feet that eased her nightmares, or at least grounded her when she woke from them.

"Play nice, you two," she said fondly.

"Do you think Daisy thinks Peri is a dog?" Pru mused. "Or that she's a rock goblin? I found her barking at a stone in the backyard yesterday like she was having a conversation with it."

"Maybe she was," chuckled Violet. "I'd rather she pick up habits from Peri than from Bartleby anyway." She shot a look at the pothos, who had managed to squirrel away her pruning shears that morning and had tried to cut her with them when she'd demanded them back.

"He's a menace," Pru agreed cheerfully. "Where'd you get him anyway?"

The bell above the front door jingled—thankfully, because Violet had no lie prepared—and both women smiled when they recognized the newcomer.

"This place looks lovelier and lovelier every time I'm here," said Quinn from the entryway, her hands trailing along the center table of pansy starters Violet had laid out this morning. At least a dozen honeybees buzzed around her head like a crown as she peered curiously around the shop, her keen eyes taking in every detail.

"Thank you," said Violet with a smile. "I think people are enjoying it."

"They certainly are. Mrs. Hemmings down at the blacksmith's said her daughter has never been so taken with a birthday gift, and of course you didn't hear this from me, but her brother's planning to propose to his partner at Solstice, so I expect she'll put in a word for you to do flowers for the wedding. You've managed to inject a little bit of joy into Dragon's Rest, and that's something we direly needed after, well, everything."

You cannot take credit for fixing something you helped break, petal, said Guy's voice in Violet's ear, cruel and seductive as he'd ever been. *You played a part in holding this town in terror, not just me.* Her smile faded.

"Anyway, I came to extend an invitation to a little weekly get-together next Thursday at my home."

"Oh, you should go," said Pru. "Guy—good Guy, not the bad one—will be there, so you know he'll bring baked goods!"

"And I'll make my honey cakes, of course!" said Quinn cheerfully. From behind her, Pru made a slashing motion across her throat, mouthing something that looked a lot like, *Do not eat them!*

Quinn cleared her throat without looking over her shoulder. "The recipe is a *work in progress*, Prudence."

Violet turned to Pru. "Will you be there?"

Pru exchanged a glance with Quinn. "Er, no. I perform at the inn on Thursdays."

"It's just a few of us," said Quinn with a smile. "We drink wine and bring dishes to pass for supper and talk through what's on our minds. We're all dying to get to know you a bit better."

There was no way she could allow them to get to know her any better. Violet imagined being honest at a gathering like that:

"Violet, tell us about where you grew up."

"Oh, me? I was raised by the evil sorcerer who cut out Guy's—good Guy, not bad Guy's—tongue. I did terrible things under his orders, and it's still a daily struggle not to return to my evil ways. Pass the charcuterie, would you, please?"

Quinn and the Dragon's Rest gossip circuit would have enough fodder for weeks of talk.

"I'm afraid I'm busy that evening," Violet demurred. "I have a lot of orders to prepare for the next day. But I'm grateful to you for thinking of me."

"Of course." Quinn winked at her, and one of her bees flew in a little loop-de-loop over her head. "One of these days we'll make it happen."

"One of these days." Violet felt a little ill about the lie but worse about the truth behind it: The people of Dragon's Rest would never be able to know her, not really, and suddenly that no longer felt freeing—it felt like just another prison. Another collar chafing at her throat.

There was no way to strip this particular rose of its thorns, not really. Violet would have to live by the lie she'd created for herself for the rest of her life, and not a single slipup would ever be tolerated. No one would accept the Thornwitch into their community; they'd run her right out of town if she told them who she really was. She pictured Jerome the Gnome with a pitchfork in his hands, and sweet Quinn sending her bees after Violet in a swarm of fury. Pru and Nathaniel would— Well. It was best not to think of things that would never happen. Violet could lock down her story and invent a past for herself that was boring and believable enough that no one would ask questions. The Thornwitch didn't exist anymore, and it would be best for everyone if Violet could manage to pretend she never had. Now if only her nightmares would agree.

"Will you be at the market tomorrow?" Quinn was asking Pru. "I'll have the beeswax Nathaniel was asking after for making his salves, but I can drop it by the apothecary if I don't see you."

"I haven't decided." Pru threw a look at Peri, who croaked at her. "The slide is protecting that spot of blight we discovered the other night, and I don't want them to leave their post if they hear me playing."

Quinn chuckled. "I wonder if we'll ever know what they love so much about you."

"Obviously they have excellent taste in music, that's what."

Violet made small talk with the two women until another

customer came in seeking a bouquet. Pru and Quinn left the shop with a friendly wave, and Violet pasted back on her sunny smile. Violet Thistlewaite, florist, was not plagued by unpleasant thoughts. Violet Thistlewaite, florist, had no problems deeper than helping the man standing before her design a bouquet for his mother's birthday.

When she bid him goodbye at last, Peri croaked at Violet with concern, cocking his lopsided head and sagging against her legs like he knew her thoughts.

"I'll be fine," she murmured to him, watching the door close behind her customer, leaving her shop empty. "I'm not that person anymore. The Thornwitch is behind me, and so it should be no problem to erase her from my past."

She pulled a broom from the corner behind the counter, and as she began to tidy up her shop, she almost believed it would be true.

MOONLIGHT

Hours later, Violet awoke in her bed with a shout, thorns prickling beneath her skin like seeds about to sprout from soil. *Violet?* Guy's voice was still in her ear, his shock evident as he struggled for breath. *Be good*, Karina the Tempest had said. The memory of that day mixed with others. *Go to Silbourne. Take care of the problem.* A ship with purple sails and a woman at the helm whose face she couldn't see. Violet's surprise at the amount of blood from his wound as Guy's eyes found hers. *Run, petal.*

There was something in her hand, and she knew without looking what it would be—a long, thick thorn, sharp and deadly like a dagger, an instinctive defense against her ghosts. She crushed her fingers around it, allowing her magic to dissolve the weapon into dust.

Violet took a ragged breath and threw off her quilt, startling Peri, who croaked. Guy was a monster. He'd lied to her, treated her abominably. How was it possible that she still missed him anyway?

It was too hot in her room; she was sweating so much she looked like she'd just had a bath in her nightclothes. She staggered to the window and threw it open, letting cool air rush into her bedroom like a balm. Moonlight from all three of the sisters, Rava, Evry, and Cesenne, beamed down over the dark rooftops of Dragon's Rest, bathing the town in their protection. Two of the moons were almost full, though Evry was but a sliver, and Violet could feel her magic respond to them like a child begging to be let outside to play. But this particular child would only cause trouble. Violet closed her eyes and drew a breath into her lungs, then held it there before releasing it. Slowly, her heart rate started to fall. As the sweat on her skin cooled, the urge to use her magic settled into the same dull longing she'd come to expect would always lie just beneath the surface now that she was no longer giving in to her villainous instincts. Violet took another breath, feeling the breeze on her flushed cheeks, and—

"Are you alright?"

She shrieked, panic flooding her all over again. She clutched a hand to her chest and looked around, finding Nathaniel Marsh leaning out of the window next to hers, his face bathed in moonlight.

He clutched his own window frame. "I didn't mean to frighten you." His voice was hoarse with sleep, lower and raspier than it was by day, and he was—oh, three moons, he wasn't wearing a shirt. She'd thought knowing he had nice *forearms* was bad enough, but even as Violet squeaked and averted her eyes, she knew that the sight of his firm chest was far worse. She'd never be able to get any work done ever again with him in the greenhouse. She snuck another peek, regretting it immediately. Had his shoulders always been so broad? The man needed a better tailor with the number of secrets he was keeping beneath his clothes. Or perhaps that would be even worse for her concentration.

Before her traitorous thoughts could tempt her with wondering just what else he—her *landlord*!—was hiding beneath his apparel, Nathaniel spoke again. "My bedroom shares a wall with yours . . . and I heard you cry out."

The roil of Violet's emotions turned all at once to embarrassment, settling heavy in the pit of her stomach. She flushed bright pink and had to physically fight the urge to crawl back into her room and hide under the bed. She knew she did more than cry out—sometimes she spoke in her sleep. What if she said something about Guy? What if she revealed herself as the Thornwitch? What if the image that had suddenly taken up residence in her mind—of him in bed at night, shirtless with that *chest* and those moons-cursed *forearms*, only mere inches of wall separating them—refused to vacate?

Gratifyingly, Nathaniel looked mortified as well. His gaze was fixed firmly somewhere just to the right of her as he waited as patiently for her answer as a naturally impatient man unexpectedly awoken from sleep was capable of being.

"I'll try not to disturb you in the future," Violet said, her mind already aflame with plans to switch her tiny parlor with her bedroom so she'd be farther from the offending shared wall.

"It's no trouble," replied Nathaniel, his eyes on hers. "I only wanted to make sure you were well."

This stopped her.

"I'll be fine, thank you," she said softly.

"Do you want to talk about it?"

She found, to her surprise, that she really, *really* did. "I don't know if I know how," she said, feeling pathetic. "I'm not used to having people to talk to."

Nathaniel looked out over the moonlight casting warped reflections on the glass roof of the greenhouse as Violet collected her words.

"My adoptive father didn't really encourage friendships," she admitted finally.

"Why?"

Violet held her face to the light of the moons and closed her eyes. "I was born on a night when all three moons were full," she said finally, imagining that she could feel the power of the three sisters lighting her up like a beacon.

"A Convening," Nathaniel marveled. Sometimes centuries passed before the cycles of all three moons matched up this way. "No wonder you're so powerful—you're moonsblessed."

"Blessed," she repeated with a humorless laugh. "To most people in my life, I was a commodity, or competition. The man who raised me was . . . not always kind."

Nathaniel made a sound she couldn't decipher.

"I left him recently," she continued, halting and slow, avoiding the one word her lips wanted to form. Avoiding the word *dead.* "No going back. But I wonder sometimes if I will ever really be free of him."

Nathaniel was quiet for a moment. "There is no force so vengeful as a ghost from the past." His words were laced with some meaning she couldn't quite parse. "It is no simple thing to rise anew from the ashes of your old life."

"It is not," she agreed softly. "The worst part is, until fairly recently I never questioned that everything he told me was true. Isn't that horrible?"

"No." The resolve in his voice surprised her. "He raised you. You trusted him. Family is complicated."

"It stopped being simple a long time ago, but at some point it got *too* complicated. I don't know how to move past that."

"One day at a time," said Nathaniel, and Violet realized then that he was speaking from experience. "One step, one breath, one heartbeat after another. However slowly, they'll all move you forward."

Her look must have been full of consideration, because he smiled wryly and confirmed, "You're not the only one in this town trying to escape the past."

Picking through her words like she was sifting a garden plot for stones, she asked, "And what are you trying to escape?"

He was quiet for so long that Violet began to regret asking, but then he said, "I don't suppose it's a secret to you that being an apothecary was never my ambition."

"No," she admitted. "I don't suppose it is."

"I've always wanted to be an alchemist. I was quite well respected in the Crucible, if that's not too presumptuous of me to say."

Violet made a sound somewhere just shy of a chuckle.

"I loved it," he continued after a long moment. "The *scholarship* of it all. The *magic*. But some of the things we were doing . . . some of the things we were creating for the Queen and her war . . ."

It was a dangerous topic of conversation, and Violet recognized the vulnerability of even broaching it. She waited for him to continue.

"I left the Crucible and came home to focus on finding ways to make my family's business better. I'm aware my field has traditionally been used for warfare or parlor tricks. But my goal was always to invent new medicines, improve upon the ones my family had been selling for generations. Alchemy and herbal medicine, I thought, could have been a powerful combination. I could have invented an entirely new branch of medicine."

The past tense confused her. "I don't know much about alchemy, but it seems to me there's incredible potential there."

"I thought so too."

"What happened?"

Nathaniel's voice was hushed like he was telling a secret. "I failed. I came home, as I'd promised. The apothecary used the whole building then, and the half where your shop is now was the workspace where my parents mixed herbs and made balms and medicines. My father made room on his worktable for me and my experiments alongside him. I'd had some early successes with concoctions for headaches and the flu, but I knew I could do more." He ran his fingertips along the window frame, watching them closely. "I was brewing the base for a solution I thought might be able to ease the symptoms of fire-cough."

She waited as he paused again, gathering himself.

"It was . . . volatile. I should have been clearer with them about that." He turned his head, but he wasn't really looking at her at all, or at least not really seeing her.

No force so vengeful as a ghost from the past, she thought wryly. She understood the look in his eyes, for it mirrored her own in the weeks since Guy's death. Unbidden, delicate tendrils of vines sprouted from her fingertips and clung to the rough stone exterior of the building, gently reaching toward Nathaniel's window in a way that could almost be accidental.

"I don't know what they were doing," he said. "If they touched it or tried to move it, or if it exploded on its own. If it was a stupid bloody accident no one could have prevented." She watched his face harden to anguished stone. "I never got to ask, because they were dead by the time I found them."

Violet couldn't help herself; she gasped softly. The creeping vines froze in place.

She imagined Nathaniel coming home. Discovering—

"So now I'm here," he continued, "running the apothecary like they always wanted. Trying to keep their legacy alive even though I'm the reason they're gone." He raised his eyes to hers at last, searching her face. "And who am I now to be delving into that field again? To delude myself into thinking I can reverse this blight?"

"Everything you're doing is trying to help." She kept her voice soft. "Why diminish your own skills when Dragon's Rest needs you, and you have the expertise and knowledge of alchemy that no one else here has?"

He grumbled something in response that she didn't quite catch.

"Pardon?"

"Nothing," he said dismissively. "Just some new competition in town. It'll be fine."

"Another alchemist?"

"Yes. It's made me realize just how much I miss it," he admitted. "Following the trail set out for me by nothing but my own ambition and creativity. Researching, experimenting, the thrill when I find the perfect balance . . . I hadn't realized how much it had become a part of me until I opened that door again to try and reverse the blight."

"Then why not let that part of yourself out once more?" She kept her eyes on the moons while he gathered his thoughts.

"What if I make another mistake?" he whispered finally. "What if I hurt someone else?"

Violet considered his fears, his passions, the raw way he was laying himself open to her right now. "It's terrifying to know you have the power to hurt someone," she acknowledged, "and it's tempting to lock that part of yourself away entirely. But that doesn't make it disappear."

She paused, thinking of her flower shop, of the smiles on her customers' faces, of Karina the Tempest in the garden that horrible day. *You could be good.* "That power of yours goes both ways, though. Perhaps it's not a matter of asking, 'What if I hurt someone?' Perhaps it's about asking, 'What if I could help someone?'"

Between them, a delicate white flower budded and unfolded, glowing almost blue in the moonlight. Lady's favor, she recognized, the flower that had been given to the goddess Cesenne by her lover as a symbol of hope in impossible circumstances. It only bloomed at night, under the light of Cesenne herself.

Nathaniel froze, watching it grow, but when he spoke next, she knew by his tone and the way he was back to the stiff, formal shopkeeper that she'd lost him. "That is an admirable thought," he said politely. "But I suspect this is something you couldn't possibly understand."

I do understand, she wanted to say. *I know what it is to carry power that can destroy everything you love. I know what it is to feel the weight of death on your shoulders.* With urgency now, she ignored the pain in her fingers and coaxed the vine closer to his window, the flower like a ship bobbing on the waves.

But he was already closing the shutters, already telling her, "Good night, Violet."

Already gone.

Rough Around
the Hedges
FLORAL & GARDEN SHOP
PEONY FOR
YOUR
THOUGHTS?

NOTES

Shame bubbled in Nathaniel like a cauldron beginning to boil. For more than a year, he'd kept these emotions at a low simmer, even among the people who knew him best. Pru had begged him to let her in, and old Guy—who had been so close with his parents—had sat with him more than once while he cried, but he'd never talked about it.

He saw the wreckage of the workroom whenever he closed his eyes, as though it had been tattooed to the inside of his eyelids against his consent. He felt his mother's cold skin whenever he shook hands with a customer. Even the smell of the elixir he worked on now—a pet project, and nothing unsafe—brought to mind the scent after the explosion, the acrid sharpness of alchemist's fire so strong that even experimenting on the blight made Nathaniel have to step outside more than once to settle his nausea.

But he'd prided himself on his ability to keep it all together, to hold steady so not a drop spilled where it shouldn't. So why in the name of the three sisters had he chosen to overturn the whole damn flask? To *his bloody tenant*?

The witch was anathema to his self-control. A distraction he didn't need or want at a time when he certainly couldn't afford the disruption. Nathaniel had far too much to worry about—his struggling business, the new competition, his sister, and now this blasted blight—to be letting Violet worm her way through the protective structure he'd built inside himself. Nothing good lay inside those walls, he knew, only rotting, empty buildings haunted by old ghosts best left undisturbed. He was spent, past his prime, a broken thing. There would be no point to letting her in; he would only cut her on his edges.

For two days, he changed his schedule or conveniently popped back into the apothecary whenever she came to the greenhouse. He was subtle about it, of course; he didn't want to offend her. But on the third morning after their conversation, he came down to the greenhouse an hour earlier than usual, while Violet was sure to still be asleep, to find a note on his worktable, next to his glass box of blight and the simmering cauldron that held his other work.

In her blocky script, it said,

Are you finished avoiding me yet?—Violet

Shame warmed his cheeks for entirely new reasons. Not so subtle after all. She'd called him out, and what's more, she was entirely correct. Nathaniel raked a hand through his hair and looked around as though she might be waiting in the shadows, hiding behind the ridiculously large hydrangea bush she'd installed in the corner by her door. But of course the sun wouldn't be up for another hour or so yet, and she was likely fast asleep in her bed.

The bed that was just on the other side of the wall from his, where he could hear her toss and turn each night. Where he spent more and more of his own evenings wondering if he could—

Get it together, Nathaniel.

Still, he supposed he owed her an answer. Calmly, Nathaniel tore a leaf of paper from one of his notepads and wrote back.

V–

Apologies. I've been very busy.

–N

He rushed it to the other side of the greenhouse and set it on her messy worktable next to a pungent bucket of compost, feeling guilty about the lie, then went about his day, adding a dash of goblin bane to his cauldron and stirring for precisely three and a half minutes before setting it back to simmer and heading inside to take inventory in the shop.

He was delighted when the bell rang moments after he unlocked the door, but the woman who came into the shop wasn't looking to buy anything at all. "Quinn says you're the one to talk to about this blight business," she said.

"Yes," said Nathaniel, glancing out the window to Wingspan Green, where he could just see the pile of rock goblins. "We have it contained, and I'm working on—"

"Contained?" The woman laughed. "You're mistaken. The hedge separating my yard from my neighbor's is black and rotted."

Nathaniel's heart sank as he promised the woman he'd investigate and gave her instructions about what to do. About midday, after he'd served all of three customers for the morning—one of whom had asked him outright whether he knew that Sedgwick's charged *half* as much for witch's burr (*half!*) as Marsh's did—Nathaniel went back to the greenhouse to check on the blight.

Sedgwick's was coming for Marsh's, that much was clear, but it would have to wait, even if his deadline with the bank was looming closer with each day. If the blight was spreading, it needed to take priority.

The flower Violet had grown between their windows had given him the idea that he could try an infusion of lady's favor and soil from one of the Darktide Isles, which only existed at the lowest tide when all three moons hid their faces. The balance between the two ingredients, one that only appeared under the moons and one that never saw their light, might—

There was another note waiting for him.

Liar.-Violet

P.S. I know it's not part of my lease but I noticed the remains of a vegetable bed along the fence in your half of the garden. Would you mind terribly if I revived it? I shall pay you in fresh tomatoes.

He sighed and ran a hand through his hair before penning a response.

V—

I don't suppose you would believe I've been kidnapped or called away on business or, I don't know, accidentally turned myself into a decorative end table with one of my experiments, would you?

—N

P.S. Do as you wish. Pru and I certainly aren't using it.

An hour later, after he went inside for a cup of tea, another reply appeared.

I saw you flee (FLEE, Nathaniel! Like a rabbit!) back into the apothecary yesterday when I came out to the greenhouse. Am I truly so frightening?

–Violet

P.S. Thank you. Do let me know if you have requests for produce.

P.P.S. What kind of decorative end table? With shelves? Drawers? I'm still in the market for good furniture for my parlor.

Nathaniel felt ashamed all over again; he hadn't realized Violet had seen him duck out of sight.

She obviously didn't hold his confession against him, or if she did, she was playing it awfully close to the chest until she could berate him in person. But nothing he knew about Violet Thistlewaite suggested she would do such a thing. She was clever and stubborn and determined and creative and kind, but never, to his knowledge, judgmental. He picked up his pen and tore a new scrap of paper from his notebook.

V–

You caught me. My distance had nothing to do with you. The story I shared with you is not one I often discuss. What you must think of me.

Yours in cowardice,
N

P.S. Strictly out of curiosity, do your conjured vegetables provide any nutritional value or do they only taste like they do?

P.P.S. Between you and me, Quinn and her wife have a storage shed full of extra furniture. I suspect she'd be inordinately thrilled to donate an end table, a sofa, or a whole bloody dining room set complete with silverware if you asked.

She didn't write back that day, and his nails carved grooves into his palms at the thought that he'd offended her with the inquiry into her magic. He scolded himself the whole walk to the site of the new patch of blight, and the whole way home again too, clutching his sample vials almost tight enough to break them. He shouldn't have asked. He should have left well enough alone, even though he *was* extremely curious about the answer. He did have to blink away a suspicious stinging in the corners of his eyes when he returned home and noticed his father's vegetable garden had been cleared and tilled. But there was still no sign of the witch herself.

It wasn't as though he was waiting on her response. He was simply visiting the greenhouse twice an hour until midnight so he could check on his experiments until he gave up and went to bed.

But in the morning, relief rushed through him when he came downstairs to find on his worktable a small wicker basket of lettuce, carrots, and the promised tomatoes, as well as a folded letter in her handwriting.

What I think of you is that you're a person who feels the mantle of blame is yours to wear and who bears the weight of a responsibility you never wanted with admirable grace.

I won't try to convince you that what happened to your parents is not your fault, because even if some part of you knows it, I know that logic is seldom welcome at the table of our emotions, particularly when they disagree. I understand what it is to feel responsible for your own misery.

I failed to mention the other night that my adoptive father took me in very young, and I spent most of my life with the knowledge that my magic was the reason I had been abandoned by my mother. She left me, he said, because she was afraid of what I could do, and perhaps she was right to be. I know what it is to feel like there is something deeply broken at the core of you, and I know that whether or not the blame is earned, we wear it, and not a soul can take it from us no matter how we might wish for it.

It helped me a bit to hear your story, and to know I am not alone. I thought perhaps it might help you too.

There. Now we have both told stories we don't often discuss.

–Violet

P.S. I don't know about nutritional value, but perhaps that's something to experiment with. I promise they are fully edible and delicious–and besides, tomatoes won't be in season for months yet anywhere else.

Nathaniel blinked at the letter, unsure of where to begin. The situations weren't the same at all, not really—Violet had been a *child*, and made to feel responsible for things entirely outside of her control—but the thread of understanding wove itself into a strong braid inside of him. She understood what it meant to have power that could hurt people, even unintentionally. She understood what it was to be eaten alive by guilt. A knot built in his throat.

When Nathaniel had been a student at university, a professor had once told him that they worked in pairs their first year so they could learn from each other and share in their failures.

"It makes you a better alchemist," his teacher had said, when explaining why Nathaniel had also received poor marks for a mistake that had been his partner's. "More precise in your actions and much more in control of your work because you don't want to fail your partner."

But what the professor had neglected to mention was that sometimes failure could not be controlled, no matter how tightly one held to command. Nathaniel was surprised to find that he didn't feel ashamed for sharing his experience with Violet. He didn't feel like he'd failed her or Pru or anyone else. In fact, he felt his burden lessened somehow, as if by telling her, and by learning that she'd understood, he'd taken some of it off his shoulders and laid it on the ground. The knowledge of what he'd done didn't magically disappear—it just sort of sat there at his feet—but at least he wasn't holding it anymore.

The thought followed him through his day ("Tomatoes!" cried Pru with delight, immediately eating half of them the moment he brought them inside), and as he headed into the greenhouse one more time that evening, he wondered if Violet felt the same. Perhaps her own burden would lessen by sharing it with him. He supposed a heavy load was much easier to carry with two sets of arms than one.

Damn it all, he realized with a start, he *wanted* to help her carry her burden.

Putting his thoughts into words felt easy with her, like the cost of baring himself was lower than it was with other people. He could let himself free of his self-made bindings, knowing she'd see him without putting him through the discomfort of having to feel observed.

Sometime in the past day or so, Nathaniel had stopped pretending that he didn't want Violet Thistlewaite to know him.

The realization, when it came, shocked him. Nathaniel Marsh was not much in the business of being known by anyone but Pru, who had been grandfathered in by right of having shared a womb. He preferred to spend his days at a safe distance from people, specifically the width of his counter at the apothecary at a bare minimum. But he'd read Violet's words again and again, the paper already creased and worn inside his breast pocket. *Whether or not the blame is earned, we wear it,* she'd written, and suddenly he wanted to know more, to extract her past from her like a distillation and learn the myriad other ways he was beginning to suspect they were more similar than they were different.

Nathaniel wafted the concoction in the cauldron he'd been working on all week, smiling at the scent of spearmint and lemongrass and rose petal and magic. The sense of peace that swept over Nathaniel told him he'd gotten his old invention just right. He carefully spooned some of the mixture into a vial and screwed the lid on tight, and then he pulled out his pen and wrote one more note for Violet.

V—

It does help, thank you.

And now it is my turn, I hope, to help you. This is a tincture I invented for restful sleep and to eradicate nightmares. It's quite safe, I promise.

Add two drops to a cup of hot tea each night before bed.

I call it the Sweet Dreams Elixir.

Sleep well, Violet.

—N

He wrote hurriedly, his handwriting growing messy as his nerves spiked. With an anxious smile, he walked the bottle over to her side of the greenhouse and set it down alongside the note.

Yes, he thought as he doused the lamp and left the greenhouse, his eyes darting to the leafy vine that stitched together the space between their bedroom windows, he rather hoped he could lessen her burden too.

Tea makes
everything better.

YOU KNOW WHAT THEY SAY ABOUT THE PAST COMING BACK TO HAUNT YOU

"Thank you!" Violet waved to Fallon, who lifted a clay-splattered hand and watched her leave their shop. The potter, who had a bit of fire magic that they used to power their kiln, had agreed to increase the number of pots they made for her, and even to design a stamp for the shop. ROUGH AROUND THE HEDGES it would say, with a border of flowers and even some silhouetted dragons for the town she now called home.

"I'll wager this is the first time anyone's asked me to make a regular stream of flower pots," they had mused. After an hour of conversation with the quick-to-laugh ceramicist, Violet rather thought they'd wager anything that came their way. Thanks to a forewarning from Pru, she had been able to resist taking any of Fallon's offered bets.

Violet had had a dozen moments over the past few weeks that had made her want to pinch herself. She couldn't believe this was her life, that the specter of the Thornwitch had faded to something like a long-ago dream, half remembered and easily forgotten at the slightest distraction. The call of dark magic had mostly faded from a shout to a faint whisper, and even the question of the blight, frightening though it may be (especially to a woman whose livelihood was plant related), couldn't put a damper on Violet's mood.

And it was all due to Nathaniel Marsh.

Well, perhaps not *all*, but his Sweet Dreams Elixir had done wonders for Violet. Her sleep had been haunted by nightmares for months even before she'd left Shadowfade Castle, and Guy's death had only made them worse. She hadn't realized how *not* fine she'd been until yesterday morning when she awoke feeling refreshed and light, and without having to wipe aside a layer of dread to even begin her day.

She hummed as she made her way down the street, lifting her face to the sky. It had rained for most of the day, but now beams of sunlight pierced through the clouds to bathe the town in patchy golden light. Though snow still crested the mountaintops that crowded the horizon, Violet could feel the tendrils of spring unfurling in Dragon's Rest. She knew it wouldn't be long before she was putting out warm-weather flowers and sun-loving vegetable starters for her customers to plant in their gardens. Already, the cherry trees that lined the street had begun to blossom, and the green of their leaves wouldn't be far behind. As the sleepy town began to wake and bloom under the change of the season, Violet wondered more with each day how she ever could have thought it dreary.

"I beg your pardon," she said, skirting around a man who had stopped at the edge of the street. His hood was up as though he expected the rain to start again, and as Violet followed his gaze, she halted too, her mouth dropping open in dismay. There was a new patch of blight stretching all the way from the front of a house to where the grass met the street. It was the largest Violet had seen yet.

"Has anyone determined where it's coming from?" asked the man, still staring.

"Not yet." Violet worried her lip between her teeth, her hair falling over her face as she stared at the ground. They were learning more about it every day—someone had brought home a blighted vegetable just yesterday, and while it wasn't an experiment Violet would have ever sanctioned, they now knew, at least, that while it smelled something awful and was quite difficult to clean from the skin, the blight didn't seem to affect people at all.

Word had spread quickly through Dragon's Rest, and more and more residents were finding blight in their gardens, lawns, and fields. Nathaniel had been diligently collecting samples from each, trying to determine if they were different in some way or if he could learn anything about how they'd formed based on the surrounding areas, but so far, they seemed entirely random. Violet, Nathaniel, and Pru had done their best to spread the word of how to keep it in check—make sure it stayed away from live organic material and contain it within a barrier of stone, glass, or metal—but it was only a matter of time until someone slipped up or it spread somewhere that would be more difficult to isolate.

"Odd that it would begin after Shadowfade's demise, isn't it?" The man's voice was smooth and drawling, and it sparked uncomfortable familiarity in Violet. Perhaps the mere mention of Guy was enough to do that to her these days. "Almost as if the sorcerer had been keeping Dragon's Rest safe."

"I wouldn't go that far," she said sharply.

"No?" His attention was still on the blight, but his tone once again tickled Violet's warning bells. "A powerful magical entity is dead and now a magical blight crops up from nowhere? Perhaps Dragon's Rest is in need of a protector once more?"

He turned to her, and as his face came into the light, horrified recognition dawned on her.

Hell and Undersea, it was Tristan Sedgwick, the alchemist who had made her life miserable in his attempt to unseat her as

Shadowfade's favorite. Violet looked quickly down at the ground again, grateful for the hair that covered her face, hoping he hadn't gotten a good look at her.

"Do I know you?" he asked slowly.

"I don't believe so," she responded in a slightly higher voice, trying to calm her racing heartbeat. She turned away, fists clenched against the onslaught of thorns that pushed against her skin, begging to let them defend her from a threat. If he hadn't recognized her already, thorns would certainly give her away. "And I also don't believe a 'protector,' at least one like Shadowfade, is what this town needs."

She could feel his eyes on her back as she rushed away. It was just about the most suspicious reaction she could have had to someone asking "Do I know you?" but Violet was operating on instinct, not intellect. Like the frightened animal she knew dwelt beneath the thick bramble protecting her heart, she fled like prey, even knowing it would draw the predator's eye.

Sedgwick had the power to bring her new life crashing down around her. He could destroy everything she was building with a single word. It mattered not that she could do the same for him—she doubted his talk of a new protector was meant to be rhetorical after all. He was planning something. She suspected it was no coincidence that the blight had started appearing so soon after he arrived.

Violet rounded a corner and leaned against a building, pressing her back to a wall that was still pebbled with stubborn droplets of rain. As she sunk to the gleaming, soaked cobblestones, her breath caught in her throat.

I can handle this, she told herself, but the note sang flat in the frenzied melody of her thoughts.

A protector, that's what Sedgwick had said. He was positioning himself to take the role; she would bet her life on it. With

Guy out of the way, there was a whole castle on a hill that sat empty and a town full of people who were used to living under someone else's control. Her training kicked in, years of lessons about spotting weaknesses, looking for an opportunity. Dragon's Rest was as wide open as an abyss and Violet knew then, in her heart, that it was only a matter of time before someone came to fill it.

She still had some money. She could flee Dragon's Rest tonight. Get to Lokoa, board a ship, and make for the Shards. The massive island chain was full of pirates and criminals and *villains*, just like her. Plenty had gone there to hide from their pasts. She could be safe there.

But what of Dragon's Rest and the people she was coming to adore? They needed a protector, a real one.

It struck her then: the Tempest.

Karina the Tempest had stepped in when Shadowfade became too much of a threat. She and her band of heroes could protect Dragon's Rest. Violet needed to contact her, let her know what was unfolding. She would come and help.

Be good, she'd said, and Violet knew she would never forget the tone of her voice, the exact cadence of those words. Violet was a coward—she was certainly no hero—but for her town, for her people, she could do this before she left.

Violet's panic began to ease, but she could still barely feel the breeze on her clammy skin, barely feel her nails digging into her face as she clutched them over her eyes, barely hear someone calling her name until a hand came down on her shoulder.

Thorns burst from her skin.

CAN'T HELP FALLING

Nathaniel snatched his hand away as something stung him—a pin in Violet's cloak, perhaps, or an insect that had hidden away on her shoulder. For a moment, as she whipped her face up to look at him, he imagined malice on her features, fury and intent like he'd never seen before, that lush mouth curled into a snarl and those eyes blazing with *something* that scared him, but then he blinked and she was Violet again, albeit much more distraught than the woman he'd come to know.

"What's wrong?" he asked sharply. Grouchy though he could be, Nathaniel was not a violent man—but he found himself just then seized by the mad desire to find whoever had hurt her and make them pay. A cold gust of wind whipped her hair in front of her face, and again he saw that glimpse of a startled predator, a fey creature with glowing green eyes, all snarling teeth and jagged edges. He blinked.

Violet made a barking sound that might have been a laugh or a sob or a choke of relief. "You," she said, breathless, running her hands over her arms like she was soothing a bird with ruffled feathers. "It's you." Her voice cracked and his frown deepened, creasing his face into crisp lines like folded laundry.

"Violet." He forced his tone to soften so she didn't think he was upset with her. "What happened?"

She shook her head. "It doesn't matter."

"You're on the ground, looking like you've seen a ghost. Of course it matters." He searched her face for answers, but she only tilted her chin, searching him right back. Nathaniel knew with some inner certainty that he was undergoing some kind of test, and so despite his discomfort, he held her gaze as he helped her to her feet. Some of the tension in her eyes seemed to soften as his fingertips brushed her wrist, the flash of green he had imagined replaced once more by the warm golden brown he sometimes saw when he closed his eyes.

"Thank you," she said, brushing the dirt and damp from her clothing, her eyes breaking from his. "There was a man—I thought I recognized him from somewhere, that's all. Sometimes I—"

"You don't have to tell me anything if you don't want."

Again, Nathaniel forced himself to still as she studied him. "There's more blight," she said finally. "Bigger than any we've seen."

"Show me?"

When she led him around the corner, his heart sank. Nathaniel produced a vial from one of his pockets and, as he'd grown accustomed to doing, took a sample to test in the greenhouse. He cast his eyes around, looking for similarities, patterns, anything to help him determine why this was happening to his town.

"The man I met," Violet said quietly, "suggested that Shadowfade had been keeping it at bay." She gestured to the blight. "And that with him gone, the town needs *protection*."

She studied the rot, refusing to meet his eyes. "That monster was not a protector," said Nathaniel firmly, but his response didn't carry the comfort he intended. "We can hold our own here just fine."

Nathaniel couldn't shake the feeling that she was taking more from his words than he intended, and he didn't know how to break the flow of whatever was happening inside her head to cast such heavy sadness into her expression. This Violet looked so far from the smiling, bright, hopeful woman who lived and worked next door, the one who, despite his stubborn intentions, made *his* days brighter too.

He wanted to touch her, to tuck the wayward hair behind her ear, pull her cloak back up over her shoulders so she'd stop shivering.

He had no idea how she'd react if he did.

Moons, he wished he was better at this.

"I'm worried he could be involved," she said.

"With the blight?"

She hesitated, then seemed to come to a decision. "He's an alchemist, and the timing of his arrival in Dragon's Rest is . . ."

Recognition prickled like a bee crawling up his sleeve. "He wouldn't happen to be named Sedgwick, would he?"

She startled. "You know of him?"

Nathaniel barked a humorless chuckle. "Do I know of the man who appeared from nowhere to open a rival business that is doing its best to sink Marsh Apothecary? Yes."

"He's hungry," Violet said. "Ambitious."

Nathaniel thought of the list of ingredients Sedgwick had asked him for. "He's dangerous."

"I think the blight could be his way of positioning himself as someone powerful in Dragon's Rest. If he 'saves' everyone from a problem he created, he'd be respected and listened to."

He thought on this for a moment. "I suppose the blight could be alchemical in nature. A skilled alchemist could create a balance that only they'd be able to reverse."

"And if he lets Dragon's Rest fall to panic and is then the one to produce that reversal . . . ?"

"He would be considered a savior."

"Sedgwick could do anything he wanted in this town." Horror filled Violet's expression. "He could routinely allow the blight to continue cropping up, just to remind everyone that if his goodwill was lost, he could let Dragon's Rest fall to rot and ruin."

Nathaniel was quick to believe the bleak picture she painted. His experiences with Sedgwick had shown a man who fit quite cleanly into the role of a villain, but Nathaniel knew his view was biased. Still, the theory merited further study. He was a scientist, was he not?

"I'll have to run some tests," he said. "If I approach my experiments from the hypothesis that the rot is alchemical in origin, I might be able to find out how he's doing it. And I want to know more about Sedgwick. Where he came from. Who he is. What brought him here."

Suddenly, a sharp crack filled the air, seeming to come from everywhere all at once. Violet finally looked at him, though her eyes were filled with, of all things, horror. In a flash, she threw herself at him, knocking them both to the ground. His head knocked painfully against the wet cobblestones, and he was dimly aware of movement, a heavy whoosh and a shuddering crash that shook the air around him. His arms flew around Violet's waist, clutching her to him and rolling them both to the side as something big and heavy snatched at his sleeves.

Dust enveloped them in a cloud, and Nathaniel clenched his eyes shut, raising a hand to cradle Violet's head to his shoulder as they trembled. The air grew eerily still and, his heart thudding in his chest, he cracked open an eyelid.

A cherry tree had fallen, landing exactly where he and Violet had been standing. Blossoms rained down around them like snow, blanketing their bodies in pink-and-white petals as they lay, shocked, in the filth of the empty road. Wet branches tangled with their legs and clung to Violet's hair, and a wall of thorny bramble had appeared from nowhere, holding back a heavier branch that should have crushed them. Violet's doing, Nathaniel surmised. She was panting, her eyes wide and glowing eerily green just as they had that first night in the greenhouse and again today when he found her. Her arm was flung wide from summoning the bramble, her scar stretched tight over a tense mouth. Something vibrated against his chest, and he realized she was shaking.

Nathaniel recognized it with the distant sort of awareness he sometimes got when he spotted one of his own expressions on his twin's face—Violet was experiencing the same sort of attack that sometimes stole his breath and drove his heart to fighting the bars of his ribs for escape.

He pushed himself to a sitting position that left her in his lap. "Breathe," he instructed, ducking his head to catch her eye. Her teeth chattered and her body shuddered, and it was as easy as blinking to pull her into his arms. He stroked her hair, pulling twigs and petals from her curls and inhaling the scent of petrichor and fresh-turned earth that clung to her skin like perfume. "Deep breaths. Look at me, sweetheart. Focus on my face. The sound of my voice."

She dragged her attention from the tree that had nearly crushed them and scanned his features with those wide, darting eyes, which slowly faded back to their usual color.

"We're alright," he murmured, holding her tightly. "Violet, we're alright."

And then she flung her arms around his neck and burst into tears.

Nathaniel froze like a statue, his brain catching up to his body all at once with the reminder that while he was somewhat experienced in managing anxiety (however poorly), he was not very good at offering physical comfort. He felt entirely certain that there was a protocol here, that there were Certain Things One Should Do to comfort a crying woman in one's arms, but for the life of him, he could not remember what they were, if he'd ever learned them at all. (Pru would, he surmised, roll her eyes at him.)

What he did know, however, was that they'd just narrowly escaped death or serious injury, and that he was incredibly relieved to know Violet was safe. Slowly, intentionally, Nathaniel relaxed his body and allowed himself to hold her as she cried great, heaving sobs into his shoulder. He was peculiarly aware, in that moment, of her humanity, full and robust and a three-dimensional thing. The woman in his arms was not just the wild force of reckless optimism she'd come to represent to him but a person with fears and fragile pieces, just like the ones that rattled painfully within the cage of his own soul. He stroked her back, his other hand tangling in her hair, and thought to himself how curious that the knowledge made him want her even more.

"I don't want to go," she said wetly at one point, her tears soaking his shirt. "I want to stay."

"Then stay," he said into her hair. He was not entirely sure what she was talking about, but he knew he didn't want her to be anywhere else, to seek comfort from anyone but him. "Stay here with me."

He could sense the exact moment she collected herself and realized where she was, what she was doing. He anticipated missing her moments before she pulled away. The scent of her hair—blackberry and almond, like her magic—clung to his nostrils, and he found himself back in that dream. *I want* you, *Violet.* Nathaniel had pulled his desire from the flame so it would not boil over; now with proximity, he found it burned him anyway, but oh, how he craved the heat. The flustered way she made him feel was unacceptable. Wasn't it?

"Look at me," she scoffed, avoiding his eye. "Crying like some damsel."

"Violet." He caught his thumb softly, so softly against her chin to get her to look at him. "You are the least damsel-like creature I have ever met."

She hiccupped, and he managed to find it adorable. "You've quite literally just found me overcome with panic and then saved me from certain death, after which I burst into uncontrollable tears."

"Technically, you saved me," mused Nathaniel, but she wasn't having any of it.

"All of it just days after curing me of distressing nightmares—*which you could hear through the wall*."

"Ah, that." He paused, taking in her mortification. "The elixir works well, then?"

Her laugh was flat. "Like a charm. You're a genius." He pulled her against him again. It was instinctive, this need to be close to her, and when she relaxed, something within him did as well.

To herself more than to him, Violet muttered, "How did I ever think I could do this?"

He squinted at her, her hair wild where it had tangled in the branches and his fingers, her eyes glistening and red rimmed, an adorable speck of mud on her cheek that he tenderly wiped away. "You can do this because you are incredible."

She froze, their eyes locked on each other.

Nathaniel finally gave in to his impulse and brushed her hair away from her damp skin, allowing himself to trace her cheekbone with the edge of his thumb. "You moved to a new place, started over, and built a business that is already thriving. All despite, well, *naysayers*."

"Naysayers," she teased, tears still gleaming in her eyes. "Who could you mean?"

"I'm not too proud to admit I was wrong." A wry smile twisted his face. "And even if Rough Around the Hedges does fail—and Violet, I don't think it will—the point is that I admire you having the courage to try."

"Nathaniel Marsh, was that a compliment?"

"Would you like more?" He meant it in jest, but the look on her face had truths spilling from him like serum from an overturned vial. "I envy the way you approach life with such hope. I am astonished by the way you embrace obstacles in your path and I'm regularly struck speechless by your smile. I find myself looking forward to seeing you each morning in the greenhouse and I—"

He wasn't even sure what he would have said next, and found very quickly that it didn't much matter, because Violet had pressed her lips to his.

The kiss bore little resemblance to any expectations Nathaniel might have held of what it might be like to kiss Violet Thistlewaite (not that he'd thought about it in great detail or at any length or with increasing regularity over the past several weeks, because no, of course he hadn't). They came together in a way that was neither gentle nor sweet. Her mouth was demanding and salty with tears, and he momentarily froze with astonishment—Violet was *kissing* him. *Violet* was kissing *him*. Perhaps it was the adrenaline of nearly dying, or the fact that some part of him had been wanting this for weeks, but Nathaniel found the shock wore off quickly. Before he knew it, he was returning the kiss with equal fervor.

Her lips parted beneath his, and Nathaniel swept his tongue into her mouth, knowing with dreadful, wonderful certainty that he'd uncovered a new addiction. He kissed her like a problem he wanted desperately to solve, like a formula he'd yet to crack, and he knew that, like every other puzzle he'd ever been faced with, he'd not rest before he could explore and understand every inch of Violet Thistlewaite. His hands dragged down her neck, thumbs skimming the dip at the base of her throat. Unraveling her completely, he suspected as she arched against him, was an impractical pursuit. A riddle that would take him years to solve. A lifetime perhaps.

And yet. And yet, *and yet*—

It was time to stop thinking so much.

Violet's fingers tangled in his hair, tugging just enough that Nathaniel became hyperaware of her position on his lap. It had been years, if ever, since he'd felt so affected by a kiss.

"Violet," he breathed against her lips, his own mouth quirking into a smile.

But then it was over as suddenly as it began, one more firm press from her lips, as though she were simultaneously shutting him up and sealing the occasion. A ragged gasp tore from his throat when she pulled away.

Their eyes met, each searching, her mouth still just a breath from his own.

"Thank you," she said, then lurched to her feet, disentangling herself from him.

His head whirled, his brain and body struggling to catch up with each other. He missed her warmth, already craved another taste of her. He ached to touch her again, to drag her back home to his bed and allow neither of them to leave until he could sort through exactly what it was about her that made him so undone.

She reached out to help him up, and their fingers both lingered once he was on his feet.

"We need to take care of this blight," she said quickly.

"Whether or not Sedgwick is behind it, that's our first step, and you're the best hope this town has of reversing it."

She was right, as much as the responsibility of it all weighed on him, and were it not for the neck-twisting series of events that had preceded it, Nathaniel would have been satisfied. But he only felt thrown off by her brusque return to their previous conversation. It stung. *We should still be kissing right now* said some part of his brain. Perhaps he should—

"Goodness, are you alright?" A woman leaned out her window across the street, calling down to them. "What happened?"

Violet dropped his hand in a rush, as though she'd only just remembered they were still touching.

"A tree came down!" Nathaniel called back, voice hoarse. "Thankfully we were able to get out of the way."

"The cherry tree?" The woman looked puzzled. "It was perfectly healthy just this morning."

Nathaniel looked back at the tree. He'd registered the pink-and-white petals when it fell, of course, but only now did he allow himself to really notice it. She was right; the entire fallen canopy was laden with fat blossoms that should have hung low with fruit later this season. There weren't even any dead branches. He frowned and followed the trunk to the break, where streaks of black rot stained the splintered wood. The base of the trunk, still anchored in the ground where it had broken, was entirely black at its core.

"The blight must have infected its root system," said Violet from where she stood, not nearly close enough to him. "The roots probably reached the rot we were looking at."

"We'll have to make sure to clear all the debris so it doesn't spread," said Nathaniel, agreeing. He had already spotted more blight in the grass, a large chunk of black wood at its center where it must have fallen with the tree. "Can you call upon your rock goblin friend to help?"

"Peri," Violet corrected. "I'll try."

Nathaniel turned back to the woman in the window. "We've got to go and get help. Can you keep watch over this mess and make sure no one touches it?"

"Aye," said the woman, nodding. Many of the villagers in the central district of Dragon's Rest were well familiar with the protocol now. "I'll send my son down to gather some helpers and lend a hand."

"That would be most appreciated," said Nathaniel. He searched his pockets for a pair of work gloves but only came up with the fine suede pair he wore to ward off unexpected cold. His hands would have to do.

"I'll get Peri," said Violet. "And I'll ask Pru to get more people."

He wanted to call after her, offer to come with her, pull her back to him by the sleeve and kiss her again, but she had already dashed away.

A VISIT FROM AN OLD FRIEND

By the time Violet, Nathaniel, Peri, and Pru returned home, the sky was growing dark.

"I suppose I should count this skirt ruined," said Pru with a sigh, inspecting the rot staining the hem.

"You could trim it off?" Violet suggested. Her own clothing was in no better shape; at this rate, all her trousers were on track to becoming knee-length knickers. She'd fit right in with the gaggle of young children who played in Wingspan Green each day while their parents shopped.

Pru looked thoughtful. "Sounds to me like we're on the cutting edge of a new fashion. Short skirts and bare shins for all! A new age dawns in Dragon's Rest, just in time for spring!" She flung her arms wide and called out, "Everyone, quick, fetch your sewing scissors! I want to see those legs!"

Nathaniel had, of course, managed to keep his clothing spotless, the blackened tips of his fingers the only evidence that he'd just spent as much time in the muck and mire of the rot as they had. Violet swallowed hard, watching those careful hands flex at his sides, trying to banish the memory of them firm around her waist, those fingers ghosting across her cheek, in her hair, at her throat. She'd kissed Nathaniel Marsh. No, correction, she'd cried on him and then practically mauled him, and had then spent the better part of an evening helping him clean up a biohazardous ooze from the muddy street.

Romantic, Violet. Well done.

Deep inside her, the Thornwitch smoldered with resentment at being made to look so vulnerable. And now . . . now she had to leave. Violet tore her gaze away, staring at the ground where Peri the rock goblin chattered up at her, his head cocked at an angle that made the peridot in his chest gleam.

"Hopefully this new age for Dragon's Rest includes a bath in my near future," said Violet loudly, as if the volume would clear her mind of those other thoughts. "I cringe every time I think I might bring even a speck of this blight into my shop."

"I should have mentioned it earlier," Nathaniel said, perking up, "but I've created a special soap to remove it. You're welcome to it if you like."

"Oh, that would be marvelous."

"Fair warning," interrupted Pru, "it will also remove any evidence that you've ever had fingerprints."

Nathaniel clucked his tongue. "I've solved that particular issue, as you well know."

"Yes, but have you solved the smell?" Pru cocked her head, an equally crooked smile aimed at her brother.

"Perhaps that's just your natural odor."

She elbowed him. "Violet, tell Nathaniel that I smell wonderful."

Nathaniel had smelled like mint and rosemary. He'd tasted of it too.

"Violet?"

She jerked back to the present. "Hmm? Yes, you smell . . ." She wrinkled her nose. "Like blight, if I'm honest."

Pru's sigh rivaled a gale-force wind. "I'm almost tempted to say it smells better than Nathaniel's soap." She sniffed her spattered collar. "Almost."

Nathaniel leveled his sister with a lopsided smile that made Violet's heart stutter. "It's either this or scrub yourself raw trying to remove it with regular soap."

Violet looked between the twins, amused.

"Sounds like either way I lose my fingerprints, then," said Pru. "No matter, I've never been particularly fond of them anyway."

"For the last time, it doesn't—"

Pru laughed and winked at Violet. "He's so easy, this one."

They reached the apothecary doors. "Which of us has the cleanest hands?" Violet asked, but Pru had already taken a handful of her ruined skirt and used it to cover her hand so she could turn the key and open the door. The siblings maneuvered easily through the dark apothecary, Prudence announcing loudly that she was ready for a bath and heading up the stairs with a hurried good night.

"Don't you dare touch Daisy without washing first!" Nathaniel called up the stairs as he led Violet to the back door to the garden and their shared greenhouse. He looked down at Peri with suspicion. "And you, I'm watching you."

The rock goblin croaked at him, keeping close to Violet's heels. Violet's heart pounded so loudly Nathaniel must have been able to hear it. She was alone with him again. Three moons, how had that happened?

"Here," said Nathaniel once they'd reached his worktable. He handed her a tin of some pungent-smelling cream.

Violet scrunched her nose. It was herbal and bitter, with a

peppery quality that made her want to sneeze. "Pru wasn't kidding."

"I'd tell you that you'll get used to it but it honestly smells worse every time I open the tin."

"I suppose it would be shortsighted to tell you to stop working on the antidote for the blight in order to find a way to make this smell less awful, wouldn't it?"

His lips twitched. "Believe me when I say I'm tempted."

She looked at the tin to distract herself from the way her neck flushed with heat at the sight of his smile. "Is there anything special I should do?"

"Just rub it into your hands. I'll fetch us some water."

Violet nodded to her half of the greenhouse. "There's some in the pail by the door."

He dutifully fetched the bucket from the ground near her worktable. They were each standing on the other's territory, and it made Violet entirely too aware that she now knew what this man's mouth felt like against hers, that later tonight she would draw to memory the scratch of his stubble against her skin. As he returned to her side, his eyes darted across her face in a way that made her think maybe he was thinking the same thing. Moons, what had she done? Silence settled over them as they washed the blight from their hands. Violet couldn't hold back her embarrassment any longer.

"About earlier," she began at the same time he said, "Can we discuss—?"

They both cut off abruptly. "You go first," he said awkwardly, and Violet wanted to call the earth to bury her where she'd never have to have this conversation. Why was this so difficult?

"You and I have been in a better place lately, haven't we?" she began. "The chalkboard signs aside—and to be clear, those are all in good fun—we've been getting along."

"We have."

She kept her eyes on her hands as she scrubbed. Horrible though the smell might be, Nathaniel's soap really did make it easier to remove the rot. "I've enjoyed getting to know you better. And I didn't mean to jeopardize that earlier by presuming anything."

"You haven't."

His words took a moment to catch up to her, and her thoughts stuttered. Violet dragged her gaze to his and found him watching her, the dark brown of his eyes almost black in the dim light. It was a different type of watching than she'd grown accustomed to from him. Heavier. She felt naked under this kind of attention. How much could he see?

He offered her a clean handkerchief to dry her hands and dipped his hands in the bucket to wash his own. The soft slosh of the water in the pail played harmony to the pounding in her ears. When Violet offered him back his handkerchief, he clasped her fingers in his, the damp cloth held between them like a spiderweb hung between eaves, gossamer and delicate, so easy to break.

He came closer, tugging her by her fingertips until her hand lay against his chest, and fear tugged at Violet's heart even as she felt the reckless pounding of his. She was leaving. She couldn't stay. Couldn't risk her future for this man, beautiful and infuriating and igniting as he might be. The way she felt right now, like he'd turned aside the soil that buried her heart and found the glowing seed that took root beneath, was nothing but a passing fancy. No matter that he'd listened to her, no matter that he'd helped her with her nightmares. Violet had worked too hard to escape her identity as the Thornwitch to let it all come to light now. She couldn't bear to see the look on his face—or Pru's or Quinn's or any of her other new friends—if they found out about her past.

Nathaniel's mouth hovered over hers, asking for permission, and Violet wanted so badly to grant it.

But no, it was better that she leave. Without complications.

"I'm sorry," she whispered, pulling her hands from his. "I'm so sorry, Nathaniel, I can't."

She mourned the light when it left his eyes, wanted to snatch away the familiar stiff mask when it settled back over his face. He scraped a clean hand through his hair, missing a single curl that she wished she could push back from his eyes, and cleared his throat. "I understand."

"It's not that I don't—"

"No, I understand," he said stiffly, offering her a weak smile. "It's . . . this would be a distraction. I have the shop and . . ."

If Violet could wind back the clock just a moment and redo it, she would have, if only to bring back the look he'd had, like he truly saw her, instead of the wooden expression he wore now. "Nathaniel . . ."

He jerked at the sound of his name. "I should check on Daisy. I've left her alone too long. She's probably eaten another of my shirts by now."

He rushed for the door, turning back to her with his hand on the knob.

"Good night, Violet," he said, then disappeared.

She waited until he was back inside the building before leaving the greenhouse and darting into her shop. Violet closed her eyes and pressed her back to the closed door, taking in the familiar scent of flowers and dirt and plant life. Moons and stars, but she loved this place. Every shelf she'd grown from a stick, every plant she'd conjured from a thought—even Bartleby had settled into his corner shelf above the counter with the territorial ease of a jaguar waiting to pounce from a tree branch.

She'd be sorry to leave it.

Violet opened her eyes, looking around at the space she'd so lovingly crafted. Her gardens at Shadowfade Castle had always felt like her safe place, a respite from the chaos and the constant infighting among Shadowfade's other minions. But at the end of the day, they'd always belonged to him. She'd only been able to grow them on his good graces, and more than once he'd burned her hard work to the ground in retaliation for a job that hadn't gone as expected or, in the end, for saying no to a job in the first place. Guy's love, when betrayed, soured quickly, but still, he'd allowed her to grow, to flourish, to build as she pleased in those gardens, and it was more than she'd ever had before.

Until now.

She'd crafted this shop not just of magic but of hard work. She'd sought out the space, planned the layout, strategized her business plan, given it a name, grown to know and appreciate her customers . . .

Rough Around the Hedges was a love letter to the person Violet was trying to become, one who'd left the Thornwitch behind and grown into something new. Change, she was beginning to discover, grew like a seed. Its roots began to sprout beneath the surface long before the leaves burst through the soil. But how would she ever blossom if she had to continually uproot herself?

As she left her spot by the door, Violet knew she would be unable to try this again. Wherever she ended up next, she'd lie low, find some other way to make a living. Flowers were too close to the Thornwitch's magic, and she couldn't risk someone from her past finding her again. Wherever she went next, she'd . . . cut her hair or pay an alchemist to change her eye color perhaps. Maybe she'd give up magic altogether, as much as the thought felt like plucking out a vital organ. But it had been too close a call with Sedgwick. She couldn't possibly start over while her past kept looking her in the face.

Still, her heart tore at the seams as she remembered Nathaniel's words in the street. *Stay here with me*, he'd said as she cried nonsense into his shirt.

How she wished she could.

It was with this thought that Violet registered the knock on her door. Who else could it be but Nathaniel, probably here to berate her and maybe—hopefully?—kiss her again? She was surprised at the jolt in her pulse, the sudden drumming in her heart that begged her, please, just once more.

"Perhaps I owe him another truth before I leave," she whispered to Peri, but the rock goblin had already scampered upstairs to bed.

She swept to the front of the shop and opened the door, only to find Tristan Sedgwick leaning against the jamb.

"Hello, Thornwitch," he said, smirking at her. "I thought that might have been you."

So. She'd been recognized after all.

"Sedgwick," she replied, schooling her face into an expression she hadn't worn since she'd left Shadowfade Castle. "I was hoping I'd been mistaken."

He laughed, low and unpleasant. "Thought I'd check in, make sure our plans don't interfere with each other."

"My plan is for you to leave," said Violet darkly.

He perused her wares, flicking a potted springleaf and watching it twist into a tightly bunched coil as a response. Violet felt the same, a tensely wound spring that could release its unpredictable force at any moment. She breathed through her fear, keeping her magic at bay, but just barely.

Deep breaths, Violet, she thought in a voice that sounded curiously like Nathaniel's from earlier.

"Leave?" He tutted. "Not likely. This town is ripe with fear, just waiting for someone to pluck it from the vine. Better you or me than, say, Cannibal Craig or the Bone Hag." She repressed a shudder at the mention of two of Guy's nastiest associates, though her heart sank at the implication. Dragon's Rest was unprotected, and once she left . . .

"But they're not here," she said firmly, feigning more confidence than she felt. "I am. Now get out, Sedgwick. Find somewhere else to terrorize."

"We could work together, Thornwitch. As partners."

Her skin prickled at the name.

"Absolutely not," she hissed, and was surprised to see a flash of real emotion in his expression. Was he disappointed? Could it be he truly wanted to work with her? She wouldn't believe it of him. For the first time in weeks, Violet allowed dark magic to flood her body, her eyes burning with sinister light as she glared at him. "This place is *mine*."

She hoped the display was enough to make him think she was still the Thornwitch, that she was working on something big and dangerous here.

But Sedgwick only smirked. "For now."

Her voice dropped to a growl. "What?"

"Oh, don't play dumb." Sedgwick narrowed his eyes. "I know you're looking for it too. Why else would you settle yourself *here*, in this miserable shit stain of a town? Why else would you ingratiate yourself with these peasants if not to find it?"

Find *what*?

Violet hid her surprise beneath her meanest mask of disdain and clutched the disguise of the Thornwitch around her like a cloak against the hard wind of winter. "Don't deign to pretend you understand my plans," she said haughtily. "Unless you have information you'd like to share. You've always bragged about your connections, haven't you, Tristan?"

"Remind me," he said slyly, studying her. "How did those connections pan out last time? I've only ever told you the truth and you know it."

Violet clenched her fists and tried to appear unaffected. *Don't think about Silbourne. Don't think about Silbourne.* She scoffed to rid herself of the knot in her throat. "Of course. You're incredibly trustworthy." Her words dripped with sarcasm.

Guy's voice came back to her in a rush. *Wield your cunning not as you would a sword, petal, but like coin. Watch them slip it into their purse for an even trade—and be gone from their sight before they realize it is counterfeit.*

Right. She needed to be smart about this. Sedgwick had always been a talker. She could use that now, so long as he believed she was still the monster he thought her to be. "Tell me what you know and you'll be rewarded," she said, her magic crackling and echoing through her voice with the ill intent it was made for.

But someone had apparently taught Sedgwick some sense since she'd last seen him because he shook his head with a teasing smile. "Ah ah, nice try, Thornwitch. What could you have to offer me without Shadowfade standing behind you?" His words were too close to the fears that endlessly circled her mind in Guy's voice. Sedgwick continued. "If you want information, find it yourself. And once I've found it and you're the one working for me, you'll wish you'd taken my offer. You might have been Shadowfade's favorite pet, but you're nothing alone."

Thorns bristled inside Violet's skin, and for once she didn't stop them, letting him see the way her natural defenses itched to remove him as her problem, reminding him who held the real power here. She felt her body change, twisted thorns bursting from her temples like horns, vines creeping from her back, itching to bind, to strangle.

Even if she knew he was toying with her, being the Thornwitch again was seductive. Breaking the dam of her dark magic and letting it flow slaked a wicked thirst she hadn't realized had grown so severe. Her body soaked it up like rain in the desert, her limbs crackling with power that pushed for release. There was no sting, no ache, only the dazzling current of magic. Oh, but she'd forgotten how *wonderful* this felt.

Sedgwick knew who she was, what she'd done, what she was capable of, and for the first time in weeks, Violet allowed herself to be that monster.

"You have no idea what I am," she warned. Her voice, her stance, the soft threats and veiled displays of her power—it was as comfortable as slipping on a broken-in pair of shoes, perfectly molded to her feet and well suited to planting a kick between his sorry legs. "You have no idea what I could be."

He cowered for only a moment, his surprise quickly tempered by arrogance. "I think you're a sad, scared little girl who has lazed so long on the arm of Shadowfade's throne that she doesn't know what happens now that he's gone," he taunted. "But let me tell you something, Thornwitch—you will find out. And I'll be glad to teach you the lesson."

She whipped out a hand to grab his arm, and he yelped when she let her thorns pierce his skin.

"Try it, you pitiful excuse for a man," she hissed. "You have no idea who you're dealing with."

He jerked his hand back, cradling his bloody wrist against his chest. "And neither do you," he spat, but backed toward the door, his narrowed eyes glued to her like she might pounce at any moment. She wasn't positive that she wouldn't, if she was being honest with herself. "I'll get to the bottom of the legend before you do, Thornwitch. Your magic won't help you."

She gathered her bravado and shot him a haughty look. "We'll see."

It was only once he was gone and the door locked behind him

that Violet allowed herself to sink to the ground. Unbidden, the floor became cushioned with soft petals as she shed her Thornwitch guise, letting her unused power dissipate around the shop as it pleased. The lilies on the shelf behind her burst into bloom, and a potted ivy grew about three feet to weave through her hair and wrap comfortingly around her shoulders like a shawl. She felt nauseous as she came back to herself, banishing the Thornwitch to the farthest reaches of her consciousness.

You're nothing alone, Sedgwick had said, and Violet feared he was right. Without Shadowfade to tell her who to be, she was flailing. Karina the Tempest had misplaced her faith; Violet wasn't *good*, she was a bloody coward.

She could still leave; she *should* still leave. Start a new life far from Dragon's Rest where Sedgwick could never find her.

But it didn't seem like the smart option it had been earlier that night, when Sedgwick recognizing her had felt like the worst thing that could happen. It *had* happened, and she'd held her own, and now she knew he was looking for something.

Something he could only find in Dragon's Rest.

Violet knew it must be something that would give him power—Sedgwick was a deviously talented alchemist, yes, but he would never dare to try to stake a claim over Shadowfade's former territory unless he knew he could maintain it. Whatever he was looking for, he thought it would allow him to hold his own against the Thornwitch and probably much more.

And he'd mentioned a legend.

Violet could find it first. When she thought about Nathaniel and Pru and Quinn and (Good) Guy and all her new friends and neighbors living under the rule of someone like Sedgwick, she knew she couldn't leave this place unprotected.

Running away was out of the question now.

She had no choice. Violet had to stop him.

Sup-herb
solutions to all
your
aches and pains!

Marsh Apothecary

DROWNING

What kind of monster uses a red envelope? Nathaniel wondered as he slid a finger beneath the flap and broke the bank's official seal. It seemed unnecessarily aggressive, like leaving a bottle labeled POISON on the supper table next to a bowl of soup.

Nathaniel skimmed the short letter and tossed it aside, his heart kicking into a gallop. He had six weeks until he had to start making the extra payments—did they have to keep sending him notices like this, as if there weren't already a voice in his head loudly counting down the days? All it did was send him spiraling.

"What am I going to do?" he asked Daisy, who trotted over at the sound of his voice to sit perfunctorily on his feet, where she continued the imperative business of gnawing on a thick length of braided fabric Pru had made for her. The weight of her little body calmed him a bit, giving him something to focus on besides the crushing disquiet that heated his skin like a forge and tunneled the edges of his vision. She was here, which meant he was not alone, he reminded himself through the ringing in his ears. Nathaniel bent to pick Daisy up with clammy hands, holding her close to his chest as she notched her head over his shoulder and began chewing on the collar of his shirt.

He was going to lose the shop, he thought with devastated certainty as he focused on the texture of her soft fur and forced another breath through his lungs.

The barest drop of relief fused through the roiling mix, asking if perhaps this was better. If he failed, he could blame it on their inherited debts. He would no longer be bound to a business he didn't want, and he would be free to . . .

To do what? Continue ignoring the siren call of alchemy? Go back to the Crucible to build weapons for the Queen? Spend the rest of his life in the same state of constant guilt and worry for the people he cared about, only unable to provide the security that he and Pru needed? Failure wasn't a relief. It was defeat. It was his family's legacy, his home, his and Pru's livelihood—*Violet's* livelihood—gone.

Disappointment sank into Nathaniel for the umpteenth time since last night. His shortcomings were taking center stage from every angle, it seemed. After Violet had rejected him—and so soon after their kiss on the street—Nathaniel had replayed the entire encounter in his mind until he could recall it in vivid detail. She was attracted to him, he'd decided, at least a little, or she wouldn't have kissed him and wouldn't have looked at him the way she had in the greenhouse before she pulled away. He was certain there was *something* between them and that she must have felt it too.

Perhaps she was afraid of more—he knew she was running from her past life with her adoptive father (who quite frankly sounded like a piece of work), but perhaps she had other reasons to fear starting anything romantic with Nathaniel, reasons that could very well have little to do with him. Despite the logical reasoning and the answer upon which he'd landed, Nathaniel found it difficult to ease the sting in his heart when he remembered her wincing away and telling him, “I can’t.”

He couldn’t out-logic his emotional response or the rejection he felt. He wanted her—and even more than that, he *liked* her, dammit. The flower witch had wormed her way past his defenses, and all the tonics and remedies in his apothecary couldn’t get her out of his system now. But it wasn’t up to him. She’d made her stance clear, and he could do nothing now but give her time and space, he decided. Nathaniel Marsh was not a man known for his patient manner, but for Violet, he could try.

“Until then, it’s just you and me, Daisy-girl,” he murmured. She looked at him with her big brown eyes and licked his face, her tail thumping against his abdomen with a flat, rhythmic thud. With a little whine, she transferred her attention to chewing on Nathaniel’s sleeve.

“No bite,” he told her firmly, detaching her mouth from his clothing with practiced ease.

Daisy accepted a toy as a suitable alternative and snuggled into his chest as she teethed.

“Sedgwick is taking my business,” said Nathaniel, pressing his cheek to the top of her head. He had grown accustomed to talking through problems in his experiments with his colleagues in the Crucible, but since coming home, Nathaniel hadn’t realized how much the habit had grown rusty. Although the puppy in his arms couldn’t offer any feedback other than a slobbery kiss or the occasional chewed-up pair of shoes, he still appreciated her attentive ear as he worked through his thoughts. “But my family’s been doing this for generations. We survived Shadowfade, we can survive this too.”

She licked his nose by way of response.

He called Pru downstairs to watch the shop and the dog, then strode into the greenhouse with determination. But the second he stepped foot inside, he knew something was wrong. A foul smell saturated the air, thick and cloying. Nathaniel rushed to his worktable and was dismayed to find that his most recent experiment on the blight hadn't diminished it at all—in fact, it had only made it grow. Like one of Pru's failed bread doughs left too long to rise, the black goo had grown puffy and inflated, with a shiny green cast to its color now that reminded Nathaniel unpleasantly of pond scum. It had taken over the glass box, filling it entirely and even seeping through the ventilation. In one place, it appeared to have grown with such force that it cracked the tempered glass.

He'd have to dispose of the whole thing, box and all, and it would take weeks to order a new one from the Crucible. Corrin, the glazier, could perhaps create something for him, but he'd have to explain to her exactly what he needed, and Nathaniel wasn't sure how the box was constructed. He slammed a fist down on the worktable with enough frustrated force that his mint plant dropped a few leaves and the array of vials and bottles along the back edge shook.

He simply couldn't understand this thing, and it infuriated him. That sense of drowning swept over him again like a wave, and Nathaniel felt a heavy rock of anxiety form in his throat. They were depending on him—Pru and Violet and everyone else in Dragon's Rest—and he was failing. How could they possibly expect him, a failed alchemist with an already poor track record, to save the town? He couldn't even keep his family's apothecary afloat, and as for his alchemy, the last time he'd tried to invent something that could really make a difference, he'd only brought disaster upon his family.

Nathaniel ran a frustrated hand through his hair, pulling until his scalp protested in pain. He needed to stop focusing on what he didn't feel capable of and start focusing on what he *could* do.

He could step back and see that this most recent experiment had caused the rot to react differently than before. He could isolate the ingredient in the solution that had done that.

He could clean up the mess in the greenhouse and prop open the doors so neither he nor Violet would have to tolerate the smell.

He could start working on a few minor potions for the shop so he could make a bit of extra money.

He could march right into Violet's shop and kiss her again.

Oh. Well.

He allowed himself a single moment to replay the memory that had been on repeat since last night. The soft yield of her mouth, the press of her thighs against his lap, the little mewling sound she'd made when he— No. Moment over. He simply couldn't allow himself to be distracted right now, and that's what Violet Thistlewaite was. A distraction. A lovely, bright distraction that made him yearn for things he'd never before thought he might want, but a distraction nonetheless. And moreover, one who *didn't want him*.

Nathaniel simply had too much upheaval in his life right now to allow himself to fall under the witch's spell, and besides, he'd resolved to wait. Perhaps later, after he'd eradicated his current messes, he could consider a future in which he felt happy as well as secure, but right now one of those two needed to take precedence, and as usual, his happiness would take last priority.

Support a

local business!

Buy from Marsh!!!

MARSH APOTHECARY

RESEARCH

As the postmaster took her message, some of Violet's worry disappeared along with it. One week. The letter would be delivered in one week, and then Karina the Tempest would know what to do.

After all, she'd come once before.

Still, Violet's thoughts were dark as she made her way down the street, shaking out her hands to try to eliminate the ache that had set into them. She kept her eyes on the paved walk before her, her brow furrowed as Sedgwick's words replayed in her head once again.

You're nothing alone.

She hated how much she believed him. Shadowfade had given her power and purpose. Alone, she was useless. Leaving was no longer an option, but Violet was terrified. She wanted to run. She wanted to believe she could be free of the Thornwitch, and the thought that she might have to *be* her again, even if just to scare off opportunists like Sedgwick . . .

That wasn't what "being good" meant.

But she didn't know how else to do this.

Stay here with me. Nathaniel's voice, rough and so close to her ear, rose once more, the only thought that had been able to compete with Sedgwick's taunts. She closed her eyes and took a ragged breath, stamping down the complicated turmoil of emotion that threatened to overtake her. No, she had to stay focused, no matter how tempting the alternative.

Sedgwick had spoken of a legend, so Violet made her way to the town hall building, which also held the community's small library. For the past two days, she'd been working her way through the local history section with every moment she could spare. Anything to help stop Sedgwick, though it also had the added benefit of helping her avoid Nathaniel. Inside, the musty-sharp scent of paper and ink cast Violet into memories of Shadowfade Castle, happy ones from her childhood before she realized who she'd become, as Guy read to her from ancient spell books and encouraged her to experiment with what she found there.

Violet wound her way through tall shelves of scrolls and books until she found a thick, promising-looking book and brought it to the front desk to sign it out.

"We have other texts on the town's history," said the library clerk, who recognized her by now, "older ones that can't leave the premises. If you don't find what you're looking for, you can come back and request them."

Violet returned to her shop to find Jerome the Gnome outside with his cart, tapping his feet impatiently next to the Marsh Apothecary sign, which was less pointed today than usual. Although a few half-hearted response options swam weakly through her brain, the sign failed to bring out Violet's competitive streak, and only brought a blush to her cheeks as thoughts of the other night once again rose unbidden. Here, in front of their shops—where it would take no more than a dozen steps to stand before him—it was harder to ignore the fact that they'd kissed. Or the fact that a not-so-small part of her wanted to do it again . . .

"This is no way to run a business." Jerome waved his hands at her. "You have hours of operation on your sign, don't you? Are you going to open or what?"

Violet snapped back into the present and unlocked the door. "Hi, Jerome," she chirped cheerfully, forcing herself to be Violet the Shopkeeper again. Was this what her future looked like? Bouncing back and forth between identities, constantly trying to keep up? "Give me just a second."

He grumbled while she opened the window shades and set out her own sign, which would have to bear the same message as yesterday until she was feeling more creative.

"Your door's hung crooked," said Jerome, inspecting the door that led upstairs to her living quarters. "Told the Marsh twins not to use Patchett as their carpenter—his prices are cheap for a reason."

She had noticed she had to lift the door a bit to get it to latch, but she'd never found it troublesome enough to tell Nathaniel or Pru. They had enough to worry about, and she didn't want to create more problems than she needed to.

Jerome ran a hand over the hinge. "I'll stop by tomorrow morning with me tool kit and fix it for you," he promised gruffly.

Violet was taken aback. "You don't need to do that."

But the gnome wouldn't hear otherwise. "We take care of our own here." Before the words could sink in, he added, "Now take care of *me*. Am I a customer or not? I'm here for more soil."

With Jerome close behind, Violet made her way to the back garden and hefted a sack of the soil mixture she'd made specifically for him. She noted his eyes catching on the neat pile of flat, decorative stones she'd just had shipped in.

"They're for folks whose lawns or fields have been marred by blight," she explained. "So they can cover the area and stop it spreading."

"You heard about the Feldspar farm, then?"

Violet stopped in her tracks. The Feldspars were one of the biggest farming families in Dragon's Rest and supplied nearly half of the town's grain. Horror tinged her voice as she asked, "Not the blight?"

Jerome nodded. "Took about ten percent of the crop. A field hand noticed and they were able to contain it, but we're looking at a hard summer of high prices."

"It's getting worse," whispered Violet. "Spreading faster than before."

"Aye. We're all facing ruin, and your—" He sneezed as if to punctuate his point. "Your flowers won't help."

She ignored his jab at her business. "A tree nearly killed Mr. Marsh and me. It wasn't directly next to a spot of blight, but its roots must have touched it beneath the ground."

"I heard he was working on some type o' fix for it."

"As far as I know, still no luck." She glanced at the greenhouse. It was empty at the moment, but she knew he had about four different experiments going. It had smelled absolutely foul in there this morning, and she hoped that meant good news, despite olfactory evidence to the contrary.

"It's bad." Jerome's voice was as serious as she'd ever heard it. "Folk are starting to talk, wondering if it's a result of Shadowfade being gone. Some curse he put on us in his dying moments. The timing, you know? Feels like revenge."

Anger hummed to life in Violet's veins. It was too similar to what Sedgwick had implied. Was he spreading that drivel? There couldn't be truth to it, could there?

"This has nothing to do with Shadowfade," she said acidly, noting as she did how the grass beneath her feet shriveled and died. "What reason would he have to take revenge on a town like Dragon's Rest?"

"Right." Jerome stared nervously at the dead grass, as though it would turn to blight before his eyes.

"Sorry." Violet shook herself and breathed life into the grass, which sprung back up, green and lively as ever. "I just can't bear the thought of that monster."

He watched her, thoughtful. "You're not alone in that."

She helped Jerome load the soil into his cart. "We're going to fix this," she promised, sounding more confident than she felt. "You send anyone who needs help containing the blight to me, alright?"

The gnome nodded solemnly. "We'll pave the whole town in stones before long, and then what?"

She let her expression fall. "I haven't the foggiest, I'm afraid."

As soon as she was back in her shop, Violet slumped. This was bad. A blighted food supply meant trouble. Violet could help the farmers regrow their crops in an instant, but Nathaniel had struck fear into her about her conjured plants. She'd eaten apples from trees she'd created, and vegetables from the garden out back, but as Nathaniel had pointed out, did they provide any real nutritional value? Would conjured grain keep a town's worth of bellies full if it was all they had? She'd told him in their notes that she would experiment. Perhaps it was time to do so.

"Experiment!" she muttered, unable to keep a smirk from pulling at her lips. "That man is rubbing off on me."

There was no one else in the shop, and she'd already finished the arrangements that were due for pickup today, so Violet pulled out one of the books from the library and spread it open on the counter. She'd never been much interested in reading anything that wasn't about plants, and the long, dry accounts of the town's history as home to an exiled prince and of musty depictions of battles fought by people long dead weren't exactly riveting. In between customers she flipped through the pages, keeping her eyes open for the words *artifact* or *legend* or anything that might lead her to understand what Sedgwick had been on about, but the book appeared to be rooted firmly in dates and figures, with no sign of any lore that might help her.

All the while, Sedgwick's words repeated on a loop. *You're nothing alone. You're nothing alone.*

You're nothing.

This was never going to work. Not only did she have no idea what she was looking for, but Sedgwick was right—her powers wouldn't help her here.

Violet turned the page and swatted Bartleby away when he tried to flick back to the previous one. "Are you trying to read with me or just being annoying?" she snapped, but left him to his own devices when the front door opened. More customers—perfect. She needed a distraction.

"Hi, neighbor," said Pru. "You've been making yourself scarce, haven't you? I figured I'd come and check that Nathaniel didn't melt you into a puddle the other night."

Violet could feel her blush down to her toes. "Pardon?"

"With his magic soap," clarified Pru, her brow furrowing. "For the blight. You used it, right?"

"Oh. That. Yes!" Of course Pru wouldn't know about the kiss. Of course she couldn't possibly know the tangle of emotion that knotted in Violet's chest. She'd been far too open, and though letting the Thornwitch out in front of Sedgwick had been a calculated and necessary move, there was no denying that Nathaniel had seen far too much of her to make Violet comfortable.

She stood by her decision to pull away from him, but now that she'd resolved to stay in Dragon's Rest, it felt— No, she needed to stay on task. Outsmarting Sedgwick would take all her energy. Now more than ever, she needed to put her former life under lock and key if she intended to stick around, and spending more time around a man who made her want to spill all her secrets was not the way to do that. No matter how much she longed to.

Banishing her thoughts, she asked Pru, "How are you?"

Pru hummed, her face serious. "Frustrated. Did you hear the news about the Feldspar farm?"

Violet nodded. "Jerome mentioned it."

"Did he also mention one of the field hands accidentally tracked it on her boot and it spread to a second field?"

Violet groaned. "He did not."

"Idiot," cursed Pru. "It's common knowledge now that it spreads—what were they thinking?"

"People are scared," said Violet, "and when they're scared, sometimes it's easier to pretend problems don't exist."

"Well, I hope they've learned their lesson over there," said Pru with uncharacteristic bitterness.

Violet grimaced. "I suspect we'll all learn the lesson of their mistake."

Prudence leaned against the counter, propping her head with her hands. "What do we do?"

"I'm working on something," she said, gesturing to the useless book open in front of her.

"For the blight?"

She hesitated. If her suspicions were correct, then stopping Sedgwick *was* stopping the blight. "Yes. Do you know anything about ancient artifacts in Dragon's Rest?"

Pru's dark brow furrowed. "Artifacts? Oh, you mean the legend? Sure, everyone does."

"Seriously?" Violet threw her hands up and glared at the book like this was its fault. "This town's library is useless."

Pru laughed good-naturedly. "Well, don't judge us too much for it. All our good books ended up at Shadowfade Castle. Not that we had much to offer in the first place."

"Right." She supposed that made sense—Shadowfade Castle did have an extensive library full of books and scrolls about magic and history. As the years had passed, Guy had made sure to build the collection of books on botany, gardening, and herbalism to satiate Violet's endless appetite for plants. It was in those books she'd discovered her penchant for poisonous plants and the exact species of carnivorous flowers that she could work to her advantage—but she'd also pored over books on vegetable gardening and propagating and greenhouse cultivation. It was where she'd learned the basics of flower arrangements (of course, it was for the purpose of sneaking blades into the bouquets for an enemy's gala) and how to grow plants by hand rather than by magic (that one was meant for a rival sorcerer who could sense magic on plants, so she'd started the vines the old-fashioned way before sneaking them into the garden beneath his bedroom window and using them to— Never mind).

How she wished for the resources of that library now.

Violet was ashamed to realize she'd never given any thought to where all those texts had come from. But if the books that would have proven useful to her were missing from Dragon's Rest, it carried a sort of logic that she was on the right track if Guy had found value in them as well.

"We could break in and steal them all back . . ." Pru was musing. "No one's using them now, and as far as I know the castle's sat empty since all his minions cleared out."

The very thought of returning to that place pumped ice into Violet's veins, but she forced the feeling away. "Before we go committing any crimes, I'd love to start with that legend," she said with a strained smile. "What can you tell me?"

Pru's expression turned thoughtful. "How much do you want to know?"

"As much as you've got."

"Well, the story goes a bit like this . . ."

THE WITCH AND THE WARRIOR

". . . A thousand years and a day before you or I were born, when the moons were young maidens still painting the sky, these mountains were home to a powerful dragon who terrorized the land, seeking riches for his hoard— Don't look at me like that, Vi, I'm a performer. If I'm going to tell the story I'm going to do it right."

Violet pressed her lips together and settled back to listen. Pru the Neighbor was gone and Pru the Bard stood before her as she continued. "His scales were impenetrable as the stone mountains that surrounded him, and his breath wrought fiery despair upon the land. The dragon was stronger than most, for besides his own magic he knew how to draw power from his vast hoard of riches, which was hidden deep in a cave inside the mountain.

"Knights and mages came to steal his treasure, but the dragon defeated them all, leaving a field of scorched bones scattered across the mountainside. No one lived here then. No one could; the dragon would take them as his next meal. So when a great warrior came to the mountain with the intent of defeating the dragon, the dragon thought little of it. But this one was different, for the warrior did not come alone, you see. He had fallen in love with a witch who had lived many lifetimes and watched the rise and fall of kingdoms while she stood unchanged. The witch carried around her neck a great, glowing gemstone that granted her power immeasurable. It was even said to hold dominion over life and death, and indeed the amulet had saved her from many mortal wounds and had kept her young and beautiful across many human lifetimes. 'This amulet will help us defeat the dragon,' the witch confided to her lover, 'because it was once the serpent's left eye.'"

Violet sucked in a breath as Pru spoke, for she realized she knew the story, or part of it at least. Guy had been obsessed with finding the Eye of the Serpent. He believed, like the witch, that it would make him all-powerful. Could it be that this was what Sedgwick searched for?

"As the centuries passed," Pru was saying, "the witch had grown lonely in her power. Her heart shattered again and again when those she loved grew old and withered away, all while she remained young and powerful. When she fell in love with the warrior, she knew the only way to avoid another heartbreak was to grant him a life as long and unending as her own by capturing the dragon's other Eye.

"'I will defeat this dragon for you, my love,' said the warrior when they made camp that night upon the fields of bone and ash. 'No. We will defeat it *together*,' she insisted firmly. 'For the brightest constellations shine not from a single star, but many.' The warrior kissed her sweetly and took her to bed, but after, as she slept soundly in his arms, he slipped the Eye of the Serpent from her neck and stole away from camp. Many had perished in pursuit of the dragon, and he did not want the witch, powerful though she was, to meet the same fate. When she woke and found him gone, the witch knew instantly what he had done.

"Without the power of the Serpent's Eye she felt weak. Mortal. But more than that, she was filled with a terrible fear for the man she loved. He had lied to her and stolen from her, but if he were to be killed, her heart would never recover, not in a hundred lifetimes. Her love for him fueled her as she made her way to the dragon's lair.

"The sound of a great battle reached her ears—the roar of the dragon and the clash of steel against hard scales. A wave of heat rocked the witch, hotter than any forge, and she saw the warrior bravely fighting the dragon, his sword flashing with deft speed. But the dragon was bigger and stronger, and she could see her love was beginning to grow tired.

"When the dragon's blind side was turned toward her, she summoned a great cyclone of dust and ash, sending it toward the beast. But though the witch had once been a formidable power in her own right, she had relied for centuries on the Eye of the Serpent as a source, and the river of her magic had slowed to a trickle with disuse. Casting such a powerful spell without the Eye weakened her, and the witch watched in horror as her right hand grew withered like a crone's, for all magic bears a cost. The cyclone struck the dragon's good side, blinding his remaining Eye temporarily. The dragon roared, lashing out with his great claws and striking the warrior to the ground.

"The witch worried for her love but kept to her cause. She lunged toward the dragon and with inhuman strength plucked out its other eye. The dragon bellowed a deafening roar, thrashing in agony, and the witch clutched the eye as she ran back to the warrior. The strength it had taken had required more of her magical essence, and even as power from the second eye filled her, her withered limb crumbled away to ash. Dread overcame her then, for the witch used her hands to cast magic, and though there were other ways to wield power, she would have to learn them all over again—if she survived that long. Tears ran down her cheeks as she reached the warrior, still prone on the ground, and she realized his legs were broken. 'Why is the Eye of the Serpent not healing you?' she asked, and he said, 'Because I do not know how to wield it. I'm sorry, my love. I stole from you and did not consider that I could not use it.'

"The dragon roared again and let out a jet of deadly flame that missed them by inches.

"'Even blind, it is still dangerous,' said the witch.

"'We must defeat it, or it will take innocent lives in vengeance,' agreed the warrior, 'but I cannot stand to fight.'

"The witch looked to where her arm should have been. 'And I cannot do magic like this.' The warrior grasped her remaining hand and looked deep into her eyes.

"'The brightest constellations shine not from a single star, but many,' he said. 'I shall be your hands.'

"He slipped the amulet back over her neck, then took the second Eye and grasped it in their conjoined hands.

"'And I shall be your legs,' she replied. Magic flooded her once more, only this time, she could feel his body as well as hers. The pain in his legs was agony, but she summoned strength enough to lift him onto her back. Together, left hands still clasped, they turned as one to the dragon. The witch carried them toward the beast as the warrior held aloft his sword. The blinded dragon turned to them, opening his great mouth to show flames forming in the back of his throat. The warrior threw his sword like a javelin into the roof of the dragon's mouth, and as he let go, the witch summoned the power of both Eyes, using their hands to channel magic into the weapon. Guided by her spell, the sword struck true, piercing the soft flesh inside the dragon's mouth and driving into his skull. A wave of power pulsed through the air, throwing them both back until they lay outside the cave's entrance, still in each other's arms. The ground around them began to rumble and they watched in shock as the dragon froze, the fire never leaving his throat, and turned to stone before their eyes."

Pru's next words broke the silence like a plucked bowstring. "The cave trembled around them, and the witch used her remaining strength to drag herself and her warrior farther from the cave while it collapsed to a great pile of rubble, taking the dragon with it.

"'We did it,' said the witch with no small amount of wonder.

"'Together,' added the warrior, pressing a kiss to his love's lips. 'I'm so sorry I left without you.' The witch clutched her amulet, determined to heal the warrior's legs, only to realize it was gone, as was the second Eye. In fact, the entire hoard of the dragon had disappeared entirely, lost in the wreckage of the cave. She cried out, searching, but the Eyes were gone."

Even Bartleby was captivated, his vines curled up beneath him in tense wonder, and it took Violet a moment to understand that the story had finished.

"What happened to the Eyes?" she asked, and Pru waggled her brows.

"No one ever managed to find the dragon's hoard, or the Eyes of the Serpent. The witch, it is said, believed the dragon had taken them back, for dragon magic is not something we understand. 'Anyone who searches for it,' she claimed, 'must first find the stone dragon.'

"Before long the story became just that—a story, powerful magic in its own right, as all stories are. As the years passed, the land began to heal from the dragon's rampage and the collapsed cave began to grow over with grass and wildflowers until it was indistinguishable from the rest of the mountain. The place where the great stone dragon took his eternal rest became a bustling town, and the witch and the warrior lived out the rest of their days there—mortal, yes, but together. Starting over wasn't easy, and came with its share of challenges, but as the community of Dragon's Rest grew and grew, the witch and the warrior knew they never need be lonely again."

Silence rang like the after tone of a struck bell. Violet's chest felt tight.

"So we start with the stone dragon," she said finally, setting her troubled thoughts to rest until she had time to examine them.

"Maybe." Pru's smile turned wry. "If the story's true. Personally I think it's a load of dung. People have been searching for the dragon's hoard for centuries. If it ever existed, they'd have found it already."

Violet frowned. Shadowfade had not been known to chase ghosts.

"But the Eye of the Serpent has a reputation that expands beyond the legend."

"Of course it does. The Eye was always a big tourist draw for the town," said Pru. "Back when, you know, we had tourists."

The name *Shadowfade* hung in the air between them, because of course no one would want to visit a windy little mountain town that also happened to be within spitting distance of a dark sorcerer with homicidal tendencies. Violet was working on that, of course, but even once she managed to get rid of Sedgwick, that wouldn't change the fact that Dragon's Rest was tainted with fear. *Just another story*, she thought, but the seed of an idea began to take root.

"What if it could be again?" she asked. "What if we could bring the tourists back? More business for both our shops, as well as everyone in town—and you'd have a larger audience to play for. You wouldn't have to travel so much to find work if you didn't want to."

An image struck her then, of Pru up on that stage, telling that story—accompanied by music and costumes and a few actors to play the different roles—to a rapt audience each week on Market Day.

Pru cocked her head, thoughtful. "I suppose there's an entirely new generation of people out there who have never heard of the hoard of Dragon's Rest."

"Exactly." The idea had sprouted now, unfurling leaves and opening to the sun. Violet could feel it budding as it took on life. "We could build a town-wide treasure hunt that takes tourists through all the major business districts. Talk to Quinn and Fallon and the other business owners in town, and we could cast *ourselves*"—she stumbled over the word—"the businesses and all the people who live here, I mean, as the 'treasures of Dragon's Rest.'"

Pru looked intrigued by the idea. "If we could boost tourism, we could offset some of the hardship folks are facing and even head off some of what's coming now that Feldspars is . . ." She trailed off, frowning.

"Right," said Violet. "What about the blight?" For a moment, she had forgotten all about the blight and Sedgwick and the reason she was trying to learn about the legend to begin with.

But just as quickly, Pru waved a hand to dismiss the thought. "Do you honestly think my brother will rest until he's found a solution?" she asked. "Nathaniel's even more pigheaded than the warrior in the story, and he won't hesitate to fight this particular dragon alone if he needs to. I'm not saying this isn't a serious problem. It is. But it's not a bad thing to look toward the future even as we're still figuring out the present. The point is, with Shadowfade gone, Dragon's Rest *has* a future now, and we can help be the ones who make sure it's a good one. It's a great idea." She grinned. "We'll call a meeting of local business owners and start planning. They'll want to help, and they'll have even more ideas than what the two of us can devise alone."

As they chattered about festivals and themed market days, Violet reflected that Pru was right—Dragon's Rest did have a future now, and Violet was flattered and a little sheepish to be a part of it. Maybe this was how she could redeem herself and put the Thornwitch to rest. Planning community events was about as far from villainous as she could imagine. Was this what it meant to be good?

But despite Pru's optimism, Violet knew that in order for Dragon's Rest to truly have a future, she had to keep it from sliding back into the past. She committed details of the legend to her memory.

She was certain now that Sedgwick believed the Eye of the Serpent could be found in Dragon's Rest, and she had to stop him from taking over, not just for her own sake, but for the sake of the community she was growing to care about. Guy had been a lot of things, but he wasn't stupid: whether or not all the details of the legend were true, Violet believed the Eye existed, and even if Sedgwick had a head start, no one had known Shadowfade like Violet did. She would follow his logic and pick up the trail where he had left off.

She would find the Eye first, and she would destroy it.

RISK

A sliver of light streamed from the crack beneath the door that separated his half of the upstairs hallway from Violet's, and Nathaniel knocked before he could convince himself not to, turning the thick, brass key in the lock for the first time since she'd moved in.

"Don't look at me like that," he muttered to Daisy, who sat at his feet with her tongue lolling from her mouth. "It's late, I'm just checking to make sure she's well."

When there was no answer, he convinced himself she simply hadn't heard him, but he didn't want to knock louder and risk waking Pru, who would certainly have questions he didn't feel equipped to answer right now.

He turned away and was steps from his own bedroom door when he heard the clink of the lock on her side. Daisy whined and rushed for the door, her tail thumping on the carpet.

"Hi," he said, feeling inexplicably breathless as he turned back.

"Hi." Violet was wearing nothing but a dressing gown, which left her lower legs bare. Instantly, Nathaniel wondered if he'd made a mistake in knocking on her door. After all, he was supposed to be avoiding distraction and giving her space. She bent down to scratch behind Daisy's ears, and Nathaniel averted his eyes when he saw the way the garment gaped at the collar.

He cleared his throat. "I saw the light, and it's so late, I—I wondered if perhaps the elixir wasn't doing its job."

Her face melted into a soft smile that made him recall exactly what it had been like to feel those lips under his. "It's not the elixir," she said, standing, and he stepped closer so they could continue to speak in low voices, unheard by Pru down the hall. "I can't remember the last time I slept so well."

His relief must have been evident on his face, because she looked at him oddly.

"Why? Should I expect it to stop working?"

"No, no, nothing like that." Nathaniel leaned against the door frame and stared at the ceiling as he admitted, "It's only, I've spent the past few days wondering if I can do anything right at all."

Behind Violet, Peri appeared, which was apparently the best news Daisy had received all day. With a soft yip, she leapt toward the rock goblin and the two of them tore down the hallway, wrestling and pouncing on each other. Violet and Nathaniel both followed their movements for a moment until Violet said, "Why don't you come in?" and stood back to allow him past the doorway.

As Daisy and Peri continued zooming and wrestling, Violet led him to her small kitchen. Nathaniel felt his shoulders loosen as he took a seat and looked around the room that had once been his mother's study. It was undoubtedly Violet's space now, with flowers and plants everywhere and an open book on the small table next to a bowl of vegetables from the garden and a plate of pastries. Nathaniel could smell them from here—they were the same delicious brown butter, pear, and cardamom tarts Guy had brought him today. It didn't surprise him one bit that Violet had managed to charm the old man into giving her baked goods.

Nathaniel plucked a cherry tomato from the bowl and rolled it between his fingers. "The vegetable gardens were my father's," he said, staring pointedly at the tomato instead of meeting her eyes. "He would be happy to know they are being used."

"I'm honored to make use of them," she said softly. "And let me know if you'd like me to grow anything in particular. I'm still getting the hang of squash—Pru said my last attempt tasted of cinnamon."

"Was she complaining? Pru loves cinnamon."

Violet's laugh was clear and sweet as ever. "No, she was inquiring as to whether harvesting the seeds from that particular squash would grow *more* of the same flavor."

"That sounds like my sister."

"She said something similar," Violet divulged. "About your father's love for the vegetable garden."

"That's because it's true. Neither of us liked seeing it fall to disorder last summer. And I suspect my mother would be pleased that the greenhouse is being used for growing plants again." He made sure to smile so she'd know he was teasing as he added, "Even if they're for bouquets and not medicines."

"Har har." A kettle was already steaming atop the woodstove, and Violet pulled down a jar from a shelf. "Tea?"

"Got anything stronger?" he drawled, scraping a hand through his hair.

She smirked at him. "Was that a joke?"

"I am capable of humor, you know."

"Oh, I've seen your chalkboards, if that's what you're calling humor."

"And yours are any better?"

They stood grinning at each other until Nathaniel forgot what they'd even been saying.

Violet looked back at her jar of tea. "I mix my chamomile with mint before bedtime," she explained as she retrieved a second jar. "I call it mintomile."

"That sounds perfect." He frowned, his brain snagging on the name. "Have you considered chamomint as an alternative?"

"I have not." She brandished the tea at him like a weapon. "Is this going to be on your sign tomorrow?"

"Frankly, if the superior wordplay option is up for the taking, I'd be remiss if I didn't use it."

"Superior! Haven't we just been over this?" Violet's laugh soothed him more than any cup of tea could—and Nathaniel really, really liked tea.

"Now what's all this about you not doing anything right?" Her eyes were on the shelves as she pulled down a jar of Quinn's honey, but Nathaniel felt her attention nonetheless. "I'll assume you haven't made progress with the blight today, then?"

He shook his head and thanked her when she set her place with a mug and handed him another. It was one of Fallon's, heavy and glazed in pale green. Their fingers brushed for the barest moment, and he responded, "Not even a little. My experiments are limited until I can get a new workbox. Corrin says she'll make it her top priority, but it will still be a day or two at the soonest."

"You're doing all you can," said Violet soothingly, taking the seat opposite his and pushing the book aside to make space for the teapot. She poured them both a cup. "And more than anyone else knows how."

"That's the problem," he said with enough force that her gaze sharpened on him. "It's still not enough."

Gently, Violet reached across the table and laid her hand over his. Her palm was warm from her mug, yet still nothing compared to the heat that coursed through him at her casual contact. "No one is asking you to solve this on your own. No one expects that of you."

"*I* expect that of me." He turned his palm, lacing his fingers with hers, and marveled at the very act—was this what they were to each other now, or was their closeness something they could only achieve late at night with the moons their sole witnesses? "It feels sometimes like everyone I know is depending on me. I'm the one they're relying on to solve the blight, but what if I can't do it? What if I'm not clever enough to fix it and more people lose their crops or livelihoods? And then there's the apothecary—it's my family's legacy and I can barely keep it afloat. If I can't make my next bank payment, I'm going to lose the shop. And then I must make it again the next month, and *every month following*. We've had entire days lately without a single customer."

He wasn't sure what he expected. He thought she'd demand to know what would happen to her own livelihood or try to solve his problems for him or even insist that things would suddenly turn around on their own. But she stayed silent, the pressure of her fingers warm and comforting over his, and just listened.

Nathaniel continued. "My sister and I have inherited so many problems from our parents and now it's on us to solve them all—but neither of us even really *want* to run an apothecary. If I ask Pru for more help, I know she'll give it, but then she'll have to stop playing music at the inn and the market, and I won't do that to her. Even you—" He turned a tortured gaze on her. "If I fail to keep the apothecary open and the bank takes the building, what will become of your shop? I can't let you lose it, not after you've worked so hard."

"Thank you for saying that." She squeezed his hand. "But Nathaniel, what about you? What is it *you* want?"

He could feel himself closing down, shuttering the windows through which he was suddenly afraid she had seen all his dusty rooms and dark corners not often exposed to light. "It doesn't matter."

"It does," she insisted, and suddenly his hand was clasped in both of hers. "Nathaniel, of course it matters."

He resisted the urge to pull away from her, settling instead for closing his eyes, focusing on the warmth of her fingers wrapped around his. "I want what I've always wanted. To make a difference. To invent medicines that can help people."

"Then do it," she said simply.

"I tried. I failed."

"So try again."

Nathaniel scoffed. "Yes, because it's that simple."

"Isn't it?"

She made it sound so easy.

"You studied in the Crucible, didn't you?" she cajoled.

"And what a waste that was."

"I see it very differently." She stared at him evenly. "You have an education and experience to help you toward your goal. That puts you leagues ahead of me—I had exactly *zero* business knowledge before opening my shop, but it was my dream. And if I hadn't done it, I would have always wondered if I could. Am I still figuring it out? Yes. But is it worth it? Absolutely. You can long for something all you want, but you'll never unlock the door if you're too afraid to turn the key."

"I can't afford the risk," Nathaniel said immediately. It was the excuse he'd used with Pru again and again, and by now she'd stopped arguing with him.

But Violet wasn't Pru, and she didn't allow him to keep those tidy boundaries. She only looked at him with those shining eyes and said with more patience than he deserved, "What do you think you're risking? Your reputation? Everyone in this town respects you, admires your intellect and your resolve. That won't change." She cracked a smile. "Your friends and family already know you're a bit gruff and particular, and they love you not in spite of but *because* of it. Because it's part of the rest of you—the determined, loyal man who adopts stray puppies and helps a neighbor with her nightmares and enjoys wordplay more than he'll openly admit. You won't lose the people who care for you if you fail. You'll only have to accept their hands to help you back up again."

Nathaniel wondered if she was telling him she was one of those people.

He wanted to believe she was, or could become so.

"Without risk, there can be no hope of change," Violet continued. "And believe me, I've made a *lot* of changes recently. You tell me you want to create new innovations in alchemy, make a difference to the world. The elixir you gave me *has* made a difference to my life."

Her words struck him at first with embarrassment that he should forget something so simple, and then with a burgeoning sense of light he soon recognized as hope. She was right about all of it. He did have the experience and the schooling, and that wasn't worth nothing. He had made mistakes—big, terrible ones—but he'd made a difference too.

He wondered when he'd forgotten that in order to truly consider himself an inventor, he had to be unafraid to try something new.

"You're right," he said finally, and the words struck such a chord that he repeated them. "You're right."

"I'm often right, these days," she replied with a wink. "Now what are you going to *do* about it?"

His mind raced. "There's not much I can do about the blight

at the moment, but the apothecary . . ." A laugh escaped his throat when he discovered the answer had been there all along. He met her eyes. "I have some ideas."

"Good." She extricated her hands from his and took a sip of her tea. How could he have thought this woman a distraction? If anything, she was a driving force, a guiding star. She had come here, fresh from a past that clearly troubled her, and started anew. She took risks. She made changes. He could do that too, couldn't he?

When they finished their tea and collected Daisy from where she'd passed out curled up with Peri at the foot of Violet's bed, she led him back to the hallway door.

"Thank you for tonight." He used the hand that wasn't full of sleeping puppy to tuck a stray lock of hair behind her ear. "I needed someone to be honest with me."

"I'm always glad to be the boot in someone's arse," she quipped, scrunching her nose as she smirked at him.

"It's been a while since I had someone to talk to like this."

"Me too." She tilted her head to catch his eye. "You're going to figure it out. The apothecary, the blight . . ."

A lingering wave of doubt crashed over him, the tide rising once more. "And if I can't?" he whispered. "If I lose the building? If Dragon's Rest suffers because I can't fix the blight?"

She surprised him by pressing up onto her toes and looping her arms around his neck, pulling him close enough that he could smell the bright scent of her magic that clung to her like perfume. In his ear, she told him, "Then we band together like the community we are and figure it out."

Her words had the intended effect; he felt calm once more, confident under the beam of her belief. And then—the softest pressure of her lips against his cheek. Nathaniel didn't dare move or breathe. He knew she was afraid, but perhaps this was Violet taking a risk. Perhaps they could take a chance together. She lingered before pulling back, tugging her lower lip between her teeth as she fought a smile, and scratched Daisy between the ears one more time. “Good night, Nathaniel.”

He couldn’t remember the last time the roiling sea that churned constantly in him had calmed its waters like this, clouds parting and leaving nothing but clear skies full of endless stars above him.

“Good night, Violet.”

He stood there in the hall after she closed the door, listening for the sound of her locking it. The sound never came, and he didn’t turn the key on his side either.

Rough Around the Hedges
FLORAL & GARDEN SHOP
GOT BLIGHT?
WE CAN HELP.
WE WILL GET THROUGH
THIS TOGETHER,
DRAGON'S REST.

What she said.
MARSH
APOTHECARY

TRUST

The facade of Violet Thistlewaite had begun to grow tattered, and the thorns of her past were beginning to snag on the weave. The truth was that her conversation with Nathaniel had shaken loose something she normally kept screwed tight. It didn't take much to understand that he'd allowed Violet to see a part of him he showed to few people, and she wanted to return the favor.

He would understand.

He would still care for her if he knew.

Wouldn't he?

Her doubt hovered over her like a storm cloud all day. Whether he knew what he asked for or not, by trying to get close to her, Nathaniel was asking for her truth. She wasn't sure she could act on her feelings without giving it to him. But could he be trusted with her past? Could anyone?

Another of Guy's aphorisms came to her. *Even secrets told at a whisper grow wings, petal. We must clip their feathers by never letting them fly from our mouths and shoot down any birds that take to the skies.*

She couldn't help the part of her that still believed him to be right.

"You're distracted today," said Jerome. "More'n usual. Mind, you're not the most attentive shopkeeper I've met even on a good day."

He'd shown up bright and early with his toolbox to fulfill his promise to fix her door.

"Tea with milk, and I like me eggs scrambled, not fried," he'd said by way of greeting.

Violet hadn't argued, just gone upstairs to make him breakfast. The ache in her hands was growing worse, the sort of raw, chapped feeling that made every movement uncomfortable, especially magic, so doing something as mundane as making eggs and toast for Jerome was a welcome distraction. Violet liked the old gnome; his blunt gruffness was a respite from some of the others in Dragon's Rest—as kind as they could be, Violet wasn't *used* to their friendly drop-bys or kindly invitations to get-togethers (or Pru's recent plans of breaking and entering at Shadowfade Castle on a "book rescue mission"). Her instincts insisted they wanted something from her, but Jerome was about as direct and undiplomatic as a person could be, and she found that strangely comforting.

"Just thinking," Violet replied now. "Have you ever had a secret?"

He took a leisurely sip of his tea and studied her carefully. "Sure."

"Is there ever a right time to share it with someone?"

"S'pose that depends on the secret, and what's at risk in the telling."

"Quite a bit," she admitted.

"And what's the cost of keeping it to yourself?"

Violet slumped against the wall. "Also quite a bit."

Jerome turned back to his work, measuring out where to realign the hinge in the jamb. Violet almost thought he'd abandoned the conversation when he said, "Everyone's got secrets, just as everyone's got a past." He held a mouthful of nails between his lips so it came out slightly garbled. "We're none of us the people we once were, but it's still scary letting others through that gate. But those that're worth it, they'll let you know. Might be in different ways than you expect, but they'll show you that they're worthy of your trust."

"How?" Bartleby snuck a vine into her hair; she only caught him seconds before he hacked off a sizable lock with the pruning shears he'd stolen *again*. "I will prune you until you don't *have* vines anymore," she warned him, and he retreated.

Jerome spit out the rest of the nails, chuckling. "I s'pose trust comes from the way they make you feel part of their circle. The way they make you feel safe." He eyed the pothos with mild, almost-amused derision. "Safe like leaving your hair be and not hoarding weaponry."

"You can imagine why it's difficult for me," she said dryly, gesturing to Bartleby, who froze at the attention, trying desperately to look like he wasn't in the process of pilfering a few fallen nails. She sighed, mentally tasking herself with disarming him later, and massaged her hands.

Did Violet feel safe around Nathaniel? She wasn't sure she really knew the meaning of the word or if it was something she felt around *anyone*.

"I'll take another cuppa if you're just going to stand there," said Jerome, jerking her from her thoughts. She took his empty mug and went upstairs to fetch him some more tea.

Long after he'd left, her door now hanging straight and proud on its hinges, the conversation swam in Violet's head. Violet wasn't sure she'd ever had cause to truly trust anyone.

Your mother saw who you truly are and she abandoned you, Guy had told her.

You are so lucky I found you, petal.

The rest of the world may fear you, but you will always have a home with me.

It had taken her nearly all her life to realize that he had orchestrated all of it that way.

Her memories pressed into her consciousness like ivy climbing a wall, finding any hole, any foothold where it could stick.

Funnily enough, it was Sedgwick who had lit the spark that burned her relationship with Shadowfade. He had spent years trying to get under her skin, to unseat her and take her place as his favorite. None of it had worked until the day Guy sent her to the city of Silbourne.

"They're amassing a militia against me," Guy explained when he summoned her to his study, "led by some 'great warrior' or other who wants to make an impression upon the Queen."

"What would you like me to do?"

"Go to Silbourne. Take care of the problem," he told her, flicking his ring-laden fingers as if sending a child off to play. "I will follow in three days' time."

"Of course," she said, and he dismissed her.

As Violet mounted her horse, Sedgwick had strolled into the stables, a folded piece of paper in his hand.

"What's this?" she asked haughtily when he offered it to her.

"A little parting gift, Thornwitch," said Sedgwick, winking.

"I want no gifts from you."

His eyes glittered with mirth. "Believe me, you'll want this one."

Violet had rolled her eyes and shoved the paper into her pocket, riding away. It wasn't until she made camp that night that she remembered it, unfolding the creased paper carefully as though it might explode—with Sedgwick, one could never be sure. And as her eyes scanned the letter there, her life changed forever.

She'd heard Sedgwick brag about his connections, of course—anyone who was in a room with him for more than five minutes had heard him boast of his ability to procure information—but he must have been exaggerating, never mind that Shadowfade trusted his network. He must have been a liar because this couldn't possibly be true.

No, because if the letter before her eyes were true, the one that contained words like *Captain Marigold Thistlewaite* and *missing daughter* and *kidnapped* and *still searching*, then it would mean that Guy had lied to her about *everything*. It would mean she'd done terrible things because the man she trusted told her she was evil—and all the while there had been a ship somewhere in the Stained Glass Sea with purple sails called the *Violet* and a captain at its helm who had never abandoned her on an island after all.

It had been a long time since the Thornwitch cried, and when she noticed the hot moisture that tracked down her cheeks, it only made her angry. Sedgwick was lying. He had to be. She couldn't trust him, not when he was so openly trying to replace her. Her thorns shredded the letter until nothing was left but a few scraps drifting in the wind.

And so the Thornwitch had ridden to Silbourne, the swirling vortex of emotion forming into a cyclone of anger. As she drew closer to the city, she announced her presence as she always did, by desiccating whole fields of crops, her smile growing as cries of dismay and fear rose around her.

They shot at her with arrows, as they usually did, but the Thornwitch simply opened her saddlebags, laden with soil, and grew strong vines that wove around her like tentacles, pulling arrows from the air and breaking them to pieces until they littered the packed dirt road behind her horse like a carpet of rose petals beneath a queen's feet.

To either side of the road she grew tall, thick hedges, their wicked, long thorns just as toxic as their vivid purple flowers, and the armed men who rushed at her drew back just as quickly when they were overtaken by hacking coughs from the poison. It was a performance she had played out countless times, and she knew each line of the script by heart.

Her mouth curled in a wicked smile; *this* was what she was made for. As her purple cloak whipped around her, she—

Purple sails. A ship with purple sails.

No.

Violet snarled, and her thorns grew. She was the Thornwitch, fearsome and powerful, and that was the truth. That was what she'd been taught, and Guy wouldn't lie to her. He'd taken her in. He'd protected her from those who would have called her a monster and punished her for the evil that was inherent in her. He'd cared for her, given her a home when no one else wanted her.

Hadn't he?

Violet wavered, and her hesitation was enough for someone to get lucky. An arrow knocked her from her horse; a sword she barely dodged sliced open her lip. And by the time Guy found her, three days later as promised, and fought his way through the city to free her from the dungeons, she'd had time to let her thoughts fester.

"What *happened*, petal?" His voice had been a low hiss, and there was a shallow gash on his temple that dripped blood across his brow. He was still a man, she remembered thinking. For all that he had become, he could still bleed. The sounds of fighting had stopped; she imagined he must have won, as he always did. He wanted Silbourne, and Guy Shadowfade got what he wanted.

Like Violet.

"My mother," she said, tucked back into the farthest reaches of the cell where she'd been kept. Cuffs on her wrists stopped her from accessing her magic, and the skin beneath them felt just as raw and angry as she did. The cut on her face had grown infected, and while it was agony, it wasn't the worst pain she felt. "Did my mother abandon me?"

"Why are we reliving the past?" he said smoothly. "You know she did. I found you, and I took you in because I knew no one else would. I gave you a home, petal."

"Tell me the truth. Did you *rescue* me? Or did you take me from her?"

He was a good liar, one of the best, but he hadn't been prepared for this conversation, and in the instant before his mask settled into place, Violet saw it—alarm. Just how much truth there was to the story Sedgwick's informant had shared remained to be seen, but there *was* truth to it.

"Let me get you out of here," Guy said soothingly. "We'll destroy this place, raze it to the ground for what they've done to you, and then we'll go home and I'll get one of the healers to fix that dreadful wound on your face. Really, petal, how did they manage to get the better of you? Frankly I'm a bit disappointed."

She let him remove the cuffs from her wrists, but the second he did, she let her thorns grow long and vicious, forming twisted horns at her temples and vicious, spiky pauldrons at her shoulders. The wound on her face was torture, but this was armor in the best way she knew. Before she could think twice, she'd reached for Guy's throat.

"You lied to me," she growled. "My *entire life*, you lied to me."

He gasped for air, pawing at her hands. "Petal, let go."

She found she was crying, for the lies she had been told, yes, but also, for the first time, for the person she could have been if he hadn't taken her and raised her to be a monster. If she'd been allowed to grow up on that ship in the Stained Glass Sea. If she had been *loved* instead of used.

"Violet . . ." Guy got himself together then, and his skin grew red-hot beneath her fingers until she was forced to let go. He coughed and collected himself quickly, and when he spoke again, his voice was a growl, his eyes lit with the threat of more magic. "That is *quite* enough."

She shrank back from him like a dog who had been beaten.

"Those idiot sailors didn't know what they had in you," Guy snarled. "Born under a *Convening*. You were made for so much more than they offered. You would never have reached your potential if I hadn't taken you in."

"You don't know that."

"Of course I do!" he roared, and when she winced at his anger, he schooled himself back under control. Just like that, he was her father again, the man who'd raised her. Beseechingly, he said, "The past is the past, Violet. Haven't I loved you well enough? Everything you are, you owe to me. *Me*, not some merchant nobody on a floating death trap. *I* made you."

A monster, she thought, smelling the smoke of destruction though the tiny window of her cell. *You made me a monster.* The realization broke something within her, though she was careful not to show it.

He searched her face, and whatever he found there, he was satisfied. After all—as he said—he had made her. He swept from the dank stone corridor, leaving her to follow at his heel.

Guy had done more than destroy Silbourne's militia that day. He had destroyed nearly the entire city, leveling buildings and allowing his minions to do as they pleased. Violet hated him. She loved him. She wasn't sure what to think, what to do, where to go from here.

When they finished, Shadowfade stood above the destruction

before his team of assembled villains, handsome and charismatic, and said, "All of this thanks to your Thornwitch."

They took it like a celebration, but Violet knew it then for what it was: a warning. She came home to Shadowfade Castle to all the accolades she had yearned for, but they felt hollow now, a snakeskin from an animal that had already shed. Guy celebrated the sack of Silbourne by giving her full rein over the southwest lawn. That seed of something inside Violet had taken root, though, and she found she couldn't enjoy the act of growing as she once had. She hadn't been abandoned, and the man who raised her wasn't her savior. What would her life be like now if he hadn't taken her? Would she have drifted toward dark magic anyway, or was that affinity, so lovingly nurtured by Guy, just another lie?

A complicated hedge maze grew on the southwest lawn from Violet's tattered thoughts, unnavigable by anyone but her unless she wanted them to find their way through. The vivid, tropical-looking flowers were carnivorous and toxic, and the thorny hedged passageways often shifted, trapping unwary visitors inside the maze until they had no choice but to crawl out through its wicked thorns. Guy thought it hilarious whenever one of his cronies emerged into the hall radiating fury and covered in scratches, their clothing torn. Before long, everyone learned to treat the misleadingly beautiful new garden like any other danger on the grounds of Shadowfade Castle.

As for Violet, the cut on her face never quite healed, and she learned never to trust anyone again.

Now, as she tidied her shop, cleaning soil and leaves from the counter, straightening the displays, Violet marveled at what that day had brought. The very worst of her reputation, yes, for Silbourne would follow her and haunt her for as long as she lived. But another seed had taken root as well.

The next time Guy had asked her to become the Thornwitch, Violet had said no.

He had not liked her answer. He'd threatened her, burned one of her gardens, and, after she'd refused to change her mind, locked her in her room. But he had not replaced her, hadn't given Sedgwick or any of the others the seat at his side.

"The Thornwitch is indisposed," he'd told the other villains of Shadowfade Castle. He hadn't wanted them to know she'd disobeyed. After weeks in her tower room like a princess of legend, with only Bartleby for company, Violet had stopped moping and decided enough was enough. She couldn't get rid of Shadowfade herself, but she knew of someone who could.

She'd written a letter and sent it before she could think twice.

Violet did not know it at the time, but it had been the beginning of the end.

THRILLED

"What's got into you today?" Pru asked the next morning as she finished measuring bite root for a customer. "You've got your thinking face on. Is the blight bothering you? Quinn said there's a patch of it now in her neighbor's garden."

"What?" Nathaniel looked sharply at his sister. "Has she contained it?"

"No, I told her to spread it on her morning scone like butter." Prudence rolled her eyes. "Of course she's contained it."

The familiar cracks of dread began to spiderweb through Nathaniel's confidence. "I've still never seen anything like it. I'm considering reaching out to some of my old colleagues from the Crucible for their take."

"What if you asked that new alchemist who opened up shop?" Pru asked. "Sedgwick, yeah?"

"Sedgwick, *no*," Nathaniel disagreed. "He's blatantly stealing business from us. And besides, Violet thinks he might be behind the blight."

"What?" Pru reared back. "Really?"

"He has some kind of reputation. It sounds like she knows him from before she came to Dragon's Rest."

His sister's expression flattened to stony solemnity. "That's serious, then. Who else knows?"

"I'm not sure. We don't know anything for certain yet." Not that Nathaniel would be upset if, say, word got out to Quinn and spread through Dragon's Rest until Sedgwick was forced to leave town. His vehement dislike had only grown with Violet's suspicion that Sedgwick might be the one causing the blight, not to mention with every one of his customers who'd stopped coming into Marsh's. And if those reasons weren't valid enough, the man had *made Violet cry.* He had to go.

One good thing had come of it all, he supposed. The Sweet Dreams Elixir that he'd made for Violet would spoil after a month. He'd resolved already to brew her more whenever she had need of it, but even the smallest batch would leave him with more than she could use in that time. So Nathaniel had taken to heart the ideas that had sprung in Violet's kitchen and bottled the rest for sale. He'd placed it on display this morning . . . and already sold four bottles at a significant price point.

A few more days like this, he thought with something dangerously like hope, and they might be able to make their first monthly payment to the bank.

The Sweet Dreams Elixir wasn't volatile, he reasoned with himself. Even in its early experimental days, he'd never seen any sort of adverse reaction—no explosions, not even a bad smell—and even before he perfected the balance of ingredients and the precise details of the method, he'd never experienced any side effects.

"What do you think about offering a few other alchemical medicines?" he slowly asked his sister now. He'd started working on several this morning, inventions from his days in the Crucible, but had resisted floating the idea to Pru. Now that one of them was not only on their shelves but doing well, however, it was time to ask. "Nothing big, mind, and certainly nothing dangerous."

He was still resolved not to experiment on anything brand new without a proper work setup, especially now that he shared the space with Violet. Nathaniel would never put the people in his life at risk for his own ambitions again—but he did have alchemical solutions for some of the regular problems of folks in Dragon's Rest that were tested, safe, and effective. He could sell them in the shop without risking fire, injury, or death upon the people closest to him.

And maybe keep his business afloat in the process.

"Yes," said Pru before he'd even finished talking. "Nathaniel, *yes*."

He could feel his cheeks growing warm. "It's just that the Sweet Dreams Elixir is doing so well already, and I thought—"

"I already agreed, you silly bat!" She flung her arms around him. "It's a wonderful idea, brother. Exactly what the shop needs."

"Well," he said again, feeling sheepishly pleased. "We'll need to buy some specialty ingredients, and it won't be cheap, but I think with the markup on the inventory once it's ready for sale, we can—"

"Still yes. You're not going to talk me out of it, and I certainly won't let you talk yourself out of it." Prudence looked feverish with excitement. "I'm thrilled, Nathaniel. Thrilled."

"But are you *thrilled*?"

She slapped his shoulder, grinning. "Thrilled!"

He felt his own smile grow as he watched his twin walk away from him and scoop Daisy into her arms. She stopped at the bottom of the stairs. "Thrilled, Nathaniel!"

It was settled, then. Marsh's would start selling his inventions. Nathaniel would officially be an alchemist once more.

Guy—Regular Guy, that was, not Big Bad Evil Guy—watched with an approving smile from over by the window display. The old man held a bottle of Sweet Dreams Elixir in his gnarled hands.

"You heard all of that, then?" Nathaniel asked, scratching at the back of his neck self-consciously. Guy had been close with his father and grandfather and had been a regular fixture at Marsh's all of Nathaniel's life.

Guy nodded.

"And what do you think? Am I setting myself up for disaster?"

Guy ambled over to the counter and set the bottle down. Slowly, so that even Nathaniel with his extremely basic knowledge of sign language could understand, he spelled out the word *proud*.

"Well then," said Nathaniel, feeling unendurably pleased. "If you say so."

Guy paid for the elixir and left the store, leaving Nathaniel behind the counter with entirely too much emotional energy for a person to safely contain. Pru was thrilled. Guy was proud. He'd spent so long being ashamed and horrified about what he'd done, he'd assumed everyone else in Dragon's Rest felt the same. When he'd packed away his alchemy gear and vowed to keep the apothecary as it was, he thought everyone else must have been relieved. No risk of anyone else being hurt by his actions; no chance that more of his experiments would go wrong in other, even more disastrous ways.

But both Guy and Pru had known him his whole life. Was it possible they'd seen the way it had affected him, not being able to do the thing he loved most? Was it possible they didn't hold him responsible for his parents' deaths? Was it possible there were others in town who felt the same?

When Nathaniel had worked for the Crucible, he felt swallowed up by the big city, secure in his own anonymity. Coming back to Dragon's Rest had made him feel uncomfortably on display. But perhaps there was safety to be found even in a space where everyone could see him. Perhaps Violet was right—these people knew him, flaws and all, and they would not let him fall.

As a child, Dragon's Rest had felt stifling—everyone knew everyone's business and made it their own, and for an anxious, introverted boy finding his own way, that was more of an imposition than anything. But a community, he was finding since his return, was about much more than a lack of privacy. It was about help, and support, and family. Nathaniel still didn't look forward to surprise visits from neighbors and the way Quinn inserted herself into gossip—but he loved the way Jerome pretended to be reluctant and grumpy while simultaneously offering to be everyone's handyman, and how Guy gave away leftover pastries at the end of the day, and how Nathaniel could easily remember his customers' names and regular orders. He even loved sharing the greenhouse with Violet.

He could never have planned for this, *would* never have wanted to plan for it, but perhaps unexpected bumps in the road didn't have to be a bad thing. Perhaps change could lead to good as well as bad, and he could adapt more easily than he gave himself credit for if he just gave himself the space to pivot and explore. He'd spent so much time focused on everything he was getting wrong, it never struck Nathaniel how much he had gotten right.

Nathaniel's thoughts buzzed as he shut the apothecary for the night. He locked the doors, closed the blinds, and updated his ledgers as quickly as he could, all while a different type of energy built within him, one that flowed like fire through his veins as he extinguished the lamps and strode out the back door.

Nathaniel had never been the type of person who wanted to

gloat over his victories. He'd always kept the particulars of his life tidy and private—even Pru had to drag information from him. But Violet didn't make him feel like she would judge or gossip or pander; she made him feel *heard*, and *safe*, and a number of other words Nathaniel would have scoffed at only weeks ago. He wanted to share his news with her.

He opened the door to the greenhouse, and there she was, the warm lamplight from her worktable painting her hair with streaks of gold. Her greeting cut off as he strode purposefully toward her, bypassing his own half of the greenhouse.

"Are you alright?" she asked instead, cocking her head.

"Never better," he said honestly, and swept her up into his arms, lifting her off her feet in a tight embrace that made her squeal with laughter. He pressed his nose into the waves of her hair as he swung her around, smelling that blackberry-and-almond scent that meant he'd interrupted her doing magic, no doubt preparing bouquets for tomorrow morning.

"I did it," he said without bothering to mask his joy. "I put the Sweet Dreams Elixir on our shelves, and I'm going to sell more alchemical medicines in the apothecary. It's really happening."

"That's wonderful." She laughed again and pressed a hand to his cheek, thumb grazing his stubble. He leaned into her touch. "Nathaniel, I'm so happy for you. I want to hear everything."

"I've got so many ideas," he told her, setting her back on her feet, though he didn't let go of her waist. Her hands settled at his shoulders as he explained his inventions. A lotion to encourage hair growth. A tincture that straightened crooked teeth. A powder that ensured new shoes would not give the wearer blisters. "They aren't life-changing cures and medicines, but they're a start. And it's all thanks to you."

"Certainly not." She beamed at him. "*You* invented these."

"But I'd never have done anything with them if you hadn't

talked sense into me." He drew a deep breath. "Violet, I've been an idiot. I've spent so long worried about repeating past mistakes and maintaining my parents' legacy I didn't consider the legacy that *I* want to leave. Who *I* want to be. You helped me see that. You helped me be brave enough to take the risk." His gaze roamed her face, drinking in her wide eyes and long lashes, those thick brows and bow-shaped lips separated by that scar. She was perfect, his flower witch, and he needed her to know it.

"And in the interest of taking risks," he said, before he could convince himself not to, "I need to tell you something."

She took in the change in his expression, pulling her lip between her teeth in a way that made him want to bite it himself. *Easy, Nathaniel.*

"I meant every word I said the other night." His voice rasped as he told her, "I find you incredible, Violet Thistlewaite."

Her breath caught in her throat.

"The notes back and forth, our conversation at the window, last night in your kitchen, that kiss—" He cut himself off, suddenly nervous, but nothing done by halves, he supposed. "I care for you, Violet. More than I ever intended. If you tell me you don't feel the same, I will understand. But with the way we left things, I wanted to—"

"But I do," she said, and his heart stuttered in his chest. "I do feel the same."

"Oh." Nathaniel took the small smile she showed him, held it in his chest, and let it warm him like a fire on a wintry night. He knew, then, that she was scared too. His thumbs brushed small circles over the fabric of her waistline, urging her to talk to him.

"Nathaniel, I'm not good at this." He watched Violet swallow her words and commanded himself to pay attention to what she was saying instead of closing the space between them to press his lips to the place where her throat met her collarbone. "I'm terrified

I won't be able to be the person you think I am. I don't want to ruin everything."

He ducked his head to catch her gaze. "Someone very wise and lovely once said that without risk, there can be no hope of change."

She narrowed her eyes, looking at him sidelong. "Has anyone ever told you it's incredibly rude to use someone's words against them?"

"I'll make a note of it." He dared to move closer, and trailed a hand up her arm until his fingers brushed her neck, then her jaw. *She* was terrified? He wondered if she could hear the way his heart staggered in his chest. Nathaniel had been brave today—perhaps it would prove contagious. "All I know is that I feel lighter than I have in a long time, and *you* are the person I want to share that with."

She dropped her head to his collarbone as she huffed out a breathy laugh he could feel against his skin.

"And besides," Nathaniel continued, tipping her chin back up so she was looking at him, "I've recently become somewhat of an expert in taking risks."

He took the biggest one of all, then, and lowered his mouth to hers.

MAGIC

Nathaniel cupped her face in his palms like water and drank from her lips all the words she had said in their notes and under cover of moonlight, as well as a few she hadn't yet. Violet gasped, feeling again that great intake of breath from deep within her, the delicate sprouting of an emotion she'd only just dared to expose to sunlight.

This was not a kiss. It was comprehension.

"Is this alright?" he murmured against her mouth.

"Yes," she sighed, and never had she meant the word so much. "*Yes.*"

Her hands roamed his waist, his back, pressing herself ever closer to the hard lines of muscle beneath his clothes. Nathaniel maneuvered them backward until her lower back was flush against the edge of her worktable, and she pressed closer still.

He tasted of mint and rosemary. As Violet kissed him, she was of a sudden mind to grow an herb garden, a constant reminder of him that would drive her wild every time she drew near. But there was no need when he was right here before her, his hands on her body and his tongue demanding of hers.

"You are all I have been able to think about," he murmured against her lips. "The sound of your voice, the feel of your skin, the taste of your mouth . . ."

He hissed in pleasure as she slipped a hand between them, brushing her fingers over the fabric of his trousers.

"Violet." He stilled.

"Mmm?"

"I'm afraid you're going to have to be very direct with me here. What is it you want?"

She pulled back just enough to look up at him through her lashes, and a spark of the Thornwitch buzzed through her just then, devilish, powerful, confident. She couldn't tell Nathaniel who she really was, and that had started to eat away at her, but perhaps she could show him, just a little.

She smirked up at him. "I don't want to go slow," she said carefully, watching the way his throat bobbed and trying to judge his reaction. "Perhaps we should, but . . . I don't want to be good right now."

A matching smile began to form on his features. "You know, I rather think being good is overrated."

Her heart swelled, and their lips met again. One of his legs parted hers, and she rocked against his thigh, delighting in the friction at her core, her hands winding around the back of his neck to tangle in his thick hair.

No, they weren't being *good*, exactly, but Violet struggled to think of a time when she'd felt better than this.

Her head fell back when his teeth nipped at the exposed skin of her throat. "Oh, that is . . ." Violet's words rode the low hiss of her breath like a leaf on the breeze, quickly losing track of their destination and fluttering aimlessly in the air.

He chuckled against her neck, and from this angle she could still see the quirk of his eyebrows as he asked, "Is that so?"

She moved against his leg again, satisfaction and heat curling together low in her belly, and greedily reached for the back of his head so his mouth could once again meet hers. "Shush."

But he didn't.

"I have imagined us a hundred different ways," he admitted in a rough voice. His thumb traced the hills and valleys of her knuckles, lingering in a moment's caress along each one and banishing the soreness in her hands to the furthest reaches of her mind.

"Have you?"

"Mmm." A press of his lips to the corner of her mouth. "Here in the greenhouse, the other night in your kitchen . . ." His lips trailed up her jaw until his teeth nipped her earlobe, his whisper rough enough to make her shiver. "You have been endlessly distracting to my work of late."

His words thrummed through Violet like a surge of electricity after a lightning strike. She was buzzing, she was galvanized, she was recklessly, splendidly *alive*. She nudged the hollow of his collarbone with the tip of her nose, her hands roaming his arms. "And what, exactly, have you imagined?"

A growl of playful laughter escaped his throat, and his hand slipped between her thighs. Violet had never doubted for a moment that the alchemist would have talented fingers, and yet as he began to move against her, circling her sex through the fabric of her trousers, she gasped, still managing to be surprised.

"I've imagined *this*," he said, low and rough in her ear. "You just like this, right here against this table, and touching you just like this, and hearing you make sounds just like—" He circled his fingers again, just so, and Violet moaned. "Yes, *just* like that."

Her laugh was breathy and strangled. She grasped his shoulders and threw her head back, eyes fluttering closed as he touched her. "And how does reality hold up to your fantasy?"

Nathaniel nipped at her earlobe again and pulled back until she looked him in the eyes. "Violet Thistlewaite, never doubt that you are a thousand times better than anything I have ever dared imagine for myself."

She drew a shaky breath, unsure of what to say to that, and settled for grinding wantonly against his hand. Her hips jerked when, together, they found a rhythm that made her vision darken at the edges. Nathaniel's mouth twisted into a smug grin. Violet clutched at his shoulders, pulling him in for another kiss so he could swallow the rather embarrassing cry she couldn't contain.

"Whatever you do, don't you dare stop," she commanded against his lips.

"Sweetheart, I wouldn't dream of it."

In the past, Violet had sought her pleasure while in disguise, as well as from people who knew who she was and feared their own attraction to her. Before now, she'd have considered those dalliances satisfying. But here in the greenhouse, still fully clothed as she rode Nathaniel's hand to chase her release, Violet had the sudden thought that all those times she'd been fumbling in search of something she could not name.

Until now.

When she came, it was with a cry that choked in her throat. Her hands flew behind her, grasping for purchase on her work-table, and she was dimly aware of knocking over a pot of soil. Violet blinked hard, her breath uneven, and found Nathaniel watching her with something like awe. She wondered what he was seeing when he looked at her. She wondered how much she had let her mask fall. How much further she could drop it before he saw all the parts of her she kept hidden.

Her hands went to his biceps and trailed downward, tracing the tendons and muscles of his forearms through his shirt as she gave a self-satisfied little smile.

"Do you want to know what *I've* been thinking about?" she asked then, her expression conniving as she watched the way his eyes grew hooded at her touch. She mapped the line of his shoulder, then ventured down across the plane of his chest. Touching him like this was even better than stolen looks and late-night imaginings, she decided.

"If it's anything to do with this, then yes, desperately."

"I could tell you." She teased him lightly with her fingers, one hand finding his belt. "Or I could show you."

The sound he made then could only be described as a growl. "Show me," he demanded, squeezing with the hand he'd wound into her hair, and there was the bossy apothecary she wanted, the one who more and more filled her thoughts and featured in the hazy, pleasure-filled fantasies she had begun to allow herself at night before slipping into a blissfully dreamless sleep.

She made short work of the buttons at his waist, and he let go of her long enough to help slip the fabric over his hips, stepping out of his trousers and underthings until he stood before her, lips swollen, hair a mess, in nothing but a shirt and an unbuttoned waistcoat that had seen better days. He was beautiful, and Violet couldn't take her eyes off of him.

"This too," she said finally, her hands sliding up his arms to the collar of his shirt, where she began to undo his buttons. He reached for her as well, unlacing the top of her blouse.

"Fair is only fair," he said, and she laughed as they shrugged out of their shirts.

Nathaniel's hands dropped to her waist, quickly skimming over her hips and to the backs of her thighs. He pinched the fabric of her trousers playfully and said, "These will have to go as well, you know."

She laughed again and repeated his words, shimmying out of the rest of her clothes. "Fair is only fair." Then he lifted her to the surface of her worktable, right there in the spilled dirt, and she wrapped her legs around his hips, pulling him closer to her until she could feel him everywhere.

To her surprise, he froze, extricating himself from her. "Hold that thought for precisely one moment," he said urgently as he dashed across the greenhouse and pulled open a drawer in his worktable, riffling through the contents until he procured a slim silver bracelet and slipped it onto his wrist. He returned as quickly as he had promised and drew her legs around his hips once more.

"It's infused with a contraceptive solution," he said with a self-conscious smile, showing her the bracelet. "I can get you one too if you like, but they work for either partner."

"Did you invent this?" Violet caught his hand in hers, gaping at it as he nodded curtly. "Nathaniel, that's marvelous. You'll have to sell them in the—"

He cut her off with a hungry kiss that she suspected had as much to do with embarrassment as it did passion. "You can tell me all about how clever I am later, how does that sound?"

Entirely perfect was how it sounded. She smirked. "Impatient, are you?"

"Little witch, you've no idea," he rasped against the skin of her throat, drawing a delighted laugh from her.

This, now, was entirely new to Violet. She had never laughed so much during sex. Playfulness and fun, so closely interwoven with pleasure that they became one and the same. The tension between them was as tightly wound as ever, but now instead of caustic banter in chalked messages, they exchanged touches with fingers and mouths and tongues, counting each other's shivers and gasps like points in a game that was all their own. She had never wanted so badly to win. She had never wanted so badly, full stop.

She let out a moan as he cupped her breasts, his thumbs cir

cling over her sensitive flesh. "You've been hiding these under all those oversized shirts of yours? All this time?" His voice was mildly scolding as he dipped his head to appreciate them further.

"You're one to talk," she teased on a gasp, running her hands over his forearms like she'd been wanting to do for weeks. "Besides, a woman's allowed some secrets." He peppered her with biting kisses that had her grasping at his shoulders to ground herself.

"I want to know all your secrets."

He sensed the change in her, lifting his head until they were eye to eye once more. He cradled her jaw, thumb brushing the jagged scar that reminded Violet every time she looked in the mirror of the dangers of trusting someone.

No more, she decided.

"I want you to know my secrets too, I think," she told him, struggling to keep her voice steady. She wanted to take him at his word. She wanted to trust that he wouldn't feel differently about her if he knew she was the Thornwitch. But this version of Nathaniel, the one who spoke to her like this and held her like this, was still too new. There would be a time and a place to tell him, she decided then and there. Her secret would not stay a secret for much longer, or it would salt their soil before they ever had a chance to see what could grow between them. But that time and place was not now. Not here. She couldn't bear it if he stopped looking at her the way he was now.

So she shoved away the guilt and pressed her cheek to his, delighting in the slow rasp of his stubble on her face as she said low in his ear, "But we've got more important things to be doing right now, haven't we?"

With one hand, she reached between them, wrapping her fingers around him and stroking, guiding him toward her.

"Much more important," he agreed, leaning into her touch.

He kissed the edge of her mouth where her scar pulled at her lips and kept his eyes on her as he entered her, making Violet feel once again exposed. She forced herself to look right back as their breaths grew staggered and they began to move. The table beneath them rocked and creaked until Violet used her magic to strengthen its legs.

"Clever, clever woman," said Nathaniel, breathless.

"Don't you dare stop," she responded before he could inspect her handiwork.

"Impatient, are you?"

She beamed against his lips and repeated his words from before: "You've no idea." A tendril of something she could not name grew between them, grasping for his heart like the reaching corkscrew coils of ivy climbing a wall, seeking a place between the cracks to bond, begging him without words not to cut her down when the weight of what she carried grew too heavy.

As they moved together, discovering the turns and play of yet another new game between them, Violet reached back to grasp her worktable for purchase. Her hands in the spilled soil, she felt another release begin to wind tight within her. With Nathaniel inside her and his hands and mouth on her, she came again, and dimly, amidst the pulse of heat and the tunneling of her vision, she felt her magic release as well, flowers sprouting from the dirt beneath her hands, the drawers of seeds on her worktable suddenly bursting with color and sharp, floral scents. Chrysanthemums and peonies, lilies and orchids—suddenly, she and Nathaniel were lost in a jungle of her own making, and Violet cried out a laugh as she sank her fingers into the dirt, feeling the tender roots that were beginning to form. Nathaniel's thrusts became quicker and more erratic, and as he followed her into bliss, the greenhouse continued coming to life around them. Her eyes glowed green, but for once she didn't care, because this wasn't dark or evil; it was *magnificent.* Violet let go of all control and allowed the energy within her to sprout as it pleased, and she was amazed to find no thorns grating against her skin.

There was only life and color from her magic.

Things that grew.

Things that blossomed.

Now *this*, she decided as Nathaniel grew still and leaned against her, their breaths loud within their shared space, his body sweaty against hers and his heart beating hard against her chest as they held each other close—*this* was magic.

BREAKTHROUGH

"I've never been so pleased to be covered in dirt," said Nathaniel smugly, kissing her bare shoulder.

She laughed, low and throaty, and looked around them. They'd ended up on a bed of their own clothing on the greenhouse floor, illuminated only by the moons. "You know we both have bedrooms within sight of this place, right?" She nodded toward the building, blurry through the rain that had begun to splatter and run in rivulets down the warped glass.

"I don't mind," he said honestly. They would have to make a run for it eventually, and would likely end up drenched in the process, but Nathaniel had exactly zero desire to leave this place, or her, anytime soon. "This is perfect."

Violet snuggled closer to him, and Nathaniel allowed himself a few more moments of this gorgeous, relaxed freedom, because for once even the incessant buzz of anxiety in the back of his brain couldn't convince him that any task or obligation was more important than the woman in his arms.

"I never expected this," he said suddenly. "I never expected *you.*" He drew a hand up her arm, fingertips brushing along soft, pale skin, charting their path by way of freckles.

"Sometimes life gives us unexpected turns," she responded softly, her voice barely audible over the drumbeat of rain against the glass.

He couldn't argue with that. If he'd been asked only a few weeks ago, he'd have said there was no way he *wanted* this—with anyone—but now that she was with him, now that he knew what it was like to be with her, he wanted to shake Past Nathaniel for his stubbornness, for his inability to let himself have something good.

He held her tighter. "I'm beginning to discover that unexpected turns aren't so bad."

To his surprise, she sobered, her gaze drifting to the floor.

"What is it?"

"It's nothing."

He *hmph*ed. "I don't believe that for a second."

She sighed and said quietly after a moment, "It's just that I wonder if you'd feel that way if you knew everything about me."

He chuckled. "I can't imagine there's anything about you I wouldn't like."

But her answering smile was limp and sad. "You don't know the parts of me that have been trying to get out. My past."

"We've all done things we're not proud of. You certainly know I have."

"Coming here was meant to be a fresh start. A way to be someone new. But I . . . I do want you to know me."

His puzzlement must have shown on his face because she quickly shook her head.

"It's a conversation for another time," she said. "Perhaps when we're fully clothed."

"That might be tricky," he said, trying to cheer her up. He wanted to hold on to his good feelings, not be drawn into his usual dark thoughts. "I plan on keeping you naked as often as possible from now on."

He was rewarded by her smile, a real one this time, that struck him to his core with how it lit up her face. Desire stirred in him once more. Moons, she made him feel like a teenager.

"I can't say I dislike that plan." She stroked a hand over his hip in a way that brought his skin to life with interest and laughed at the trail of dirt her fingers left.

"Your hands are filthy," he noted primly, sending her into a peal of giggles. "What?"

She grinned. "I'm over here trying to entice you with more sex and you're—that was the most *Nathaniel* response ever."

He froze, waiting for defensiveness to rise, but found there was none. "You're right," he said, cracking a grin of his own. "We're literally lying in a bed of dirt. I'm being ridiculous."

"I like your ridiculousness," she said fondly, kissing his nose. "But if you're really so worried about it . . ." She pressed another kiss to his jaw, then his throat, then his chest. "Then I suppose I'll just have to avoid using my hands."

Well. He wasn't going to argue with *that*.

They continued in that vein for some time, and Nathaniel, for his part, was quite content to let go of the subject altogether. But afterward, her head on his chest and her hair fanned out across his shoulders, she said, "I think the difference is that your past was spent working toward an admirable goal, but you were blown off course. Unveiling who you were means brushing the dust from something that has the potential to be great. Looking into my past would be more like unchaining a beast."

His post-orgasm focus was admittedly hazy, but even so he could sense that she was trying to tell him something important.

"I'm still finding my balance," he said carefully, "but I do believe there's a balance to be found." He brightened at the thought. "It's like alchemy, you know?"

She laughed, surprised. "No, I don't."

"Alchemy is balance, remember?"

She nodded.

"The bracelet I'm wearing, for example." He held up his wrist. "The solution that gives it power is made with raspberry leaf, which actually *increases* fertility, but it's balanced by pennyroyal and red cedar, which, by canceling out the raspberry and then some, creates a focal parity for the magic. I can then adjust that center through careful measurement and the addition of other ingredients until I achieve the results I want."

"Oh, well if it's that easy," Violet teased, as though she was about to spring up and start brewing potions naked at his worktable. Blatant safety hazards aside, Nathaniel mused, he wouldn't mind that at all. In fact, it was a mental image he was absolutely going to revisit later.

For now, he tamped down his hormones and said, "Well, not quite. But it is about finding balance. All magic is, at its core." He looked around the greenhouse, and the mess of flowers that had sprung up on her table during their . . . activities. "Or at least, it should be. I still can't work out how your magic powers itself."

"What do you mean?"

He waved his hand around the greenhouse. "I mean *this*. I've seen you perform incredible feats of nature magic that would bring a practiced mage to their knees. You keep your entire shop stocked and fresh with plants that I have on good authority come from other parts of the world and are more long-lived than their natural counterparts. You just did"—he gestured to the worktable behind her and the jungle of botanicals that had sprung from the spilled soil and burst from the drawers—"*that* without breaking a sweat."

She smiled devilishly and nipped at his jaw. "I seem to recall exerting myself quite a bit during that last one."

Warmth swept his body. "You know what I meant. Don't you ever experience magic burn, woman?"

She raised her hands. "Oh, you mean like this."

"Your hands?" Nathaniel frowned.

"The way they hurt when I do magic." She clocked his face. "Is that not what you meant?"

Nathaniel tugged her hands into his lap, tracing her fingers with his. He'd never heard of anyone whose magic reacted like that. "Can you explain what it feels like?"

As she spoke of stinging nettles and pulling magic through her system like she was forcing it through a straw, Nathaniel grew more and more tense.

"Has it always been like this?"

"No," Violet admitted. "Just since I . . . since I came to Dragon's Rest, really. And it's gotten worse lately. I assumed it was cumulative—that's what magic burn does, right? It comes from overuse?"

Nathaniel's brows drew together. "Well yes, but magic burn doesn't happen while you're doing magic, it happens *after*, as a result of drawing on too much of it," he said with confusion. "And it's more of a full-body exhaustion than a concentrated injury. Violet, this is something else."

She sat up, trying to pull away from him, but he kept hold of her hand, massaging circles into the pad of her palm with his thumbs. "I don't think it's anything to worry about," she said, studying him. Every word sounded as though it was being torn from her. "It isn't comfortable, but it's my cost. For acting against my nature."

Now he was *really* lost. "What does that mean?"

She shifted, looking supremely uncomfortable. "My magic isn't . . . it's not *good*."

"What do you mean?"

"What I said." She shrugged as if it were that simple, as if she weren't spouting nonsense. "There are two types of magic inside me—one that's very powerful and doesn't hurt, and one that takes more effort. If I let the first one have its way, it wouldn't be growing flowers for people's weddings, so I use the second, even if it's not comfortable."

"Violet," he said gently, tipping her chin so she couldn't avoid looking at him. "Magic is energy. Energy isn't good or evil, it's just energy." He wondered for the hundredth time who she'd been before she came to Dragon's Rest, and who had let her believe such a thing.

"So you're saying Guy Shadowfade wasn't evil?" she asked skeptically. Even with his tendency to ignore social cues, Nathaniel could sense there was something dark and hulking behind her words, some missing puzzle piece in the picture that was Violet Thistlewaite.

"I'm saying his *magic* wasn't—it was what he chose to do with it that was evil. Just as Sedgwick choosing to do evil with the blight doesn't say anything about alchemy as a whole."

"Hmm" was all she said, and he could tell she didn't believe him.

He gestured to the colorful jungle she'd made of her worktable. "*That* isn't evil. A bit of a mess, perhaps, but a good one. Did making *that* hurt?"

"No, it didn't." She looked puzzled, and the most adorable little wrinkle appeared between her brows. Her eyes darted to him, and a blush crept up her neck. "It felt wonderful. Even if I'm going to have to replace all those seeds now."

Nathaniel's eyes wandered to the small chest of drawers, barely visible beneath the flower bed that had sprung from it. "Those were *seeds*?"

"Mm-hmm. I'll harvest more from the plants that grew."

He remembered her telling him in the Smokewood that using her magic to manipulate an existing plant was easier, which meant whatever was hurting her when she used magic wasn't at play in the same way. The little scientist who lived in his brain began taking notes, and Nathaniel sat up, dislodging Violet with a squeak of surprise. He pressed an apologetic kiss to her temple and stood, ignoring the protests of his limbs after lying on the hard ground.

"I need to try something," he said, excitement bubbling in his chest as he pulled her to her feet. He tugged on his trousers, not bothering to look for his belt. Behind him, he heard a rustle as Violet donned clothing too. Nathaniel plucked one of the flowers that grew from the seed chest and examined it, sniffing the flower and rubbing the stem between his fingers. He turned to look for one of the conjured flowers as a comparison, his eyes flaring a moment when they settled on Violet wearing his shirt and nothing else. "That's yours now," he said, pausing to kiss her again. He wanted to see her wearing his clothes every day.

She chuckled against his mouth. "Good. I wasn't planning on returning it."

Scratch that last thought, he wanted to see her wearing nothing at all every day. He couldn't even bring himself to be frustrated at how easily she distracted him from his task.

"How am I supposed to stay focused when you look like that?" he muttered, dragging his gaze over her from head to toe once more.

"Go on," she said, shooing him toward his workstation with

an indulgent smile, following close behind. Her expression turned sly. "Teach me, *professor*."

Pleasure leapt through him, and any restraint he had mustered instantly vanished. Perhaps she was evil after all—she was trying to kill him, it seemed.

"Oh, we'll be revisiting *that*, believe you me," he growled, catching her around the waist and drawing a delighted laugh from her as he hauled her against him. He kissed her soundly once more before tugging her over to his half of the greenhouse. "But for the moment, would you conjure a flower for me, please?"

Now that he was watching for it, he noticed the tight set of her jaw and the little wince of discomfort before a round, yellow flower with spiky-looking petals appeared in her hand. He had a number of salves and creams at the apothecary; as soon as they were done here he'd fetch her a whole selection to see if any of them would help her hands.

Nathaniel took the flower from Violet and held it aloft in his free hand. "This, erm, flower," he said, gesturing with the spiky one.

"A dahlia," she supplied patiently, albeit with an amused smirk. "You work with plants for a living, shouldn't you know this?"

He treated her to a look of practiced disdain. "If it has no medicinal or alchemical use, then no."

"Aren't they used to treat intestinal ailments?"

He paused mid-retort—dammit, but she was right—and booped her nose with the dahlia. "You're awfully clever today, aren't you?"

"Just today?" she teased, pulling the flower from his hands and twirling it between her fingers. He could feel himself getting distracted by her (again), and was very grateful that she didn't seem to mind, though not so grateful when she pulled away from him, once again directing him back on track. “Now what’s this about the dahlia?”

“You envisioned it and created it using nothing but magic, and despite appearances, it didn’t actually grow from anything but your mind. It’s more like a fancy illusion brought to life. It’s real and corporeal, and like we proved with the mugwort, it’s at least partially organic. But it’s not a genuine flower.”

She shifted on her feet, looking defensive. “So?”

“So you’re absolutely brilliant, Violet. You’re creating flowers that have a scent and texture and—forgive me, I’m not as familiar with flowering botanicals as I am with herbs—seem to bear an exact resemblance to the real thing, and you’re creating them using nothing but your mind and memory. That’s incredibly advanced magic.”

She seemed appeased, if a bit puzzled. “Thank you?”

“But it’s not all you can do.” He held up the flower he’d picked from the overgrown worktable and the mound of flowers that had once been her seed collection. “This flower—” He waited for her to fill in the blank.

She grinned placatingly. “Freesia.”

“It grew from a seed, not your imagination.”

“Bulb.”

“Pardon?”

“It grew from a bulb.”

He shot her a look. “My point is you used magic not to form the flower but to encourage the *bulb* to start and complete its life cycle. Everything in the world has its own reserve of magical energy, you see, but some things far more than others.”

“Like the Eye of the Serpent,” said Violet thoughtfully. “It has its own magic, which users can draw on.”

“Exactly, but not everyone *can* draw on the magic inherent in everyday substances because they simply don't have much to spare. An artifact like the Eye contains an immense store of power compared to a single seed—er, *bulb*."

She smirked at his correction.

Nathaniel continued. "By pouring your magic into the bulb and asking it to grow, you evoked the energy that was already within it, the same way a water mage can bring a kettle to boil, or how the Clerics of Rava can shape structures from raw earth."

"So that one's an actual flower, then?" Violet asked. "And the dahlia isn't."

He shook the dahlia at her and turned to his worktable, where a sample of the blight was contained within a large glass jar while he waited for his new safety equipment to be delivered. "If my suspicions are correct, then yes," he clarified, opening the jar.

He dropped both into the jar, Violet looking over his shoulder, and watched with satisfaction as the rot crept over the dahlia and, just as with the mugwort, slowed and stopped. The freesia, however, was quickly overtaken in its entirety, collapsing within the jar to become a stringy mess of black goo, soon indecipherable from the rest.

"So what does that mean?"

"Well, it means that the blight reacts to magic."

"We knew that already, didn't we? It pushed back when I tried to use my magic to reverse it."

"Yes, but *why*? Magic is balance, remember, so what is the blight balancing by pushing back?" He looked up at the rain-splattered panes of the roof, his mind whirring. "When did you say the pain in your hands started getting worse?"

"Not long ago. It stopped going away just after—" She sucked in a breath, her mouth falling open. "After I saw Sedgwick."

Nathaniel took her hand between both of his and absently began massaging it again. "Magic shouldn't hurt," he murmured, kissing her fingers. "You said it first started when you came to Dragon's Rest?"

She nodded, frowning. "I—yes."

"Sedgwick came here that very same week, did you know that?" He looked down at their clasped hands. "And the ingredients he came looking for when he first came to the apothecary—how could I have forgotten?" Nathaniel thought back to that list. Minotaur horn. Mane of marea. Both were elements of magical creatures that could be used to perform powerful magic—or inhibit it. "What if Sedgwick is trying to obstruct your magic? The blight affects plants. Wouldn't it make sense that he'd identify a powerful plant witch as a threat to his plans? That he'd take steps to deter anyone who could potentially stop the blight otherwise?"

Violet's eyes widened. "You think Sedgwick is targeting *me*?" She appeared thoughtful. Quietly, almost to herself, she added, "That . . . makes a lot of sense."

Nathaniel squeezed her hand. "If we can figure out how he's affecting your magic and counteract it, we could stop your magic from hurting you anymore."

"And get rid of the blight," she reminded him.

"Yes, the blight. Of course." He smiled sheepishly. *Distraction*, he thought again, with no shortage of fondness. "That too."

He'd been focusing too hard on the blight, but the answer had been staring him in the face all this time—*Violet* could reverse it. If Sedgwick saw her as such a threat, then it meant her magic was the key to stopping the blight. He only needed to help her unlock whatever alchemical means Sedgwick was using to hurt her, and luckily Nathaniel had a lifetime of experience as an apothecary. He knew how to combine alchemy and medicine.

Nathaniel reached for a pair of gloves. "I need to test a theory. I need to—"

"Get dressed," Violet finished, smirking at him. "You need to put your clothes back on before you do any experimenting. I'm not an alchemist, but even I know you probably want to be wearing a shirt."

He looked down at his bare chest. "Ah," he said. "You are correct."

"I often am, much to your chagrin," she teased, and reached for her buttons. "Do you want your—?"

He grabbed her wrist, stopping her, and they stared at each other for a moment. "You undressing right now is going to lead us in one direction and one direction only," he told her, smiling. "And as much as that's a road I'd happily travel down again, Dragon's Rest needs a solution to the blight, which means *you* need a solution to Sedgwick."

She redid the offending button and stood on her toes to kiss him again. Nathaniel allowed himself to sink into the kiss for just a moment before pulling away. Truly, he felt he'd never be able to get anything done again in this greenhouse. If it weren't for the matter directly at hand, he didn't think he'd actually mind at all.

Sweet Dreams
Elixir
now available!
MARSH
APOTHECARY

Rough Around
the Hedges
FLORAL & GARDEN SHOP
LAVENDER SACHETS
50% OFF WITH PROOF
OF PURCHASE OF
SWEET DREAMS ELIXIR
FROM NEXT DOOR.

BOOKS AND BURGLARY

Pru waited for Violet at the edge of town, an empty satchel slung over her shoulder and a linen-covered wicker basket in her arms.

"You said you were running an errand," she said with her Prudence-iest smile. "I thought I'd keep you company!"

But Violet's nerves wound tight around her heart, kicking her pulse into high gear. She did *not* want company today. "Pru, you've done enough."

"Please." Her friend flapped a hand. "All I did was tell you a story, and that wasn't helping, that was me confirming that you do *not* listen to my performances at Market Day because I'm pretty sure I've told that one at least three or four times since you moved here, so really, you're the one who owes me."

"Maybe later?" Violet squeezed her eyes shut. "I'll buy you a pint at the Claw & Hoard?"

"Nope," said Pru immediately. "I feel useless, I need to help, it's a personality flaw, deal with it. So what are you doing? More research about the blight? Planning for the festival so we can present it at the town meeting next week? Ooh, are we taking a trip to the library?" Pru clapped her hands. "I'm a *very* good research assistant."

Violet tried one more time. "I'm sorry, Pru. You can't come with me."

"If you're saying that because you've talked to the librarian, I can assure you my being banned was a big misunderstanding."

"I'm not going to the Dragon's Rest library," Violet blurted. "I'm going to Shadowfade Castle."

Now why had she gone and admitted that? She felt naked under Pru's stare—she shouldn't have said anything at all—but then Pru cocked her head and smiled a smile that Violet had never seen on her before.

"I *knew* it!" She pointed a finger at Violet. "Breaking into the castle library was *my* idea, Violet! I knew you were trying to go without me!"

"It could be dangerous," Violet warned.

"I *love* danger! I eat danger for breakfast, right alongside my buttered toast."

"I don't want to draw attention to myself in case there are . . . other people there or . . ."

"So I should leave my violin at home, is what you're saying." Pru snorted. "I *can* be quiet, you know. Besides, I brought snacks!" She hefted her basket and showed Violet the collection of flaky fruit pastries beneath the linen. "Guy gave me some of his leftovers from this morning's market. Rhubarb turnovers and raspberry and vanilla cream tarts!"

Violet could feel herself losing control of the situation. She wanted to get to the castle, poke around the library to see if she could find some information about Sedgwick or the Eye of the Serpent, maybe have a good cry in her old gardens to take the edge off her emotions. She certainly didn't want to have to explain to Pru how she knew her way around or have to hide what it meant to her to return to the place she'd called home most of her life.

But against her judgment, she could feel her resolve weaken when Pru's mouth pulled into a pout. "It's just, Nathaniel's going to sequester himself in the greenhouse as soon as he closes for the evening, and I know he's doing important work but I'm *lonely*, Violet!"

She chuckled, more than aware of Nathaniel's singular focus. Her hands ached in response—she couldn't say she had complaints about the new direction his experiments had taken. "Because your brother is usually such a charming conversationalist when he's not busy?"

Pru's expression turned sly. "*You* certainly seem to think so, don't you? Although I suppose the two of you haven't been doing much conversing this week."

Violet blushed; she'd walked directly into that.

"Oh, don't be embarrassed," said Pru. "You've earned me ten stelle from Fallon!"

That took a moment to sink in, but when it did . . . "You *bet* on us?"

"Half the town's been betting on you two. Quinn was convinced you'd hold out for another month, but I know my brother. He's great at denying himself what he wants—until he isn't."

Violet groaned, her face going even hotter. She snatched a baked good from the basket and shoved it whole into her mouth, but even the buttery, flaky crust and tart rhubarb filling didn't dispel her embarrassment.

Pru threw her head back and cackled. "You're wearing his *shirt*, Violet. Don't think I wouldn't recognize it—I'm the one who spilled the tincture that stained the sleeve. You can't have wanted it to be *that* much of a secret."

Violet's fists bunched beneath the too-long sleeves. The

truth—that the shirt smelled like Nathaniel and she wanted to feel comforted as she revisited the castle—felt too private to divulge, so she said, "It's not a secret, it's just . . . new."

Pru smiled triumphantly, and Violet got the sudden impression that she'd passed some sort of test. "I'm glad for you both. Nathaniel's been through a lot—I think you're aware of that."

Violet nodded, averting her eyes.

"I was always jealous of him, you know. For following his dream. For *leaving* Dragon's Rest. I wanted that—I've spent my whole life fantasizing about playing my way across the countryside, performing in Lokoa and Belakry and the Shards and everywhere in between. But then when he came home, and Mum and Da—" She cleared her throat. "Anyway, it never seemed to be in the cards for me. But he's doing better now, and I think a lot of that's because of you."

Violet felt uncomfortable in an entirely new way now, one that made her feel warm and cold and light and heavy all at once. It wasn't as if Nathaniel had changed, exactly—he was still grumpy and meticulous—but once the sunlight of that focus became trained on her, she found she could bloom. She rather enjoyed knowing that beneath the buttoned-up alchemist was someone playful who made her work for a smile and challenged her to understand herself and her magic on a different level. He made her feel like she truly could be better, but more than that—he made her feel like she was *already* so much better than she saw herself, like she could borrow his belief in her until she believed it too. She hoped that he felt the same, but she'd never been as good at *people* as she was at plants.

"I don't know if I can take responsibility for someone else's happiness," she said finally.

"Perhaps not, but you're a big part of it. And it's good, really good, to see my brother happy again"—she pulled a face—"even if I never, ever, *ever* want you to explain the reason behind your redesigned worktable."

"Oh, moons . . ." Violet muttered again. She'd cut the majority of the flowers from her accidental garden for bouquets—and Nathaniel, adorably, had insisted on keeping a few for himself—but it was hard to hide the way the table itself had sprouted a few leafy branches, which rained blossoms down on her work area, as well as two extra legs, which admittedly made it much sturdier even if her face went pink as a peony every time she looked at it.

"That's all I'll say about it, I promise," Pru said, and her eyes glittered mischievously. "For now at least. Just know that the next time you two step foot in the inn, you're going to be the center of attention in a way that will turn you both as red as one of these raspberry pastries, so either leave Nathaniel at home or let me know you're going so I can be there to see his face. Now come on, I've always wanted to see what Shadowfade Castle looks like on the inside."

So that was how Violet ended up on the steep mountain road with Pru at her side, a trail of flaky pastry crumbs falling behind them like they were marking the way back home.

Was the castle smaller or had Violet only built it bigger in her memories, she wondered as they drew nearer. Shadowfade Castle looked as dark and imposing as ever, its black stone ramparts shining like onyx in the aftermath of the day's rain, mist rising from the mountain to cloak it as though its towers pierced the clouds themselves. She'd lived most of her life behind these walls, and for a long time she thought they would be all she'd ever know.

"So how do we get in?" Pru asked, munching on a pastry, crumbs fluttering to her bodice like autumn leaves on a forest floor.

"The gates are open," said Violet quietly, gesturing to the sinister entrance, all black wrought iron bent at sharp, jagged angles. The gates barely hung from their hinges after the Tempest and her crew of heroes had destroyed them, and as she and Pru passed beneath the gaping arch of the wall, Violet shivered, suddenly paranoid that those doors would trap her here once more.

"Oh, wow," said Pru, and Violet followed her gaze to the southeast gardens, where Violet's hedge maze, overgrown with two months of neglect, was as vibrant and colorful as ever against the drab darkness of the castle itself. "I don't think I expected the grounds to be so . . . gorgeous."

Violet swallowed around a sudden knot in her throat, feeling strangely touched as well as extremely, unbearably exposed. "Yeah, well, the Thornwitch must have needed something to keep her busy," she said, her voice strangled.

"The Thornwitch," said Pru softly, eyes firmly on the greenery, "had a spectacular talent for landscape design."

Those gardens were once the center of Violet's life. And they were huge and gorgeous and grandiose, it was true—but all they made her feel now was sad for the woman she'd been, who had little else to live for. Violet was struck by the sudden realization that she'd lived more in the past few months in Dragon's Rest than she had in over twenty years at Shadowfade Castle.

The feeling deepened as they opened the huge oak doors to the castle. It was musty inside, the air stale with disuse, though there was a cold draft coming from somewhere that swirled around them and made Violet tug her hands back into the sleeves of Nathaniel's shirt like a turtle retreating into its shell.

"This place is massive," said Pru in a hushed voice. "I can't get over the fact that people *lived* here. It's too big for me—though I bet the acoustics are gorgeous in some of these rooms."

"Let's hold off on testing those acoustics in case we're not alone."

As Violet's eyes feasted on the banisters she'd slid down as a child and the ugly tapestry she'd once tried to set fire to as a moody teenager, Pru opened the door that led to the Great Hall, where Guy had celebrated campaigns and received guests.

"Violet, look at this." Pru's voice was grim. "Someone's been here."

Violet darted to the door and looked inside. Sure enough, the big space had clearly been in use. Tables had been shoved to the edges of the room, and the platform at the other end where a dais led to Guy's seat was now set up with a workstation that looked decidedly alchemical in nature.

"Sedgwick," said Violet. "It has to be."

"Do you think this is where he designed whatever toxin is causing the blight?" Pru asked as the two of them crept forward.

Or whatever is inhibiting my magic, Violet thought. "It has to be."

There was no sign of anyone else in the castle, but Violet still looked around nervously, checking the floor ahead of her feet. "Be careful where you step," she warned Pru. "He seems the type to set traps." She *knew* he was the type, she wanted to say, but she also knew she couldn't explain how.

The workstation at the head of the room consisted of several large cauldrons, one of which was actively bubbling with something orange with an overpoweringly bittersweet scent. There were a few stoppered vials on a rack, each glowing vaguely green. Violet pocketed one. "For Nathaniel," she explained. "Maybe he can make sense of it."

Violet so desperately wanted to believe Nathaniel's theory, that using good magic shouldn't hurt her at all, that the pain in her hands was Sedgwick trying to stop her and not her own natural resistance to being good. And though Nathaniel couldn't possibly understand the intricacies of why, it did make sense that her former nemesis would target her like this. If Nathaniel could fix it, then maybe Violet *could* stop the blight. Maybe then she could tell him the truth about herself, and he'd be so overjoyed at their success that he wouldn't be upset with her.

She found an empty vial and carefully spooned a bit of the orange concoction into it, sighing wistfully as she slipped it into her pocket too. Hope, Violet was discovering, was as dangerous a poison as any, for it had spread through her veins quickly and ruthlessly, and it made her dread finding an antidote.

Meanwhile, Pru searched the table for clues about what Sedgwick was doing.

"'Rate of decomposition,'" she read from a scribbled piece of scrap paper. "'Time of revival.' Is he talking about the blight, do you think?"

"He must be," said Violet, looking for any notes or books that might tell them more, but there was nothing there. A large metal box, longer than Violet was tall, rested on one of the tables against the wall. Looking at it nearly bowled her over with a wave of unease.

"And what's this symbol, do you think?" Violet's gaze rose from the box and looked to where Pru pointed to the margins. Sedgwick had drawn a curling spiral slashed through with some kind of rune.

"I have no idea."

"He's drawn it several times," noted Pru, turning over the scrap of paper and pointing.

Violet shivered. She didn't like this. "Let's see if we can find anything in the library."

So Sedgwick had taken up residence in Shadowfade Castle, she mused, even if just part-time. And he was working on something in addition to looking for the Eye of the Serpent. It had to be the blight, and hopefully the sample in her pocket would give Nathaniel the edge he needed to reverse it.

But Sedgwick's being here presented a different problem—if he was searching for the Eye, then he would have looked in the library. He was a person who knew the value of information, so he would have found and read any useful books already. Violet needed to get on the same page as him. Even if he was ahead in the race, she needed to catch up before she could surpass him. Sedgwick hadn't been part of Shadowfade's inner circle, though. Perhaps he wouldn't have known where to find the truly rare texts.

Violet was lost enough in thought that she barely noticed they'd reached the library until she threw open the doors and noticed Pru looking at her strangely.

Right. She wasn't supposed to know her way around.

"I, um," she said awkwardly. "I found the library."

Pru looked like she wanted to say something but closed her mouth. Finally, she said, "Yes, you did." Then that odd expression disappeared, and she smiled, looking like her cheerful self once more. "I can't wait to steal some books. I should have brought a bigger bag."

Violet laughed, relieved that the subject had shifted. "Eat some more pastries and you'll be able to fit a few books in that basket."

While stepping through the gardens and into the castle had brought Violet sadness, being back in this library washed her with nostalgia. How many evenings had she spent here with Guy as a child, poring over magical texts and practicing her magic? The battered armchair in the corner still had the split in the leather where she'd accidentally grown a tree through the armrest, and over there at the window seat was where she'd sat anxiously before her first solo mission, looking out over the mountainside. She had been fifteen years old.

"You can do this," he'd told her, his voice as warm as the father she'd pretended he was. "You are capable of so much more than anyone knows, petal, and we're going to uncover it all together."

Violet had kept her eyes on the window as she admitted, "I want to make you proud."

"Ah, my darling, there is nothing under the moons that I am prouder of than you."

That was the thing no one had ever understood about her relationship with Shadowfade, what Violet herself still struggled with. It wasn't just that she'd worked for him; it wasn't even completely that he'd raised her. It was that he'd encouraged her, trained her, empowered her.

Guy Shadowfade had *loved* her.

He'd done terrible things as well—to her and to others—and she wouldn't, couldn't, forget that, but moons, how she'd loved him too. And even now, with the full knowledge of what he'd done to her and what he'd taken from her, Violet knew that part of her always would.

Pru lurched toward the shelves, head cocked to the side as she scanned titles for anything that might be of use to them. "*The History and Mystery of Rock Goblins*!" she exclaimed, pulling out a book and opening the cover.

"Maybe you can figure out why they're so obsessed with your music," Violet teased.

Pru guffawed and began to read aloud, "'Rock goblins are magical beings, not biological creatures. They do not, to the knowledge of the scientific community, reproduce, and are only created when a being of immense magical power is—'"

"Why don't you take that one home with you?"

"You're right. I'm getting distracted already." Pru tucked the book into her bag and resumed searching the shelves. While she was occupied, Violet made a beeline around a corner shelf to another row of books against the wall next to the dark, empty fireplace. She looked over her shoulder to make sure Pru was out of sight and twisted the ugly brass candlestick on the mantel, triggering the mechanism that opened the door to Guy's private library.

It was clear even from a glance that Sedgwick had never set foot in this place. The study felt messy in an in-progress way, as though Guy had simply left the room and would return at any moment. An empty teacup on the desk. A notebook open to a half-scribbled page. A high-backed, overstuffed chair pulled out as if waiting for him to sit back down. Behind the desk, Violet spotted a dried rose in a vase and recognized it as one of hers. Softly, almost reverently, she touched the stem and tugged magic through her stiff fingers until the rose blossomed once more, petals soft and as vibrantly purple as the Thornwitch's cloak. For the first time in weeks, the color didn't make her recoil.

There was a bookshelf on the opposite wall, and Violet began her search there, abandoning her emotions in favor of single-minded purpose. Keeping an eye out for Pru, she found books on sorcery and on the Merethi Empire. Scrolls that contained workings for spells to raise the dead or curses that would make the target forget the people they loved most. But nothing that referred to the Eye of the Serpent or a magical blight. With a sigh, she moved to the desk, opening drawers and searching inside.

It was more of the same—detailed sketches of magical daggers, maps of the Darktide Isles, a contract in a language she didn't recognize that appeared to have been written and signed in blood. And then—

A book, hardly bigger than the palm of her hand and embossed on the leather cover with the same symbol that Pru had found in Sedgwick's notes. Frost blossomed through her veins. She opened the cover to begin reading the first page.

She wasn't sure how long she sat there reading. She took in

words she didn't understand and some she *wished* she didn't. She traced her fingers over long-dried ink in Guy's familiar handwriting, notes he'd pressed into the pages, probably in this very room, sitting in this very chair. She caught snippets she recognized from Pru's storytelling, things about the Eye of the Serpent, and more about its power over life and death.

Hell and Undersea, the box in the Great Hall . . .

By the time Pru wandered into the open door of the study, Violet was slumped in the chair, staring out the stained glass window.

"This is a great room," Pru said admiringly. "Shadowfade had *style*, I'll give him that." She held up a book and continued. "I found some great information about the legend. Apparently, there's actual evidence that the witch and the warrior were real people who founded Dragon's Rest. But while the story is the same everywhere it's told, and there are reports of a dragon living in this region a long time ago, scholars take issue with the idea that they defeated the dragon as easily as they did. They must have—" Pru stopped, catching sight of Violet's expression. "Violet? What's wrong?"

Violet dragged her eyes up to meet Pru's. "I know why Sedgwick wants the Eye of the Serpent," she said quietly. "He's not trying to seize power himself. He's trying to resurrect Shadowfade."

Marsh Apothecary
closed today—
for urgent matters,
please inquire next door.

(Ignore Violet's terrible wordplay.)

MARSH APOTHECARY

Rough Around the Hedges
FLORAL & GARDEN SHOP

READY TO "SPRING" INTO THE SEASON BY PLANTING A GARDEN? THERE'S STILL "THYME" TO GET STARTED!

(RUDE, NATHANIEL. JUST FOR THAT YOU GET TWO PUNS.)

HAPPY

Night had long blanketed the sky by the time the greenhouse door creaked open and Nathaniel looked up from his work.

"Is that a cup of tea?" His voice carried more excitement than the prospect of a hot beverage probably merited, but Violet didn't seem to mind as she strode across the greenhouse to hand it to him. The scent of spearmint and lemongrass rose enticingly from the cup in a comforting trail of steam.

"For you," she said with a smile.

Nathaniel wiped his hands on the rag hanging from his belt and took the teacup from her, setting it on the edge of his worktable so he could lean in and steal the breath from her lungs with a kiss. It still felt shocking—baffling, almost—that he got to do this now. It didn't add up that someone like Violet would be interested in someone like him, but for once in his life, Nathaniel wasn't interested in doing the math as long as the result amounted to this. Every kiss still felt so new, and he hoped the swoop of his stomach and the giddy intoxication that came with her proximity never went away. He threaded his fingers into her hair, holding her to him, savoring the taste of the tea she'd clearly sampled before bringing it to him.

"Have you moved at all from this spot since I saw you this morning?"

"Certainly doesn't feel like it." Nathaniel had been running on sheer stubbornness for two days now, keeping the apothecary closed under Violet's and Pru's urging so he could focus on the blight. He'd barely stopped to eat or sleep unless one of them made him do so. If Sedgwick was truly trying to resurrect Shadowfade, they needed every advantage they could get.

"Doesn't look like it either." He knew his hair was mussed and his shirt untucked, and there was a middling to high chance that he had some dark circles beneath his eyes. But Violet only looked at him with fondness as she reached up to fix his collar, her fingertips just kissing the skin of his neck. He wrapped her in his arms, trapping her in place. "Anything yet from the vial we brought you?"

Nathaniel pressed his lips together and buried his face in her hair. He still wished she and Pru had not gone to that place, but he couldn't deny that what they'd learned was invaluable—and the book Violet had slipped him, an old text called *Fundamentals of Alchemical Healing*, had been one of the kindest gifts he'd ever received, even if it was technically stolen.

"Nothing about the blight," he said. "The orange vial appears to be some kind of paralytic, which *might* be a component in how he's inhibiting your magic, but it's hard to be sure." Nathaniel twisted around and pulled a small tin of balm from the shelf above his worktable. "That reminds me, I want to try this one." He'd rolled out an entire arsenal of salves and liniments over the past few days, trying to see if any of them soothed Violet's hands.

He opened the tin and the scent of menthol filled the air. Violet turned in his arms so they were both facing the table and loosed a soft sigh of contentment as he began rubbing it into her hands.

"As for the green vial," he continued, voice low and directly in her ear, "my guess is it contains a weapon of some kind. It's hard to tell without testing it on a live subject, which I will not be doing. Any more progress on the Eye?"

"Nothing." Violet leaned into his chest, huffing in frustration. "We know he's trying to use the Eye of the Serpent to power a resurrection spell, and I know he hasn't found it yet, but as to how *we* can find it first, I have no idea."

She seemed so distraught, Nathaniel had to remind himself she had never lived in Dragon's Rest under Shadowfade's rule—she had no idea how bad it was, but he was sure she'd heard stories. She must be worried for her shop and for her future—not to mention her magic. For years, Shadowfade had a habit of making magic-users in Dragon's Rest disappear. Nathaniel's resolve hardened; he would not let that happen to Violet. "We'll figure this out."

Her concern clung to her like smoke, and Nathaniel felt it start to overtake him as well. There were obstacles coming at them from all sides now. Violet felt like the only thing keeping him grounded. He finished massaging her hands and reached for the cup of tea, groaning with delight when the flavors hit his tongue.

"You should rest," she said, still leaning against him. He held her with his free arm, unwilling to let her go.

"I'm getting close, Violet," he said by way of answer. "I know I am. I'm going to fix this for you."

"I believe you." She nuzzled into his sleeve. "But what time did you come to bed last night? And what time did you get up this morning?"

Nathaniel took another sip of his tea instead of answering. He had slipped through the unlocked door between their apartments a few hours before dawn to slide between the covers with her and pull her close. It had felt like a dream, one much too short because she was, in fact, correct with her implications—he'd been up again before the sun and back in the greenhouse.

Her expression turned wry. "Come on, then," she said, tugging him away from his work. "You're done for tonight."

He was larger than her, enough that her gentle tugs barely registered, but when one of her hands, soft and fragrant from the balm, slid down his arm, clasping his hand and pulling, Nathaniel went willingly, leaving his teacup behind on the worktable.

"Done, am I? And what, might I ask, would you have me do instead?" His voice was teasing, his innuendo clear.

"Why, Mr. Marsh, are you propositioning me?"

His hand tightened on hers. "I might be."

"Well, then." A slow, dangerous smile grew on her lips, one that promised long hours of the sweetest torture imaginable. He liked her like this: mischievous, sultry, playful. In a husky voice, Violet said, "I should tell you that what I have planned for you involves taking you upstairs."

"Oh?" His interest was officially piqued.

The slow trail of her fingertips down his chest was like a branding iron. "Taking off those filthy clothes you're wearing."

"I'm listening."

"And allowing you to sink deeply into my soft, warm . . ." Her smile flattened as she shifted to a serious voice. "Bed. You need to sleep, Nathaniel."

He threw his head back and laughed a deep belly laugh that immediately made him wish he gave himself occasion to do it more often.

"I'm serious," she added firmly. "You're no use to any of us if you're dead on your feet."

He pulled her by their clasped hands until she was close to his chest. "Will you be joining me? In your soft, warm bed?"

Violet stood on her tiptoes and pressed a soft, chaste kiss to his lips. "Just to sleep."

He nuzzled her nose. "We'll see about that."

"I mean it, Nathaniel."

She did not.

Shortly after, when their clothes were on the floor and their hearts were in their eyes, Nathaniel wondered at how he could feel so at peace. He should be pulsing with anxiety right about now, downing another vial of his calming draught to keep his symptoms under control and his focus clear. His mind—and body—should be back in the greenhouse, inflicting eviscerating thoughts upon himself for his own failures to solve the blight. But instead, with Violet atop him, legs straddling his hips and her soft skin beneath his hands and her lips on his and the tight heat of her all around him, he felt utterly at home with himself in a way he couldn't remember *ever* feeling. But it wasn't just the sex. It was the way she made him feel known just as he was, all his rough edges cradled in a way that didn't make him feel like she was trying to smooth them but to understand their shape.

"*Just to sleep*," he taunted, trailing his fingers over the curve of her waist.

She rolled her hips in a way that made him groan and her grin turned vicious. "Would you like me to stop?"

"Never." His hand continued its wandering, dipping to the tight bud of nerves between her legs where their bodies were joined. She laughed out a moan, and his eyes remained bound to hers as he brought her to a cresting, gasping peak. With her hair wild and her lips parted, she looked beautiful. She looked like she could be *his*. "Moons, Violet, you make me so happy."

She paused her movements to lean down and kiss him, slow, lingering. "You make me happy too, Nathaniel Marsh."

And when they awoke in the soft blue hours just before dawn, Violet, warm and drowsy, was tucked against his chest like she belonged there. As they reached for each other once more, something old and bitter that had long since splintered in Nathaniel worked its way to the surface and finally, effortlessly, let go.

Marsh Apothecary,
where magic and medicine
meet in the middle.
Ask us about
our new product line!

MARSH APOTHECARY

Rough Around the Hedges
FLORAL & GARDEN SHOP

SO LONG AS WE'RE IN THE MOOD FOR MAGIC...

CUSTOM BOUQUETS CONJURED RIGHT BEFORE YOUR EYES!

THE OAK AND THE WEED

"He thinks the Eye of the Serpent is here in Dragon's Rest," she muttered to Peri, who was batting at Bartleby in a half-hearted duel. "But *where*?"

Bartleby swung a vine over her shoulder, curling lazily around her neck until she pushed him away. "Not now."

The town commerce meeting was due to start in two hours, but Violet couldn't shake the sense that she was running out of time. Sedgwick was trying to bring back Shadowfade. Violet knew what would happen to Dragon's Rest if he returned, and she knew exactly what her fate would be. There was no place she could run that he wouldn't find her, not after everything that had happened. Not after everything she'd done. Best-case scenario, she'd be forced to become the Thornwitch again, but after a taste of who she could be without that part of her identity, Violet knew she could never go back.

And Shadowfade would know it too.

He would seek out everything she loved—every*one* she loved—and he would destroy it all. Her shop. Her flowers. Her friends.

Nathaniel.

All to prove a point: that she was no one without him, and it was foolish of her to try.

No, she couldn't let Sedgwick bring him back.

Her best chance was to stop him before that ever happened, and it was there that she felt she had the upper hand. Magic was her strong suit. Sedgwick was a powerful alchemist but a weak mage; his own natural magic barely registered as a threat. It was why he'd put so much effort into alchemy, which could gift him power far beyond his innate abilities.

She shuddered to think of the things he'd done—the things they'd done together. The havoc they'd wrought, the destruction . . . until she met Nathaniel, she hadn't realized alchemy wasn't limited to explosions and devastation. Nathaniel used his knowledge to help people in a way that was utterly brilliant—and it wasn't just her lust-addled brain telling her so.

Perhaps your magic isn't so bad either, said a small voice, one that had been growing bolder recently. Violet still didn't understand the garden she'd grown that night in the greenhouse, not fully. But she knew with certainty that even if she'd pulled it from deep inside herself, it wasn't evil, not in the way she'd always been taught her power was destined to be. Perhaps Nathaniel was onto something after all. Perhaps it wasn't about the magic itself; perhaps it was how she used it that mattered.

Nathaniel had faced so much, carried the weight of his family's legacy on his shoulders, and yet he was still using *his* magic to overcome the fear that harried him. Despite the tragedy of his past, he was moving onward, and Violet took inspiration from his actions. She had never fought with anything to lose, not really, and she found now that she wasn't sure she liked it. But if Nathaniel could push past his fears, then so could she.

She had never been in love before—how could she, surrounded by villains who saw emotion as weakness? But though the word itself frightened her for its foreignness, she wondered if it explained what she had come to feel of late and what she was feeling now, this almost uncomfortable fullness in her chest, like a plant grown too big for its pot. She wanted to expand, to grow, to see where it took her, but there was still something holding her inside, trapped within the walls of her own secrets.

For the thousandth time that week, she wondered what would happen if she told Nathaniel the truth about her past. He cared for her, that much had been made *abundantly* clear, but could he care for who she'd once been? She could explain it tactfully, warn him ahead of time that her past would upset him. Once he knew, perhaps they could find a way to tell the rest of the town. Pru, Quinn, even cranky Jerome . . . they were her friends, weren't they? They would understand that Violet was no longer the Thornwitch. They would see how much she was trying, how she had become someone new and better and good. They would understand that she was trying to stop Sedgwick from bringing back Shadowfade, and even more, they would help. Wouldn't they?

But what if they rejected her? What if they feared her? What if, all this time, Violet had been fooling herself? What if her brief escape from villainy was just that, brief, and she succumbed to the training of her past? It wouldn't be on purpose, but she couldn't deny that her first reaction to being surprised or caught off guard was still to protect herself with thorns, to wrap the threat in a stranglehold of vines.

If she told them the truth, she might let her guard fall. She might hurt one of the people she cared about, and as Nathaniel would tell her, even accidents could have dire consequences. Then all of it—her shop, her friends, Nathaniel—would be lost to her.

From his place on the counter, Peri *creeaugh*ed at her and butted his stony head against her arm.

"I don't know how to tell them the truth," she said sadly, stroking her thumb over the bumpy surface of his head.

Bartleby reached over her shoulder and idly flipped a page in the book she was reading, the one they'd found at Shadowfade Castle about the resurrection ritual.

"I know," she told him. "I'm done moping, I promise. Back to work with me."

The bell above the door tinkled a gentle greeting, and Violet looked up, her smile freezing when she saw it was Sedgwick. She slammed the book closed in front of her and passed it to Bartleby, who curled his vines around it until it was entirely obscured.

"What do you want?"

He tutted at her scowl. "Now, now, Thornwitch. I know you're not known for your bedside manner, but is that any way to greet a customer?"

"You're not a customer."

"Sure I am. I'm here for . . ." He looked around and plucked a packet of seeds from a display. "These."

"They're not for sale." Violet crossed her arms across her chest.

"Interesting way to run a business."

"They're not for sale to *you*," she clarified, glaring at him. "What do you want? Come to gloat? Interfere with my magic some more?"

"I came to see if you'd reconsider my offer."

She scoffed. "In other words, you're stuck and you need my help with your little resurrection plan."

His eyes widened in surprise for only a moment. "I'd have thought you'd be more pleased. Although, now that I think about it, I seem to remember the two of you having a little bit of a disagreement at the end there—but no, that can't be right. You were his favorite."

"And now I'm on my own, making my own plans," she said coldly. "I don't need him."

He looked her up and down with disdain. "Don't fool yourself. We all need him. He made sure of that—none of us were allowed to have the vision to make it on our own."

She swallowed hard, the words ringing a little too close to something that felt like truth.

Sedgwick continued. "But once I resurrect him, things can go back to the way they were. I won't have to hide like this anymore, in this horrible little town where no one understands that I *am somebody*. I'll have a place by his side again. And if you're set on getting in my way, *petal*, then perhaps he'll be on the lookout for a new favorite."

"You're an idiot if you think being favored by him won't cause you anything but more grief." For the barest second, she stopped hiding and let him see her. Not the Thornwitch, not Violet the florist, but the little girl behind them both who had been taken in by a villain and manipulated and brainwashed until she had no idea who she was anymore. "It's not the picnic you think it is, being the one he depends on. The things he will ask you to do, the ways he will make you hurt if you fail him—the reward is greater, it's true, but so are the punishments. Are you prepared for that, Sedgwick?"

She saw the moment he wavered—and the moment he shoved it away in favor of arrogance. She could work with arrogance.

"Tell you what," she said casually before he could speak. "I'm growing tired of this business with the blight. It's interfering with my plans. If you put a stop to it, I'll hear you out. Maybe I'll even help you."

But she was met by a look of utter confusion, quickly masked by Sedgwick's usual insufferable smarminess. "The blight? I thought that was you."

"Excuse me?" This *did* stop her in her tracks.

"It has *Thornwitch* written all over it, doesn't it? Blighting plants and wrecking crops? Isn't that what you're known for?" There was no guile in his expression, only puzzled uncertainty.

Had she been heading down the wrong path all this time? Was it possible Sedgwick wasn't behind the blight?

He watched her closely, tracking her open shock. "If it's not you, then I've no idea where the blasted rot is coming from."

"I don't believe you," she said, trying to mask the quiver in her voice. "What about my magic?"

"What about it?" He seemed genuinely confused. There was no crowing tone to his voice, no smirking glory in his expression. If Sedgwick truly had nothing to do with the side effects of using her magic, then that meant Nathaniel was wrong. The pain was coming from her because Violet using good magic just wasn't natural. It meant her magic really *was* evil after all.

Sedgwick scoffed. "Come on, Thornwitch. Even I know better than to—"

"Don't call me that," Violet hissed, her mind racing *evil, evil, evil* with each beat of her wicked heart.

"Thornwitch? Why? It's who you are." Sedgwick cocked his head. "Unless . . ."

She whipped her attention back to him.

"You couldn't possibly think you're fooling anyone with this getup, could you?" His expression turned delighted. "Don't tell me this is more than a gambit? You're not actually playing house here with this sad little shop and these sad little people?"

"You have no idea what you're talking about."

"Oh, I think perhaps I do. Poor little Violet felt unloved and unappreciated by Papa Shadowfade. He betrayed you, after all. Stole you from Mummy."

Violet hardened, the panic of that day in Silbourne coming back to her.

"You thought you could run away from it all and no one would notice one of the most powerful sorceresses in the world had set up as a florist, practically still in view of the castle?" Sedgwick laughed cruelly. "You're not that stupid."

"Leave," she spat at him.

But he had wrested control of the reins, and the power made him brave. "I don't think I will. You've gotten soft, Thornwitch. You've gone and thrown in your lot with this ridiculous little town, and unless you want them to suffer, you're going to help me. Or I will raze this sorry place to the ground and tell everyone about your secret."

"You're mad. You think telling them I'm the Thornwitch will work for you? I know your secret too, Sedgwick. You'll be ruined here just as much as I am."

"I couldn't care less about them knowing my identity. The shop was a necessity for me, and a temporary one at that. But no, I'm talking about your other secret."

Her blood froze in her veins. He couldn't know. The only other person who knew was Karina the Tempest.

Sedgwick smirked. "I have spent weeks preparing for this ritual. I have built the space in his Great Hall, preserved his body for his return. I have cared for his wounds, Thornwitch. I know exactly the weapon with which he was murdered. I know who drove it through his chest. And I can put a bigger price on your head—yours and the heads of everyone you care about—with that information than you ever could on mine."

He knew.

Three moons, he knew.

And whether or not he managed to bring back Shadowfade, he would use that information to his advantage—and put not just Violet but everyone she loved at risk in the process.

Thorns erupted from beneath her skin, and from his fearful expression, Violet knew exactly how she looked: eyes glowing green, thorny vines snarling through her hair, skin spiny with armor that hadn't been there a moment ago. Her clothes would be shredded, and as the buckets of flowers behind her shriveled and withered away with the force of her anger, she knew she'd have to regrow all her commissions before tomorrow. Magic flooded from her body, radiating around her in a way that felt almost like relief. It erased the residual sting in her palms, leaving only delicious, wicked power. Sedgwick wanted her to be the Thornwitch? Fine. Evil came as easy to her as breathing.

"What makes you think you can demand anything of me?" Violet's voice was low, and she watched with satisfaction as he swallowed hard, trying to mask his fear.

"I demand nothing, milady," said Sedgwick, backtracking. Violet's mouth pulsed in a cruel smile at the deference in his tone. A part of her had missed this, the fear, the groveling. She was powerful, and why shouldn't she show it? Sedgwick continued. "Although I am pleased to see you are still yourself."

But there was still that tone to his voice, the one that said he knew he had something over her, something that could ruin her. He could control her with the knowledge of what she'd done. She would be his puppet, his plaything—unless she put a stop to this right now.

She laughed, knowing it sounded arrogant. Her magic swirled and eddied inside her, rejoicing. Being without this power had been like breathing with only one lung. The other magic, the one that hurt, had never felt this way. Somewhere inside her, Violet

Thistlewaite the florist pounded against the inside of her chest, begging her to remember . . . *something*. But no, she needed to scare him. She needed him to think she would end him, that he couldn't intimidate her or control her. No one would ever force her into their service again. No one.

"You know nothing," she told him. "Of me, of my power, of what Shadowfade was and was not. How could you? You are a weed, seeking opportunity to grow wherever you can. But a weed cannot uproot an oak. You do not know the extent of my power. You will never understand how far beneath me you are, how easily I could crush your roots. Leave this place and do not return."

Sedgwick's eyes had gone wide, and again triumph thrummed through her. She was proud of making him feel fear; she *wanted* to crush him. Tear the building down over his head. If he was dead, he couldn't talk. She was—

Something bit her hand, hard, and Violet rushed back to herself, panting. Peri had latched his stony teeth on to the skin between her thumb and forefinger, not biting hard enough to draw blood, but enough to snap Violet out of the bindings of her past. She didn't want to be that person anymore. She *wasn't* that person anymore.

Sedgwick was still staring, but no longer at Violet. Complex thoughts raced across his features, too fast for her to follow. "That rock goblin," he whispered, then cut himself off, his eyes darting back to Violet. "I'll leave," he said slowly, drawing his cloak around himself like a shield and curling his hands into his pockets. "I yield."

It was meant to soothe her ego, and a moment ago, it might have, but Violet had shaken off the Thornwitch like snow from her cloak, and all she could feel was cold disgust. She didn't want this. She didn't want anyone to fawn over her or fear her. The people at Shadowfade Castle had never known her, never wanted to know her, because they were too afraid of ending up like Bartleby or one of the hapless victims in the towns she destroyed. She would never have been able to build a friendship like any of the ones she had created here. She—

Glass shattered on the worktable in front of her, and a faint orange mist rose in the air. Before she could stop herself, Violet inhaled, registering an overwhelming scent like bitter wormwood and sickeningly sweet hyacinth. She wanted to grimace but suddenly found that she could not move her face. Her eyes darted to Sedgwick, who smiled triumphantly and used his cloak to cover his nose and mouth.

"I would apologize for this," he said, "but I'm not actually sorry at all."

Violet tried to lunge for him, to twitch her fingers and use one of the plants on the shelves to wrap him in bindings so tight he couldn't move, but she was the one who was frozen in place. Her arms and hands felt tight, and her feet felt heavy. She teetered where she stood as Sedgwick chuckled.

"It will wear off," he said smugly, "but by then I'll be well on my way to completing the ritual." He reached for Peri, who had also been rendered motionless by the contents of the vial. "I do thank you, however, for solving the final piece of the puzzle for me." He tapped the big peridot in Peri's chest. "I had just about given up on finding the Eye of the Serpent, and here it was right in front of me all along."

Her heart pounded hard in her chest as she struggled to stay on her feet. Peri! How could she have missed it? *No!* she wanted to shout. *Let him go!* But her mouth wouldn't work, her muscles wouldn't listen to her brain's demands. She crashed to the floor, her balance giving way at last, and took down a shelf as she fell, half burying herself in fallen plants and broken pottery. Her vision began to blacken, and consciousness began to leave her.

Sedgwick smiled at her again, clearly amused. "It appears," he said, flipping the sign in the front window to CLOSED as he left the shop, Peri under his arm, "that the weed is capable of felling the oak after all."

HUNCHES

Hunches had preoccupied Nathaniel his entire career. It was part of being a scientist, this endless questioning of his circumstances and the need to follow those questions to a solution. The problem was, sometimes those hunches led nowhere, and sometimes he *knew* they would lead him nowhere, but they wouldn't leave him alone until he tested them anyway. And sometimes he dismissed a hunch entirely only to discover, after testing every other avenue, that it was indeed the answer.

The former was what he'd thought was happening with his current experiment.

He couldn't wrap his head around the latter.

All day, this hunch had haunted him: the vials Violet had taken from Sedgwick were leading him to dead end after dead end. If Sedgwick were truly behind the hindrance to Violet's magic, Nathaniel would be able to find a magical signature in the flowers she conjured, but there was nothing there except Violet; he was sure of it.

And then there was the matter of the blight.

The blight had started after Sedgwick came to town. He had

a motive, and through alchemy, he had the means. It also didn't hurt that Nathaniel disliked the man and was quick to assign blame to his corner. But his feelings had gotten in the way, for there was another new arrival to Dragon's Rest at that time—Violet herself.

Nathaniel was loath to think that Violet could have anything to do with the blight. He believed she truly loved Dragon's Rest and wanted to make a home here. But the fact that he had ignored the timing of her arrival carved a deep pit of anxiety in Nathaniel's stomach, one he remembered from his days in the Crucible whenever he realized he had missed something big. Even if he hated this thought, he needed to test it, just to get it out of his system.

It would come to nothing, of course. Coincidences happened all the time. But why had Violet's hands begun hurting the way that they did? And at the *time* that they did? And she never had explained to him just why she thought her magic was evil . . .

Nathaniel mentally cataloged what he knew about Violet's past. Complicated childhood, no knowledge of her own heritage, adoptive father who did a real number on her self-image. Powerful magic, but no formal education in it. She had run away from something, but what? There was still so much he didn't know about her. While even hours ago he had been content to let her share herself slowly, now Nathaniel was struck by impatience. Was he really entertaining the idea that there could be more nefarious reasons for her hesitation?

He assembled the samples before he quite knew what he was doing—plants, both Violet's and not, and blight from a variety of sources. *Nothing will come of this*, he told himself again as he filled a dropper with the solution he had created to test for Sedgwick's magical signature.

Now, hours and dozens of tests later, Nathaniel stared at the empty jar on his worktable, which moments ago had contained blight.

"I did it," he said aloud to the empty greenhouse. He had managed to eradicate the blight, but he felt none of the satisfaction he thought he would, only disappointment that he had allowed his own feelings to blind him to the truth. Sedgwick wasn't behind the blight at all.

It was Violet.

All of the samples he tested, even the blight that had formed from plants she had never so much as looked at, contained her magical signature. Even now, the blackberry-and-almond scent he had grown to love permeated the air, taunting him.

It had to be a mistake, Nathaniel thought for the thousandth time. Violet wouldn't. She was working with him *against* the blight!

But she was convinced her magic was evil, Nathaniel reminded himself. Why would she think that? This couldn't be a coincidence.

That was why the blight had pushed back against her magic, he realized. Because it was *made* of her magic. That was why it had appeared only after Violet had settled in Dragon's Rest. How could he have been so stupid?

Nathaniel's thoughts were a complicated roil of emotion and anxiety as he made his way over to her shop. The town meeting wouldn't start for another hour, so she'd probably still be working. He could just picture her, cheerful smile as she greeted a customer, watching them with light in her eyes as they took in the colorful flowers and plants she'd arrayed artfully around her shop. It couldn't be a lie, because then what else was a lie? Was she only pretending to care for him? Nathaniel squeezed his eyes shut; more than anything else, he found, he didn't want to believe that. She would have an explanation. He knew she would. His Violet wouldn't have done this on purpose.

The door was unlocked, which was not unusual, but the shop was dark, and there was a terrible smell Nathaniel recognized immediately: blight. Every muscle in his body tensed, and something crunched beneath his feet as stepped inside. Broken pottery, he realized, squinting in the dim light.

"Violet?" he called, but there was no response. All his suspicions turned to ash in his stomach, replaced by concern for Violet. Something was seriously wrong.

Nathaniel looked around him at the blighted remains of her flowers. Bartleby cowered in his corner, apparently unharmed, though his vines were curled up into his pot in a tight ball, like he was hiding from the blight that surrounded him. Nathaniel lifted him from his shelf, and Bartleby didn't even try to choke him after he set him down on the counter, which Nathaniel took as gratitude.

"Where is she?" he asked the plant, and for a moment, it didn't look like Bartleby would answer, but then he stretched out a vine toward a shelf that had fallen near the counter. Beneath it, curled in a heap, was Violet.

Nathaniel rushed to her, dropping to his knees and ignoring the crunch of more broken pots as he lifted the shelf and shoved it away from her. "Violet, what happened? Are you alright?" His heart pounded. *Please, love*, he thought, frantic, *please be alright.*

But as he rolled her onto her back, brushing her hair from her face, he recoiled in horror, for it wasn't Violet he found, but a monster.

Nathaniel snatched his hands back, taking note of the viny tendrils coming from her hair and the nasty-looking thorns protruding from her skin like some macabre beast. The Thornwitch, he realized with a spike of fear. Shadowfade's trusted second-in-command. But what on earth was she doing here? And what had she done with Violet?

Horror of a completely different kind set in when Nathaniel recognized his own shirt, shredded by thorns, on the witch's body, and only deepened when he looked past her monstrous features to find Violet's own.

Like solving a formula on a blackboard, Nathaniel began to work the variables in front of him until the answer became clear.

Violet, his Violet, hadn't just caused the blight.

She was also the Thornwitch.

TRUTHS

Violet came to on the floor of her shop to the sound of broken pottery tinkling. She lay frozen, eyes still closed, as memory came back to her. Sedgwick had Peri. Peri had—or *was*—the Eye of the Serpent. She had to stop Sedgwick, or he would bring Shadowfade back from the dead. She was out of time.

Her eyes snapped open to find Nathaniel sweeping dirt and broken pots into a neat pile. He'd folded his jacket and placed it beneath her head, she realized, though when she reached up to touch the familiar green wool, she saw thorns on the back of her hand.

Oh no.

Oh *no*.

Quick as a flash, she reined in the Thornwitch, returning to herself as he watched. She was Violet again, but it was too late. He knew—and not because she'd told him.

"Nathaniel—"

"Please don't." His voice was clipped, terse, back to the version of him she'd known in her first weeks in Dragon's Rest, only worse because now there was something else in his tone she'd never wanted to hear from him: fear.

"I can explain," she tried again. "Sedgwick, he's got—"

"What is there to explain?" His sweeping grew frenzied, and he still refused to look her in the eye. Violet clutched the shredded remains of her shirt—*his* shirt—around her as he furiously cleaned her floors. "You are the Thornwitch, are you not?"

Her voice was small. "Yes."

"You came here after Shadowfade's death to, what, hide?"

"To start over."

"As a *florist*?" Disbelief was written on his features.

"Yes."

He laughed, but there was no humor to it. "And the blight?"

She reeled. "What about it?"

"You're the one causing it. Don't bother trying to deny it. I've figured it out. Your magic is all over it, after all. Were you lying about your hands to throw me off the scent?"

"*What?* No!" But a nasty seed of doubt was germinating in her heart. It was the second time today she'd been accused of being behind the blight, but something about Nathaniel's words struck home. Her hands. That other spring of magic—what if it had never come from her at all?

With a sick feeling in her stomach, Violet searched her shop for a bloom that hadn't been ruined and spotted a spider plant. She conjured a flower, a daisy, just like that day in the woods, only this time she concentrated on the spider plant too. The daisy sprung to her hand with a stinging tingle just like it had every time she practiced her new "good" magic. But her heart shattered when she saw the spider plant shrivel and blacken with blight. Violet had thought herself so clever, learning to use a source of magic that was different from the Thornwitch's. But it had never been her magic at all.

Just as Nathaniel had explained to her, everything in the world had its own small reserve of energy. And Violet had been using the plants around her instead of her own magic, sucking them dry until there was nothing left but rot.

Magic had a cost, and every bouquet, every blossom, every sprout she'd grown for her shop had been paid for by the *blight*.

It was all her fault.

Nathaniel watched her prove his theory correct and nodded, as though checking a box on a list.

"I didn't know," she said, her voice cracking. "Nathaniel, you have to believe me, I didn't know."

He gripped the broom tighter and continued tidying her shop with stiff, wooden movements.

"I was right," he said quietly, and the tone of his voice was worse than when they'd met, when he had disliked her. It was worse than disdain or annoyance or even the unreadable tone that had driven her mad in the beginning—this was disappointment, it was heartbreak, it was something shattering between them, and she'd caused it. "Shadowfade's death did create a vacuum; I just never expected it would be you coming in to seize power and take advantage of us."

"That's not true!" Tears burned at the corners of her eyes. "I wanted to start over. I wanted a new life. I'm trying to stop Sedgwick before he—"

He stopped sweeping and glared at her. "Why should I believe you? How much of what you told me was a lie? Your sob story of growing up in a bad home, running away—you only left because he was dead, didn't you? You only left because you knew you'd be hunted down like an animal if people knew what you were, what you'd done."

"I was trying to find a way to tell you," she said beseechingly. "But everything I shared with you about my past was the truth. I left some details out, yes, but I never lied to you, Nathaniel. I wanted you to know me."

"Leaving out an ingredient in alchemy could mean the difference between a harmless solution and a dangerous explosive. It's still a lie, Violet. You lied. To the whole town, to *me*. You—"

"I didn't want you to look at me the way you're looking at me now!" Violet blurted. "I didn't want to be the Thornwitch anymore. I just thought—" She shook her head, feeling foolish. "I didn't want to be a villain anymore. I wanted to be good."

She shrunk beneath the force of his glare, feeling stupid and small and wrong in a way she hadn't felt since Shadowfade was alive. For a solitary moment, she hated Nathaniel for shoving her back into this role. Desperately, she whispered, "I wanted to tell you."

"Tell me what? How you've killed people? Destroyed their homes and livelihoods? Violet, I spent years in the Crucible serving an organization that made me complicit in terrible things, but I left. I didn't just stand by and allow it to happen."

"I left too!"

"Once he was already dead."

"*Yes, because I killed him!*" Violet clapped a hand over her mouth, and Nathaniel stared at her in shock.

There it was. Her secret.

It was the first time she'd said it aloud.

"Karina the Tempest killed Guy Shadowfade," said Nathaniel slowly, his voice low.

Violet swallowed. "I'm the one who sent for her. I told her how to get past the castle wards. But in the end, when she had us cornered, she wasn't strong enough. He was going to kill her and I—" She choked on the words, remembering her hand on his back and the way her dagger-sharp thorn had burst through his chest. She remembered the way his blood had splattered on the Tempest's shirt, and the betrayal in Guy's eyes. His gaze had darted to the Tempest and right back to her.

Run, petal.

They'd been his last words.

She'd fled, and he'd haunted her dreams, his voice present through her waking moments ever since. He thought she'd been in danger, she realized much later. Even after she'd betrayed him—*killed* him—he told her to run. He wanted her to get away.

One way or another, Violet would have been responsible for Shadowfade's downfall. She just hadn't expected it—hadn't *wanted* it—to be done by her own hands. Because she was a coward. Because she'd loved him.

Yet even after all that, even with confirmation that he cared for her too, at least a little, she couldn't bring herself to regret what she'd done. She'd killed a man—the man who'd raised her, who'd lied to her and forced her to do terrible things in his name, but also the man who had encouraged her to learn more about plants and given her space to garden and showed her not to fear her power but to embrace it. She'd killed him, and as much as she would always mourn the aspects of him that she loved, she wasn't sorry for ending the monster that Guy Shadowfade had become.

Violet wasn't sorry for trying to start over afterward, for trying to do what he couldn't, or wouldn't: change.

"I killed him," she repeated, her tone even this time. "I have lived every moment since that day knowing what I've done, not just in the end but in the years that preceded it. I *live with that*, Nathaniel. I will keep living with it for the rest of my sorry life."

He was still staring at her, only now instead of outright anger, his face was a blank mask, and that was worse. Would he hate her forever? Drive her out of town? A tiny voice inside Violet asked if he would forgive her, but she banished it, knowing she couldn't allow that thought to take root.

"If Sedgwick brings him back, he'll harbor no fond feelings for me, never mind all our history together," she continued. "I stood by and let him be a monster for far too long, and I did monstrous things in his name. I know that. It took me too long to understand what he was turning me into, what I was becoming, and believe me, I know that too. But don't tell me I didn't try. Don't tell me I did nothing."

When he didn't say anything, she swallowed, their eyes still locked on each other. It was striking Violet again that she would have to leave, and this would already be the hardest goodbye she'd ever had to say. There would be no hope of forgiveness. After all, how could she expect him to forgive her when she couldn't forgive herself?

"I want to fix this," she said quietly. "I will do what it takes to prove to you I'm not the Thornwitch anymore. But you have to listen to me: Peri is the Eye of the Serpent, and Sedgwick has taken him. He's going to bring back Shadowfade. We have to stop him. And after we do, I'll—I'll leave Dragon's Rest. You'll never have to see me again, but please believe that I want to stop him. And I need your help to do it."

His silence pierced her as if one of her thorns had grown inward, digging through her heart rather than bursting through her skin. "Say something. Talk to me. Please."

The spell broke, and he twitched away from her. "I . . . I can't do this."

"You can't do this," she repeated lamely.

"I need time. To think. To . . ." He trailed off, his silence so complete that Violet swore he could hear her heart breaking. That was it, then. She was too monstrous for Nathaniel, for Dragon's

Rest. Lies about her mother aside, there was truth to what Shadowfade had tried to teach her—there was no use in showing people who you really were. They'd only abandon you once they knew the truth. She was the fool who had chosen to delude herself otherwise.

"Right," she said finally. Sedgwick was right—Shadowfade had broken them, made sure that by his side was the only place they would ever belong.

For a moment Nathaniel hesitated, clutching the broom like he wasn't sure what to do with it, but then he leaned it against one of the shelves that was still standing, and with one last look at her, he was out the door.

Violet crumpled the moment he was gone, leaning over her counter and crying long, deep sobs while Bartleby wound his vines through her hair and around her shoulders without even pretending like he was attempting to strangle her.

She felt alone and lost, her worst fears confirmed. Nathaniel knew the truth, not just about her identity but the terrible thing she'd done, the thing that would bring the entire world crashing down on her. She'd be hunted for being the Thornwitch by the Queen and anyone with a taste for vengeance or glory, yes, but Shadowfade's supporters would kill her for being a traitor. Nowhere was safe for Violet.

And apparently, no one was safe *with* her either.

The blight was all her fault. She was the reason for the rot in Wingspan Green and the fallen cherry tree downtown and the wreck that had become the Feldspar farm's crops. Her intentions had been good, but her own ignorance had caused harm.

Despair crashed into Violet like a wave at highest tide, when all three moons were full in the sky. No matter what she did, what she told herself, where she ran, she would always be a villain. The Thornwitch would never leave her.

And now, if Sedgwick successfully brought Shadowfade back, she'd have no choice. If Guy didn't kill her for what she'd done to him, he'd force her back into service, especially now that Sedgwick knew she could be extorted. All it would take would be a threat against one of her friends here in Dragon's Rest, and Violet knew she'd be helpless.

He had the Eye of the Serpent. He had the spell. Nathaniel needed time, but the clock had run out: every moment she stayed here moping was another moment Sedgwick had to prepare.

Perhaps it was a futile endeavor, but Violet's life was over. She would never be Violet Thistlewaite, the florist, ever again. Rough Around the Hedges was done. Nathaniel would tell everyone else, and she would be finished.

A clattering at the door drew her head up hopefully, but of course Nathaniel wouldn't have returned. Of course he wouldn't want to talk this out. No, it was a letter in the mail slot, fluttering to the floor.

Violet approached it with shaking hands, knowing there was only one piece of post she was waiting on, and there it was, a seal marked with forked lightning and a sword—Karina the Tempest.

The missive was short:

You cannot keep calling me like a dog.

You've done this before.

You can do it again.

Be good, and don't make me regret this.

—K

That was it, then. The Tempest wouldn't come to help.

Violet shut her eyes and clenched the letter in a tight fist. She had nothing to stay for and no one to help her. There would be no hero coming to save them. No knight in bright armor with a team of laughing, glorious companions riding to victory.

And Violet? She was the Thornwitch, dammit, a villain proper. A monster.

But she was powerful. And determined. And heartbroken and angry, and protective as hell over the people she'd come to love. The Tempest was right—she'd done this before. She'd killed Shadowfade, and she could very well be the one to make sure he stayed dead.

Whether they loved her back or hated her for existing, she would help the people of Dragon's Rest. The people of her *home*.

Like it or not, she was all they had.

SUPPORT

"Violet is the Thornwitch," Nathaniel said miserably as he burst through the door of the town meeting, scrubbing a hand through the mess of his hair. His neighbors and friends stared at him in shock, eyes wide and jaws slack. "She's behind the blight. I—"

"Hold on now," said Quinn, putting her hands up. "Start over."

Nathaniel sighed, feeling completely drained, and leaned against the wall of the inn, closing his eyes as he explained to them what had happened. He could still see her, holes in her shirt, covered in thorns, that unearthly glow in her eyes when she'd first regained consciousness.

"She came here after his death, trying to hide," he said on a sigh, "and she played us all for fools." *She certainly played me for a fool anyway.*

The collected residents of Dragon's Rest were silent long enough that Nathaniel had to open his eyes to be certain they were all still there.

"You idiot," said Pru softly, Daisy curled up in her lap. "Nathaniel, go after her."

He reeled. Of all the reactions he'd been expecting, this wasn't one of them. "Excuse me?"

"Of course she worked for Shadowfade," said Pru. "You thought it was a coincidence that she showed up here a week after he was defeated, all mysterious-like?"

"You knew?"

His sister shrugged. "It was an easy guess."

"And you didn't think to *tell me*?"

Pru exchanged a look with Quinn, and Nathaniel got the impression that she hadn't been the only person in on it. "Hang on now . . ."

Quinn stood to place a hand on Nathaniel's shoulder. "It wasn't anyone's secret to tell but Violet's, honey," she said, and smiled a sheepish smile. "Just like it was my secret when I left that castle."

His brain stopped working for a second. Nathaniel wasn't sure how many more surprises he could handle tonight.

"Y-you?" His mouth dropped open. "What? When? How?"

"A long time ago. I was known as the Hornet Queen back then," she said evenly. One of her bees buzzed around her hair as if to prove her point.

Nathaniel's mind reeled. "What?" he repeated.

"Leaving Shadowfade was one of the hardest things I've ever had to do, and Dragon's Rest became a soft place to land after a difficult fall."

"A place to start over," piped up Jerome. "Where none of us had to be who we used to." The gnome sat on his tall stool, arms crossed, legs dangling, glaring daggers at Nathaniel. "Where we could be someone other'n what he made of us."

Us?

"You too—?" Nathaniel choked out, feeling absolutely flabbergasted.

"For many years," began Quinn, "Shadowfade farmed this town for mages like you'd harvest an orchard for fruit. Those of us he could control, whose magic he wanted, he took from our homes."

Quinn continued. "There was no leaving him, not while he still had use for us. And if any of us tried, well . . ." She looked over at old Guy, who opened his mouth, displaying the grotesque remains where his tongue had once been. His mouth snapped shut, and he winked at Nathaniel with a toothy grin.

Jerome scowled. "He worked us until we burned out and then kicked us to the bloody gutter."

"My bees are all I have left of my magic," Quinn explained, "and Jerome has none of his strength left at all. Fallon used to be a powerful fire mage, and now they barely have enough power to keep their kiln running."

"Some days I don't," said Fallon with a shrug, brushing crumbs from one of Guy's black currant tarts off their shirt. "Gotta do it the mundane way, and let me tell you, that feels like a kick to the face after what I once was."

"Who else?" Nathaniel looked around the room.

"Are the four of us not exciting enough for you?" Jerome growled. Quinn shushed him.

"We're the only ones left, but there were once more. Remember old Harriston? And Corrin's grandfather Otho?"

"And Mum's sister Althea," added Pru quietly. "She was an alchemist for Shadowfade, taken from Dragon's Rest. She didn't just disappear like Mum said—she was killed working for him before we were born."

Nathaniel drew his eyes up to meet his twin. "That's why she didn't want me going to the Crucible," he said, putting it together.

Pru nodded. "Shadowfade stopped kidnapping mages from the town when we were young—probably around the time he found Violet—but Mum didn't want to take any chances. She was terrified for you. It's why she never fought you when you told her you were staying in Lokoa. She didn't want you anywhere near the castle."

"We've all lost friends and family members to his cruelty." Quinn gestured around the room. "Dear loved ones who were brainwashed into believing his madness or were killed fighting his battles, or who burned through their magic and couldn't survive the result."

More heads were nodding in the room.

"And you knew all along?" He cut his gaze to each of them, the people he'd thought he knew well. "All of you?"

Pru shrugged sadly. "You were away for a long time, brother."

Nathaniel stood shocked, taking it all in.

"I was there when he first brought Violet to Shadowfade Castle," said Quinn. "She was such a scared little thing. I'd never seen so much power in a single being, and it was clear he hadn't either. He banished many of us from his service and put all his focus into turning her into the Thornwitch. She never stood a chance of escaping his clutches."

"And you just let her move in?" Nathaniel could feel his anger rising again, his betrayal a fresh wound ripped wider and bloodier. "You didn't think any of us needed to know? You put our lives in danger, Quinn."

"My bees kept an eye on her," said Quinn with a careless wave of her hand. Nathaniel filed away this fact—that apparently the woman he'd known most of his life could *spy on people* through her insect friends—for later, when he'd have more capacity for intelligent thought. "And on that Sedgwick too. It's clear to us when someone comes here to rebuild versus when they come to Dragon's Rest to destroy, and we knew exactly which one each of them was trying to do."

"We almost had her too," grumbled Fallon. "Another week or two and she'd have trusted us enough to come clean on her own."

Quinn shook her head. "I really thought she was going to say yes to the Thursday support group when I asked her the other day."

"Support group?"

"Well, yes. Every Thursday, those of us who used to work for Shadowfade meet to chat and see how we're all doing."

"Guy always bakes the best snacks," added Jerome.

"Violet was trying to start over, honey," Quinn said. "She moved here to see if she could be someone other than the Thornwitch, and she wasn't the first. Those first years right after leaving—they're hard. Shadowfade makes you think you're nothing without him, and the things you've done in his service . . ." She shuddered. "Well, it's important to have support while you're rising from those ashes."

"The Thornwitch was infamous," he argued, though doubt bubbled in his heart now. "She was known for being evil. She did terrible things—she killed people!"

His sister rose from her chair, her eyes ablaze in a way that reminded him, terrifyingly, of their mother. "Nathaniel Marsh, did you or did you not work for the Crucible?"

"That's different." Nathaniel thought back to those years. "I never killed anyone."

"No?" Pru snorted. "You built weapons. Explosives. Devices that were made to hurt, to kill. Don't deny it."

He met his sister's eyes. "I don't."

"You can parse the differences until your face turns blue, but the truth is you did things under the orders of someone with more power than you. It doesn't make what you did right. But it also doesn't mean we don't understand." Pru's face softened. "I know it's scary, Nat, but people change. They're *allowed* to change. They're allowed to try and be better than what they were before. And when we care about them, then we need to support them."

Nathaniel wanted nothing more than to bury his face in his hands. He'd already known Violet was trying to start over; she'd made no secret of that fact. Moons, he of all people should know how important that was—coming back to Dragon's Rest had given Nathaniel the space to grow. Here, back where he'd started, and especially since Violet came to town, he'd awoken from the sleepy half life he'd been living since he came home from the Crucible and since his parents' passing.

He'd learned he could be more than his family's legacy and more than what he was in the Crucible. Here, he could build his business on his own terms, in a way that spoke to all his skills and aspirations. It was like Nathaniel had removed an ill-fitting shirt he'd worn for so long he hadn't realized that he'd grown out of it, only continued letting the seams dig into his skin and the buttons strain at their stitches. Now that it was off, he could see how it had kept him warm through the years, but he couldn't fathom putting it back on. That was the thing about change, after all. It meant letting go of the person he'd been in the past.

Even here, among people who knew every last one of his wretched mistakes, no one had brought up his parents. They had given him the grace to start fresh, and he knew what it meant to him. Why hadn't he been able to give Violet that same chance?

"But she's behind the blight," he said miserably. "She's the one causing it."

"And that's serious indeed," said Quinn. "She did that maliciously?"

He saw her face again, her horror, her shocked realization. *Nathaniel, you have to believe me.* And he hadn't.

"No, I—I don't think she knew she was doing it." He averted his gaze, which was dawning with the realization that he'd acted every bit the monster he'd accused Violet of being. "She worked hard right alongside me to try and find the cause of the blight. I know she wanted to stop it. And I threw it all right in her face."

And now she'd . . . *oh no.*

"Sedgwick," he whispered, remembering her words. "She went after Sedgwick and Peri."

"Pardon?" Quinn asked.

He told them what he knew. "She said Sedgwick had the Eye of the Serpent, and that if he could bring back Shadowfade, he'd—" He gritted his teeth. That Violet had killed the sorcerer was something she'd clearly held close to her chest. He'd spilled enough of her secrets tonight; he didn't feel right sharing this for her too. "He'll kill her if he returns. Thornwitch or not, Shadowfade'll kill her. And then Dragon's Rest will be right back where it was . . ." Another horrible thought struck him. She said she'd do what it took to prove herself. "And I let her go alone."

He'd been such a spectacular idiot.

Pru was at his side. "Violet's powerful. She can hold her own, can't she?"

Nathaniel's heart sank. The wreckage of Violet's shop, of her crumpled form on the floor, flashed through his mind. "He's dangerous. And after I accused her, with the blight . . ." He looked around the room. "I know I made a mistake, but I *know* her. I don't know *how* exactly she caused it, and I don't know if she does either, but she'll hold back if she's afraid her magic will cause any more blight." He swallowed hard, pulling the vial from his pocket. "She doesn't know I discovered the antidote."

Pru's face lit with surprise. "You did?! Nathaniel, that's—"

"Not the time, Pru. She needs help." He felt wild, like something had been set loose inside him.

Pru put a hand on his shoulder. "Then help she will receive. Violet's as much a part of this community as anyone."

"But we're already too late."

Quinn held up a finger, a smile spreading over her face though her eyes looked distant. "Maybe not," she said, and turned to look at Jerome. "How fast can you be?"

The gnome was already on his feet and on his way out the door. "Don't let the short legs deceive you."

Nathaniel and Pru exchanged a long look, the kind that said more than words could. Hope flared in his chest. If Peri was the Eye of the Serpent, then it might not be the only part of the legend that was real.

"Pru," Nathaniel said slowly. "Did you ever finish that book on rock goblins?"

SHADOWFADE CASTLE

For the second time in a week, Violet returned to Shadowfade Castle. Bees buzzed happily through the colorful flowers of her overgrown gardens, probably thrilled for the out-of-season nectar. But Violet felt sick looking at anything her magic had grown.

She couldn't believe she'd been so stupid. *No more dark magic*, she'd vowed when she came to Dragon's Rest, but it had been there all along, letting itself free through the windows even as she carefully guarded the doors. She understood now what Nathaniel had been trying to say about magic and energy. Pulling life from the plants around her? *That* was evil, even if the magic she had taken from those plants wasn't. Violet had brought destruction to her community, all because she was a naïve little girl who wanted to be good and had no idea what that truly meant. She dragged a hand over her scar, a permanent reminder of her own stupidity.

What would the Tempest, that shining hero, think of her now? Would she see the blighted remains of Dragon's Rest and regret her decision to leave Violet alive? Would she see Sedgwick's plan and understand that Violet couldn't possibly be good because even if she wasn't evil, she was nothing on her own? She was a tool in someone else's hand, only as good or evil as its wielder.

Misery overtook her anew as Violet realized even that wasn't right. Shadowfade had forced her hand at the end, yes, but she'd been the one who destroyed those towns, who killed those people, all because she wanted him to care for her as something other than a master would his favorite hunting hound.

Violet's innate well of magic was never dark or evil; it was what had grown the greenhouse jungle that night, after all. It was what had sprouted rosebushes on these lawns and calmed her moods with the gentle touch of branches and vines on her shoulder. No, Nathaniel was correct here as well—her magic was never bad; she was the one who had used it so poorly.

But that stopped today.

She crept toward the castle, avoiding the front entrance. Sedgwick had set up his workspace in the Great Hall, so it would only make sense that was where he'd taken Peri. Violet made her way toward a side entrance, the same one she'd used to make her escape after Shadowfade had— No, it was time to stop talking around it. After she'd killed him.

Violet slipped through the servant's corridor and peered into the Great Hall. Sedgwick stood exactly where she'd stabbed Shadowfade and had watched him bleed out before she ran. Intricate ritual symbols had been painted onto the parquet floor, forming a circle around the metal box she'd seen that day with Pru. He was preparing to do the spell, then.

In Sedgwick's hands was a large yellow-green gemstone, about the size of his fist. The Eye of the Serpent. Violet looked for Peri and found the rock goblin lying motionless at Sedgwick's feet, a cavernous hole in his chest.

"Thornwitch," said Sedgwick with a smile, turning to look directly at her. "So good of you to join us."

"My name," she said, stepping fully into the hall, "is Violet Thistlewaite. *Not* Thornwitch. What have you done to Peri?"

"Who?" Sedgwick looked around, following her gaze to the rock in his hand. He laughed. "The rock goblin? Oh, Thornwitch, you *have* gone soft."

She breathed a sigh of relief when she saw Peri move. She had little understanding of rock goblin physiology or what it took to injure one, but her friend was alive at least. She could work with that, but now she needed to focus on Sedgwick. Remembering the nasty vial he'd thrown at her before, she glanced around for traps. Sure enough, there was a line of some glittering substance about three feet in front of him, and above them hung a curtain, no doubt coated in some devious powder that would immobilize her. She did not want to bring blight or other consequences, so she abandoned everything she'd taught herself about magic during her time in Dragon's Rest and allowed her own eager power to flood her senses. Her eyes gleaming green, she conjured a careful mass of creeping vines that slowly bound the curtain so he could not shake the powder loose.

"Tristan, stop this," she said to Sedgwick, deliberately using his first name just as he had deliberately avoided using hers. All she had to do was keep him talking. "He's gone and we're better off for it. What will bringing him back do for you?"

"Shadowfade had vision," said Sedgwick, his jaw tight. "He had power and he wasn't afraid to use it, unlike you." It was clear from how he spat the words that he saw it as an insult.

"You're right. For a long time, the power he wielded gave me purpose. I didn't belong anywhere else but with him. But *you* are the one who set me free, Tristan. You're the one who woke me up when you gave me that letter about my mother. You made me realize I could be something else."

He reared back like she'd struck him, and she recalled the moment the alchemist wavered in her shop. She wasn't the only one who felt aimless without a master to follow. Only Sedgwick never had anyone to show him there was more. He'd never had anyone to offer him a second chance. Gently, Violet gave him the words she wished someone had said to her years ago. "You can be more than what he made of you."

Sedgwick's face twisted. "What are you talking about?"

"He won't love you for bringing him back," she said softly. "You might think it will win you his favor but he'll resent that he needed you. Whatever you're looking for by resurrecting him? You won't find it."

For a moment it was as if she could read his every thought: He wasn't powerful like she was; he couldn't command respect through his magic alone. But he was smart, the kind of man who had clung to power all his life, a pilot fish over the shoulder of the shark, knowing the chum upon which he fed was all due to his patron. Following someone like Shadowfade lent him protection, armored him in someone else's power, made him feel he had a purpose. Made him feel needed.

Violet could relate.

"You can build what you need without him," she cajoled in the same voice she'd used to get Daisy out from under the bush. She wished she had one of Guy's pastries to offer, but all she had were the same words that drew her out of her own personal darkness. "You could be so much better. You could be good."

Sedgwick froze.

"Good?" Sedgwick scoffed, but his voice trembled. He wanted to believe there was more to life. She could see it in his ragged expression even as he shook his head. "People like us are not *good*, Thornwitch. You think you're a hero now?"

"No." It was the truth. "I'm not a hero. I don't even know if I *can* be truly good. But I'm not the Thornwitch anymore either. I'm something different. Something better. You could be too."

His jaw tightened. "You're grasping for a fantasy."

"I found it," she said quietly. "Even if just for a little while, I found a home and a community. I built a life on my own terms, without Shadowfade. Don't you want to try?"

For a moment she thought she had him convinced. They could end this without bloodshed and lay to rest any chance of Shadowfade's return. Sedgwick could start over just like Violet had, and she'd help him do it.

But then his mouth twitched into a sneer, and cruelty clanked over his voice like a bolt sliding shut over a door. "I'll never be anything other than this," he drawled. "And neither will you. I didn't set you free, I *broke* you. You're fooling yourself, Thornwitch. For all your power, you're weak."

She let her eyes fall closed, his words sinking into her like knives. "I was afraid you might say that."

"And now what? You're going to turn all Thornwitch on me? Going to kill me? Go ahead and prove me right, *Violet*. Prove you'll never be anything but a villain." He spat her name like a curse, like a lie.

And maybe it was true. Maybe the Thornwitch would never truly leave her. Maybe she would always be a part of Violet.

But maybe . . . maybe that wasn't such a bad thing.

Violet was different now than when she lived at this castle, and it was because she wanted to be. Because she was choosing to be different every single day. She might not yet feel worthy of her home and the love of those around her, but she was working at it.

Perhaps that's what it meant to be good after all. Goodness wasn't something you could just *be*; it was something you *did*. Violet had done terrible things, but it didn't mean she needed to be a villain for the rest of her life. Just like her magic, she was not good or evil until she chose to be, and she could *choose* goodness and love and take steps every day to make sure she was worthy of her friends and her home and herself. It would never undo the past, but she owed it to herself and others to change her future.

To do better.

Be better.

Be *good.*

And it started right now, because her job today had never been to duel Sedgwick; it had been to stall for time.

"You were right about the Thornwitch, Tristan. She's not as powerful alone." Violet's power buzzed within her, and from somewhere behind her rose the sound of a solitary violin.

The door to the Great Hall thundered open, just as they'd planned before she came up to the castle. Plan B.

The brightest constellations shine not from a single star, but many.

And as her friends poured through the doors of the Great Hall, armed and ready to defend their home—defend *her*—Violet's smile grew. She breathed a sigh of relief when she saw Nathaniel among them; until that moment she hadn't been sure he would come. But he caught her eye and nodded at her, removing a vial from the bandolier across his chest, and the feeling that grew inside Violet then felt a lot like hope. She didn't know where they stood—didn't know if he could forgive her for deceiving him—but he was here. That counted for something, didn't it?

Violet turned back to Sedgwick. "I'm not alone anymore."

THE DRAGON AND THE HOARD

Relief thrilled through Nathaniel as he caught sight of Violet through the open doors. Jerome had found her before it was too late, and she'd bought enough time talking to Sedgwick for them to catch up, just as they'd planned. There was so much he still needed to say to her, but he felt more hopeful than he had an hour ago that they would have time for that conversation.

And now here he stood next to his sister, who wielded her violin like a weapon, and Quinn, whose bees buzzed around her like a cyclone. Fallon, who held fire in their hands like clay. Even Bartleby, who was strapped to Jerome's back with a dozen knives, real and improvised, clutched in his vines. Nathaniel felt his chest swell with a pride and loyalty he'd never felt while in the Crucible.

"Idiots," screeched Sedgwick, pulling on a rope behind him. The curtain above them shuddered, caught in a web of vines clearly grown by Violet. Still, powder spilled from the edges, casting the room in a cloud of smoke.

"Don't touch it!" Nathaniel cried, and hurled a vial toward the trap on the ground in front of Sedgwick. Sure enough, it exploded with force and even more smoke.

"Watch out for Peri!" Violet yelled when Fallon followed up with a ball of fire, aiming for the unnervingly coffin-like box on the platform behind Sedgwick. Their magic was weak these days, as they'd explained to Nathaniel, so they'd filled clay bottles with accelerant. Fallon only had to light the hemp cord that protruded from one side and throw it in Sedgwick's direction.

"Aye, watch your own end!" Fallon responded with a wink, jovial as ever. "I'll bet you a dozen of Guy's pastries my aim's better than yours."

Nathaniel looked for Peri and found the rock goblin in a heap on the ground. Sedgwick had recovered from the shock of being faced with a crowd of angry villagers and was scrambling to protect the ritual circle as well as the sinister coffin at its center. He wore his own bandolier of bottles and vials, and he plucked one from its bindings to throw at Violet. It shattered before her feet and an orange mist rose in the air, but she summoned a wall of leafy, thorny plants to block her from the mist. The vines froze in place, hardening with a loud crackle.

"You can't try that one again!" she called to him. "I know your tricks now, Sedgwick."

"Keep him distracted," Nathaniel told Quinn, who nodded and sent her bees in an angry cloud toward the other alchemist. "Pru! How are we doing?"

His twin smiled a smile he'd seen a million times throughout their childhood when she was about to loose a prank on him or their parents and couldn't hold in her excitement. "Should be any moment."

"Good. You know what to do." As Pru tucked her violin under her chin, Nathaniel selected another vial and threw it to the ground before Sedgwick's feet. A cloud of viscous, horrible-smelling smoke arose, clinging to the first living organism it found—in this case, Sedgwick. The other alchemist shrieked, and Nathaniel took off toward Peri as Pru drew her bow across the strings and began to play.

He had an entire arsenal's worth of military secrets at his disposal when it came to alchemical weapons, but his options had been extremely limited due to time. Still, he'd managed a few quick and dirty tricks. Sedgwick was no idiot, though—he'd realize in a moment or two that the smoke only hovered in the air from chest level up. Before he could duck free, Nathaniel swept the motionless rock goblin into his arms, noting the gaping hole in his chest where the peridot had once been. He tucked Peri beneath his arm and bolted for the wall of vegetation Violet had created.

"Incoming!" He grabbed hold of the wall's edge and swung himself behind it, coming face-to-face with Violet for the first time since the disastrous fight in her shop. "Hello."

"Hi," said Violet, avoiding his eyes as she took Peri from him.

"You know, despite being made of literal stone, he's still heavier than I anticipated," Nathaniel quipped, catching his breath.

Violet scanned Peri for injuries, grimacing at the hole where the stone once was. "Do you think he'll be alright?"

"I hope so." At the edge of the room, Pru coaxed a lively tune from her instrument as if she were onstage at Market Day or dancing between tables at the Claw & Hoard, not in the castle of an evil sorcerer while her friends fought around her. "But you? You're unharmed?"

"I'm fine." As she set Peri down gently behind the wall, Sedgwick finally ducked free of the smoke. Nathaniel tried to focus on the fight, but inwardly he was kicking himself—there was so much he needed to say to her, and this was all he'd managed?

"Jerome, Bartleby—watch out!" he yelled, and the pothos, who had been helping Jerome scuff the ritual marks from the floor, chucked a paring knife and a straight razor in quick succession toward Sedgwick.

"We still need to get the Eye away from him," said Violet. "I don't think he can perform the ritual while we're here distracting him, but we can't risk it. I don't know if he's capable of using its power for anything else, but if he can . . ."

Nathaniel nodded. If Sedgwick could wield the Eye, they were in even bigger trouble. "Can you trap him with magic? Hold him still?"

"You're not worried I'll cause more blight?"

"Violet, I should have—"

"It's fine," she said flatly, her eyes on Sedgwick. "I figured it out. That second source of magic I told you about? *That's* what was causing it, not my own magic. So you don't have to worry."

"That's—" There was a time for this conversation but it wasn't now. He settled for telling her, "Anyway, I solved it, Violet. I discovered the antidote."

"You did?" Her eyes widened, and he basked for a moment in their light before she turned her attention back to the matter at hand. "*Hey!*" she cried, curving her hand into a claw and gesturing at Sedgwick, who tripped over a vine that hadn't been there a moment before, therefore landing short with the potion he threw at Pru.

"I'm so proud of you," she said, turning back to Nathaniel and beaming. For a moment it was like they were back in the greenhouse, not surrounded by an actual battle. "I knew you could do it."

Nathaniel took a deep breath. He supposed now was as good a time as any. "I owe you an apology." He paused to throw a potion at Quinn's feet, sending up a temporary shield that blocked the worst of a trap she'd triggered.

"*You're* apologizing to *me*?" Violet's mouth hung open in shock.

The vine wall they were hiding behind crumbled to dust, finally spent, and Violet threw herself toward Nathaniel, taking his hand and leading him away from the noxious orange smoke that began to rise in its place.

"I was scared and surprised, but I should have listened to you," he said, pulling her toward him to dodge a trap.

"But I'm the one who lied!" said Violet, flinging her free hand to his chest to catch her balance. "I should have told you the truth weeks ago—I wanted to, I did, but I was afraid of losing you."

Nathaniel threw another vial, this one releasing a harmless smoke that provided cover as they bolted for the other side of the room near where Pru played her music.

"And I confirmed those fears," he said miserably. "I'm so sorry."

"I mean, it's a lot to take in," acknowledged Violet, panting to catch her breath. "I'm pretty famous, and not in a nice way."

"But I should have heard you out. I should have stayed and listened, and I regretted it the moment I walked out of your shop."

She searched his face, her eyes softening, and again he felt drenched with shame. He knew Violet's heart even if he didn't know everything about her past, and he would spend as long as it took trying to make up for his knee-jerk reaction.

Because he loved her, he realized with a start. He loved Violet Thistlewaite, villainous origins or no. Hope bloomed in his chest as he opened his mouth to tell her—

"Oy!" Jerome hollered from where he had been blown back by one of Sedgwick's bombs. "Can you two idiots stop making moon eyes at each other long enough t'help us *stop the evil sorcerer from returning*?"

Nathaniel and Violet exchanged a sheepish look.

"Pru, how are we looking?" Nathaniel called.

His twin cackled, playing a fast and rousing melody that echoed through the cavernous space and set Nathaniel's heart pounding in time. "Just about ready for phase three!"

Things happened quickly from there. Violet put out her hands, and a tangle of vines emerged from the ground in front of Sedgwick, tearing through floorboards like paper as they wrapped around his legs, holding him in place, and curled tight around his arms, pinning them at his sides.

"You think you can hold me forever?" Sedgwick taunted, sneering at Violet. His face was red and spotted with beestings, which were already beginning to swell. "You're weak, Thornwitch. You've shown your hand already; I know you won't kill me."

"No," she said coldly. One of her vines crept over Sedgwick's mouth, silencing him. "I won't have to."

A rumbling sound echoed through the large room, and Nathaniel turned to his sister. "Pru, now!" he yelled, and she dropped her instrument, her job done.

"I was totally right, by the way!" she called out in the silence that fell over them all, her voice echoing. "The acoustics in here are *great*!"

The rumbling grew louder, like percussion to the absent tune, and all at once, a massive creature burst through the open doorway, taking part of the wall with it.

Nathaniel had seen a couple dozen rock goblins at once who sometimes combined to make a bigger form. But this must have been the entire slide, and it was enormous. The rock goblins took the shape of a four-legged creature that towered over everything else, dripping dust and bits of gravel from their joints as they moved as one. Nathaniel ducked to avoid a bit of plaster that flew at him as the rock slide spread a pair of giant, stony wings, and his eyes widened as he realized what it was, the way its long neck swept from side to side, seeking the source of the music the rock goblins had followed here. There were no eyes in its head, but the shape of the creature was clear.

Together, the rock goblins had formed a dragon.

"Got him?" Nathaniel called out.

"Aye!" Quinn yelled back.

"All good!" Violet added, her hands in front of her as she added more and more of her plants to Sedgwick's bindings.

"Pru!" Nathaniel yelled again. His sister danced toward the front of the room, brought her instrument back into position, and began to play again. The rock goblins, entranced by her music as always, followed like a giant, unwieldy moth fluttering after a lantern.

"He's the one," Violet cried, sparing a hand to point at Sedgwick, who had begun to struggle furiously against his bindings. Her voice echoed through the hall. "He hurt Peri! He has the Eye of the Serpent!"

The stone dragon roared, a great groan like the clearing of a pipe, and as its head whipped to the side, Nathaniel caught a glimpse of one of the dragon's empty eye sockets. A missing piece, just about the size of Peri.

His hunch had been correct, but the truth of what he was looking at struck Nathaniel like, well, a stone. Peri didn't just have the Eye by chance—Peri had it because the Eye was part of the dragon. Years of storytelling wound complicated paths through his thoughts. The witch and the warrior. The dragon turned to stone. It was all real.

And so the rock goblins, like the dragon they had once been, narrowed their gaze on the hapless alchemist who held the Eye of the Serpent. It barreled forward, as unstoppable as a boulder crashing down the mountainside, and smashed the horrible metal coffin beneath its mighty feet. As one, the rock goblin dragon surrounded Sedgwick, sweeping its tail around to trap him. It roared again, a cacophony of scraping, croaking sounds that hurt Nathaniel's ears, and reared its head, smashing through the rafters with a massive crack that shook the castle.

"We have to get out of here!" Nathaniel cried, looking around them. "It'll take care of Sedgwick and will make sure Peri is okay!"

"Come on!" Violet cried to their companions. She swept an arm toward the door just in time for them to see the crack in the ceiling spread like forked lightning and take down a rafter. The huge beam of wood, and the chandelier connected to it, crashed to the ground, blocking the exit.

Nathaniel looked at Violet in horror.

They were trapped.

A BETTER GARDEN

From the moment Jerome caught up to her on the road to Shadowfade Castle, Violet had felt a confusing mixture of warmth and confusion.

"Just stall 'im," Jerome had insisted. "Keep 'im talking long enough for us to get a few things together. And know we're right behind you."

So she'd expected her friends—but the rock goblins? A *dragon*?

And now they were trapped.

The dragon roared again, and though she could hear no trace of Sedgwick amidst that mountain of angry stone, she winced to know he was at its core. The dragon's wings brushed the walls, shattering what was left of the windows, and the castle shook again. It was coming down all around them.

"How do we get out?" Pru wailed, her violin clutched to her chest. Quinn and her bees, gathered in a swarm that crawled on her arms and torso like armor, weren't far behind. Violet looked for the others and found Fallon on the other side of some fallen debris, crawling toward them, and Jerome at their side, digging through the plaster and stone trying to make a path, Bartleby at his back flinging rubble out of their way.

"We're going to die," said Quinn, and there was agony in her eyes for all that her voice sounded serene. "But we've done good for our home, and the people of Dragon's Rest will be safe because of us."

Nathaniel pulled Violet toward him. "I'm so sorry," he said, leaning his forehead against hers. "I wanted to make it up to you."

"Hush," she told him, her mind ricocheting between options. "It's going to be alright."

"I never got to tell you." His eyes were wild and his breathing erratic. "I—"

Violet put a finger to his lips, silencing him. "After."

"But—"

Three moons, this man!

She said firmly, "Nathaniel Marsh, you tell me after. Now do as I say and *hush*. I'm busy saving all of our lives."

He frowned, and she went about ignoring him entirely, focusing on Fallon and Jerome. Her eyes began to glow as she used her vines to help destroy the debris in their way. This destructive urge she felt to crush and throttle was the Thornwitch's influence, years of habit rising to the surface, but for the first time since Silbourne, Violet leaned into it without guilt. The Thornwitch was part of her, and so was her magic. It was neither good nor evil, only a tool in her hands. And Violet was determined—*choosing*—to use it for good.

When the path was clear, her friends rushed to her side.

"That was a handy trick," said Jerome, and for once he sounded impressed.

"Wait until you see this one," she said with a tight smile as her eyes darted around what was left of the Great Hall. "Stick close to me!"

She led them toward the western wall, where she pressed a secret panel. The door opened haltingly, and though the corridor behind it was already collapsed, the doorway itself stood strong. Violet gathered her friends to her as the dragon reared its head and took a chunk out of the ceiling.

"Get close!" she cried, and they huddled around her as she drew plants over them like a blanket, building a wall of thorns that grew ever thicker, smashing through walls and forcing its way through cracks in the stone. *Destroy, destroy it all*, she urged her plants, gripping tightly to Nathaniel's hand like a lifeline keeping her tethered to herself. *Bring this terrible place to the ground, only protect me and mine.* Magic rushed through her veins, pushing from her body and eagerly overtaking the castle with vines that gripped and tore. As she channeled more and more power from the well of magic inside her—the one that was well and truly hers—Violet could feel the thorns tearing through her skin as the Thornwitch truly unleashed her might. Faintly she heard Nathaniel cry out, but though she tried to pull away, he wouldn't let go of her hand.

Violet focused on her spell, weaving thorny hedges dozens of feet thick as the ground shook and heavy weight pressed into their bubble of safety. Ever more, that horrible loud roaring of the dragon tore into their ears. It went on for minutes or hours, she couldn't be sure, but when it stopped, she was stiff and sore and disoriented. Her vision swam at the edges, and she let her eyes drift closed as she was guided slowly to the floor.

"Violet," came a voice. "Violet, it's over."

She was faintly aware of Pru standing over her, hands on her face. Violet jerked away, and Pru hissed as one of her thorns scratched her.

"I'm sorry," Violet mumbled. She tried to retract the Thornwitch, but it hurt to even think about magic after all of that. She groaned.

"Think she finally gave herself magic burn?" Jerome asked with a chuckle.

"Not sure anyone took that wager," mused Pru.

"Jerome did," confirmed Fallon.

Quinn chuckled. "I can't decide if I'd be more impressed or flabbergasted if she *didn't* have magic burn."

Then she heard Nathaniel's voice, became aware of her hand still in his as he squeezed it. "Don't try to get up. Rest a bit."

When she came to again, there was a painful throbbing between her temples, but her thorns had receded. Her head was in Nathaniel's lap, and he stroked her hair absently. One of Bartleby's vines coiled loosely up her arm, for once not squeezing like a boa constrictor. The others sat in a loose circle around her, close within the small space, Quinn's bees buzzing with a comforting rhythm.

"Awake?" Nathaniel smiled down at her. "Feel any better?"

She shook her head. "I feel like someone just dropped a castle on me."

"I'll make you a tincture for magic burn when we get home," he murmured, brushing his thumb across her cheekbone. His hand was bandaged with what looked like a strip of Pru's skirt, and she felt a twinge of guilt that swirled confusingly with warmth when she remembered how he'd refused to let go.

"Eh! She *did* get magic burn!" Jerome cheered. "Fallon owes me a beer!"

"I'll buy everyone a round if Violet can get us out of here," said Fallon, laughing.

"True," added Pru. "Beer's a bit hard to find in this, er, cave of thorns?"

Violet sat up, reaching behind her to squeeze Nathaniel's knee. "Give me just a second."

"Take all the time you need," said Quinn with a smile.

"Did we do it? We stopped Sedgwick?"

"We did." Quinn's smile grew.

"And Peri? The rock goblins?"

Pru shook her head. "No idea."

"What happened there anyway?" Violet asked. "How did you know they'd become a dragon?"

"Well, *that* part was a surprise," admitted Pru. "But remember the book I found in the castle library? I learned all about them—as much as anyone really knows anyway. They're formed when beings of immense magical power are turned to stone, and all that magical energy needs to go *somewhere* so it kind of animates itself. When a slide gets together, it can re-form into whatever creature it once was. There were so many of them, we knew it would be big. We just didn't know it would be . . . that."

Nathaniel scoffed. "Do you think they knew they were trapping us in here?"

"No idea." Pru shrugged and threw him a look. "Haven't gotten to that chapter of the book yet. Plus, Violet kept us safe. That was downright heroic."

Through the weariness in her bones, Violet's body heated in a head-to-toe blush.

"But can you get us out of here?" Jerome asked gruffly. "Reckon I'd take some more heroics if it means we don't die like this."

She looked at the wall of bramble around them, various bits of stone wall or wooden door frame wound tightly in its grasp. She stood on wobbly legs and closed her eyes, pressing a hand to the thorns.

Thank you, she thought to them, and instead of letting the magic that created them dissipate, Violet drew it back into her body like a great inhalation. Almost instantly, her headache disappeared, and though nothing else seemed to change, she knew it was working. The magic filled her, pouring back into her vast reserves until even that well felt close to overflowing.

Eyes still closed, Violet began to imagine a garden. She pictured her greenhouse and all the flowers in her shop. Daisies for Daisy and bee balm for Quinn. Hypoallergenic hydrangeas for Jerome, fiery red camellias for Fallon, and fragrant, edible herbs and spices for Guy. Vining plants for Bartleby. She added yellow tulips for the sunshine in Pru's smile and marsh roses for the twins and the home they'd given her. Snapdragons for Dragon's Rest.

For Nathaniel, she thought of the clematis that had knocked over his potion the night she'd met him and the mugwort she'd grown for him in a misguided attempt to help. Cherry blossoms for the tree that had nearly crushed them the night they first kissed, and dahlias and freesias and all the flowers of the riotous jungle that had grown from her worktable the night they'd made love for the first time.

The garden of her life grew and blossomed in her mind, full of color and life, but there was one person she was forgetting.

So for herself she added blankets of violets, purple as the cloak she hated and the sails of the ship she hoped she'd be brave enough to look for someday. For the Thornwitch—and for Guy, both of whom would always be part of her—she added a few rosebushes, beautiful and fragrant and, of course, thorny.

Violet took the magic gathered inside her and poured it into that image like a vast waterfall of power. There was no stinging or pain or even thorns beneath her skin. This felt good, yes, but even more, it felt *right*. The bramble beneath her hands melted away, and when she heard the harsh intake of breath from her companions, she knew she was done.

Violet opened her eyes and saw what she had created.

It was night now, but they no longer stood in a castle, or even the ruins of one. Violet's magic had destroyed it all as surely as she had once sunk entire towns into bogs, but she hadn't stopped there. Thick ceiling trusses had been grown into benches, shaped from the dead wood into something curving and elegant. Stones had been hauled by her bramble to form fountains and pools and pathways, and all around were the flowers she had imagined and so many others. They spilled from stone planters and beds that lined the paths, bracketed by hedges and flowering fruit trees, most of them a bit out of season. Under the approving eyes of the moons, everything shone silver.

"It's beautiful," whispered Pru, stepping out of their circle onto one of the paths.

Jerome sneezed loudly, pulling a polka-dot handkerchief from his pocket. "Great," he muttered, setting off down a path to explore. "More flowers."

Quinn's bees shot off in all directions as she turned to Violet. "You made all of this?"

Violet drew a staggering breath. "I had some extra energy to burn."

As her friends discovered the nooks and walkways of the garden, Nathaniel took Violet's hand and led her in a different direction, awe painted on his features.

"This looks like much more than 'some extra energy.'"

"I pulled my own magic back from those thorns," Violet explained. "I wasn't sure it was going to work."

Nathaniel had the look on his face that told her he was in scientist mode, so she swallowed hard and set loose the thought that had been flitting in a frenzy since he'd found her in her shop. "I got the idea from the blight. I was so afraid of being the Thornwitch that I accidentally used every drop of life and magic I could source from the plants in Dragon's Rest rather than touch my own. I wondered, maybe, when I spent so much of my own power to protect us, if I could repurpose it in the same way. Only, you know, without accidentally hurting anything around me, because it was my magic in the first place."

He looked down at the ground.

"I'm sorry," she blurted again, blinking away tears. "I was scared, and trying to be good, and I thought—"

"Violet, I get it."

Her breath caught. "You do?"

"Well, inadvertently blighting your neighbors' crops and half the local flora? No. But I do understand desperately trying to avoid a part of yourself that has hurt people in the past." He took a deep breath. "You're the one who helped me see that it's not the answer."

"You had an accident," she rebutted gently. "I was the trusted right hand of an evil villain. They're not exactly the same thing."

He rolled his eyes to acknowledge her point and let out a weighty sigh that cast dread into her bones.

"I'm going to ask you a difficult question now." He waited for her to nod, her heart thrashing the whole time. "Will you tell me about the Thornwitch?"

And though it scared her, Violet did. As they walked along the paths of the garden she'd built, she told him the truth about Shadowfade and Silbourne and that day with Karina the Tempest. She recalled memories of growing up here and the gardens she created and the ship with purple sails and the day she realized she had been stolen rather than abandoned.

"I didn't know how to trust myself after all of that." Violet kicked at the grass beneath her feet. "I knew he'd lied to me but I still felt like he was right and that there was something wrong with me."

"Do you feel that way now?"

"Sometimes," she admitted. "That's why I came to Dragon's Rest, to learn who I was without him, to see if I could build something all my own. But I built it around a lie because I thought it was the only way to escape my past."

Nathaniel took her hand as they turned a corner to discover a gazebo that appeared to have been grown from the ornate window frames of the Great Hall. Some of the panels were still fitted with colorful stained glass.

"None of us can truly escape the past," he said as they climbed the stairs. Light poured in around them, casting them in a dappled rainbow of light.

"I know that now. The past is a compass; it's what guides us to the future we want—and away from the one we don't."

"Even when that future means facing the unknown. Even when it means *change*." He said the word like a bitter curse, and Violet laughed.

"I *want* to change. I *want* to be better than I was."

"It sounds like you already are."

"I'm certainly trying. And I'm going to keep trying."

He drew them to a stop and turned to her, taking her other hand and gathering both in his. "I've never been someone who deals well with change," he said, inching closer. "I turn inward when I fear I might fail. I lie to myself or I ignore it or I run. But I don't want to do that with you. I know now who you once were and I can't say if that woman would ever have made me feel the way I feel for the woman you are now. But I see how hard you've worked to create a life you love, and I want that too, even if it means change. I want a life that I am passionate about, in my business and my family—and with you."

Her chest tight, Violet whispered, "I want that too."

He tucked an errant curl behind her ear, letting his thumb linger on her cheekbone as he regarded her with bright eyes. "I love you, Violet Thistlewaite. For all that you are, I love you. For all that you are working so hard to become, I love you. I see you, thorns and all—and I love you."

Violet's heart was a bud, and in that moment it blossomed, petals unfurling, expanding, stretching toward the light of a sun she had thought lost behind the clouds.

"I love you too, Nathaniel Marsh."

And that was the last she could say of it just then, for he hauled her against his body like he couldn't wait a moment longer and kissed her soundly. Violet laughed against his lips, tasting mint and rosemary and the salt of tears that might have been hers or might have been his. It was the most perfect sort of alchemy she knew, because it all combined in this moment, with his hands in her hair and her lips beneath his and their hearts beating a harmonized duet against their pressed-together chests. Together, the way they were meant to be.

He *loved* her.

Pru's voice cut through the air. "I hate to interrupt, because this is obviously A Moment, but you're going to want to see this."

Violet and Nathaniel broke apart, foreheads resting against each other, chests heaving, arms still entwined. They had more to talk about, but Violet felt better. They had *time* now. Time for talking and more mistakes and making up and everything in between.

"Come on," she said, feeling positively giddy. Hand in hand, they took off toward the sound of Pru's voice.

Pru was standing with the rest of their group in front of a massive statue. A stone dragon curved around a lone figure, glaring at him with its eyeless face. It was Sedgwick, freed from his thorny bonds but trapped by the dragon's huge body. Held aloft in his hand was the Eye of the Serpent, the gorgeous peridot gleaming in the moonlight, and at his feet was Peri, still and frozen as the rest.

"So it wasn't a myth after all," murmured Nathaniel. "Rock goblins really can turn living beings to stone."

"Including themselves, apparently," said Violet, crouching to stroke Peri's still form. "Poor little thing."

The group crowded around Peri.

"I can't get over it," said Fallon. "All this time, the legend was real. The Eye, the dragon . . . it was all around us."

"Where's the second one?" Jerome asked. "I see only one Eye."

"I don't know," said Violet. "I didn't see it back in the castle either. It must still be missing."

"And now the dragon has come to rest," said Pru, patting the beast's stone tail. "Maybe someday the other Eye will find its way back."

They stood in silence and Violet leaned her head on Nathaniel's shoulder as his arm slipped around her waist. She allowed herself a moment to mourn her friend. "Peri deserved better," she whispered.

Nathaniel squeezed her shoulder. "So we'll do better."

Her answering smile was teary. "Yes," she agreed. "We'll do better."

It was a battle she'd fight her entire life, she suspected. Being good—*doing* good—wasn't easy, but perhaps that was true for everyone, not just recovering villains. As Violet looked down at the statue of her friend, and the dragon it had come from, for the first time in her life she truly looked forward to that fight.

DARKNESS AND LIGHT

When Nathaniel woke, Violet was gone. He panicked only briefly before he registered that Daisy had disappeared from the foot of the bed as well. Moments later, the bedroom door opened, and there they both were, a tray of pastries and a steaming teapot in Violet's hands.

"I should be bringing you breakfast," he muttered, rubbing his eyes and adjusting his hold around the sudden armful of dog that threw herself onto the bed. "You're the one who brought down a whole castle. You need more time to recover."

"It's been two days, you big worrier. I'm fine, I promise. And besides, we need to get back to real life eventually."

"Can't say I see much wrong with spending the rest of my days in bed with you." He was delighted as ever to watch her blush.

"Flatterer." She stuck her tongue out at him and settled her focus on the puppy. "Off the bed, Daisy. These aren't for you."

Nathaniel sat up and moved his legs to make room for the tray *and* Daisy, who did not appear interested in going anywhere, and took a scone from the plate. It was one of Guy's, obviously, for no one else in town used flavor combinations like he did, and peach and basil was one of Nathaniel's favorites.

"Where did he get the peaches?" Nathaniel wondered through a mouthful of pastry. "They're not in season for months yet."

Violet sat next to him, toying with his free hand. "I wanted to talk to you about that actually."

He turned to her sharply. "You?"

"Me." She laughed sheepishly. "You're the one who put the idea in my head, all the way back to that mugwort and the vegetable garden. I knew that my plants were edible and wouldn't hurt anyone, but I wanted to see how they'd hold up for cooking and baking. Guy has been more than happy to help. Didn't you wonder how we've all been eating strawberry rhubarb and pomegranate and lemon pastries for the past several weeks? None of it is in season! Most of it doesn't even grow here!"

"I was distracted by the blight," he said sheepishly. "I never thought twice about it."

"We're still learning what does and doesn't work, but if I grow the fruit from seed, like we figured out that night in the greenhouse"—he grinned as he recalled *everything* about that night, and she scrunched her nose at him—"then they *do* provide nutrition like real food."

"Violet, that's incredible." Nathaniel's mind was whirring. "Think of all the people you can help with that skill!"

"I'm going to the Feldspars this afternoon to ask if I can help regrow their crop. It's the least I can do. And I was thinking of going back to Silbourne and some of the other places I've hurt." She choked on her words. "I don't want them to know who I am, but I can try and help them rebuild. I could go in the night and help their crops along, you know? Get a few saplings to fruit-bearing age in the blink of an eye." Violet's smile turned nervous. "But I'd like to start with you, if it's all the same."

"What do you mean?"

"Get dressed and come with me to the greenhouse? I have something to show you."

Nathaniel all but tripped over himself as he threw on his clothes and poured himself a cup of tea to take with him downstairs. She laughed at him the whole time—until he kissed her to shut her up.

That worked quite well too, though it did delay them somewhat.

By the time they finally made it down to the greenhouse, the tea had gone cold and Nathaniel's fresh shirt was irredeemably rumpled, but he couldn't bring himself to mind.

"Now what is it?" he asked, looking around as though she might have left him a surprise wrapped in colorful paper and tied with a ribbon. But there was nothing except a pile of fresh-cut sage on her worktable.

"I've been doing some more thinking about my magic," said Violet.

"Have you?" He wasn't sure where she was going with this.

"I can pull energy from plants, but if I take it all, then it causes the blight. So I started thinking, what if I intentionally took only a little from a plant? Just enough to . . ." She reached for the sage and held it tightly in her fist, then closed her eyes. Nathaniel watched as every part of her seemed to come to life, her hair growing lustrous, her cheeks rosy. Magic suited her, as did the bouquet of purple flowers she'd grown from thin air.

"Beautiful," he said, but she only laughed at him.

"Don't you see?" she asked, and held up her other hand. The sage had dried up, looking exactly like the bundles he had wrapped and hung from the rafters to eventually use in the apothecary. "Nathaniel, I can help you restock the apothecary. If you can get me live plants, I can dry them for you in an instant, without any of the waiting. Teas, medicines, even ingredients for your alchemical products, as long as they're plant-based. And if you get me some seeds, I can grow them for you on the spot. And I can use the excess magic I pull from the plants to grow *more* plants."

Understanding wove its threads through him. Seeds were much cheaper and easier to procure for most of his ingredients than the entire plant. *Growing* them was the costly part, for it required so much time, space, and effort.

"If you could help me keep my shelves stocked . . ."

"Then the money you're saving on supply would cover the gap in your bank payments, wouldn't it?" Too casually, she added, "Plus what you'll make from the increase in my rent."

It took him a moment to catch her meaning. "Violet, no. You're already doing more than enough. I don't want your charity."

"It's not charity," she said firmly. "I'm not going to let you lose the shop when I have more than enough money—taken from the estate of an evil sorcerer who certainly did not gain it lawfully himself, I might add—to help you."

He prickled with the uncomfortable sense that he was being managed—but no, he corrected. He was being *cared for.* There was a difference.

Nathaniel Marsh had made a lot of mistakes in his life, but what he had come to realize recently was that good things lay buried beneath the wreckage, and being scared shouldn't stop him from digging for them anyway. He could grow, he could change. He could learn to accept help when it was offered. Nathaniel was already so different from the man he had been when he and Violet met, and he was beginning to look forward to who he could become. Someone unknown, yes, and perhaps that was frightening, but with the right people beside him, Nathaniel knew he could find it in himself to be excited about change rather than afraid of losing what he once had.

After all, love had nothing to do with holding on tight for fear of letting it escape. Love needed space to grow, to put down roots, to blossom. He was finally giving himself that space, and it was due, in large part, to the witch who had captivated his thoughts and his heart.

"Besides," Violet cajoled, "once you're out of this hole, you can hire someone to help you in the shop and won't need to rely on Pru so much."

This, more than anything else, decided the matter. "She could finally travel."

"And *you* could focus on your alchemy."

Nathaniel weighed the image Violet painted against the one he wanted for himself and found that the scales balanced almost perfectly.

"On one condition," he said. "Instead of rent, you let me sell your half of the building to you."

That caught her by surprise, he could tell.

"You said you moved here because you wanted something of your own. Well, here it is, if you want it."

For a moment he thought she'd say no. Maybe Rough Around the Hedges *wasn't* what she wanted for the rest of her life. Maybe *he* wasn't. Maybe she had plans to leave someday or—

"Is the greenhouse part of the deal?"

Hope bubbled in his chest like a cauldron about to boil over. "Of course not," he said sternly. "This is my *workspace*, madam. I have delicate experiments in here that aren't to be disturbed."

She stepped closer, nudging him playfully. "Well, this *is* a greenhouse and I *am* a florist, you know. I'm afraid I must insist. Besides, the advertisement did promise it to me . . ."

Nathaniel narrowed his eyes and huffed as he pretended to consider. "Well, I suppose you could have half."

"Half?!" Violet gasped, taking another step until their chests pressed together. "You mean I'd have to share? With whom?"

"A rather grouchy alchemist, I'm afraid. He'll decide to dislike you from the moment he lays eyes on you, but that's only because he's a stubborn fool." Nathaniel hid his smile, but she saw it anyway.

Violet looked him up and down like she was sizing him up. "Do you think I could win him over if I tried?"

Nathaniel wrapped her in his arms and kissed her forehead. "Violet, he's already yours."

She tipped up her chin until her mouth was a breath away from his. "That's awfully convenient," she said with a smile he would remember for the rest of his life. "Because he's stuck with me for good. I accept your offer, Mr. Marsh."

And she sealed it with a kiss.

So this was what bone-deep contentment felt like, Nathaniel marveled. This was what it felt like to be so in love that all his little anxieties sank into the ground like summer rain. He wanted to bottle this feeling and sell it in the apothecary—no, he wanted to hoard every vial for himself so he could open them whenever he wanted to remember.

Or perhaps that wasn't right either. Perhaps Nathaniel's happiness lay in the knowledge that rooted deep in his heart: that it didn't need to be preserved at all, and he could feel this way forever, whenever he wanted, because that was what it meant to be with the person he loved.

"Dragon's Rest will be all the better for having you as a permanent fixture," he declared. "You've helped this town bloom into life again, Violet." His hand crept to her neck, his thumb tracing her jaw. "You've certainly helped me see that there's more to life than just surviving it."

She clasped his hand beneath her own, holding it to her as she looked up at him with shining eyes. "You've taught me that too," she said. "I want to be more than I was."

"And you will be."

He could practically see that weight disappear from her. It wouldn't be gone forever, he knew. She would feel the burden of her past as surely as he did his, but they would carry it together.

"I love you," she sighed, and pressed up onto her toes to kiss him.

Nathaniel's heart soared. "I love you too, Violet Thistlewaite."

"Thorns and all?"

When he kissed her again, he never wanted to stop. "Thorns and all."

Rough Around the Hedges

FLORAL & GARDEN SHOP

She can't spell but her flowers will still put you under her spell.

IT'S CALLED POETRY, YOU NERD!

EPILOGUE
THORNS AND ALL

The Serpent Gardens of Dragon's Rest grew famous for always being in season, no matter the time of year. Once word began to spread, people came to the mountains from far and wide to wander the grounds and hear of the sorcerer who once lived there and the dragon who'd stopped him from coming back.

Karina the Tempest wore a red cloak, hood up despite the summer heat. It was hard for her to be in public without being recognized, Violet supposed. Violet's own part in the tale of Dragon's Rest had sometimes made it uncomfortable for her among the tourists who flocked here in droves—and that was without anyone other than her friends knowing about her past as the Thornwitch. She couldn't imagine being recognized everywhere she went.

As the hero approached, Violet took a deep breath. Nathaniel squeezed her hand.

"It's going to be alright," he assured her. She took comfort from his presence at her side and the way he could tell from the quaver of her breath that she was nervous. She remembered the days when she was afraid to let anyone see her emotions and not a single soul in the world really knew her.

The way she lived now was much better.

"You look well," said the hero when she got close enough. "Civilian life seems to agree with you."

Violet cleared her throat. "It does. I own a flower shop in town." She felt oddly formal, like if she was anything but polite, the Tempest would pull out her sword and strike her down for not living up to their last conversation in these gardens.

"And the Thornwitch?"

Violet knew what she was asking, but she still felt nervous answering. Thankfully, Nathaniel took over, rattling off a speech like he'd rehearsed it. He might well have; she wasn't sure.

"The Thornwitch's magic was never the problem; it was the way Violet learned to use it."

The Tempest looked at her. "Is this true?"

"Yes." Violet cleared her throat and repeated herself. "Yes. I've spent the past year learning more about magical theory than I ever thought possible. Thanks largely to this one." She nudged Nathaniel with a grin, and the Tempest stared.

They both seemed to realize at once that there had been no introductions. He stuck out a hand and said, "Nathaniel Marsh. I'm Violet's fiancé."

He beamed as he said it, and Violet blushed, twisting the ring on her finger that they'd forged together—woven from delicate vines and miniscule flowers she'd conjured and transformed into gold with Nathaniel's alchemy. Pru was beside herself with wedding plans and had already made Daisy a fancy wedding collar to wear on the big day. But Violet wasn't in a hurry, and she knew Nathaniel wasn't either. For the first time in her life, she had a real future, and she had no plans to rush it.

The Tempest looked between them, amusement plain on her features. "Congratulations."

"Thank you," said Nathaniel happily. As their dog, now fully grown and huge, wagged her tail and barked, he added, "And this is Daisy."

It never failed to astound Violet how openly proud Nathaniel was to be with her, how he wore their relationship like a badge of honor. Family had always been important to him, she reasoned, but this was her first go at it, although he'd offered many times to try to help her find her mother's ship.

Someday, Violet answered each time. When she was ready.

She worried often whether she was doing it right, this family thing, and whether she knew how to be normal, how to be good, as well as she wanted to be. But as Nathaniel reminded her often, she was making the right choices and he was there with her every step of the way.

"Shall I show you the spot?" Violet asked, turning the attention away from her impending nuptials.

"Please." Karina strolled with them along the garden path toward the statue. "Reports in town are of a loud noise in the middle of the night, and then . . . ?"

"Yeah, that's about it." Violet shrugged. "But I don't think it's a problem."

"And why is that?"

They reached the central plinth, where Sedgwick stood frozen and stony in place as usual, but that was all that was recognizable about the now-famous landmark.

The precious stone the statue had grasped in his hands was gone, as was, more startlingly, the massive figure of the dragon that had stood guard over him for more than a year.

Best of all, the space at Sedgwick's feet was empty too.

Karina frowned at the empty space where the dragon once stood. "The rock goblins are dangerous. You've no idea where they went?"

"None. One of our neighbors said she saw them fly away into the night."

"If someone gets their hands on that jewel . . ."

"I know."

Karina examined the area closely, pocketing a few crumbs of stone that had fallen.

"The Queen wants me to find the Eye of the Serpent and bring it into her treasury," she admitted. "But if what you say is true, she'll have to make room for a slide of rock goblins in the Lune Vault as well."

"That would make quite the hoard for that dragon," quipped Violet.

The Tempest nodded. "It's a problem I don't think she's prepared for, and I'll tell her that myself. In the meantime, if anything suspicious happens, you'll contact me?"

"We'll let you know at the first sign of danger," Violet promised.

"Very well." The Tempest nodded curtly. "You've done good here, Violet. I'm glad I made the decision I did that day."

Violet's breath caught in her chest, and Nathaniel held her closer as she responded, "I'm glad too."

As the hero wrapped up her investigation, Violet and Nathaniel bid her farewell and watched her take off at a fast clip down the hill.

"She couldn't get out of here fast enough," Violet mused warmly.

"It's just as well," said Nathaniel, squeezing her fondly. "We've enough heroes in Dragon's Rest these days."

As soon as she was gone, a gravelly croak brought their atten tion behind them. A familiar pair of onyx eyes peered out at them from one of the flower beds.

Violet's mouth dropped open. "Peri?"

The rock goblin crept from the greenery, and only when Daisy lunged in excitement did he throw himself at them. It was hard to tell once he was wrapped in a heap of Daisy's pale fur, but Peri looked good as new, the Eye of the Serpent safely back in his chest where it belonged.

"Where's the rest of your slide, my friend?" Violet asked.

Peri let out a long *creeeeauuugh* and then went back to playing with Daisy.

"We're taking him home obviously."

"Obviously," said Nathaniel, but his voice was distant. Violet raised her brows at the new light that shone in his eyes.

"What is it?" she asked. "I know that look. You've grabbed hold of a puzzle, haven't you?"

"It's reversible," said Nathaniel, staring at Peri. "The stone enchantment. It wears off, and that means the magic could be sped along. I could end the spell."

"But Peri and the rock goblins are back already."

"Sedgwick isn't though."

Violet looked thoughtfully at the stone form of the man she once knew. Dragon's Rest was much different than the version Sedgwick had last seen. Still, she wondered aloud, "Is that a road we want to travel?"

"What happened with the rock goblins tells me it's going to happen anyway," said Nathaniel with a shrug. "We might as well be able to control it. But you're right. He could be dangerous."

Violet considered the stone alchemist. He was one of Shadowfade's best, just as she had been. But in the end, he had faltered. Even if it had flickered out before it could truly burn, a flame of hope had sparked in him briefly that day in the castle. She'd seen it.

"I was dangerous too once," she mused. "And even if he didn't mean it as a kindness, Sedgwick was the one who woke me up. I could try to return the favor . . ."

Nathaniel squeezed her hand. "Think there's room for one more in the Thursday support group?"

"I'll tell Quinn to bake extra honey cakes."

Nathaniel pretended to gag, and Violet burst into laughter.

They began the walk down the mountainside, back to town. Back home.

Daisy yipped cheerfully as she and Peri followed, rolling in the grass and wrestling like no time had passed. The dying light of the fading sun glinted off the peridot in the rock goblin's chest. The Eye of the Serpent. Or one of them anyway—they still had no idea what had happened to the second one. Violet wondered if perhaps that was where the rest of the rock goblins had gone, to find it.

Nathaniel followed her gaze. "The Tempest warned us what could happen if that stone ends up in the wrong hands."

"Do these look like the wrong hands?" Violet held up theirs, still conjoined. "Need I remind you, Mr. Marsh, I am no villain." She leaned up to kiss him but stopped, her mouth a breath from his, to reconsider her words. "At least, not anymore."

ACKNOWLEDGMENTS

I've wanted to be an author since I was five years old, which means that I've dreamed about writing my acknowledgments the way some people practice their Academy Award speeches in the shower (though in the interest of full disclosure, I've done that too). So of course now that the time has come to write them for real, I have promptly gone and forgotten the names of every single person I have ever met in my life.

No, for real though, bringing a book into the world isn't something you can do alone, and I'm so immeasurably grateful to all the people who have stood alongside me on this journey.

First, a huge thank-you to my agent, Brent Taylor, for his relentless support and advocacy on this whirlwind ride, and for always answering my "This might be a silly question . . ." emails with patience, humor, and a whole lot of knowledge.

An equally massive thank-you to my editor, Sareer Khader, who not only believed in this story but helped me bring it to new heights in ways I could never have fathomed. Your expert guidance, enthusiasm, and incredible insight have been everything to me, and I can't believe how lucky I am to have won the editor lottery. I'm so grateful to you for taking a chance on Violet, Nathaniel, and—let's be real, we all know the truth of the situation here—Bartleby.

Thank you to Katie Anderson for your genius cover direction and to Chaaya Prabhat for the beautiful cover and endpapers. You have no idea how much squealing I have done over your gorgeous artwork.

You would simply not be holding this book without Angela Cowan, who read the first draft, which I'd been calling my "fuck it" book, and very gently said, "Em, I think you might regret it if you didn't at least send this out to a few agents." You were so, so right. Thank you for being an incredible critique partner, cheerleader, and friend.

Pip Davidson has been an unwavering supporter of this book and an even more unwavering best friend. Thank you for innumerable coffee walks, patiently reminding me that yes, in fact, my wins *are* worth celebrating, and for being my unofficial PR man.

Thank you also to Marshall J. Moore and Megan McElroy Moore, who read this book long before it became the version it is now and who were the best kind of support when it felt like there was an entire hive of bees buzzing beneath my skin.

To Mackenzie, Jasmine, and Jamie for countless hours writing, and probably just as many *not* writing. Also a big thanks to the many baristas who kept me caffeinated (especially the ones who gave me a free latte when I ugly-cried all over the bar after accepting my book deal). And to Jason Buchholz, Nirmala Nataraj, Sarah Bossenbroek, and Donna Galassi, whose camaraderie kept me from losing it while I was writing this book.

Thank you to the Berkletes for welcoming me with open arms and being an incredible source of wisdom and support over the past year. To the 2025 Debuts discord, especially Noreen Nanja, Deidra Duncan, Melissa O'Connor, Sasa Hawk, Lauren Okie, and Maggie Eckersley, and to the 2025 class of the Author Debutante Ball. As one of the cabooses of this year, I can say it with certainty now—we did it!

Endless gratitude to my amazing parents, particularly my mom for getting back into reading just in time to understand how wild this whole publishing ride has been (and for falling in love with the same types of books as me so we can talk about them all the time). To my brother and sisters for giving me plenty of fodder to make my editor say "I can tell you have siblings" when Nathaniel and Pru bicker. I love you nerds. Special thank-you to my talented sister Katie for my author photos.

A huge shout-out to my therapist, who has more than earned her keep during my debut year. And to the writers of TikTok, who took it in stride when I made the awkward leap from teaching about writing to sharing more about my own, and whose support and excitement for this book have been incredible.

Last but certainly never least, to Zak, who listened very attentively that early-spring morning when I said, "I need you to go for a long walk with me so I can talk at you about a story idea." Thank you for encouraging me to take myself seriously. Thank you for bringing me *so many* cups of tea and making me dinner when I'm in a writing trance and forget to eat, and for celebrating every single win with me, no matter how big or small. For your support and your sense of humor and your big kind heart and your unfaltering belief in me. You are the brightest star in my constellation. Thanks for loving me, thorns and all.

And wait, I have one more thank-you from the very bottom of my heart—to *you*. If you turn back the pages in the book of my life, you'll find a little girl scribbling stories on scraps of paper, dreaming of the day she might call herself an author. Whether you loved this book or hated it, thank you so much for picking it up and reading it.

Thank you for making my dreams come true.

Katie Krempholtz Photography

Emily Krempholtz is not a supervillain, nor has she ever served as a minion to one. She lives in Colorado, where she does not have an evil lair hidden deep in the Rocky Mountains, and the baked goods she loves to make are definitely not poisoned. She is a bestselling ghostwriter, editor, and book coach, a job where she helps authors plot *stories*, not the end of the world.

When she's not writing or reading, Emily can be found hiking, playing board games, making terrible puns, or stage-whispering, "Look, a *dog*!" while out walking with her partner—which are all totally normal things that have absolutely nothing whatsoever to do with world domination.

She does, however, command a small army of houseplants, including one named Bartleby.

VISIT EMILY KREMPHOLTZ ONLINE

EmilyKrempholtz.com

WritersOfRohan

EmBakesBooks_